Dedalus Europe 2017
General Editor: Timothy Lane

Portrait of a Family with a Fat Daughter

Margherita Giacobino

Portrait of a Family with a Fat Daughter

Translated by Judith Landry

Dedalus

This book has been selected to receive financial assistance from English PEN's "PEN Translates" programme, supported by Arts Council England. English PEN exists to promote literature and our understanding of it, to uphold writers' freedoms around the world, to campaign against the persecution and imprisonment of writers for stating their views, and to promote the friendly co-operation of writers and the exchange of ideas.

Published in the UK by Dedalus Limited
24-26, St Judith's Lane, Sawtry, Cambs, PE28 5XE
email: info@dedalusbooks.com
www.dedalusbooks.com

ISBN printed book 978 1 910213 48 3
ISBN ebook 978 1 910213 53 7

Dedalus is distributed in the USA & Canada by SCB Distributors
15608 South New Century Drive, Gardena, CA 90248
email: info@scbdistributors.com web: www.scbdistributors.com

Dedalus is distributed in Australia by Peribo Pty Ltd
58, Beaumont Road, Mount Kuring-gai, N.S.W. 2080
email: info@peribo.com.au

Publishing History
First published in Italy in 2015
First published by Dedalus in 2017

Printed in Finland by Bookwell
Typeset by Marie Lane

A C.I.P. listing for this book is available on request.

The Author

Margherita Giacobino was born in 1952 and lives in Turin. She is a writer, journalist and translator from English and French. Her first novel *Un'Americana a Parigi* was published in 1993 and was written under the pseudonym of Elinor Rigby.

Portrait of a Family with a Fat Daughter, published in Italy in 2015, has already been translated into French and German. It is the first novel by Margherita Giacobino to be translated into English.

The Translator

Judith Landry was educated at Somerville College, Oxford where she obtained a first class honours degree in French and Italian.

Her translations for Dedalus are: *The House by the Medlar Tree* by Giovanni Verga, *New Finnish Grammar*, *God's Dog*, *The Last of the Vostyachs* and *The Interpreter* by Diego Marani, *The Mussolini Canal* by Antonio Pennacchi, *The Devil in Love* by Jacques Cazotte, *Prague Noir: The Weeping Woman on the Streets of Prague* by Sylvie Germain and *Smarra & Trilby* by Charles Nodier.

Her translation of *New Finnish Grammar* was awarded the Oxford-Weidenfeld Translation Prize in 2012.

For Maria, my mother,
for all my family,
and for Claudia

The Fresh Air from the Door

She was sixty-one when I was born, and throughout my childhood, despite my mother's urgings ('You must call her *aunt* Ninin!'), she was always and only Ninin, a diminutive which served as a foothold for my small impertinent feet in my efforts to subvert an authority to which in fact she never laid any claim.

In the parish register she was 'Caterina', like her grandmother – her father's mother – but pronounced 'Catlina', with that particular throaty 'n' found, in Italy, only around our way. That she had been given this name was only to be expected: if the first-born girls of the sons of the old Catlina had not been christened Catlina the *granda* would have been offended, and the guilty parties would have been the first to know it. With rules like this, a family was bound to include several people with the same name, and endless diminutives were resorted to so as to avoid the ensuing confusion: Catlinin, Catlinota, Catlinetta. She herself was known as Ninin, from Catlinin, but in our dialect ninin also means a babe in swaddling clothes, something small and new which may or may not stay the course, a scrap of a life stirring within a worm-eaten cradle between a woollen blanket and a pallet made from maize, and you don't give it a real name until it has learned to crawl. And Ninin she remained, even when a whole string of brothers and sisters began to follow after, including my grandmother.

She was the daughter of a Domenica and a Giuseppe, and her nursemaid was a cow. The story goes that they put her under this cow when her mother's milk dried up before the newborn baby was old enough to eat polenta, and the other sister-in-law couldn't feed her because she already had a strapping great lad who was drinking her dry. So they took Ninin into the stable and attached her to the long pink protrusion beneath the cow, and on hearing her famished shrieks, that kindly creature, it was said, just stood there quietly as though at milking time, with bovine patience, while Ninin sucked with all the force of her infant gums. She came to no harm at all. In those days people rubbed along with germs better than they do now; and any way children were often born in stables, which were the only warm places during winter, and they came into immediate contact with straw, and animals' warm breath. They either grew up strong or they didn't grow up at all. Ninin survived both the lack of mother's milk and the remedy for it. The only damage she suffered, according to family legend, was a slight deformation of the mouth, due to having sucked for months on a cow's big teat; her teeth, when they came through, stuck out, and remained that way until a set of false ones came to improve the picture.

We're in the last decade of the nineteenth century. Throughout the year, women wore a coarse, scratchy undergarment known as the *camisa*, which you stuffed into your drawers, when you wore any, which was hardly ever. On top of it, any number of cumbersome skirts and bodices concealed the all too frequent pregnancies. Men too wore a version of the *camisa*, with detachable collars and cuffs for washing purposes; on high days and holidays they put on dark woollen suits, always three piece: trousers, jacket and waistcoat. In those days hemp was still used, cool yet heavy, unsuited to winter wear. All adult males sported a moustache, and wore hats; all women, from earliest childhood to old age, forced their hair into plaits or buns.

A photograph, in those days, was a rare and momentous event, you had to sit still for quite some time, looking as solemn as though you were posing for your own funeral portrait, and indeed some whiff of funeral parlour finality can still be sensed in the magical ritual conducted by the photographer when he hides his head behind the piece of black cloth. No one is smiling, that levity so apparent in our digital clicks is still in the distant future. In those family photographs that you find stowed away in the bottom of chests-of-drawers, no one is the least concerned with looking happy, and certainly not radiant. Indeed, everyone looks peevish, gloomy, if not actually ferocious; guarded, crotchety.

I have no photographs of Ninin as a baby or young girl, or of her family, in the years around the turn of the century. Perhaps they have been lost, or perhaps spending money on a photographer struck people as a scandalous luxury. So I have been obliged to invent one.

It can only be a group portrait, with the old people seated in the middle, stiff and impassive, as though dried out by age, no hint of benevolence softening the hardness of their lips and looks; behind them and around them are their sons and daughters-in-law, some fully grown, indeed prematurely aging, some still almost children. The men stare fiercely at the lens as soldiers might stare at enemy cannon; the women, doomed yet expressionless, like so many Iphigenias ready for sacrifice, proffer white bundles balanced on their outstretched arms, with children of various ages clustered at their feet, staring out in surprise, their eyes like so many black buttons in astonished faces. At one of the edges of the family portrait, a woman in miniature, dressed like her mother, and like her determined to act and to resist: Ninin.

I see this image as though through running water, which is gradually eroding features already flattened by their pose and the direct light. Who, really, were these men and women? Were they as gruff and stern as they appear? Did they love each other, or merely put up with each other? What would they have to say to me, if they could surface from that water which is carrying them off a bit further day by day, above all if they were in the habit of talking about themselves, as they almost certainly were not? Have they anything in common with me, with the world as it seems to me today? The only one I can see clearly, the only one I can still just touch, dipping my hand into the flow of that past, all relatively recent though it is – little more than a century old – is the child Ninin; through her, the images of her brothers and sisters also take on life.

For me, Ninin is the *fons et origo*. Ninin the indefatigable, *Mulier Fabricans*. My Lucy, the first human form emerging from the slime.

Unmistakable, unique, my DNA, as deep in me as the marrow of my bones, her thoughts the substratum of my own. And, at the same time, wider, a super-personal being, a spirit permeating the very idea of what it is to be human.

Young or old, she's always my Ninin. As when I called to her when I was a child, with the imperious possessiveness of a lover. Passion is not a prerogative of youth and it has little in common with sexual desire, with which it is often confused; sometimes, intense and total passions are experienced during the least sexual parts of life, in infancy and old age. I can only define as passion the feeling that bound me to my mother and the old people of my early childhood, among whom Ninin was the most reassuring yet most inaccessible, the most loved and necessary.

If I had to describe what, over the years, became my personal cosmogony, Ninin would be at its core: the small, clear-cut keystone of my universe, a symbol of the most absolute, unvarnished and pragmatic woman's love.

The firstborn daughter of Giuseppe and his wife Domenica is destined to survive many another trial after the cow's teat, including typhus, two world wars, breast cancer and a starveling's pension after fifty years of working in a factory. She will bring up three generations: her own brothers and sisters (before she herself dies, she lays flowers on all their graves), her niece Maria, my mother, and me, her great-niece. She sees the history of almost a century unfold before her, with its events and portents: electric light, ships full of emigrants, cars, cinema, Mussolini, liberation and the republic, the Madonna Pellegrina, Kennedy, Pope John, the popular variety programme *Canzonissima*, the first man on the moon, the miniskirt. Always in danger of being crushed by history, she stands resolutely aside from it, absorbed in weaving a story of her own, and of her folks, small-scale, persistent, ever to be cobbled together anew and then shored up, an everyday adventure which keeps her holding her breath. However monotonous her deeds and days, Ninin is never bored. Throughout her eighty-five years on this earth, she works tirelessly (except during her last year, spent in bed complaining of her aches and pains and inability to carry on working) without putting aside anything for herself, or asking for any respite; quickened, to the very last, by a desire – all the stronger for being purely instinctive, indeed almost unconscious – to care for those who have been put into her care. To help them to negotiate today with honour and dignity, and to lead them to safety tomorrow; beginning afresh each day.

Work is to be her sacrament, and duty her religion – duty, a mysterious word whose very utterance tears at her lips like a sharp blade. Duty is a cruel god who demands that you rise early and go to bed late, that you give your bones no rest and your eyes no peace, that you curry-comb your very soul. Duty consumes its worshippers like an undying flame; you can sometimes glimpse it in her eyes, that little flame, storm-tossed but never quite put out. Ninin's sense of duty has nothing to do with the law of the land, and on occasions may be at odds with it; her very personal theology is spliced with curious and contradictory dogmas, but its beating heart knows no words, it is inarticulate, pure élan vital. As prosaic and down-to-earth as the heart which pumps blood into the veins. While there is life, come what may, Ninin will push on.

She was born at the beginning of March, when it was still winter, in the stable among the cows and donkeys like Jesus Christ, as everyone was born around her way in those days; there was certainly an ox, and probably a little donkey, but no angels, and instead of the Three Kings there was grandfather Bartolomeo, with a yellow moustache which reached almost to his ears, and his teeth even more yellow than his moustache, his son *barba* Giacu, stinking of wine, and the primordial Catlina, the *mare granda*, the grandmother, with her little black eyes, dressed in seven layers of skirts and bodices, with deep pockets between one layer and another, and knotted bundles containing handkerchiefs and snuff, and cheese rind – and the countless fine blades of her own viciousness. The gift Bartolomeo brought to the birth was the willow rod he was always quick to send whistling around his grandchildren's grubby legs; Catlina's gift was the bitter taste of countless injustices to come. *Barba Giacu* brought nothing; it was he himself who was brought back from the wine shop.

After her came a Maria who was to be my grandmother, and then a Domenica known as Michin; a Bartolomeo known as Mecio; a Margherita who died at the age of three, drowned in a nearby stream where they did the washing; then a Giuseppe known as Noto (from Pinot, which was the usual shortening of Giuseppe), then another Margherita to replace the first. By the age of four Ninin, the oldest, was already busy rocking cradles, changing nappies, peeling small potatoes for which grown-ups' hands were too big. Her mother Domenica – once she'd finished milking cows and goats, cutting grass, carrying logs and making cheese – would sit down at the loom, which stood in a corner of the big kitchen, in a niche in the ground, where she would settle with a rustle of petticoats, her feet flying over the pedals while her arms would lower and raise the bar. It was hard work. What she spun was coarse hempen cloth, for sheets and shirts, off-white in colour like cream when it's time to take it off the milk to make it into butter.

Twice a year they would go to the market at Chivasso to buy hemp yarn and sell their cloth. It was neither Domenica nor the other current daughter-in-law who struck the bargains with the dealers, but *la granda*: 'You two don't even know what the weather's like outside, they'd eat you for breakfast,' Catlina would say to the daughters-in-law. And off she'd go, her donkey laden with bundles, together with a young son or a grandson who was no longer wet behind the ears.

It was Catlina who was in charge of all the women's money, and her pockets gave out a faint clinking sound. It was always she who went to the local market of a Saturday, to buy flour, cooking pots, salted anchovies and clogs. The daughters-in-law stayed at home, looking after the animals and the kitchen garden.

The hierarchy which reigned in the house of my ancestors was a tribal affair, with hints of matriarchy. When, as an arts student in the Seventies, despite the professors' objections, I insisted on doing a thesis on witches (a subject which was becoming popular among feminists at the time, which was why I, eager for revelations about myself and life in general, was so keen to engage with it, and also why my teachers were so against it, one of them expressing the view that witches were a phenomenon of no importance, or, to use the terminology of the time, 'a boil on the arsehole of history') what I discovered as I painfully transcribed late medieval Latin court proceedings written in a bastard Gothic script, was a stretch of the past whose smoke-filled gloom put me in mind of nothing so strongly as my own house, before my birth. At the end of the nineteenth century as in the fifteenth, families were large, and the women were under the thumb of the oldest among them. As in a harem, perhaps, or a Chinese house where many wives live together, with the first one having the whip-hand, in the stone houses of the villages in the foothills of the Alps *la granda* lorded it over the daughters-in-law and, if she was firm and had them in her grip, the young men would serve as her armed right hand. She was a royal madam, a regent who had to watch out both for women's plots and for vendettas fuelled by male pride. It was a world untroubled by finicky matters of democracy, nothing but power and submission, and it was no coincidence that the daughters-in-law referred to their mother-in-law deferentially as *madona*, which comes from *mea domina*, my lady, even if they didn't know it.

What I was reading then, at the age of twenty, in those courtroom proceedings, spoke to me of the fragility of women's power, enclosed and contained as it was within those walls of stone, within those caves of beaten earth, amidst domestic objects transformed by a collective nightmare into instruments of witchcraft. Whether kindly or ill-disposed, the witches of bygone days – peasants, mothers, midwives, herbalists, witch-women or quite simply women – lived their lives exposed to a wind of pure barbarism, that same wind which was still worming its way into the house where Domenica gave birth to her first-born.

The other daughter-in-law of the family was called Rita; a woman of few words, she kept her eyes lowered and would nod her head without ever moving her pale lips. She was a see-through woman, the colour of the cold morning air; Domenica had tried to befriend her, to have someone young to talk to, but Rita was too timid, she didn't know what friendship was, she'd grown up under the protective wing of a fat and jealous aunt and then fallen straight under *la granda*'s iron rod, without even a whiff of freedom in between.

Domenica had something *invisch,* something vibrant about her, which Catlina didn't like. Furthermore, Domenica's oldest children were all girls, while Rita had given birth to two boys, and it was this too – apart from her docile nature – which caused her mother-in-law to view her in so favourable a light.

Right from her poverty-stricken, hard-working youth, Ninin realised that she belonged to a persecuted tribe. *Magna* Rita's sons received larger portions of polenta, and if there was any full-cream milk it went straight to them. Domenica's daughters looked on, and knew better than to complain. 'Men eat more,' their grandmother had decreed, and this was true for all males, even as children (though in the future Domenica's male children would eat less than Rita's). In that cavernous kitchen, beneath the long beam, the men would be seated at the massive table, blackened by the smoke of many meals, while the women crouched by the stone hearth, feeding their babies, or managed to gulp down the odd mouthful while they served the men, and the girl children would perch on stools with a plate balanced on their knee. Only Catlina would be seated at table, among the men, dividing out the portions on the chopping board and keeping an eye out to see that no one sopped up too much of the anchovy oil along with their slice of polenta, or helped themselves to both cheese and milk.

'Cheese is made from milk' – her voice would fall like an axe on greedy, guilty hands – 'so if you drink milk you won't be eating cheese, and if you eat cheese you won't be drinking milk.'

Ninin never shook off this culture of dearth. Born into poverty, she never adjusted to the idea of being comfortably off, regarding it as some new-fangled fad, even when in the Sixties our house, like so many others throughout Italy, suddenly filled up with objects and foodstuffs which had not previously existed and which soon seemed indispensable. When, within the space of a couple of years, any number of tinned or frozen foods became available, along with household appliances and plastic buckets and televisions and man-made materials – things which in the immediate postwar years had come in parcels from America but which you could now buy here as well – she remained faithful to her cotton overalls and evening cup of milky coffee. She watched television, but only after supper, when she had done the washing up and all the other household chores. Her great friend was the washing machine, which she treated with the respect due to a hard-working individual which plays its part in the household economy.

Food, for Ninin, always retained the aura of the truly precious, worth more than gold, because you can't eat gold. The fruit of hard work, food had to be made by your own hand; food made by others, don't even mention by a machine, was suspect. Particularly precious were the slightly burnt meatballs so gloriously combining all the remains from the previous day, the leftover pasta (always overcooked) reheated, the *panada*, dry bread cooked in broth, over-ripe fruit with the bad bits cut out, then cooked with a bit of sugar and lemon rind, and fresh cheeses made at home in hollow moulds, soft white blocks which you mashed up with your fork and ate with a ripe tomato and a bit of salt. In private, like someone practising a secret and barely tolerated religion, Ninin would eat up any leftovers which were beginning to go off, because food is like people, you have to show it respect even in its old age and decline.

For her – as I imagine for a Bangladeshi widow with a gaggle of children to look after – wastage was sacrilege. She would never have accepted today's unisex, one-size-fits-all label of consumer: my great-aunt's sole aim was to avoid consumption. For her, it was as though you had to creep up to things on tiptoe, leaving no sign of your approach, and, above all, never let the source run dry. She was an ardent ecologist *avant la lettre*, not for political reasons, but genetic ones: what shall we do tomorrow if there's no more light, water, wood, bread, sun? 'Turn the tap off. Turn the light out. What are you doing, still reading at this time of night? What a waste!'

She spoke these words in a harsh and somehow ancient voice: a voice calling me back to a world of poverty which is no more. Poverty may still linger on in many parts of the world, perhaps even more desperate and primitive than that which was felt around Catlina's stone hearth. But nowadays poverty is always and everywhere reflected back to us through our complex, anguished wealth. For Ninin, on the other hand, when she was little, poverty was the whole story, all 360 degrees of it. Affluence was so far off that she couldn't have glimpsed it even through binoculars, had she had any.

What she did have, right to hand, was that continual pain in the stomach which is known as hunger.

Not that her family were the poorest of the poor. They had some land, even if it didn't yield much, scattered bits of field and woodland up in the mountains, which could only be reached by clambering up hill and down dale for hours on end, possibly with a load of hay or firewood on your back, or a sack of chestnuts over your shoulder. And there were animals in the stables, which gave milk to make cheese that you could sell. But people who lived in the mountains did not have an easy time of it, even if they did have the odd cow and a bit of workable land. My family numbered up to eighteen at times, what with the two *grand*, and their children and grandchildren; there was food to eat, but you rarely ate your fill, and what there was, was divided up not in an equitable fashion, but according to power and privilege. The bread was never white, but *d'melia*, made of maize mixed with wheat or rye and bran, and it came in hard, solid cob loaves. It was good, though, for children it took the place of sweets, which they never ate except perhaps at Easter, when they might have a little sugar egg, or at Carnival a *bugia* fried in bacon fat. It wasn't every day that you ate a piece of bread, and it was quite a treat. Once when Ninin has crept into the cellar lured by the smell of fresh bread and cut herself a slice, footsteps behind her cause her to freeze in the damp darkness which smells of stone and mould.

Two hands clamp down on her shoulders in a vice-like grip, followed by Catlina's voice: 'What are you doing here? Thief!'

Scarcely has she bitten into the slice of bread than it is snatched out of her hands to end up among the folds of her grandmother's petticoats. Ninin's saliva turns to acid in her mouth.

That evenig, polenta and nothing else.

'Why aren't you giving any milk to the *cita*?' Domenica objects.

'Because she's a thief.'

'But she's a little girl, that's no way to carry on!' protests Domenica, bravely raising her voice.

'That bread didn't belong to her! And pipe down you, let's have a bit of respect round here!'

Catlina in a rage is like a snake, swaying and spitting – this is one of Ninin's earliest memories, a true revelation of things to come, and it will remain with her for ever.

Domenica is about to strike back, but her husband Giuseppe bangs his fist down on the table to silence her. She swallows her words and bites her lip. Bartolomeo, the *pare grand*, looks at her and tugs at his moustaches, first one side then the other. His eyes darken, then brighten, and for an instant a Saturday night smirk enlivens his set patriarch's mask.

'She can season the polenta with a bit of *aria d'l'uss*,' says Catlina with a disdainful gesture which sets her seven petticoats aflutter.

Ninin is all too familiar with the *aria d'l'uss*, the fresh air from the door; it's a common expression in everyday parlance. It refers to the lightness of what is absent, as opposed to the solidity of what is present; food seasoned with the fresh air from the door is flavourlless and dull, only extreme hunger can spice it up; but faced with such unsustaining fare, the unsatisfied stomach constructs dream banquets. Child that she is – that is, still in thrall to the splendidly literal nature of the metaphor – Ninin moves towards the door with her slice of cold, hard polenta, hoping that it will change taste as she approaches; and, be it the power of the imagination or hunger, pure and simple, if you concentrate, it does indeed seem that, in the space between inside and out, that piece of polenta suddenly begins to taste of the cheese and butter it so sadly lacks.

They are called Davito Gara, and the village where they live is called Ca' d'Gara, the Gara houses. So they are the Davito of Gara, they've left their mark on that terrain and have been marked by it in their turn.

It's a little cluster of houses huddled above the village of Rocca Canavese, six or seven hundred metres above sea level, on an Alpine foothill covered in chestnuts, ilexes and birches. We are some thirty kilometres from Turin, but in another world. The Canavese is a region of Piedmont with shifting borders, not quite sure where it belongs. Its history goes back to the old Celtic peoples defeated by the Romans, and it knew the usual sequence of war, occupation and repression, including by the Lombards, king Arduin of Ivrea, small local feudal lords, the Savoy and Napoleon's conquering armies. But for my family, rough and ignorant as they were, history consisted of nothing more than births, deaths and seasons, harvesting chestnuts and potatoes, and – since we were too numerous and too poor all to survive on a single patch of not very productive land – of the gradual appearance of small factories, particularly those making textiles, which grew in size and offered more and more work, especially to women, who cost less, so gradually replacing weaving at home. There were already foundries and metalworks down in the cities and towns, at Castellamonte they made ceramics, stoves and pots, and there were mines in the Val Chiusella. Migration was the great event: people migrated a few kilometres down to the plain, or to another world across the ocean, just for one season or for good. Either way, it meant a change.

From Rocca, a village in the Malone valley with nothing to boast about except a frescoed medieval chapel – the castle, or Rocca from which it takes its name having been reduced to a ruin centuries ago – a road, or rather a wide path, leads to the chapel of Our Lady of the Snows, perched on top of a steep hill, the goal of summer processions. It is by no means the only Our Lady of the Snows, around these parts they're two a penny, built on their lofty pinnacles with the idea that Our Lady must have been particularly attracted by the chill and solitude of such places. And, as it climbs, this path branches out into many smaller ones which end up in dozens of little hamlets.

Ours, Ca' d'Gara, stands right by the main road, enclasped in one of its loops; two rows of houses to either side of a road of stones and beaten earth with a stone fountain in the middle. Any passer-by can drink the water – cool in summer and icy cold in winter – from a copper-plated ladle hanging from a chain. Ca' d'Gara has eighty, perhaps a hundred inhabitants. Dogs, goats and the odd donkey mingle with the humans, all of them bound by chain or habits; only the hens wander about more or less at will, with their idiotic air. Cats lead a dog's life up here, obliged as they are to keep an eye out for birds and mice if they don't want to become vegetarians and make do with the watery remains of polenta which the women leave out for them. And they've learned not to be too trustful of humans, who tend to associate them with witches, and hound them accordingly. At night, stone martens stalk the hen-runs, tethered dogs bark, angry and powerless. Night here is the land of shadows, there are no lights apart from the moon. You grope your way to bed, hands and feet made expert by previous experience. Beds rustle, since mattresses are stuffed with maize leaves, home to tribes of ravenous fleas. Parents and children sleep in the same room; alarming sounds may alert children to the unplumbed mysteries of married couples' nights, but childhood sleep is merciful, it lays you out within minutes, before mother and father have even come to bed.

The rhythms of life vary according to the seasons. In summer you get up before dawn, go out into the fields, stay up in the hills until late at night threshing such little wheat or rye as succeeds in growing there, and stripping the maize. In winter you have supper early, then go into the cattle-heated stable and stay there, saying the rosary and telling stories. You give yourself only as much light as you need to work, to card wool, to string beans, to cut wood; when you've run through your ration of oil, you sit there in the dark. The stories are always the same, they're about witches who turn into animals, nanny-goats or tom-cats; their identity is revealed when the cat is injured or the goat becomes crippled, and the next day it is the witch who comes on to the scene, bedraggled or limping. These stories tell of strange and horrid deaths, of ghastly miracles, of talking animals and human stupidity.

Ninin's favourite is the story about the wolf and the fox, the mangy, famished denizens of a world no less penurious than her own, and thus worthy of a certain fellow-feeling, rogues though they be. One fine day this pair, driven by hunger and their natural tendency towards thievery, decide to go and eat up the *quaia*, the curds belonging to a certain Pinin, who lives not far away, behind some crag or other. Scrawny as they are, they have no trouble getting into the *crotin*, the little dry-stone shed half built into the hillside where the milk and cheeses are kept, they slip in easily through an air vent and instantly start lapping up the curds. But the fox, who is a sly one, occasionally goes back to the air vent to see if he can still fit through it, whereas the wolf gobbles away without a care in the world. So when Pinin, hearing the kerfuffle, arrives on the scene with a big stick, the fox manages to slip away in time, while the wolf, with his bloated stomach, gets stuck in the air vent and receives a healthy thrashing. And the fox is not just cunning, he is also spiteful: while his unfortunate partner in crime is howling under the blows, the fox espies a *cornaj*, a cornelian cherry tree, and rolls around in the ripe fruit that has fallen to the ground. And when the wolf at last manages to escape Pinin's wrath and extract himself, who does he see but the fox, all stained in red, and groaning wretchedly: Oh brother wolf, what a state I'm in! I can hardly walk for the beating I've taken! And the wolf – a duffer, but a kindly one – takes the fox on his back, while the fox sings: *Now we tramp down the marshy track, one bag of bones with another on its back, now we tramp through the narrow vale, the sick one carrying the hale!*

This story has several morals: stealing is wrong, but hunger may drive you to it; in this world, it pays to think ahead; never trust anyone; and, last but not least, a good joke is worth more than pity. How they would laugh, Ninin and her sisters and little cousins, at the expense of the poor thwacked and bloodied wolf, so irredeemably stupid. There is something bracing about this story with its artless cruelty, you find yourself laughing, but reluctantly, you feel yourself both the giver and the receiver of blows, at once robbed and robber, but luckily you also feel yourself a bit of a fox, as well.

Hearing these stories sixty years on, I find them at once stale and primitive, like the air in an attic, a cave of dust and cobwebs, but also a realm high among the rooftops, strewn with the gnawed bones and blackened tatters of the past, the launching-pad from which the childish imagination will take flight towards a future that is still in part a dream. Those colours, those smells, neither seen nor smelt, but simply imagined in words only half known: are they not in fact the most vivid?

Then there were the French stories about Gribouille, who burned down his house to sell the ashes and cut off his nose to spite his face, stories which left us children open-mouthed, wondering whether you could indeed sell ashes (might they be worth more than the house itself? Who would buy them? What was this topsy-turvy world where Gribouille lived?) Children would listen to these tales in silence: the fact that they were so often repeated made them as familiar as landscapes, places you go through time after time, yet without ever forgetting their potential to take you by surprise, feeling out the terrain under your feet for pitfalls, sensing the shadow cast by the hill at sundown, questioning the messages carried on the wind. With the passing of time, that distant figure of Gribouille ceased to be bizarre and unfathomable and became the yardstick for gauging human stupidity; you might stumble upon him anywhere. I like to think that our Italian Gribuia was not just the echo of the French Gribouille, but that he added a particularly Italian flavour to the popular legend which inspired George Sand and Mme de Segur. That business of cutting off one's nose to spite one's face is the first piece of home-grown nonsense I remember: little blazes of meaning which shatter the fabric of everyday speech, laughter staking its claim, declaring its presence. Why deny oneself this necessary luxury, particularly since it's free?

In other contexts, within the family the word is a pathway as narrow and stony as that leading to the Virgin of the Snows, it serves to transmit unvarnished orders: get up, be quiet, get to work! All emotions – fear, wonder, pain, joy – have to find expression in set phrases. The idea that siblings, or parents and children, might talk to each other, confide in each other, is unheard of. Individualism is heartily discouraged, to the point that it is, indeed, unthinkable. Everyone who comes into this world has a model right there before their eyes, fathers for sons, mothers for daughters, and no arguing about the unspoken rules which govern life here below: respect for authority, devotion to the land; prudence, sobriety and modesty for women, a covert cockiness for men, deference towards the powerful and acceptance of one's lot for all. Old stories too could serve as models, but also – in their own mysterious way, in their apparent ambiguity – as possible ways out.

The school is down in the village, one big room crammed with some sixty children, heated by a stove to which each pupil contributes fuel, arriving with a piece of wood under his or her arm. The teacher, who is remarkably energetic and determined, teaches three classes at once, grouping the smallest children at the front and the oldest at the back. While those in front are chanting *a, o, u* together and the second class are saying their times tables, those at the back are roving over Italy with its rivers and seas and hills. The noise level is barely tolerable, voices interweave and jar, but our teacher conducts that jangling concert like a true maestro, skillfully deploying her long baton so that it reaches into the furthest row and falls pitilessly on the ears of the mischief-makers who, in cases of particularly serious misdeeds, are summoned to the blackboard to have it fall on their bunched fingers, *tac*, a sharp rap which hurts most in winter when it lands on chilblains and *scravasse*, bloody patches in chapped skin made stiff by cold.

Because she sees her mission as dinning education into heads as hard as the stone which bred them, and since their attendance is far from regular – in winter children almost always come to school, even through deep snow, but with the arrival of spring the older ones are sent to work in the pastures and the fields – she has patented her own personal educational system which consists of multiplying each class by itself: you're in the first class for one year, in the second for two and the third for three. Like that, one way or another, something will get into those shaved and lice-infested heads; it's better to spend the winter on benches rather than in the stable, at least they're obliged to wash their hands and faces and learn to count and utter a few words of Italian, which no one speaks at home, and when they go down into the valleys everyone laughs at them and cheats them.

Ninin likes the teacher. For all its severity, in comparison with that of *la granda* her regime is like a breath of fresh air. At school Ninin encounters the hitherto unknown concept of fairness, by which she is much taken. One day the teacher brings a sack of chestnuts into class and roasts them on the stove; each child is given the same number. Everyone gobbles them up at high speed, burning their tongues because the chestnuts are still hot, before someone else can come and filch them, although in their heart of hearts they know this will not happen, not here. The teacher distributes raps and praise impartially, according to the principle of what's sauce for the goose is sauce for the gander, which will become one of the linchpins of her pupil's credo.

Knowing herself to be a citizen of the world, feeling that

she has a certain dignity, young though she is, being able to do her duty with her head held high rather than humbly and shamefully with eyes cast down: Ninin likes school. She attends as often as she can, it doesn't matter to her if her feet in their clogs are sopping wet and her damp dress steams as she sits next to the stove. The teacher has faith in her – perhaps those young eyes already show the first glints of that steely tendency to take care of her neighbour which was to reach such a pitch over the course of her lifetime – and makes her her assistant. Ninin busies herself in helping with the little ones, just as she does at home.

One winter night she is awoken by the voice of her mother, down below. She is not shouting, she is not even talking particularly loudly, but Ninin, heart beating loudly, immediately sits up, so that the mattress starts to creak. She throws off her little sister Maria who is sleeping on top of her, jumps down from the bed, doesn't put on her clogs so as not to make a noise; runs barefoot on to the wooden landing, goes down the stairs leading to the courtyard and peeks through the gap beneath the shutters, which is just at her own level.

In the kitchen Domenica and old Bartolomeo, one to each side of the table, are glaring at one another; red in the face, she's breathing heavily, the palms of her hands resting on the wood. Still wearing his cloak, he is one dark and threatening mass. It's Saturday night, he's just come back from the wine shop, before his sons.

'I married one, not two,' says Domenica choking back the tears; steeling herself by pressing a hand on the dishevelled knot in her handkerchief.

Then she turns round and moves away. He takes a step towards her, sways, holds out a heavy arm. The door swings open, Ninin flattens herself against the wall, between the window and the bench. Domenica flies up the stairs without even making them creak, in the kitchen the *pare grand* is blaspheming and spitting on the ground.

Ninin follows her mother into the bedroom. Domenica gives her daughter a look which alarms her, as though asking for help. But then she takes her in her arms and they sleep together in the grown-ups' bed until morning, when Giuseppe wakes them up by crashing down on to the mattress like a dead weight.

From then on the old man is ever more alarming, an irate, inscrutable god who casts a cold shadow on the beaten earth that is the floor. Ninin shrinks at the very sight of him.

That phrase 'I married one, not two', buzzes around in her head, it sounds sinful and threatening. Her mother seems to be being driven towards some strange abyss, from which she can rescue herself only by some dizzying acrobatic feat.

'Marriage is the union of man and woman for the founding of a family,' says the teacher. 'Honour your father and mother,' say the commandments. 'A bit of respect, if you don't mind,' thunders *la granda* if anyone dares step out of line.

The idea that unfairness and evil could work themselves into the very roots of power fills her with pained astonishment. Yet that is how it is, she's always known it, and now she senses it in her mother's timid gestures, in her downcast eyes, in the thumping of her heart, so loud it seems to find a echo within her own ribs.

La granda, all-seeing as always, now takes an even greater dislike to her young daughter-in-law, becomes even more brusque and demanding. One day – it is some holiday or other – while they are turning the cheeses in the *crotin*, Domenica tackles her mother-in-law head on with the words: 'I can hold my head high, I've never brought dishonour on my husband's house – your son's, that is.'

Her eyes bright with malice and loathing, the old woman proceeds to pour a bucket of milk over Domenica's feet.

'Look what you've done,' she says to her, 'that means that tonight you and your daughters will go to bed without any supper.'

Domenica sees that she has said the wrong thing, it is not reassurance that the old woman is seeking. She should have held her tongue. Perhaps she should even… but she dare not think along those lines. If *la granda* has not previously been her friend, she is now her enemy. Domenica becomes increasingly nervous, clutches Michin, her youngest, to her, holds her in her arms as though the presence of a child were enough to keep her out of danger, while it has been clearly proved that, that is not the case, because there are always plenty of children around, in those cramped spaces, and things happen anyway.

One day, at milking-time, when Ninin is in the stable peeling chestnuts almost in the dark – her fingers are so expert they don't need light – *il grand* comes in and shuts the door behind him. He walks forward, slightly bent, his black jacket turning twilight into night. Seated under the brown cow, *magna* Rita trembles as he approaches. There's a brief rasping sound, is it a stifled cry or just the three-legged stool knocked over by a clumsy gesture of the woman doing the milking?

Ninin is seized with a sudden sense of danger and also a strange fascination, as though one of those devilish portents described in winter evening gatherings were taking place before her very eyes. She'd like to run away, to disappear, but she daren't take a step, she's afraid she'll be seen and meet the same fate as the woman, who's been set upon by the man, and shaken, and repeatedly knocked against the wall. She doesn't seem to be putting up any resistance, her body is acting as a shock absorber for *il grand's* gasping frenzy, or has he actually killed her?

Ninin is probably crying, or more likely whimpering like a dog. She certainly wets herself from fear, as she can tell afterwards from the state of her dress and drawers.

Suddenly *il grand* turns round, scans the shadows, catches sight of her. His blazing eyes are those of a beast-god ready for a good meal. His hands are fumbling through the woman's dishevelled garments, she's slumped against him, he's pushing her away. The child forces herself into action and runs out of the room, followed by the crack of the willow cane, taking with her for ever the memory of the half-dead woman, *magna* Rita, floppy as a rag doll.

Ninin runs up the road to the shrine of Our Lady of the Snows, pauses for breath, mumbles a hasty Ave Maria and checks that no one is running after her. It's pitch dark by the time she gets home and they are already out looking for her, her grandmother is not going to forgive her but she couldn't care less about missing supper this evening, all she cares about is snuggling up close to her mother and fervently thanking Our Lady that it wasn't she who had been in the stable, that it hadn't been Domenica's turn to milk that evening and die that strange death.

In fact Rita is still alive but she's not in good shape. Every day Ninin checks to see whether she's ill, if she's bleeding, dying. Women bleed, they often have strange illnesses, sometimes the washing in the stream is all red and there are bloody sheets each time they buy a baby at the market. But Rita survives, she's just paler and quieter than usual, that's all.

'She's sensitive, she's missing her man,' says *la granda*.

Her husband, *barba* Nando, went off at the end of autumn

and no one knows when he'll be back.

'Isn't she the lucky one?' comments Domenica quietly; she has not forgotten her sister-in-law's rejection of her attempts at friendship. 'Sensitive, is she? I haven't got the time.'

Spring arrives and Giuseppe says that he's off too. Every family has men who go off, and sometimes even a woman; they go to France to work. Domenica looks up and seems to want to say something but then doesn't.

Ninin hears her parents talking in the stable, in the kitchen garden, keeping their voices down so that the old folk can't hear them, Domenica runs after him, tugs at his sleeve. He says: 'No, not you! You're staying here.'

She follows him, 'Don't leave me alone,' she says beseechingly. 'No,' he says again, 'you're staying here.'

But one day in fact it's the pair of them who leave, knapsacks on their backs, and Maria bursts into tears and says: 'Ma, where are you going?' and Michin, just out of swaddling clothes, joins in the blubbing, even more loudly, she's teething, so Ninin can't join in, because she's the oldest.

'Look after your sisters,' her mother says to her. 'Look after yourself.'

She strokes her hair and off she goes, her clogs sinking into the sodden ground.

At school there is a map hanging on the wall. France is on it too, its original pink colour now somewhat less bright because of the smoke from the stove. Italy on the other hand is greenish. The teacher tells them that their parents, uncles and brothers are seasonal emigrants. They go to France to work as day labourers, picking grapes, walnuts and lavender, or flowers for scent, they work the land, some of them also work in factories, they do this because here there isn't enough work to go round, not enough to keep their families. Children who have emigrant relatives must behave themselves, because their parents can see them; just as the eye of God can see all that man does and thinks, so mothers and fathers can see into the hearts of their own children, far away though they may be.

It's lucky the teacher explains this to her, no one in the family has ever put it so clearly. At first Ninin has difficulty in understanding quite what France is, she tries to imagine her mother surrounded by pinkish grey land and that frightens her. How could land be that colour? Is the countryside as flat as the map? Are its frontiers really marked by brown pencil rather than by ditches and stone walls?

It's a wet spring, it rains a lot, it's still cold and the children sneeze. She helps the little ones to hold their pens, she blows runny noses, keeps an eye on the stove. When school is over she takes Maria by the hand to stop her from running all over the hills like a goat, and they walk down the path together, poking around in the grass under the chestnut trees, with all this rain there might be mushrooms.

After a few days she begins to feel her eyes are prickling, it gets stronger, becomes a burning feeling. One evening at supper, in front of all and sundry, she feels two fat tears roll down her cheeks and a choking little voice utters the words: 'When will ma be back? Where is she?'

'Where is she, where is she?' says Catlina mockingly. 'How should I know? Maybe she got lost on the way. Ask the fresh air from the door. Nice women stay at home.'

'She went to France with your father, surely you know that?' says *barba* Giacu sniggering, his mouth full of polenta.

When her grandmother's head is turned, aunt Rita ladles another portion of milk and chestnut soup into Ninin's plate.

These are the last chestnuts of the season and, as it's been so wet, they are dark, maggotty and bitter.

'Come on,' says Catlina to anyone who dares complain, 'one good chestnut washes down a bad one.'

Maria eats fastidiously, trawling cautiously through what's in her bowl with her spoon.

'What are you doing?' they ask her.

'Looking for the good chestnut,' she says, 'but I can't find it.'

Ninin gets up and goes to stand at the door. The sun is setting, and there's a streak of pinkish grey – the colour of France, only cleaner, without the smoke from the stove. Over there lies France, she knows it does, that's the way they went when they left. They went towards the higher mountains, and then they would have gone down the other side.

And suddenly Ninin realises that beyond those peaks are other peaks, beyond those villages other villages, beyond those goats and cows and pastures other goats and cows and pastures until the end of the land, namely the sea. *Mare*, the same word she uses for her mother. How odd words are.

And now notions acquired, and words heard, begin to come together in her head to form a picture which is beginning to make sense, suddenly the map represents something real, the symbols become part of life, tingeing it with their colour. She imagines her mother climbing up through the grey-mauve mountains, towards the pink sunset, pink France. She sees her going down the other side, through a country which is not so different from her own, but which basks in the sun's last, loveliest rays. She sees her mother milking goats and hoeing potatoes under a soft reddish sky, in a land where the sun is forever suspended above the mountains. Together with her mother but smaller and more distant, is her father, with a big basket of grapes on his back, grapes which are not bitter likes those on the *topia*, the pergola in front of her house, but sweet and white.

And, she now sees, the air over France is the same as the air over here, and so is the sky, and the clouds. The earth is dark and hard and it stays put, but the air moves, that's what the teacher told her, that's what people say, the other day Bastian was coming up the hill with his old hat jammed down on his head and he'd said to her: 'You'd best be getting back, *cita*, there's a storm on its way from France.' And not long afterwards there was rain and hail. Now, with immense relief, and gratitude, Ninin realises that her mother is not so far away, she has not disappeared, as she sometimes fears, but is surrounded by the same air she breathes herself, and that same air may be alive with messages sent by Domenica to her daughters, and perhaps if they listen carefully they might hear her voice, coming here straight from France.

Barba Nando, Rita's husband, comes back at the beginning of summer. He's quarrelled with a mate in France and has had problems at work; some months ago they'd written to him to tell him that his brother and sister-in-law had left for France, and he'd thought his folks would be pleased to see him back because they needed men to work the land.

But his return is greeted with unusual solemnity, even a sense of alarm. *Il grand* is more irritable and sullen than usual, the old woman just looks inscrutable. *Barba* Giacu is gloomy and tense. Rita, all bundled up despite the heat, is pale as death.

Supper is unusually silent, Nando ventures the odd comment about his journey, his work, his pay. He's hardly glanced at his wife, let alone kissed her. It's not done for husband and wife to show affection in public, nor indeed is there reason to think that it's in much in evidence in private. After a bit the words die on his lips – perhaps he is exhausted, or defeated by the general unease.

For once there's some wine on the table, so the men drink, in silence.

The storm breaks out at night, and there are shouts, and blows.

Because he's had a drink, Nando is talkative, indeed he never stops, shouting out repeated questions, particularly: 'Who? Who? Who?' – and his monosyllables take on the rhythm of the blows.

The stream of talk is broken by one particularly loud shriek. *La granda* comes into the bedroom saying: 'Now that's enough, you don't want to kill her,' and Nando lifts an arm as though to fell *la granda* too, then crumples on to the floor and weeps like a baby.

'Now that'll do,' *la granda* says, addressing him with some disdain, towering over him with all five foot of her stringy frame, 'you don't want to make a laughing stock of yourself.'

'You'd better call the doctor, and quick!' says Tonieta, the neighbour. The whole village has woken up and is looking on.

La granda answers haughtily, you only call the doctor when things are truly desperate, and what's so serious about a woman bleeding? The two of them will handle matters, and perhaps the priest, if that's God's will.

The children don't know what happens next, because they are sent to bed with the threat of a slap. There's no need to call the priest because Rita doesn't die, not this time either. After a few days she's back at work, slightly bent and stiff because she's cracked a rib in falling. Nando carries on drinking, his work suffers, Giacu complains, he and *pare* can't manage on their own. When Nando sobers up he's a changed man, he has a different look. At the beginning of autumn he returns to France.

Weeks pass before Ninin learns what has happened; she learns it from Main, Tonieta's daughter and her own distant cousin, a few years older than herself: Rita wanted to buy a baby on her own, without telling her husband, Nando didn't want this baby and that's why he hit her.

'But did she buy the baby or didn't she?' asked Ninin.

'No,' said Main. And, repeating what she has heard at home, she adds: 'Luckily, it died.'

So, a corpse at last. In Ninin's mind an obscure link is forged between that evening in the stable, months ago, and the mysterious fate of this baby that hasn't been bought. Could Rita be a witch? Is that why *il grand* had wanted to kill her that night in the stable? Is this why *barba* Nando hit her? Is it she who's caused the baby to die?

From that time onwards she has approached her aunt with a strange feeling of unease, with something like repugnance. That helpless woman, incapable of raising her hand or voice, has a sort of curse upon her, one that cannot be lifted. Since she has been punished, she must be guilty, that's what the stories Ninin is always hearing tell her, the ones where the witch is betrayed by signs of her beatings and wounds and disfigurements. So Rita too has committed some sin, the most unforgivable, the most awful sin imaginable, and that's why she suffers in silence and puts up no defence.

It's a long summer, spent almost entirely out of doors. Looking after the animals until dusk, and careful you don't lose them, goats leap around like anything and vanish in a trice, and she'll put Michin down to run after the goat and Michin will crawl off into the grass and Ninin must run after her before she falls into the ditch, and in the meantime the other goat has slipped its halter, and Maria is no use, she too gets lost, she plays at hide and seek, and so the days go by, with everyone running here and there, nervous as kittens, under the boiling sun or freezing wind, with the mountains looming behind you fit to take your breath away.

Lunch is a slice of cold polenta and the odd fig, or a handful of *ramassin*, sweet little plums which get squashed in your knapsack and go all sticky. And the whole day is spent looking for something to put into your mouth, bilberries and wild strawberries and blackberries and *ciriboit*, those tiny bitter wild cherries with big stones, you might think they were hardly worth eating, but such little flesh as they do have is more fragrant than that of any cultivated fruit.

You're bound to feel sleepy when the sun is at its height, after all you got up at dawn, so you stretch out in the shade with your head on your knapsack and beg Maria to stay awake, because you have to take it in turns to sleep, not both at once, but Maria nods off too, and when you wake up you have to go after the goats again, barefoot on the stones with an eye out for vipers, slithering down the slopes, flaying your legs on brambles.

And once she wakes up to find Michin just feet away from a long brown snake which is eyeing her, about to strike, and she shrieks in terror and waves her stick at the snake, which slithers away, and Michin, alarmed by the din, starts to cry, and Ninin doles out a few hearty slaps to the two little ones and scolds the lot of them, goats included, because they have simply wandered off instead of giving the alarm.

And when a storm breaks out you rush back home, through the pouring rain, terrified of the lightning as it rends the air, murmuring breathless *ave marias* to ward off the thunderbolts, because if they get you they leave you all scorched, dead and black. The stories you've heard on winter evenings in the stable, or in summer under the pergola, come back to frighten you, and you have to go alone along the paths and over the peaks under an uncaring sky, and you think you hear steps and voices and whispers at your back. And you peek quickly behind you, hoping that the thousand spirits which are suddenly whispering around you won't see how scared you are.

You make long detours to avoid going anywhere near certain spooky houses from which nasty men might emerge, like the one called Pinot her mother has told her to avoid like the plague, or that ghastly old scarecrow of a woman, who stinks like a polecat and is said to drink more than any man, and cackles in a way that makes your hair stand on end.

But her greatest fear is linked to her own responsibilities. A child of just eight, she is in of charge of beings even smaller and more scatter-brained than herself, as though Ninin were already a grown woman – but she's not. She's been along those paths a thousand times – but know them though she may, they're always new for her, one single cloud in the sky will alter how they look.

Her mind is painfully torn between a childish desire to marvel, to play, to concentrate on small, nearby things, and the need to focus on big, distant ones, and never to let herself be distracted. Her child's arms are barely long enough to hold the goats' ropes, the body of one sister and the hand of another; they are slight, yet they have to be as strong as pillars, to which people can cling.

'But where is Ma?' asks Maria.

'You mean you don't know? She's in France.'

'When will she be back?'

'Soon.'

'That's what you always say, but she never is.'

'Just be patient, she'll be back.'

'If Ma doesn't come back, I'm not going back home,' says Maria, who yesterday had been given a hearty slap by *la granda*, for having put her fingers in the cream from which the butter is made.

'Don't be silly,' says Ninin. 'Ma can hear you, you know, she's just over there, she can hear everything.' And she raises her arm and points towards France, beyond the mountains. 'Ma always knows what a daughter of hers is doing, even if she's far away.'

Maria, who is five, gives the matter some thought.

'So,' she says after a moment, 'if she can hear us, we can hear her.'

Ninin stops to think about it, and she can't see any holes in this argument. She thinks of her mother so often, so intensely, it's as though she sees and hears her in every corner. In the evening, when they are going home, driving the animals before them, Maria with Michin in her arms and Ninin with a great bundle of grass wrapped up in a sack on her head, scythe hanging from her belt, Maria – partly as a joke, but partly in earnest – begins to describe what Ma is doing at that moment.

'She's making supper for Pa in a big kitchen with a nice fire; he's just got back from work. She's put a rabbit in the pan, she's browning it in butter. You can smell it from here,' she says.

Her favourite dish is stewed rabbit. She's eaten it just once, a little bit as small as that, actually more bone than flesh, but she remembers it to this day.

Each evening Ninin pauses for a moment at the door and breathes in the *aria d'l'uss*, the fresh air from the door, her ally, her allotted portion of hopes and certainties. 'Come home,

Ma,' she whispers, 'make it soon, I'm waiting for you, today Maria tore her dress, Michin has tummy-ache, I learned how to do division, it's true that I also threw a stone at Martin, but it's his fault because he called me names, let me know when you'll be back.'

Fair weather or foul, come rain or shine, it's her mother who sends the weather from the other side of the mountains.

Towards the end of autumn the migrants start coming home, but her mother is never among them. They've received a letter, and *barba* Giacu reads it out loud at table. It says: 'Dear Father dear Mother we are well as we hope are all of you, here it's no picnic but we get by.' They never mention their return except in the vaguest of terms. They never talk about Ninin and her sisters, they are included in 'all of you', just as Domenica is included in 'we are well', a piece of verbal economy which leaves Ninin less satisfied than ever. The letter is signed: 'Your affectionate son Giuseppe.'

The envelope is put on the mantlepiece, under a piece of stone from the shrine at Oropa. One morning Ninin gets up early, before anyone else, to see whether that is really all that is written on that sheet of squared paper. But it is still dark, and she can't make out the writing.

Now of an evening Ninin stands outside the door and prays. She prays to the Madonna, just as her mother does, she says an *Ave Maria* and if she can get through it without drawing breath it means her mother will come back, she tries the same thing with two prayers, but fails. Ma isn't coming back, that is her punishment for having stolen the bread, for all the times she's answered her grandmother back and for the oh how many more times she's wished her ill: if only brigands would kidnap her, if only she'd loose her footing while going to the fountain and crack open her head!

(But if there's a God in heaven, if indeed heaven or hell exist, then grandmother's place is certainly in hell. For Ninin this will remain an article of faith throughout her life. As an old woman she will offer her words to God by way of challenge: 'Now watch out God, don't disappoint me – a great deal hangs on this!')

She prays and clutches the door-post with reddened fingers. The little knife she uses to peel potatoes and chestnuts has become blunted, and she's got calluses on her thumb and index finger to show for it.

'And shut that door,' shouts out *la granda*.

For some time now, grandfather has been gloomier than ever. One night, coming back from the wine shop in the village he falls over and breaks an arm. He has to pay the doctor, and now he's got his arm in a sling and can't work on the land.

'What a disaster,' says *la granda*.

Ninin keeps her head down, but somewhere within her burns a tiny, guilty, obstinate glow of satisfaction. She keeps it hidden between her dress and her chemise, between her chemise and her skin, like the chestnuts that she burns her hands on as she steals them out of the fire, one for her and one for each of her sisters, to be eaten in haste because here we're not at school, here there is no teacher to ensure fair deals.

'There's not much justice around these parts,' she thinks. 'If there is anything like justice,' she carries on confusedly, 'I too must have a part in it, it's got to be everywhere equally.' And yes, she thinks, now perhaps her mother could come back, now that the old man is huddled by the fire and seems to have shrunk; he's not so frightening any more.

All Saints Day comes, and then All Souls, and you leave them a slice of polenta, a plate of *brusatà*, roast chestnuts, and a glass of wine. Lured by the smell of the unguarded food, Maria gets out of bed and eats it. She comes back to bed slightly tipsy, she's drunk the wine as well, and she waves a bit of polenta under the nose of the sleepy Ninin. Ninin gobbles it up a little nervously, it sticks in her throat, after all it's meant to be supper for the dead! What if they take offence and come and grab her by the feet? Then, despite herself, she falls asleep again and wakes up in the morning, and nothing at all has happened.

When he finds the empty plates, *barba* Giacu swears loudly, *la granda* darts out accusing looks, but the two cousins – the older Bartolomeo and the younger Pietro, who's thick-headed and often half asleep – say that it was the dead who ate the food, both are struck dumb, they gawp at the plate, and then *barba* begins to laugh, not a sight you often see, a single man, a widower, in awe of his father and mother, but this morning he's laughing like a drain: 'Yes, that'll be it, the dead came out to eat and drink, just as we'd expected! They know which side their bred is buttered, those blessed dead!'

Fortunately Maria is in a dark corner and no one is looking at her, otherwise they would see the glint of quiet satisfaction in her eyes, and some smart spanking would follow.

With November come mists and cold and the sun does not show itself for days on end, not even as a red glow in the sky. The air is biting, it smells of smoke and frost. Standing outside the door, Ninin strains her ears listening to the empty air and feels overcome by despair.

And then, one Sunday morning while she is asleep, she feels two cool hands laid on her forehead and for a moment of pure wonder she dreams that she has been enveloped in the pink air of the heavens and lifted upwards in a journey that will never end.

Then she opens her eyes and sees her mother's smiling face. She looks her up and down, her cheeks are a little fuller than before she left, her hair is messy because she's slept in the cart on the way, and her stomach beneath her clothing already announces the arrival of her first boy child, another Bartolomeo. She's gazing at Ninin with her hazel eyes.

And Ninin, at long last, breaks out into one huge sob.

They will be separated again a few years later, but this time it is Ninin who leaves. At the age of twelve, now that she's been through the third form the requisite three times, and is capable of saying her times tables backwards and forwards, she's ready to move on into the world of adult arithmetic and economics. The family has grown, it's too big, there's not much land, nor does it yield much, it's time for the oldest to go and earn her crust of bread. Maria will stay at home to help Domenica, she's nine now and knows how to sew, mend and wash, and Michin will take the goats to pasture, she herself is like a *crava* , a goat, the way she leaps up and down the crags, never still for a minute. After Bartolomeo, known as Mecio, comes another girl, Margherita, and *il grand* has a good moan about all those females his daughter-in-law keeps on churning out, and Ninin, little and thin as a rake as she is, tells him roundly that all those females graft from dawn to dusk, scything the grass and hulling the maize and milking the cows, while he sits by the fire and is waited on hand and foot, and *il grand* goes scarlet with fury and waves his stick at her but misses, because she is so much the nimbler of the two. Anyway, that evening Ninin stays away from home, she dines on a handful of plums and figs and spends the night in the hay, above the stall, just to be on the safe side. The next day she tells her mother that she wants to go and work in a factory straight away, without waiting for the autumn.

Down in Ciriè they're taking on women and girls in the textile factories, the daughters of a woman they know are working in one of them and every Saturday night they come home with their week's pay. Her mother would like her around for a while longer, but Ninin stands her ground, she can already see herself, pay packet in hand, she'll buy material to make her mother a coat, and shoes for her sisters, and white bread and sweets. She's so determined that she doesn't mind the idea of leaving her mother and her sisters, after all it's on their behalf that she wants to go into this factory. She tells her sister Maria not to cry – Maria is prone to tears – because in a few years she'll be able to join her in the factory, and bring Michin along as well, they'll be much better off down there, down in the village where all you ate wasn't polenta and curds, and also they'd be out of the clutches of *il grand*, they'd be able to laugh and joke whenever the mood took them, and not have to keep their heads forever bowed.

And so it is that she does indeed leave, one morning, at four o'clock, together with some other girls who are already factory-workers, carrying a bundle with a bit of linen and a small bag of flour. But the evening before she leaves, while they're sitting outside after supper and her mother is sewing a button on to her shirt in the last glimmer of daylight, and she is sitting next to her in silence, slightly alarmed at what is happening, the people of Ca' d'Gara all come out into the street to say goodbye, to savour the scent of novelty which is gathering around her. They come from other hamlets, too, and Main d'la Riva comes as well, she was Ninin's godmother at her first communion. She arrives all out of breath, on the arm of a young grandson, because she is old now, and her legs are not so good. They talk about her in the gathering dusk, as though she herself were not there; one neighbour says: 'I've come to say goodbye to you for the last time, *cita*, thin and puny as you are you'll never leave that factory alive'; some agree, others do not. Ninin, who is indeed a wisp of a girl, or at least gives that impression, does not know what to say, not that it matters to her that much, old folk always like talking about death and disaster, it's meat and drink to them. Her mother doesn't say anything either, she just clutches Ninin's arm and pulls her fiercely to her, as though to say that if death has any designs upon her, it's her mother that death will have to reckon with.

It's the summer of 1903, and Ninin doesn't die. Indeed, factory life proves to be a positive tonic. By the next summer, when she spends a couple of weeks at home to help with the haymaking, she's grown nearly two inches and looks distinctly less hollow-cheeked. She'll never be buxom, but it's true that down in the valley they eat more, and much better. And an eleven hour stretch in the factory is nothing new for her, used as she has been to getting up early and capering around from dawn to dusk. Her sisters want to know all about her new life, they can't wait to follow in her footsteps.

Theirs is a modest dream, to find work in the nearby town and sleep all together in the same room – ideally with Ma, as well, if they can persuade her, if Pa gives his permission. But this is a dream which has the advantage of being realistic, and it serves to enable them to swallow the bad chestnut, to put up with *la granda's* spiteful tones and *il grand's* hawking. It even helps them to endure the assaults from the bloodthirsty fleas which emerge night after night from the *pajun,* the straw mattress, leaving furious little red marks on their tender skin.

At the dawn of the new century, they ask for nothing more

than to work together. And, by dint of doing and hoping, this dream will come true. It will leave its mark on the rest of their lives, and then on that of the only daughter any one of them will have, my mother – and, finally, upon my own. If these women had not been what they were, I would not be here at all – or I would not be what I am.

Their daughter will come from the sea, many years later, but it is as though they are already preparing themselves, even now, as children, to receive her.

The Little Girl from America

What was my mother Maria like at the age of eight, when she came back here? I know from her passport photo that she had a little round face and dark eyes; her helmet of hair is neatly combed, the soft childish curves of her chubby face make her look like a porcelain doll. On the photo, her wobbly schoolchild's signature declares her to be 'Mariana Rastler'. So, her father called her Mariana? Her face is veiled in the seamless, fragile inscrutability of childhood. I know that she was shy, she hardly talked at all… I'd like to hear her voice, to hear her talk a tongue which I imagine as a mixture of three languages, American, Mexican and that other language which no one on the boat can speak.

Chin resting on her hands, arms on the parapet, Maria is screwing up her eyes to peer into the distance. Down on the quay men and carts come and go, but they are too small for her to tell one from another. Between her and them lies a stretch of black water coated with a network of oily, iridescent reflections. It's a weak yellow spring day, with the sun dissolving and drowning in the sky.

Maria wipes her nose on her coat sleeve because she has no

handkerchief, Lina, the maid who is looking after her on board, forgot to give her one this morning, her mind is elsewhere, she's anxious to set foot on dry land after having spent an extra night on the ship to keep Maria company.

Maria is tired, she didn't sleep well last night, she'd kept on waking up to peer through the heavy curtain to see whether the sun had risen.

The journey is over. Now it stretches behind her like a great blue and golden bridge over the ocean. A bridge of light crowded with visions, with the call of sea birds, with the soft swaying of the ship which is a bit like riding a pony, an immense pony with a humming metal back; and the band that plays in the evening, the scent of the ladies taking tea beneath their parasols, the novel smell of Oswego biscuits. The rough sea with its sudden spurts of foam, the officers' uniforms with their gleaming buttons, the chrome handrails, the salt-laden wind, the clink of the glasses in the warm, dense air of the dining-room. And the sky all around, now deep and any number of different shades of blue and streaked with clouds, now flat and uniform. Sky and sea merge into each other in the evening, you can't tell where they meet, and at night you might imagine you were flying along as part of that great black, damp, shining mass which is the sky-sea, the sea-sky. Then early in the morning, before it's time to get up, through the porthole you can see the sun rising like a red fruit, which ripens in an instant and spreads its fiery flesh over the blue. In the full daylight, if you're lucky, you can see the dolphins leaping, their arched and gleaming backs executing perfect curves in the air and everyone is saying Ooh look! and Maria opens her mouth but says nothing, her wonder ringing silently within her.

The Pacific, the Panama Canal, the long Atlantic crossing

are slowly vanishing in her wake.

Now Maria is here, stock-still at last, on the unmoving ship moored in front of the city, in the middle of the water. She is alone among strangers. Only a few people are still on board, and she is suddenly seized with shyness even with those whom she knows, the maid and the barber who cut her hair just yesterday. It is as though they were different people now that the voyage is over. Missis Rose and her women friends have all gone. The only people left are men who rush around the deck without looking at her.

Maria can't make out the distant figures on the quay. She's looking for a touch of light colour among the dark: a woman's dress. A lilac or light blue or even ecru dress like the ones Missis Rose wears of an afternoon when she takes tea with her friends, and they talk and laugh, but never too loudly, with their faces half-hidden by their big straw hats.

When she imagines her mother, she dresses her in Missis Rose's wardrobe. Yesterday Missis Rose left the ship together with her husband and her maid Anne and Miss Lora, her friend, and before she left she hugged Maria and said 'Good luck my little girl', and bent over her with a swish of blue silk and her kiss stayed on Maria's cheek like a soap bubble, it shook in the wind and burst and Maria, surprisingly, felt a little pang of pain at the thought that Missis Rose was leaving her, that she'd never see her again, that the voyage was over.

What colour will her mother's dress be? Will she be wearing a hat? More to the point, perhaps, when will she show up?

Down on the quay she can see nothing white, or light blue, or lilac, or ecru.

Then it occurs to her that perhaps her mother will be wearing black. She too had been dressed in black when she'd first gone to stay with *magna* Neta. She remembers the smell of the once pink dress, after it had been endlessly boiled in the dye. Then after a few months *magna* Neta had said: 'That's enough black, at this rate you'll be upsetting Lucy as well,' and she had her put on her usual clothes, which in the meantime had become too short and tight. Even the red coat she's wearing is a bit tight, last year it had belonged to Lucy, they'd given it to her because after all she did need something decent to wear on board. Somehow or other she felt guilty, orphans aren't supposed to dress in red. And what if her mother doesn't recognise her, wearing Lucy's red coat?

She stares at the people down on the quay at Genoa. Little dark faceless shifting specks, rolling around each other. She feels a sort of pins and needles in the nape of her neck, as you do when someone you're very much expecting is about to arrive. Where is her mother? She closes her eyes: when she opens them, her mother will be in the exact spot where she is looking. But when she opens them again the only thing occupying that exact spot is an empty cart, pulled by a mule which is tossing its head.

In her mind's eye she sees the photo sitting on the shelf in the kitchen, but the face has faded in her memory, and the more she stares at it the fuzzier it gets. For a moment, fear of not recognising her mother causes her to gulp down air as though she were drowning.

Cirié is down on the plain but on clear days you can see the mountains to the east and north. It has a medieval centre with long porticoes, and having been a feud of the Doria family it has a seventeenth-century hunting lodge with a fine Italian garden and above all a splendid wide avenue of plane trees leading from the station to the church of San Giovanni and the nearby elementary school. From there, a street which is now called via Rosmini, but which used to be called via Conte Verde, leads into the countryside.

The last house at the end of via Conte Verde, before the open countryside, used to belong to my mother's family, it had been bought by grandfather Giuseppe to house him and his wife Domenica and their daughters after they'd come down from the village of Rocca to Ciriè to work in the factory, those two rooms being, for decades, the only property that the Davito Gara clan were to own down there on the plain.

Here, today, Maria, poor thing, is all alone waiting for her daughter. Ninin, her older sister, is in the factory, at the loom, because it's Friday, a working day, and Michin has already had to ask for an unpaid day off for that trip to Genoa to pick up the *cita*, together with her younger sister Margherita and her husband Ermanno. They couldn't possibly both take the day off, Ninin had said: 'You go, you're the younger sister and your shoes are almost new.' 'No, you go, you're the older one,' Michin had said quickly, but meanwhile her eyes were shining at the idea of going to Genoa, and Ninin said: 'No, I'm not one to put myself forward, you go with Margherita, I'll stay at home.' Maria, poor thing, will certainly not be going to Genoa, after all she hasn't as much as been out into the street since she's been back from America, and she has her sisters describe the little town to her of an evening, all the same, she would have liked to be asked, even just for politeness sake.

This morning she has taken longer than usual getting dressed, her dress has been washed and ironed and no longer yields so easily to the familiar outlines of her body; her hands are weak and forgetful, she keeps losing her grip, pausing in the middle of smoothing her brown stockings on her legs, doing up the buttons.

She has gone through all the usual performances, hobbled

slowly down the wooden stairs, poured out the coffee left warming on the stove, stirred up the embers with the iron poker, riddled the stove, stoked it up with a piece of wood every so often because it is still cold and the house is damp. Then, leaning in turn against the wall, the chair, the door and the pergola, she goes to the kitchen garden and bends down to pick a bit of salad.

I see her now, her movements so clear in my memory, as familiar as everything that you've known right from your earliest years and which for that reason are all the harder to describe: that way she has of dragging herself along and going down the stairs which as a child I thought must be a kind of game, pausing on every step as though to reconsider the world from that particular vantage point, cautiously lowering a foot, hands gripping the banisters, then deploying all her willpower, and her weight, to slide the other foot over the black stone and let it flop down with a dull thud. Moving, for her, meant triumphing, step by step, over the resistance put up by that half of her body that had never made it back from California. Her left side had stayed over there, making my mother a cloven viscountess who lives not without an arm, a leg, with half a torso and half a face, but rather with their lifeless presence.

Nor is her mind quite what it has been either, those around her whisper. A faint air of pity and shame clings to her, closing her in, sealing each word and gesture. Maria, poor thing, is not herself. She is treated like a child by the grown-ups, and it is only us children who regard her as an adult, who take her seriously, seated on her low chair, for ever dressed in black, reading us fairy stories and the lives of the saints. Pinocchio or Don Bosco, Alice or Bernadette, it's all the same to us, always the same wonderland. Nothing is odd or different when everything is just that. We didn't yet know that grown-up's stories have other rules.

Maria was cloven as she was giving birth, and family legend has it that it was the midwife's fault, because she was Mexican and therefore probably not very clean. Steeped in fatalism like all good legends, the family version saw the midwife as destiny's handmaid; fate had already spirited two sons away from Maria, one still-born after she had witnessed a set-to between her husband Pietro and a rival armed with a knife, and another killed by forceps in a hospital which couldn't have been more American. So it had been decided that she would have the child at home, and indeed the little girl had come out safe and sound but she herself had been stricken by a mysterious illness which had left her permanently semi-paralysed, in all likelihood an ictus, suffered a few days after a difficult birth.

In fact, fate had already carried her well and truly off at the age of twenty-nine, that's the only way I can explain it to myself, her yielding to the undisputed power of convention raised to the rank of fate, that decision to go off to America with an unknown man, abandoning her sisters and all she knew. She was in service with a family of penniless nobles from Turin, where she had learned to iron lace collars to perfection, and to make so-called *minestra maritata,* literally married soup, a very delicate dish with added beaten eggs and parmesan. She may not have been happy there, although from what we know they treated her perfectly decently. Of course, in those days a servant was a servant, she didn't address her betters in a familiar manner and she expected to be given her orders. Certainly she slept in one of those windowless rooms adjoining the kitchen, the maid's room, as it was called, you can still see them, turned into box-rooms, in houses once belonging to families who were solidly middle-class. The street where she lived was right in the centre, via Pietro Micca perhaps, in a house with a very grand entrance, with Gothic arches in the inner portico and carved balustrades running up the stairs, in a dark flat consisting of two large rooms overlooking the street and other more modest ones overlooking an inner balcony. When she went out she would immediately be bang in the middle of town, among shops and cafes. Had she ever dared to have a hot chocolate at Baratti's, with some adventurous friend, all dressed up, or had she gone out just on Sundays, to take the little Ciriè-Lanzo train to see her sisters?

Had she found her life depressing? Going into service was normal for a woman of her status and generation. Anyway, in those days women were almost always servants even in their own homes: to their husbands, their mothers-in-law, the older members of the family... Maria was in a privileged position: being in service in Turin meant sleeping on a mattress rather than on straw, eating tagliatelle instead of polenta, wearing shoes rather than clogs and not having chilblains in winter.

Perhaps she wanted children. Perhaps she dreamt of a house of her own, with her own pots and pans, her own sheets. Or was she haunted by the idea that an unmarried woman is incomplete, a sort of 'unmarried soup', and she hadn't wanted to continue to be something so lowly? Perhaps she was secretly ashamed of those two sisters who continued to resist anyone who wanted to wrench them from their first loyalties? Or was she hoping to help her family, dreaming of a state of prosperity which would free her from service and them from the loom, and that one word – 'America' – rang in her ears like a song? *Mamma mia dammi cento lire, che in America voglio andar...* Was she hoping for adventure, this timid grandmother of mine with the shining eyes?

Perhaps she was simply biddable, as her daughter Maria would be, a good character, inclined to accept whatever fate threw at her, to say yes even to an unknown quantity.

He's called Pietro; he emigrated to the States as a young boy, worked for decades as a miner in the mountains around San Bernardino, then retired and bought himself a house, a bit of land which he turned into an orange-grove, and the odd animal. Then, aged forty-five, he'd gone back home to sell some land he owned in Italy, and to look for a wife. They say he noticed her at the village fete; she wasn't dancing, she was one of the older ones and she didn't put herself about, all of which were points in her favour. He made various enquiries, presented himself at her sisters' house with a marriage broker and popped the question.

'Think about it,' Michin said to her. 'Do you at least like him?'

'There's already two spinsters in the family, at least you've had an offer…' says Ninin. Then, suddenly doubtful: 'Does he own any property? What kind of man is he? He's old – is that what you want?'

'I'm not so young myself,' says Maria. 'I've turned twenty-nine.'

'America's a long way off', says Michin. 'You know what's what around these parts. They speak American out there. You speak Italian just fine, out there you'd have to start all over again.

'A lot of people go there, though,' observes Maria. 'Including Count Francesco, the nephew of Countess Lalla and Countess Luigina. New York, that's where he is.'

'He's probably gone there to avoid paying his debts,' comments Michin. 'Titled they may be, but they haven't got much more money than we have. They never pay you your salary in full. They give you an advance, followed by a pair of shoes, and then they think everything has been sorted out, and the debt goes up in smoke.

'But these shoes are good, they're almost my size,' says Maria, looking at the black laced boots that will take her all the way to California.

'You'd have preferred Francesco, wouldn't you?' says Michin teasingly.

Maria blushes.

'I hope you haven't done anything you shouldn't,' says Ninin accusingly.

'Count Francesco wouldn't look at me,' says Maria, who has dark shining eyes and hair, but who is by now – at thirty – quite simply old! And still filled with alarm at the idea of marriage, at her age!

Pietro, known here as Peru and in America as Peter, may indeed be half foreign by now but he is a well-known type: with a waxed moustache and unsmiling eyes beneath his bushy eyebrows, he resembles her father and her uncles. He had been born in Corio, she in Rocca, their birthplaces a few kilometres apart as the crow flies, with the same views over the plain, the same chestnuts groves, stone houses, grinding poverty. Perhaps it is precisely this which causes her to hesitate and stay silent, almost melancholy.

She ends up by saying yes to that great bear of a man out of politeness rather than enthusiasm, and Peru in any case is not one to shilly-shally, it's either yes or no with him, and if it was no he'd go off and find himself someone else, so let's get on with it because we haven't got all day. Then they drink a toast with the sweet wine that the *parin* has brought along (in those days there were still marriage brokers, men or women of a certain age who knew everyone in town, and offered their services as go-betweens in all sorts of arrangements; and my grandfather had clearly turned to one of them). Then the men go off to have some more drinks in the wine shop, and the women stay where they are, surprised and a little drunk, excited, not knowing quite what has happened.

That evening, Maria is in tears because America is so far away.

'I'll come and visit you,' says Margherita, 'I'll get on a ship and come and live with you.'

Margherita is only fifteen and will turn into a beautiful young lady, everyone will want to marry her but she will remain faithful to Ermanno who keeps her waiting, at all events she doesn't need to go to America to find a husband.

Maria finishes the bottle and falls asleep with her arms on the table. That night she does not go back to Turin and the countesses.

A few days later Pietro arrives with the gold ring, a chain and a medallion of the Madonna, also gold, all for her. Now the die is cast. Even if she wanted to think again, she couldn't, now.

They get married, and for their honeymoon they go up to Corio, to Cat Rastler, the hamlet which takes its name from that of his family. The next day she goes back to Ciriè on foot and takes refuge with her sisters, weeping.

'That's enough now,' says her father, hard as stone, 'don't make such a fuss, a married woman must be with her husband.'

Ninin and Michin don't know what to say, they know nothing of married life, or perhaps they know all too much, they're suspended between all and nothing in their limbo as unmarried girls, unable to speak out, to keep her with them. They hand her over to her fate, because whoever heard of a wife abandoning her husband the day after the wedding? It'll pass, like everything else, you can get used to anything.

Not that that doesn't mean that they don't take an instant and strong dislike to that Peru who made their sister cry.

Pietro goes back to America, where he 'sorts out her papers' so that she can join him. And six months later Maria disembarks on her own at Ellis Island, and from there, after the period of quarantine, she travels on to California, by train. She makes the journey in the company of other Piedmontese emigrants, distant acquaintances of Pietro's. Weeks of solitude in the company of strangers, a fitting prelude to her married life. For five years she lives alone with that big unsmiling bewhiskered man, losing two male children and bringing a third into the world, a little girl. And all this just to go back, cloven, to where she'd always wanted to be, with her sisters. On her return she is pregnant for the fourth time, within her is a fetus which will die during its fifth month, putting her life in danger yet again.

Now, in the kitchen garden, with her good hand she unfolds the sheet of blue wrapping paper that's been folded up so many times and put in the drawer in the kitchen table. She smoothes it on her knee so as not to dirty her dress and then – practice makes perfect – plucks the lettuce with one single hand, removes the bad bits and throws them into the rusty tin under the bench. When it's all cleaned, she wraps it up neatly in the blue paper.

What kind of journey will her daughter have had? Will someone have thought to see that she gets what she needs by way of food and drink? (she still remembers how thirsty she herself was during the long airless nights on board).

'Maria, what on earth are you doing crying when you ought

to be laughing? Today's a special day!'

Maria's right side heaves. In front of her, out of the brown earth of the kitchen garden sprout the mighty legs and shapeless ankles of Ginota, her neighbour, her body like a sack of maize, formless and gnarled, her pink face avid for news, her little eyes and the white hairs of her old woman's beard aquiver with curiosity.

Maria has hated the sight of Ginota ever since they had to call the doctor urgently, shortly after she'd first come here, because she was bleeding, and afterwards everyone was talking under their breath and the unspoken truth was that the baby had been born, but stillborn, but Ginota, who always knows everything, knew what had happened and looked at Maria as though that bleeding was a mortal sin and a source of shame issuing from the deep darkness of her unfeeling body. From her left half which no longer knows either shame or logic and has to be washed like a poor child, led through doors, propped up against parapets, dragged along floors.

Usually, when she sees Ginota coming, Maria limps towards the house, and if she can't make it in time she simply spits on the ground from the good side of her mouth. But today there's an amnesty, today Maria suddenly feels that she'd like to talk to someone, so she says: 'My daughter, my *cita* – she's coming home. Today.'

And she smiles, unaware that she's still beautiful, with that crooked smile of hers and her dark eyes shining through her recent tears.

I can see Ermanno seated on a wooden bench, one of those rough, uncomfortable benches without a back, probably painted an unpleasant dark brown, the kind of furniture that's not in use any more. I can smell the smell which he too must have smelt, that man whom I have never seen except as a young face in one of those frontal, shadowless photos they used to take in the Twenties, eyes amiably half-closed. He's breathing in the smell of the port, of salt-steeped ropes, of water greasy with oil and black with tar.

There's a nip in the air, but in the harbour office the air is mild and stuffy and he has to mop his forehead and loosen his tie, for him a tie is an unusual piece of attire, where he comes from you wear them only at weddings and funerals.

I see the two women seated opposite him on an identical bench, on the other side of a corridor down which, every so often, a man in uniform strides with a busy air. It is through Ermanno's eyes that I see these women; it is to him, who has not long to live, that I attribute my own remoteness and nostalgia.

Ermanno looks at his wife in her green dress with its V-neck, her new black shoes, her neatly mended jacket which, though secondhand, looks as if it had been made specially for her. He looks at Margherita's black hair, her shining eyes, her proud aquiline nose, her white throat, the red mouth from which comes that warm voice, so full of life. He looks at his beautiful young wife talking with Michin and he thinks that rather than two sisters, they look like mother and daughter, Michin a mother from the mountains with her thick brown skirt, her ruched blouse, the kind that was worn twenty years ago, her clumsy flat shoes and chapped hands. The two sisters talk to each other quietly, heads bent, he can't hear what they're saying but would like to join in, to sit down next to them and absorb the warmth from their bodies, which smell of soap and Col di Nava lavender, together with a slight hint of sweat.

But there he has to sit, stiff and alone on his bench, on the alert, ready for when the captain calls him. He feels himself very much head of the family, he's the only male on whom his wife's sisters can rely, because Ninin and Michin are not married and their brothers are barely educated while Maria lost her husband and all her possessions at one fell swoop. So it has fallen to him to write the begging letter, selecting his words carefully as he goes and asking for advice, because it's not every day you write to the Duce, and then to the authorities when at last, months later, they condescend to write back to you.

There will have been bundles of documents, letters that have arrived by sea, consulates and bureaucrats who have made various contacts, looked into matters, stuck stamps on things. In the USA someone – a magistrate? – will have decided yes, they can withdraw the sum needed for her voyage from the account of the orphan Maria Cat Rastler, even though it is supposed to remain untouched until her majority. And then they will have found that Italian ship, a merchant vessel which also takes passengers, whose captain is put in charge of the under-age traveller.

Ermanno is proud of the part he's played in this affair. Now the bundle of papers is in his left-hand pocket, and when his wife saw him slip it in there she frowned at him as one does at children, as though to say: get that stuff out of there it's pulling your jacket out of shape, but he pretended to take no notice, because he's a man and he brushes off petty womanly concerns, well-judged though they may be. Margherita's husband is an equable man, a notional fascist who may never have actually put on a black shirt, and wouldn't have been capable of administering castor oil to anyone, but who simply felt the lure of fascist ideas, which in his view combined novelty and tradition, daring and feasibility. And, first and foremost, order, so necessary to a pleasant, peaceful life, like that which reigns on his desk, above the sawmill on via Vittorio Veneto in Ciriè, where he does his accounts and keeps his registers and reads the paper to keep himself informed about what's going on and looks out of his first floor window, at the passing carts and occasional car, where every so often his thoughts wander. He finds himself staring at the cornelian cherries which are ripening on the tree near the gate and listening to the voices of the women, his mother, his sister, his wife, without being able to make out what they're saying. They're just on the other side of the wall, he hears Margherita's light steps as she goes about the house, smells her scent, hears sometimes her troubled silences within those walls which are not, after all, her own.

He knows that she would be happier if they had their own house, separate from that of her in-laws. But there you are, there are limits to how much you can go against a mother's wishes. His wife will get used to it, time will bring changes, he is sure of it, without knowing quite what sort of changes, or how they'll come about.

And in a few months they'll be having a baby! It's odd what a novelty this still seems, each time he looks at his wife – proudly but with a faint sense of unease – he notes her slightly rounded waist and hips, you really can't see anything yet, at least that's what Ermanno likes to think, because in fact he is a little alarmed at the idea of this baby, which will have more than its fair share of its mother's attention, and topple him from the warm, protected nest which he alone occupies in the domestic realm.

How long have they been waiting? He pulls out his grandfather's pocket watch and checks: over half an hour. He'd like to get up, read the announcements in the glass cases along the walls, look out of the window, but he restrains himself, he doesn't want to seem to be behaving like a bored child, so he simply shifts his position on the hard bench.

'Women are better at waiting than men,' thinks Ermanno as he looks at the beautiful wife he's pursued despite his family's wishes, a little seamstress without a penny to her name, and her ungainly sister, Michin, who is clutching her shapeless old black bag containing the chocolate bun and banana which she has insisted on bringing along for the little girl, even though he had told her that they would be buying cakes in Genoa.

It's the little girl they're talking about, heads together, instinctively keeping their voices down in that male-dominated place; about that child whose return is folded up in his pocket, typed out on ministry paper by that friend of his who is the secretary of the mayor.

It's a pity that no one thought of keeping a copy of the letter to the Duce. Was it a formal petition, couched in the bureaucratic language of the time, or did it have something of the popular novel about it? It must have made mention of the emigrants' harsh plight, obliged as they had been to leave their homeland and their loved ones, it must have talked of the wife and mother compelled by incurable disease to return to the loving care of her sisters, of the sudden illness of the head of the family which had left his little girl orphaned and abandoned in a strange land. Had my grandmother's sisters poverty been presented as a 'state of destitution'? Certain it is that no one here in Italy had the money to sail across the seas and bring that lonely child back home.

In a flight of fancy, linking one humble personal fate to that of humanity at large, Ninin maintained that Ermanno's petition had talked of a little Italian girl whose repatriation would bring a drop of pure Italian blood back to the veins of Italy, she was a woman in embryo, a reproductive force, a future maker of fighters for the nation… And so my mother comes back home, thanks to the good offices of the Italian State, not yet an empire, but to become one soon.

The children foreseen in Ermanno's flowery plea turned out to be one alone, namely myself. I was born Italian but could have been born American, I could have talked the language of the empire, the real one, that is, the one destined to dominate the world for years to come. Who knows how my life would have turned out, how I myself would have turned out if my grandfather had not died, if my mother had remained an American citizen. The lives we could have lived branch out in our minds like so many imaginary roads, forming a labyrinthine landscape which does not exist and yet is part of us, the most insubstantial yet most pervasive ingredient in our being, and ultimately it may determine the actual course that our lives take. America, the United States, are part of me because my grandmother and mother lived there, while my Borgesian twin sister, dweller in the land of forking paths, is roaming around there still.

Does this explain why, at the age of fifteen, I begin to study English on my own with the help of a book lent to me by Aunt Margherita? And, at the age of twenty, I begin reading English and American novels and poetry, with difficulty, pencil and dictionary to hand, noting the harder words in the margin? The fact remains that I persevere, until the point where I feel more at home with that literature, and derive more nourishment from it than from our own…

It is as though the language my mother spoke on her return had been set aside and held in readiness for me: confronted with the reality of life back home, she herself will forget American and indeed her whole life in America, which will become like life in a film, something which happened to a child who resembled her but was not really her, not any more. Decades later, it will be I who will take on the task of remembering those sounds learned among people who've vanished from her memory, on the benches of a school which no longer exists.

My mother was born in California, albeit in one of its less attractive regions, among dry plains ringed by mountains and, in my grandfather's time, mines. Over the course of her first eight years of life she glimpsed nothing of the splendours of the Golden State – the sequoia forests and expanses of yellow poppies, the rocks of Big Sur and the heights of Hollywood. When we finally go to look at them together, I see them through my eyes and hers at the same time, I offer them to her as a gift, something I've long treasured and can offer her at last.

For me, America will always be a kingdom of the mind, a place tinged with nostalgia dating from before my birth. But that doesn't mean I have any desire to emigrate. I'm a stay-at-home, faithful to the land of their return, to my Piedmont of crags and hamlets, diffident and self-reliant. It is as though all that had happened to my mother and grandmother, which I knew nothing of, but learned about bit by bit, in the least dramatic, most down-to-earth way possible, had left me with the feeling that I needed to stay here and keep an eye on my house. As though the longest journeys, the truest journeys, can only take place while standing still.

Unsung yet extraordinary, my grandmother's life was severed in two for all time by those five years in America. What a lot I would have liked to know about her! As always, the desire for knowledge comes late, when the person with the stories is no longer there, or has forgotten them. Such meagre information as I have is contained in the few family papers: a handful of photos, some letters from Pietro. All I can do is turn to the internet; Virginia Woolf sought the truth about women and literature on the shelves of the British Museum, and she found a forest of opinions where the tracks of truth had been overgrown. Like most people nowadays, I use the internet to search for far more modest truths – who were my grandfather and grandmother? – and I too have trouble finding their traces amidst hundreds and thousands of false leads, similar names, approximative dates. All that remains to me of my grandmother is a note in a register, where some conscientious civil servant has entered her maiden and married name with quite unusual correctness.

In the great book of arrivals at Ellis Island, on page 517, it is stated that Maria Davito Gara Rastler disembarked at New York on 24 January 1924 from the *Colombo*, which had left Genoa on the eleventh. The information concerning her states that she is twenty-nine years old, married, a housewife, an Italian citizen born at Rocca Canavese, that she can read and write Italian, that she is 'from the North' (this puzzles me, but it's plain as a pikestaff: in the same column in the register where the word *North* appears next to my grandmother's name, certain migrants from Perugia are described as 'from the *South*''. Were the employees in the immigration office in New York really so well acquainted with Italian geography? And what did the difference between South and North mean to them?) The register informs me that 'the incomer's closest relative' is her father, Davito Gara Giuseppe from Ciriè, Turin, and that her ultimate destination is 1736 Leonard Street, San Bernardino CA, where she is already resident, thanks no doubt to the steps taken by her husband Peter Rastler, who became an American citizen in 1906. On the following page it is stated that the migrant is neither polygamous nor an anarchist, neither a cripple nor mentally retarded, that she is in good health, that she is five foot three inches tall, one metre sixty, has dark chestnut hair and eyes and no particular distinguishing features.

In the first column, a hand-written cross appears alongside the number by which my grandmother is known. In the second column, headed: *Head-Tax Status (This column for use of Government officials only)*, a number, '458129', and a date, '3/13/29', appear hand-written beside her name, followed by the initials of whoever made these annotations. Could that be the date of her return to Italy? It would be a perfect fit: on 13 March 1929, after a period of just over five years spent in the United States, Maria sets sail on a return journey which is of far less interest to the American bureaucrats, who fail to turn *'No'* into *'Yes'* in the column headed *'Crippled'* because the relevant person is leaving their country and is therefore of no concern to them.

I also learn that the *Colombo*, built in 1917 by the Palmers Shipbuilding and Iron Company, of Newcastle, England, for the Compagnia Sicula Americana, originally called the *San Gennaro* and renamed after the man who discovered America in 1921 when she went into service for the Transoceanica of Genoa, measured 536 feet in length and 64 in width, had two smokestacks, two masts and three decks and could carry 2800 passengers, 100 in first class, 700 in second and 2000 in steerage. This was a ship used mostly by migrants, and who knows how many thousands of Italians she ferried to America during her thirty years of life, before being scrapped in 1947.

A big ship, then, containing one very small passenger, my grandmother. 2800 passengers plus crew, all crammed on to three decks, 536 feet in length and, talking of feet, I imagine hers, crammed into the little boots that once belonged to the countess, feet shuffling awkwardly, moving clumsily out of the way of some busy sailor scurrying down the companionway into the hold. After landing, my imagination has less to go on, it has to resort to stereotyped pictures of migrants drawn from films and letters, I can see her while she is waiting to be questioned by some clerk or examined by a doctor, in a long queue of people in rumpled garments, smelling of sweat – might she have caught lice while in the hold? – she looks worried, she's afraid she won't be able to answer the questions, that she'll lose her things, that they'll send her back, that they won't send her back. She'd like to be as tough as Michin, as polite and lively as Margherita, but more than anything else she'd like to be with them, or have at least one sister here with her, preferably Ninin, who has so far been her prop and stay and stand-in mother.

Then comes a long train journey across an unknown continent, until, through the train window, she sees the San Bernardino Mountains, and her travelling companions tell her: we've arrived. Pietro is waiting at the station with the horse and cart, and even nervous as she is she's pleased to see him, because she was beginning to fear that that journey would have neither end nor purpose.

For my grandfather Pietro, or rather Peter, the postmodern version of the library of Babel provides me with a request for a passport: 'I, Peter Rastler, a loyal naturalised citizen of the united States, appeal to the Washington State Department to obtain a passport, and I solemnly swear that I was born in Italy, in January 1878 (either he couldn't remember the day, or knew that it didn't concern the clerk in question) of my father Barney, deceased.' Where could the name Barney have come from? It seems improbable to me that this shadowy great grandfather would have been called Barnabas, whence the abbreviation Barney; it seems more probable that it was a mangled version of Bartolomeo, a common name around our parts, or of Bernardo. As reconstructed from the scraps of information on the internet, the story is simple: Bartolomeo, or Bernardo, goes off to America at the end of the nineteenth century and becomes Barney; once he has settled, he has himself joined by his wife Anna and his son Pietro in Colorado, where they spend four years and where my uncle is made an American citizen by the county court of La Plata. Then they move to that part of California where men work in mines, as indeed he had probably done in Colorado. In the meantime Barney and Anna have other children, including one called Ferdinando, known to my mother as *barba* Nando. Barney dies, and Peter, who until that moment has been a hard worker and a dutiful son, buys himself a small ranch with his life's savings as a miner – a house, land, livestock, a plot for growing oranges – and decides to get himself a wife.

So, on 3 August 1921, he finds himself making a request for a passport, declaring that he has never previously had one, that he has never left the United States since his arrival there in 1902, and that he intends to go back and live there permanently, fulfilling his duties as a citizen. His profession is that of '*rancher*', the country he intends to visit is Italy, the purpose of his trip is '*personal business*'. The crossing, which should have occurred in September 1921, is postponed by some two years – possibly Anna's mother fell ill in the meantime, causing Pietro to put off his journey, which finally takes place after she's died.

This is all the internet tells me.

If Virginia Woolf discovered a host of legends in her fountain of truth, all I find in mine is minute fragments fossilised in the muddy matter of the past. We are both looking for written documents, but she is moving through the luxuriant forest of literature, while I am trawling through the petrified forest of bureaucracy. Nonetheless, the internet provides me too with a riddle with faintly legendary echoes. Alongside my grandfather's request for a passport is a blank page with a small photograph glued on to it.

A young man in a jacket and tie, smooth-faced, without either beard or moustache, neatly combed hair with a left-hand parting, a vague smile and a pleasant, dreamy expression. If this is Pietro, I shall have to revise my version of my grandmother's story from scratch – from being a reluctant pioneer she will become a woman in love going out to join a distant husband... But what about that flight from Corio? It's hard to imagine the mild, handsome face in the photo as that of the man from whom Maria fled in tears after the first night. This unknown man, too young, too urbane, indeed almost elegant, cannot be my grandfather – not at over forty, not after twenty-five years in the mines. So, who is he then? It's true, his forehead, his eyes, his cheekbones have something of my mother about them... Was it possible that the American State functionaries had been fobbed off with a photo that dated back twenty years? Could he himself, over the course of twenty years, have turned into the *barba*, the beard, indeed the Barbablu, the Blue Beard, who had so frightened his wife? In fact, though, who says that Blue Beard can't be handsome?

I don't suppose that internet truth is any truer than the views of philosophers and sages, but it is certainly more random. Perhaps that photo on the back of a blank sheet is connected with a different request, another man whose name appears on the previous page. Perhaps the internet is objective in this alone: that in the great search engine of the universe, the data presented are constantly reshuffled, like grains of sand by the waves, thus thwarting our perpetual desire to rearrange them into a pattern that makes sense.

My grandmother too came home alone, like her daughter six years later.

Pietro put her on a train for New York, and she took the boat from there. She had a large trunk with her, containing her trousseau, plus the blouses she had made during her time in America. A little dress that had belonged to her daughter when she was a few months old. The trunk became lighter as the voyage continued, some items given away, others perhaps handed over in exchange for favours obtained. She must have received help from someone, women must have helped her to wash and dress herself, men to carry her luggage. She could hardly walk, struggling along with her stick, she must have relied entirely upon the pity of strangers.

It seems incredible, but that is how it must have been. Pietro gave money to people he trusted, perhaps he paid in advance for her to be taken some of the way by car, or stretcher. There was no question of taking her daughter with her. How would she have fed her, clothed her? Above all, how would she have kept an eye on her, stopped her falling over, getting lost, running into danger?

I imagine the return voyage. In view of her state, would they have given her a single cabin – or, as seems more likely, did she in fact find herself in the stinking, dirty, crowded hold, her infirmity exposed to the prying glances of strangers? Did she manage, every now and again, to drag herself on deck to look at the sea? Or did she spend whole days in patient prayer down in the ship's bowels?

Perhaps it was then that Maria first became friends with God, the Virgin and the saints. She'd known them before, of course, as everyone did, but perhaps her acquaintanceship with them deepened during her exile and her suffering, when there was no one else to talk to, when the irresistible power of illness drew her ever further from the rest. A woman apart, no longer able to work, or be a proper wife and mother. Was it then that she began to murmur prayers out of a corner of her mouth, half her face frozen into silence, smooth and unlined, for ever at the age when it had happened?

There was no family talk of her adventure – of twice crossing a continent and an ocean on her own, the second time with half her body reduced to a dead weight, and a twisted mouth barely able to articulate such little American as she knew – no anecdotes, no wonderment. She makes it back, but how? She makes it back, that's all. And this silence is the most telling proof of her unimportance. Maria occupies a mere corner of the room, and of people's attention. She sits there at the edge of things, she's always been self-effacing and now she's verging on the simple-minded; her story remains untold. Her life is a dark pool like those which appeared treacherously in the moorlands of my childhood; she fell in and no one found her. Only the children, from time to time, would pause to listen to her as she read out fairy stories.

And now she's here, seated on the bench at the edge of the kitchen garden, with the lettuce in her lap and the book beside her. It's a small black religious book, with edifying stories alternating with prayers. Maria is no bigot; she prays as we children read *Mickey Mouse,* to be transported into another world. The bookmark is marking the chapter with Saint Teresa of Lisieux, her favourite. But today the book stays shut.

Maria looks at the delicate new green of the kitchen garden, at the buds on the vine which, though fat, do not yet give shade, at the daisies in the grass along the ditch. The last time she'd seen her, her daughter was not yet two. The child's little face is fading from her mind, if she does manage to summon it up it almost immediately vanishes. She feels a sense of guilt at failing to remember her own daughter, at having abandoned her; this sense of guilt all but envelops her, it's bigger than she is, like a dark cloud, like her black dress. A mother should be with her children, that's the most basic of duties, even animals know as much. But when a woman can no longer move, can do nothing, really, has become just a dead weight… She wanted just one thing, to go back to her sisters. He'd said to her: 'Go back, I'll sell up, house and land, the lot, and then I'll join you.' But then came the crash of 1929, it started in New York and then spread everywhere and he wrote: 'This is no time to sell, there's no money, the land's worth nothing now, no one's buying, we'll have to be patient.'

He talked to her about the *bebi* in his letters: 'I've bought the *bebi* some trousers, they fit her really nicely, and I say to her, "Now you're a bebi boi," and this morning she says, "Dada dada, bebi boi." '

The *bebi* was growing, but there is indeed no money. 'The people at Corio owe you at least three thousand lire,' wrote Pietro, 'if they haven't got it send your brother Bartolomeo up there to get some stuff.' The stuff which the Corio relatives gave to Bartolomeo, in exchange for the land, was the sort of paltry stuff you get up in the mountains, a few stringy vegetables, chestnuts, a cartload of wood every now and again. They claimed not to have any hard cash.

'Now things are getting better,' wrote Pietro in 1934, adding that soon he would probably be able to sell the orange groves, the livestock and the house. A few weeks later the news arrived that Pietro had died of galloping pneumonia; it had taken just three days to fell that ox of a man, that foreigner who had always remained a *barba* even when she heard him snoring beside her at night; he had been struck down by illness as though by some treacherous blow from a sledge hammer.

She does not even have a photo of her daughter. She's never asked him to send her one because photos cost money and Pietro was careful about money. She has just that one little child's dress, and at every change of season, when they hang the blankets outside or put them back again, she finds a way to sit down near the trunk and leans over to touch it.

What does my grandmother remember about California? She hasn't seen the sequoias, or the rocks around Big Sur, any more than her daughter has. What does she know about the sea lions rolling heavily on the beaches, the long Pacific waves, the red and purple blooms that brighten the hills in spring? Or of the sparkling air of the forests, pure as air can be only when never breathed by man… can any breath of such air have reached her, put new life into her, when she was alone at the stove, or milking in the byre?

I sought her California – which was not the California of my holidays – in the novels of Steinbeck and Willa Cather, before I even knew what I was looking for. Her California was a little wooden house in a neighbourhood inhabited mainly by Mexicans. Leonard Street changed its name long ago, but we've seen the house, Cousin Catherine took us to visit it; she lives in Ontario, not far from San Bernardino.

It's 1982, and my mother goes back to America for the first time since returning to Italy. Catherine has us to stay in her low, square little box of a house, it's modest enough but it's still two or three times the size of one of our own apartments, and in the kitchen there's a mammoth fridge. Catherine herself is 'king-size', and makes a joke of it: I couldn't find a dress my size, I had to use a tent. On the fridge door there's a magnet with the words: *'Holy cow, are you eating again?'* and in the freezer there are giant portions of ice-cream and pans of *zucchini* cake, a recipe which my mother will import into Italy with considerable success.

Behind the house there's a big sunny yard, with avocado bushes, a vegetable patch and little wooden sheds for tools, discarded furniture and jars and tins. In America there seems to be room for everything, and it's always sunny. Catherine, who is a widow and lives alone but fairly near her son, is almost eighty, and drives a big cream-coloured Chevrolet with the utmost confidence, going to Las Vegas twice a year with women friends to play the slot machines. She does her shopping in a shopping mall a few miles from her home, a fortress in the middle of nowhere, all unlikely colours and glass surfaces, which, in the year 1982, when Italy was still virgin territory untouched by shopping centres, struck us as every bit as exotic as an oriental bazaar.

The language in which Catherine speaks to us is Americanised Piedmontese, she tells us about how she worked in the *fabbrica delle canne*, literally, the factory of the cans, putting fruit – peaches, apricots, plums – into *cans*, and waves a tin of fruit cocktail in front of our noses. Catherine has dyed blonde hair and sunglasses and talks and laughs loudly and a lot, like a real Californian. It was she, after the war, who searched throughout Italy for the Rastler stock – whose branches had spread across the USA – and it was she who finally found my mother. The Rastler must have been migrants by nature, because this unusual name seems to have fetched up in our valleys from Germany. In my early childhood, Catherine comes to Italy with her son, a great big boy who seems to me enormous, almost grown up, even though he's just eleven (I am four), and very definitely not Italian. They are strange tanned creatures dressed in gaudy colours, and they speak, or rather shriek, a language similar to our own, but different.

On that summer's day in 1982 Catherine's Chevy does not go into the centre of San Bernardino but stops in a district which is no longer quite the country but more the edge of town, with nothing very much to show for itself. We do not see the historic buildings of which the municipality is so proud, and which include an opera house; we approach this distinctly untouristic area with something like apprehension.

The house where my mother Maria spent her earliest years is still there, but now painted a dingy olive green rather than white, and seems very small, much smaller than her cousin's house and certainly smaller than my mother remembers it. The current owners are either out, or not answering the bell. The apricot trees have vanished, all there is now is trampled grass and the remains of a dismembered car, scattered rusty pieces which someone has half-heartedly tried to turn into something approaching flower-pots. It's a neighbourhood of poor, small houses, little plots of land which, even with the best will in the world, can't really be called gardens. Catherine takes us to meet certain acquaintances dating from my mother's time who might remember her, but the only survivor from those days, an old Mexican woman, is now oblivious to anything but her television screen. We are welcomed by a daughter-in-law beset by a gaggle of children, who invites us to sit next to the old woman on a broken down divan and offers us orangeade. We decline the offer and after a few polite nothings we leave the house, with its aura of entrenched squalor and abandoned hope.

That place, where we spend barely half an hour, is where my grandmother spent the five most eventful – and most wretched – years of her life. Here she had a vegetable patch, an orchard, animals to look after – all occupations she'd known since her earliest years. She had a man to obey, this was nothing new either, except it was now her duty to lie beside him, a duty she would gladly have foresworn. (This was something she confided to her sisters on her return. Ninin and Michin, who were spinsters, never pressed her further, and anyway this was not news to them. *Those matters* were never discussed within the family. But Ninin must have thought about *those things*, and others too, at quite some length, and towards the end of her life she talked about them with her niece Maria, who was now grown up and married too, and knew what she was talking about. She pointed an accusing finger at the absent offender, *barba* Peru, who'd been dead for decades. She wanted to see him in Hell, along with *la granda.*)

During those five years my grandmother has no one who speaks her own language, except for the taciturn Pietro, who opens his mouth only to give orders, and she for her part has to brace herself before she finds the courage to ask him for anything at all. Her brother and sister-in-law, Nando and Neta, live nearby, it's true, but the two couples don't see each other much. Pietro is reserved even with his brother, and my grandmother is a timid soul.

Hot dry summers, cold winters, arid earth. By night, distant howls, famished coyotes in pursuit of little creatures. San Bernardino is one of the less attractive corners of the Eden valley. In its time it has been home to Indian tribes and Spanish missionaries, Mormons and rich cattle-ranchers, the gold rush, mines and factories. It's a place of hard grind, a crossroads, America's coast-to-coast trains run through it, and when the time will come for the railroads to be dismantled, Route 66 will follow their old course.

Yet there are green patches in the dust of this parched

terrain, the orange groves. The orange arrived here from nearby Los Angeles in the middle of the nineteenth century, and it took root in this desperately thirsty earth; Washington Navel oranges prospered, golden and seedless, imported by the American government from Brazil, and local growers grew fat on the proceeds. But for my grandmother the golden fruits of California which grew on their bit of land would always be the *portugai*, as they called them in her house, when they were lucky enough to receive one as a present at Christmas time.

Pietro ran a modest business, he probably had a couple of assistants, one or two day labourers; as well as cows, a donkey and perhaps a horse, and a cart to take the milk and vegetables to market.

She herself is shut up inside that white enclosure all day long; never goes out, where was there to go to? She doesn't even know how to speak, to make herself understood.

What will she have seen, of that country on the other side of the ocean? There must be something she likes about it, some corner of the vegetable patch, a certain quality of morning light, the smell of freshly picked oranges. Something which eases her yearnings, soothes her fears, makes her feel less alone. The sight of the mountains, white in winter and green in summer, like old friends, must have afforded her some comfort. I hope she was proud of her light-filled kitchen, her brand new pots and pans. She must have put flowers into a glass, said her prayers, always at the same time, while she undressed, but she didn't want Pietro to notice because he wasn't religious, this was America, you didn't say the *pater, ave, gloria* and *salve regina* every night. She must have had a language all her own, to talk in that tiny yet infinite country that was her mind.

Here she is then, the little girl, a red smudge among the dark clothes and uniforms. The launch is drawing up at the end of the quay, a sailor is picking up the red bundle and hoisting it out over the edge towards dry land.

Ermanno clutches his wife's arm, he is almost as moved as he was that time when the cycle race came into view and he could see the front-runner rounding the first bend behind the level crossing and it was his weighty task to register the speed. Now too, as the child's feet touch land he glances at the pocket watch he is holding and in his mind he hears the voice of a sports commentator announcing date and time with a mixture of precision and excitement: 'It's 14.42, 12 April 1935.'

At that point it will have been almost two hours since Ninin went back to work at her loom, after the lunch break. Every morning Ninin takes the train which leaves Ciriè at 6.00 and arrives at Caselle at 6.20; then she has to make a dash for it because the factory gates open at 6.30 and she sets great store on being on time.

In an old leather satchel she takes with her a standard lunch, suitable for all seasons: a bit of yesterday's bread, a litre bottle of milky coffee, a quarter litre bottle of red wine and a raw egg. For dessert, an apple or a piece of cheese. Apple and cheese may make the journey between home and factory two or even three times because times are hard and, in the economics of desire, such things are worth more if kept back for tomorrow than eaten straight away.

From 6.45, when the looms are set in motion and the air is filled with the rasping sound that accompanies her working day, until 12.15, when they fall silent, Ninin will be keeping an eye on heddles and combs, shuttles and cops; she knots up broken threads and replaces empty bobbins. The loom must be halted as little as possible, but if a thread is broken work has to cease immediately and the thread must be knotted up again, so that the piece of cloth will not be ruined. At 12.15, after a short brief interval of metallic wheezing and creaking, there is a deafening outburst of silence, and Ninin moves back from the loom with a sigh of relief, swaying the while. A throng of famished women rush into the courtyard and then into the big room with stoves and benches where each eats her own luncheon. Ninin makes an expert hole in her egg, throws her head back to drink the white, then widens the hole and dips her bread into the yolk. She takes a swig of wine, then pours out the coffee, which in winter is kept warming on the stove in an aluminium mess-tin, and makes a sort of soup with the remaining bread.

At one o'clock the loom orchestra strikes up again, and she must be on the spot to conduct it. They make blankets and carpets, thick, heavy fabrics. The looms are bigger and noisier than those in the White Goods section, where Michin works, and where they make ribbons, tapes and light cotton goods.

At six in the evening the looms fall silent again, but if there is a piece of work that simply has to be finished, part of the factory carries on humming, and Ninin will stay on for an hour or two. It's all piece-work, and Ninin works down to the last minute to finish what she's doing. She gets home after seven, sometimes eight. Luckily there's a good train service, she's never learned to ride a bicycle.

Today her satchel contains neither cheese nor apple, because this evening there's going to be a special meal and Ninin hopes she won't be too nervous, that her stomach won't knot up and stop her eating, at lunch she could hardly get down her mess-tin of coffee but she forced herself, eat up Ninin there's work to be done.

Her head too has ideas of its own, today is a special day, threads break off more frequently, the foreman is shouting but for once she turns her back on him, if you can't see him you won't hear him. Today the little girl is arriving, the second but last of her putative children (the last one will be me). That's what she calls them, in philological terms she's wrong but theologically she's right, because just as Joseph was Christ's putative father, in the sense that Christ wasn't his son but Joseph brought him up, in the same way, without being their carnal mother Ninin has brought up her brothers and sisters and then later generations, my mother and me, with more or less the same sacred commitment as Joseph devoted to the son of God.

There is no reason to believe that on that April day in 1935 she was any different from how I'd always seen her, thin, dressed in blue or brown, flat shoes, blue or brown, and when she comes in the first thing she does is to slip into a faded Provencal overall.

Actually, she must have been a bit different, because she was only forty-five and hadn't yet got false teeth, which were to make her look prettier because the false ones were more even, while her real ones had stuck out, because her palate had been pushed out of shape by her wetnurse, the cow. I wonder if she ever realised that she had something in common with Romulus and Remus – they too having been reared by a non-human female.

And her glasses – was she already wearing glasses with fake gold rims? One thing I can be sure about is her hair: it was extremely sparse, she'd had typhus as a young woman and she wore it pulled back, taut as the threads on the loom, middle parting with a *puciu*, a puny chignon no bigger than a plum, on the nape of her neck.

The child Maria walks forward hesitantly, with that sense of unreality which comes upon you when something important and long awaited finally occurs. One thing she knows for sure, and that is that her feet are no longer treading the smooth wooden planks of a deck, but firm hard soil, greasy and sticky with tar. Unsure in their white socks and open shoes, her feet take their first steps on dry land after so much sea.

She walks straight ahead, arms held stiffly a little away from her body, suspended like a tightrope-walker amidst her silent audience.

One after the other, her American patent leather-clad steps bring her towards the little group consisting of a well-dressed young man, with a tie, flanked by two women.

She looks at them doubtfully, anxiously, not seeing them properly. Which one is her mother?

Captain and officers murmur encouragement, and so she stops, raises her eyes to look up at those two women clutching their handbags, mouths half-open, barely breathing, and suddenly she is hesitant no longer and turns to the pretty, younger one in the green dress.

'Are you my mother?' she asks her in English.

The murmur becomes excited discussion. Now everyone is talking, except for the two women themselves – they bend down to look at her more closely, they dare not touch her, except with their fingertips.

Then the young man clears his throat, takes a step forward, bends down and crouches beside her, in a position which reminds her of some monkeys she's once seen at the zoo: 'I'm your uncle Ermanno,' he says loudly and carefully, as though she were deaf, rather than foreign. He stretches out his hand to her, with its big gold wedding ring.

Maria stares at him in wide-eyed astonishment. An

assortment of foreign languages burbles around her. The captain is speaking French with an officer, the barber is talking in Neapolitan to a Venetian violinist from the orchestra. Now back in Italy Lina, the maid, who has spent several years in America, is suddenly speaking a lovely Florentine.

Maria stretches out her hand, which is instantly enveloped in the ringed hand belonging to the man, then she has to say goodbye to all those who have gathered around to see her safely handed over to her family, including the violinist, whom she doesn't like because he is in the habit of pinching her cheek between his index and middle finger. And, of course, the captain, who intimidates her because he is tall and fat and serious like her father, and wears a dark uniform with a lot of buttons. Every evening when Lina had taken her into his cabin before dinner he would look up and say: *'You ok little miss?'* or: *'Que tal senorita, eres bien?'* and she would nod silently and he would carry on reading and writing in a big book and they would go off without a word.

Everyone has a lot to say about the little girl from America. She boarded at the port of San Diego, and she slept in a cabin with the maid Lina, into whose charge she had been put. She dined at table with the grown-ups, Mrs. Trevanny had greatly taken to her, such a good girl! No fuss of any kind, *such an easy child* ! She likes reading, and she speaks three languages! English and Spanish, the third is an unknown quantity, even to the captain who comes from Piombino and speaks Spanish and Portuguese, American and French. What a pity, they say that her father died… quite suddenly, in just three days, poor man! And her mother's far from well!

Lost amidst that crowd of unknown folk who are all shrieking in unison – all, that is except for the two women, who appear to have been struck dumb – Maria walks forward, between motionless walls of jackets and overcoats, without knowing where she's going, until she finds herself seated in a motor car which reminds her of the one which took her from San Bernardino to San Diego, the same smell of motor car, but a newer model. Suddenly the men start talking about the car, it's the only thing on their minds, before he opens the door of his blue Lancia Augusta saloon Ermanno shines the door handle surreptitiously with his sleeve, then he makes a quick tour of the vehicle talking knowingly of tyres and lights, lifts up the bonnet and shows off the engine, lowers it again, cleans his fingers with his handkerchief, shakes proffered hands, raises a casual, almost limp arm in the direction of a uniform, opens the door to the driving seat. Sits down, pinches the crease of his trousers between thumb and finger and stretches his legs luxuriously; the two women and the child are already installed.

The second mate now takes his place beside the driver, he's from Acqui Terme and Ermanno has insisted on giving him a lift, after all it's on their way, even if it does mean the two women have to sit in the back with the child crammed between them and the officer's case right under their feet.

So off they go from Genoa without anyone having answered Maria's question: 'Are you my mother?'

The bells of the church of San Giovanni are striking half-past six as Ninin rushes into Reviglio's bakery, and the door shuts behind her, its own bell merrily jingling along with the rest. The place smells of bread, an all-embracing warm scent of yeast and malt, and the buttery smell of maize cakes, spices, chocolate and liquorice.

I like to think that the Reviglio bread and cake shop looks to Ninin, at least on this April day, as it did to me when I was little, with its dark ceiling-high panelling, row upon row of glass jars with sweets of every hue, pastilles, chocolates wrapped in coloured paper, trays of glazed fritters and puff pastries liberally daubed with jam; a well-stocked garden of earthly delights, all nooks and crannies, an enchanted cave, a theatre of wonders, one mouthwatering daydream melting into another as far as the eye can see. Greed – first and last of life's pleasures – triggers sensual and nostalgic delirium, inspires decadent fantasies which dissolve on the tongue like those *richelieux* they don't make any more, those little meringues, pink or ivory or pale green, which crackle and then crumble the moment you bite into them like splinters of sugary foam, to yield their secret marrow, a drop of liquid sweetness secreted in their centre.

I like to think that that evening – at least that once – Ninin would have allowed herself to buy some cakes. I see her coming out of Reviglio's with her arms full of purchases and her shopping bag full of packages in that straw-coloured paper used at the time for wrapping foodstuffs, cut to size and reminiscent of giant ravioli filled by nimble fingers and speedily and expertly sealed.

Once home, Maria, poor thing, tried to be helpful by putting the tablecloth on the table and keeping the stove roaring, heating the water for the *agnolotti* – made yesterday evening, they'd been up until after midnight – and basting the roast. Then she would wait, now talking to herself, now silent, getting up to look into the street every few minutes, straining her ears for the sound of a car's engine, a rare enough sound in via Conte Verde to attract attention.

Up in the mountains the men are talking about motor cars and travel and the little girl. Ermanno, lowering his voice as you do when discussing serious matters, and generally embroidering the details, repeats what the second mate had vaguely heard on board.

'After the death of my brother-in-law Pietro, the child was looked after by his brother Ferdinando and his wife; they also took charge of the sale of the property,' and here his voice drops lower still, so that it is barely audible above the engine as it strains in its efforts to take the bends, 'and they certainly made a good killing for themselves, but what could we do, we were so far away… someone should have gone out there, but here there were only women, and it would have been expensive, and there was the language problem… I myself was not in the best of health… But,' Ermanno goes on, eyes on the road and on the valleys where young green shoots are now appearing, 'money there is, and when she turns twenty-one she'll be getting a tidy little nest-egg…'

Here the roar of the Augusta drowns out the sum, which is lost for ever among the mountains between Liguria and Piedmont, lost like the actual money which, in 1948, when Maria finally lays hands on it – depleted as it has been by a long war and devaluation – is just enough for her to buy herself one single dress.

From time to time Ermanno turns round to sneak a look at the two women with the child between them. Michin has not even waited until they're out of Genoa to bring out her chocolate bun and a squashed banana, and that's no bad thing because Ermanno, taken up with the idea of getting home before nightfall, has quite forgotten about the cake shop. Maria, who is an obedient child with a healthy appetite, has devoured the lot and then feels her eyelids drooping; she is driven up the series of bends of the Col di Nava with her head lolling between two pairs of lavender-scented shoulders.

At Acqui they stop in a café, the officer simply has to offer everyone a drink, the men have an aperitif and the women have barley water. The child had whispered: 'Thank you,' when they handed her her glass, Ermanno can't get over having a little American in his car.

'What do you mean, American?' says Margherita. 'She's as Italian as we are.'

'But she doesn't speak the lingo!' objects Ermanno. Then, turning to her: 'What language did you speak with you pa?' he asks her, so the whole café can hear.

Maria goes red and says nothing.

'Leave her be, she's tired,' says Margherita.

Maria takes refuge between the green dress and the brown skirt. When they set off again without the officer, who has arrived at his destination, Margherita sits in the front, and Michin makes a sort of cushion for the child from her jacket and tells her to stretch out more comfortably.

'Sleep, child, sleep,' she orders her.

Gently, she strokes the child's forehead, pushes the hair out of her eyes. As though that hand were the Holy Spirit, understanding of her mother tongue now descends upon Maria, not all of a sudden, but in one long drowsy glide.

Maria sleeps for the rest of the journey, and sleep loosens the knot she has inside her which has been shackling her hearing and speech. She is stretched out luxuriously upon the seat, pleasantly full, her feet in her *magna*'s lap; and now – this is truly a turning point – knowledge, memory and forgetfulness descend upon her, she doesn't yet know it but from this moment onwards she will begin to feel part of that world from which she has come and which she has never seen, a world which now resurfaces within her like the physical features which she shares with the two women she has only just met. From this moment onwards America begins to become a memory, and then to vanish.

What is my mother dreaming about on her journey home? About the *bebi boi*'s blue dungarees, the outward sign of a motherless childhood, marking her out from the other little girls at her school, who wear frothy dresses with flounces and have long hair, whereas her father takes her to the barber for a no-nonsense cut, and she does indeed look like a little boy, with that mop of soft black hair, and she is the butt of merciless teasing, particularly from Emery, the prettiest girl in the class whom Maria secretly admires, with lovely blonde curls cut a la Shirley Temple. Or is she dreaming about the white house in San Bernardino, with its apricot trees which you climb up to pluck the golden fruit and gobble it up, perched in the branches, so as not to be seen by your father who has told you not to climb the tree because you might fall down. Or about the sugar sticks with red and green spirals which a neighbour has given her, saying they'd been sent by *Santa Clos*, but her father has put them in the kitchen, on a high shelf, in a glass vase, he doesn't want her to eat sweet things in case she becomes greedy, just one on Sundays, and he doesn't realise that looking at those unattainable coloured sugar sticks from a distance brings on a craving, an agonising yearning for sweet things which will dog her for all time, causing her eyes to brighten in front of cake-shops throughout her life.

Perhaps she dreams of all these things, and more besides, and in her dream she moves away from them, bids them adieu. And meanwhile without knowing it she begins to remember that bit of Italian which she absorbed from the letters from home which her father read aloud to her, and to forget the nasty year she'd spent with *barba* Nando and *magna* Neta, who put up with her without loving her; she forgets America and its languages, English and Spanish.

Her sleep is deep, yet somehow she takes in the words spoken by Michin, who keeps a jealous watch over her but leans forwards from time to time to whisper something to her sister, telling her that this is the first time she has seen the sea from close to, that while they were waiting there on the quay she was looking at those tall narrow houses with windows like black holes; she thought that she herself could never have lived in one of them, so high up and overlooking an ever shifting expanse of water; and those narrow stinking dirty alleys full of people pushing and shoving, what a nightmare.

No, Genoa is no place for her. It's not that she hasn't travelled, she's been to the lakes, to Turin, Milan and Oropa, even to France, once, when she was little, with her father when he went to help with the harvest in Val Roia and they'd gone over the mountains. But, for her, there's no place like home. The child will sleep next to her in the bed they've brought down from Rocca, in the sheets she's hemmed this winter, indeed she's even added a monogram, M.C.R., Maria Cat Rastler.

Maria sleeps on, her aunt's voice filters into her sleep like the sound of rain on window panes, it reassures her, tells her she is coming home. She recognises the sounds of this third language, the one that no one on the ship could understand, the one she spoke with her father and indeed with her mother when she was still with her, in a time before memory began. This is the dialect spoken by the mountain-dwellers of Corio and Rocca, in the hamlets and villages which cling to the chestnut groves, places she's never seen, air she's never breathed, but something, somehow, responds to the words Michin utters as she speaks to the sleeping child. The same sounds, the same rhythms as those used by her father, or very nearly, a little less harsh and stony when spoken by *la magna*, less mountainous, as though tempered by the plain and the nearness of Turin.

'Did you sleep well, *cita*?' asks Michin as soon as she opens her eyes.

'You must speak to her in Italian, otherwise how will she ever learn?' says Ermanno reproachfully.

But Michin carries on as though she hadn't heard.

Michin has less than eight more years to live. She will die in 1943, right in the middle of the war. I have just one photo of her, full length, dressed in black, alongside Ninin and Margherita. The absence of my grandmother Maria implies that it must have been taken when she was still in America. I never knew Michin, but her features, derived both from that photo and from a blend of family faces, are engraved in my memory. Thick black hair, square face, the prominent cheekbones of the mountain-dweller, a less than perfect nose, dark eyes and a big mouth tell you nothing about her character; like the rest of her family, in front of the camera, and in front of the world, she stiffens up, takes refuge behind a shield of diffidence. The Davito girls have been brought up to think that feelings and opinions are unseemly, or at the very least superfluous, a luxury, a waste of time. They know that a woman must be what is known as 'a good sort', that is, make do with what's on offer and not fret about what isn't; according to the older folk, it's best to be no sort at all. That's why they keep so much to themselves, bow their heads, put a brave face on things. They understand each other, share a secret language which expresses the unsaid.

But if Michin reveals nothing of herself to the photographer, at home with her sisters, and even at the loom with her work-mates, it's quite another matter. She's not the type to take things lying down, she reacts, she laughs, she sings. Even as a little girl she made jokes at the expense of her elders, changing the wording of her prayers: *'Santa Maria prega per me, e per'i autri s'ai n'ai e'*, Holy Mary pray for me, and for the others if there are any left'. Michin holds her own against the boys and always takes her mother's part at home, enduring her father's hefty slaps without a word. 'She's a bold one all right, a real Garibaldina', comments Ninin, half admiring, half scandalised. During my mother Maria's childhood it was Michin who was the favoured one, the most loved and feared, at once authority figure and playfellow. The Garibaldina was the ideal captain for the 'easy child'. A pity she vanished from her life when Maria was barely into her adolescence.

Over the course of a lifetime all the *magne*, for one reason or another, will at some point have been the favourite: one will give support, another will be a confidante; one will proffer reproaches, another consolation; one will go away, another will stay.

Twenty years later Margherita, upon whom Maria's attention had been focused when she leaves the ship, will answer her question, which in reality is a request: *'Are you my mother?'* When they are both at completely different moments in their lives – Maria struggling with unexpected difficulties in her marriage, Margherita basking in the happiness of a second one based on love and friendship – the older will perform that rarest of all roles, that of an accepting mother who can smile and offer comfort. '*Piora ca t'pasa'*, crying will make it better, Margherita will say, a tenderly sardonic *mater consolatrix*, radiant in her older woman's beauty, Maria's tears falling on her high imperious breast beneath the thin silk of her garment as she ruffles her niece's black curls. But only for a moment, because such family outpourings, when they occur, will be short-lived. A moment's tenderness must last a week, like

Ninin's lunch-time apple.

It won't have a chance to last long. Margherita will die around the age of sixty, suddenly, almost without saying goodbye, over the space of a few days, two years after the death of the man who, as she had recently liked to put it, had taught her how to live.

And then the only one left is Ninin, still there as always: unflagging, a perpetual moaner, *mapon*, which means maize stalk, as we around these parts call those inexpressive creatures who can neither laugh nor cry. But that's not fair, because even she would smile, and sometimes – though very rarely – laugh, with her hand in front of her mouth. Not cry though – as far as I know, she never allowed herself to cry. It was she who continued to get up first in the morning, before the others, and say to Maria, when she seemed tired and worried: *'Povra cita, su su, piora nen, dati 'n'andi'*, poor little thing, come on now, please don't cry.

And Maria will do as she is told, because even one moment of tenderness may be enough.

While talking of these matters I realise, to my surprise, that Maria actually had three mothers. I count them up, and someone's missing. Ninin, Michin, Margherita. The one who's missing is my grandmother, her real mother. The one who brought her into the world, after two failed pregnancies. I wonder how my grandmother managed to hold her daughter and give her the breast, all with a single hand. Perhaps someone helped her, a Mexican with a lot of children of her own, who knew about such matters. And what about changing her, and washing her? When she herself was scarcely back on her feet, still unused to her infirmity: in shock, as we would say today. Traumatised. And yet it was my grandmother who fed her; hers was the face which gazed into the cradle, hers was the voice that taught her how to speak.

It's a sad thought, that of an invalid mother who can't sweep up her little daughter in her arms, or tie up her shoe laces, or give her a whole smile, because half of her face is frozen. And yet, over those first twenty-one months of her daughter's life, she must have been a good enough mother, because her daughter Maria grew up in good health, and walked and talked at the right age, and didn't stammer, or wet the bed, her only problem being shyness, which later in life became thoughtful, graceful reserve.

My grandfather Pietro, too, although brutal enough to impregnate his wife in her stricken state, must have been a good enough father. Those two spent five years alone together; he was a silent, looming presence, yet apart from the sugar sticks on top of the cupboard, which caused my mother to suffer the torments of Tantalus, no other painful or frightening memory remains; only his relentless severity, and his habit of dressing her as a boy, shaming her in front of those little Shirley Temple lookalikes. A strange Janus of a man, a husband who terrorised my grandmother and a father whose clumsy, work-worn fingers did up the buttons of my mother's dungarees…

They arrive in the evening, when the water in the saucepan has boiled dry.

'They're here, they've arrived,' says Nina, Mecio's wife. The men suddenly stand up, all together, Mecio and Noto and a pair of cousins who've come specially from the Rastler houses above Corio. Then there's Ginota with her daughter and another couple of neighbours. The men go out as they hear the Augusta's engine dying down; when car doors are heard banging, Ninin rushes to refill the saucepan with water from the pan on the stove, where there's always plenty of boiling water; Maria, poor thing, seizes her half-full glass of sugared wine and downs it in a single gulp.

Maria comes in, hair dishevelled, half asleep, collar awry. She takes in the room, with its yellowish walls, the chairs with their straw seats, an array of *agnolotti* on the sideboard. She sees faces staring at her, lips moving, she breathes in the smell of the roast and a lot of people all in a small space.

For her, it all seems to be happening in silence, even though everyone is talking nineteen to the dozen.

Amidst the continuing din, she is thrust in the direction of a woman who is seated at the end of the table, saying nothing but smiling a strange, forced, tremulous smile which looks like a grimace.

Maria, poor thing, hugs her child with a single arm, and would like to become invisible so as not to be obliged to show her feelings in public. The little girl kisses her dutifully on the cheek, thinking that perhaps this woman could indeed be her mother, she's dressed in black, so maybe she's a widow.

They give her some more to eat and talk to her and ask her questions and every so often she answers yes and no. *'T'ses contenta?'* they ask her, are you glad to be here? and she nods. *'T'na voli 'ncora?'* would you like some more? And she shakes her head, as her father has taught her (if they offer you sweets you say no, do you understand?)

Then there's the priest, the prior from San Giuseppe, a tall gaunt figure in a black cassock.

'She'll need to be baptised,' he says, because her mother can't remember whether she has been or not, and what with that priest-eater of a father, in a country of non-believers, it's anybody's guess. 'She can do it all in one,' he says, 'christening and confirmation combined, it'll be a fine do, a grand affair, as thanks to the blessed Virgin for having brought the child who bears her name back into the bosom of her Catholic family.'

The women nod, this priest is pleasant and smiling and talks like an educated man, they are somewhat in awe of him and don't know whether to press him to try the *agnolotti* or to accept his polite refusal.

'Why not christen her Maria Grazia, Mary Grace, in acknowledgement of the grace she received from the Virgin?' suggests the priest.

They all immediately agree.

'Yes, the grace she received from the Virgin,' stammers Maria eagerly eyes bright with tears brought on by a combination of wine and emotion.

Ermanno explains to the little girl that this town where she is going to live is called Cirié, while the place her mother comes from is called Rocca, and the place where her father comes from is called Corio. She looks at him solemnly, nodding, trying to understand, instantly forgetting the names. Then she listens to the women talking dialect, and is astounded to be home.

Ultimately she finds herself sitting on the knee of the boniest of all the women, the one with the sticking out teeth, and she wonders why, of all those women who are her mother, she has to end up in the lap of the ugliest of all.

'Com'a la varda,' says Michin, laughing, *'com s'a fusa'l Bambin d'Varal!'*

Everyone laughs at the way *la magna* is looking at her niece – in adoration, as though the child were the Infant Jesus from the Sacro Monte at Varallo.

Maria still doesn't say a word, she's too intimidated by all those unknown faces.

But if she were to speak, she would say: 'Are you my mother?' no longer in American but in her own mother tongue.

Or perhaps she wouldn't even say that. She's on the verge

of falling asleep, she's tired and confused but she's certainly had enough to eat; she's happy to be surrounded by those four women who are her new family, none of them is as well dressed as Missis Rose and she still does not know which one is her mother, but as she falls asleep she senses that it does not matter, any one of the four will do, or, better still, all four.

Soon it will Snow

Maria Grazia sets off home on her bicycle. Her hands are frozen despite her thick woollen gloves, her lips chapped by the winter air.

She has pedalled furiously along the road from Caselle to Cirié, between fields and rows of poplars, farms which look black in the distance and darkened houses in the midst of frozen orchards. The only people around are the odd woman worker like herself, grinding along on an ancient bone-shaker. The alarm has sounded, and everyone has dashed off on their creaking vehicles. As fast as their legs will carry them, because it's a clear evening, without a cloud, and the earth must be horribly visible from above. This evening the dark air gleams like a crystal shard, and the sharp black teeth of the mountains bite at the dark blue of the sky.

She rides into the courtyard to a screech of brakes, jumps down from her bicycle and bounds up the two flights of stairs. On the second landing two doors await her, each with the key in the lock. She hesitates for a moment, then goes into the one on the left.

Beyond the door is a large room which has been divided into two, one part having been made into a small kitchen. On the east side, in the living room which by night becomes a bedroom for Maria Grazia and her mother, two windows overlook the courtyard, with its neat piles of concrete pipes, and the small villas of the district known as 'the park', with their evergreens, cedars, magnolias, even the odd palm tree. For the moment, though, it's all pitch black, the blinds, lined with heavy cloth for added safety, have been drawn with care. In the little west-facing kitchen it's somehow even darker, and there's a lingering smell of vegetable soup and ashes. The fire is almost out, there's just the faintest reddish glow, and even that seems about to die.

How long has Maria, poor thing, been waiting in the darkness? No question of wasting electricity just for her. Now suddenly the 40 watt lamp sends out a secret, war-time glow. In the semi-darkness Maria Grazia sees her mother seated beside the stove, a black puppet slumped against the back of her chair, head lolling on one shoulder, her book slipping from her one good hand, her right. As she approaches, this human bundle opens its eyes, jumps, recognises her and gives her its usual crooked smile from the right-hand side of its mouth.

The girl takes off her coat, hangs it on the wooden peg and goes to the sideboard. She knows quite well she shouldn't, but before she can stop herself she is already on her knees before the open door, her conscience somehow assuaged by Ninin's voice saying: 'Eat, eat, *cita*, you're the one most in need.'

In the sideboard, wrapped up in a bit of white sacking there's nearly half a round loaf of black bread; it crumbles when you cut it, and it smells rancid, but it's bread, the only kind you'll come upon in times like these. And there's a chipped bowl of apples, hard and wrinkled, but sweet, from the mountains, the last of the October harvest.

She cuts herself a slice of bread, sinks her teeth into an

apple scarcely bigger than a walnut. The mouthfuls go down in a trice, as though she herself were a sort of whirlpool into which food simply vanishes; she doesn't even register the rancid tang, the doughy consistency which causes the bread to cling obstinately to the palate.

The slice of bread is soon finished, and all that remains of the apple is the bits of core caught between the teeth, even the pips have been devoured. She considers having a little more, how could she not? But she restrains herself, feeling virtuous; there are only four or five apples left, and the half-eaten loaf must be made to last until tomorrow evening.

Now her mother is kneeling down by the stove and stirring the embers with the poker. She feeds in two small branches, one at a time, alternating with bits of torn up newspaper and dry bean husks. Grudgingly, at last the fire responds.

'It's cold,' the woman says, half turning towards her, showing the good side of her face. 'Are you cold? Come and warm up.'

Maria Grazia goes up to the stove, dragging the bench behind her, and sits down, stretching out her hands towards the warmth. Maria, poor thing, takes both the girl's hands in her own good hand and presses them against her chest. The girl allows her to do so – she has nothing to offer her mother except such acquiescence, and indeed perhaps her mother has nothing to offer her except for the warmth of her body through her black woollen dress, black cardigan, black stockings, black slippers, near the black hearth.

'Poor *cita*,' says her mother. '*Ommi mi*, if only I could work, if only I could go in your place.'

Maria has become impatient with this endlessly repeated refrain, she doesn't care about having cold hands and having to go to work; what she'd like is to get out and about and talk, hear the sound of voices in darkened rooms, talk about tomorrow and set off to walk towards it. So after a few minutes she disentangles herself from her mother's grip and gets up.

'I'm going to see *magna* Michin,' she says.

She goes out on to the landing, which is always dark, day and night, because ever since the blackout started the window has been covered with a double layer of blue sugar paper. She stops for a moment to listen at the door of her aunt's room. Then she gently turns the key and goes in.

Her aunt is not asleep.

'Come in quickly,' she says to her, 'and shut the door behind you, it's so cold.'

Michin's room smells of medicine and soap, because each day, after Ninin and *la cita* have gone to work, Michin props herself up on to her elbows and forces herself out of bed; her natural desire would be to stretch out and not move an inch, but willpower must reign supreme. Cleanliness is next to godliness, above all you must avoid causing offence to others and yourself.

She puts her feet on the cold tiles, wraps herself up in her chemise and then in an old moth-eaten coat she uses as a dressing gown, and proceeds to prepare herself to face the day. She starts off by emptying her chamber pot – it's best to do the least pleasant things first, the pot doesn't smell nice and there's a danger of spilling it during the journey to the lavatory which is at the end of the inner balcony. Then, heartened by this first small victory she goes back to her room and washes herself, methodically, bit by bit, trying to keep the parts she's not washing well covered up, because it's cold in the bedroom, a cold so dense you can feel it pressing up against your chest, like something solid that's hard to work your way through.

Sometimes she imagines she's in Russia, grappling with snow that's metres deep, just like the soldiers who are out there now. Michin is blessed with a lively imagination, give her an image, a day dream, an account of a journey and she will cling to it, hoist herself into the picture with all the strength that still remains to her.

She thinks of death by freezing, the so-called white death, then tells herself what an idiot she is and almost begins to laugh. She is unlikely to die a white death. Her death is more likely to be tinged with red, like that of the blood which stains her nightgown.

But then almost anything would make Michin laugh. Even when she was little, when they were listening to eldritch tales of mangled witches and children devoured by ogres, in the cowshed at night, although she was every bit as horror-struck as all the other *masnà*, she would always see the funny side.

Laughter costs nothing. It's a luxury that everyone can afford, and she has always been loved and valued for her ability to make people laugh. 'When you laugh, it's as though your stomach were full,' her mother would say. And once, when they were going from Ciriè to Rocca on foot, one Saturday evening in summer, her mother had said: 'When you're in a good mood, it's as though you're riding in a carriage.'

But making people laugh, like every other gift, requires a bit of effort, and nowadays she has less energy to spare. Once she's finished washing she stretches out on the bed again, coat and all, pulling the covers up to her chin in the hope of keeping warm.

She is at rest, like soldiers after a battle, like a woman after giving birth; like the earth during winter. Even if her battle has been merely with the stains on her nightgown. Being so tired after such a paltry struggle makes her laugh, but the laughter has a bitter taste.

At first it irked her to be sitting there idly, with all the work there was to be done in the house. So she would alternate domestic chores with a spell in bed. Then slowly the call of bed became stronger and stronger, its voice a siren song. She told herself that she needed her strength for the factory, for those few hours she still worked there. In those autumn months, which then became winter, Michin gets up before six to go to the factory and sits down at the loom. She works in Linen, making cloth for shirts. Work too is rationed, just like bread and butter. All the more reason not to waste it.

For months they've been talking about cutting down to one day a week; indeed, about shutting up shop. All the women are afraid of losing even those few pennies that they earn. Luckily, at Magnoni's, where Ninin works, they're still holding out. That's hardly surprising, they make blankets for soldiers and material for uniforms and overcoats, there's no shortage of customers.

Michin too is afraid of losing her job; it can easily happen, above all when you've fallen behind, slackened your rhythm and need help. Nor is it politic to draw attention to your state of health. That's something that should remain unobserved, as far as possible.

Now, though – with February half over and the grey morning light brighter through the shutters, and the cold, though still biting, easing up somewhat towards the middle of the day, and a bunch of snowdrops in the glass by the bed – now, today, Michin is no longer afraid.

She's no longer afraid that they'll make comments about her at work, or that Linen will close its doors; she's no longer afraid even of the sky lit up with bombs, as though it were the village fete.

When Ninin and Maria Grazia are on their way back from work and they hear that dull roar that sets the windows throbbing, and she's waiting there at home, fists clenched, listening, trying to work out which way they're flying, what height they're at, whether it really is aeroplanes or just a storm, or her own blood pounding in her ears. Those are – were – the worst moments.

And then of course there's that other enduring fear, that of the strait gate, the bitter pill. How will it come about? When? Is it imminent, as it often seems, or still off in the future, a season away or maybe two, as she equally often continues to hope?

Every now and again she told herself that this fear was just a bad dream, and she felt that she was waking up and finding herself in the old familiar world... Then suddenly she would fear that this cramped universe, this little space remaining to her, was in fact the dream, and fear was the real thing.

'Be brave,' her sister Ninin would say to her every day, 'you'll be having the operation soon, and then you'll be better, it won't be long now.' For a time, Michin believed her. As long as she had the strength. You need strength to believe, as well.

But now a new era has begun.

Fear has somehow slipped away unnoticed, it's no longer around. In its place is a dreamlike calm, a sense of utter remoteness.

It suddenly seems to her that an all-enveloping sense of peace has descended; now that the worst of the winter is over she can sense the snow readying itself in the air, she can smell it from her bed, in the closed room. Snow always brings calm and silence, this moment of the year is a final lull before the shameless light of spring. She will enjoy this late snow, she feels as though she herself had summoned it from the February skies. She waits for it, it seems to her as though that's all she's waiting for.

'So Ninin is right,' she says to herself, warming her hands in her armpits, her arms close to her chest under the covers so as not to waste heat, 'and I'm not at all nice – I don't give a damn about them now, I no longer care whether they live or die, if a bomb intended for a factory or a military installation misses its target and destroys us instead, and goodness knows, we can't be called military or strategic targets; quite often, catastrophes take the wrong route, they don't know where they're going, and men think they're in charge but how wrong they are. I no longer think about my sisters. I don't even care about my niece, the most precious thing in my whole life. Until yesterday I was worried sick about her, she was in the flower of her youth and having to live it out in time of war, and while I was lying here I was racking my brains as to how to scrape together a couple of eggs and an extra half kilo of rice, because when you're fifteen it's not nice being hungry. As recently as yesterday I was thinking, as soon as the weather looks up I'll get myself together and cycle to Rocca and come back with a sack of potatoes and butter, the cousins will have butter to spare and probably some wood as well, I'll tie it on to the bike, behind the saddle. And today not only do I not even dream of going there, but Rocca is another world to me.

A world so far away you couldn't cycle there.

But perhaps not so far away after all, because I can see it right here in front of me, as though it were at the bottom of my bed. How odd, I think, it seems to me that I'm at Ca' d'Gara, on the meadow in front of the house, on a summer's afternoon, with the sun coming over the ridge and beginning to go down, and the cut hay pricking my feet. It's a clear day, you can see for miles, the plain is vast and down there you can imagine the great city, like a low mist quivering in the bottom of the valley. And I can smell the hay and hear my mother's voice calling me, but I don't want to go home yet, I want to stay here, I want to slide down the meadow, with the grass pricking and tickling through my dress, getting into my hair, I want to feel my weight as I roll down, laugh as though life were one big game, and I let my mother call me, I don't answer, Ninin is right, I'm not at all nice.

I let myself roll down the slope and I forget everything, my sisters, Maria Grazia, even the pain in my stomach. In my family we've always had a hole instead of a stomach, as we used to say jokingly when we were girls, because we were flat, we had neither stomach nor chest, flat as washing boards we were. Indeed verging on the concave, like a washing board when it's been used a lot. Odd to feel the nagging voice of pain coming from what used to be just a hole.

Today, though, even that voice has become weaker, more remote.

This is something that is happening in her head, Michin is quite aware of that, because the pain is still there, dogged, triumphant. Now it is she – lying there ever more motionless, heavy and distant – who is removing herself further and further from that pain by means of her own cool thoughts.

She falls asleep and dreams that the child on the sloping meadow in front of the house continues to ignore her mother, and at last it is the mother who emerges from the black square of the door and comes out to her, screening her eyes from the setting sun. And the child Michin runs away laughing, catch me if you can!

There's a subtle but strong vein of buffoonery running through the harsh ground of the generations who have preceded me, a vein which cuts through everything, withstands everything, even death and misfortune, always resurfacing anew. Where this desire to laugh came from, in people who had all too few reasons to do so, I can only explain by supposing that laughing at one's own misfortunes is a primordial need, perpetually reborn, like that of building or owning or knowing.

For me, such humour is inseparable from this remote landscape of hills and mountains, green and rainy, with its history of poverty and austerity. I breathe it in during my childhood, see it shining in my mother's eyes, and Ninin's, and those of my old paternal great-aunts as they eat their soup around the table of an evening, hands on their great satisfied stomachs. I hear it explode like an insolent burst of firecrackers in comments made by my father and his friends at the bar, and sometimes I find it again within myself, so deeply part of me that I am totally unaware of it until those wretched moments when I feel its need.

For the most part, this zany strain of humour lies doggo, hidden in wary faces and workaday lives; but it may make a sly appearance at the most unexpected moments. It may be crude and earthy and commonplace, or it may be lent wings by a mysterious, unstoppable lurch towards those heights of absurdity known as nonsense. Bawdy as it is, it raises heads which are usually modestly bowed. When it is concentrated in a single person, as happens once in a generation, it may open up realms of reality beyond the visible, kindle a sparkle in eyes made dull by the grind of the everyday.

That is the picture my mother has painted for me of Michin, and this is how I see her: her gaze pierces the frayed film of daily reality, her mountain-dweller's eyes impatient of the mists which all too often hang over the plain. She is the one in her generation, and family, whose legacy is laughter, she is its bearer, the link in the chain, handing on the gift which will come down to me, the great-niece she never knew.

No one escapes Michin's scrutiny: her sisters, her fellow-workers at the factory, the foreman, but also the mayor, the priest, the chemist, the eager beavers who go to meetings and salute. She has something to say about each one of them, it may seem nothing, just the repetition of a phrase she's heard, but there's something about the tone, the set of the head, the roll of the eyes – and suddenly the objects of her satire are revealed for what they are, unmasked in all their pettiness, their all too human silliness.

In the early days, when she was little and lived with her father and the *grand*, you weren't allowed to laugh, to waste your breath on chatter and comments and jokes. It was forbidden – a serious sin. 'Silence, be quiet, you idiots! What are you women always screeching at? I'll show you what's what! Shame on the lot of you!'

But then luckily, when she was twelve, she too went down to Ciriè to work in the factory along with her older sisters, they lived with two distant cousins but had a bedroom all their own, and in the evening Michin would fall asleep talking and laughing, and full into the bargain. They worked hard but at least they never went to bed on an empty stomach, the food was regular and adequate. They'd go home at the end of the week after work, with a bag full of stuff – sugar, coffee, matches, rice, buttons, and walk those twelve kilometres, at first along the flat and then uphill, singing to keep each other company, especially after dark had fallen, and at last they'd arrive in the square at la Rocca, where they'd slip into the church if it was still open and make the sign of the cross, and then hurry up the last uphill stretch, calling out to one another get a move on, it's late, we're there now and it would be dark, and their mother would be at the door waiting for them.

Then in 1914, just after the war had begun, their mother Domenica went down to the town as well, together with her little son Giuseppe known as Noto, and her last born, Margherita. 'Now that I'm with my children, I'm in paradise,' she'd say of an evening, when they'd walk arm in arm to the end of the piazza, or sit at home and sew. When she was with her girls Domenica would become almost like one of them, she'd laugh and chatter, and they would gather round her like young lovers around a noblewoman who usually holds herself aloof, and sometimes they would vie for the place of honour at her side.

To shatter the peace of paradise, their father too decides to join them in the valley, arriving with the oldest boy, Mecio, and with the money from the sale of the land they owned in the hills he bought that couple of rooms on via Conte Verde where the family was to live for over thirty years. He works in a sawmill, his job is to plane the trunks from which they then make planks for furniture, or floors, or railway sleepers. And down there too, as up there in the mountains, when their father returns of an evening, silence falls; a tense, guarded silence, shot through with unease. Her father's presence is always reminiscent of some unavoidable natural event, like frost or hail or thunder. You don't put up objections to such things, you just try to stay out of their way.

One winter night in 1916 a nearby house catches fire, and everyone rushes out in their nightshirts, children and old folk included, and throw buckets of water, and make ready to run off if the fire should spread. It doesn't, but Domenica catches a bad cold which turns into pneumonia and a raging fever which lead to her death. At the age of forty-nine my great-grandmother was already old and threadbare; she'd run through all her resources. Like Mrs. Ramsay, the mother in Virginia Woolf's novel, though in another context.

If they have ever thought of marrying, at this point the two eldest, Ninin and Maria, give up the idea, Ninin with no regrets, Maria unprotesting because protest is not her line. Ninin, the oldest, is now twenty-five, Margherita, the youngest, is not yet eight; Noto is eleven. Leaving them at home with their father, without a woman in the house, is out of the question.

Mecio, the oldest boy child, is called up at the end of 1918 and fights for a few months in the war, returning unhurt, thank God. Maria finds a place in service with a family in Turin, she comes back by train each Sunday and spends a few hours at home. Margherita is learning to be a seamstress.

Maria marries Pietro and goes off beyond the seas.

Then Mecio marries, a girl called Nina who also works on the looms, and he goes off to live nearby, just a couple of streets away, but when someone marries it's as though they're going to America, thinks Michin, because here we are in town, no longer up in the mountains where we were all hugger mugger, fathers and mothers and children and grandchildren, married or otherwise, but all under the same roof, whether we got on or not.

So that leaves the three sisters, with the young Noto. Margherita finds work in a smart shop in the main street selling fabrics and made-to-measure clothes, in no time at all she has become an expert seamstress and trousermaker, she cuts, tacks and sews in the back of the shop and earns a decent living. Every morning she takes a turn through the stern yet welcoming old porticoes, where you can walk out of the rain and mud, and look at the lighted windows and the shop counters, gleaming with polish, and the hats in the milliners and the shoe-trees in the cobblers. This is where all the luxury that Ciriè has to offer is concentrated, it is here that Margherita feels she is in a real town, and the sound of the steps constantly ringing out on the pavement makes her heart beat faster, as though fate, decked out in its finest, might come and seek her out right here, or at least pass by her side.

The customers eye up the little seamstress and some of them try it on: 'Will it be you who takes my measurements, signorina?'

At first she is embarrassed and hides behind the curtain, but as time goes by she learns to smile prettily and say: 'The boss will take care of that, *monsu*, it's not my job.'

But if the boss is otherwise engaged and she does indeed have to take measurements, should the customer prove skittish, she'll plunge a warning pin into flesh that rarely sees the light of day. 'Oh, I'm so sorry,' says Margherita. 'Did I hurt you? Please keep still, I wouldn't want that to happen again!'

One young man comes more often than the rest, he seems to be having a whole wardrobe made. He doesn't ask her to take his measurements, but he talks to her nicely, during fittings he makes polite conversation, asks her where she lives, what kind of things she likes doing, does she like dancing? He is called Ermanno Chiesa, his face is round and delicate, he dresses with care, his collars are always clean, he wears gold cufflinks and a tie pin with a pearl. He likes to chat, if it were up to him he'd sit in the back of the shop for hours watching her sew, hands on the pommel of his stick, talking of this and that. He's intelligent and well-informed, he reads the newspaper, he's travelled the world, he's been to Switzerland and the Cote d'Azur, to places where the air is good and life is sweet. His health prevents him from over-exertion, he was delicate as a boy. He was excused military service.

He and Margherita embark on a long, lazy courtship –

relaxing for him, sometimes slightly less so for her: are they ever going to marry? Margherita puts things aside for her dowry, prepares her trousseau, like all girls who are getting married. But she continues to hand over most of her wages to her sisters, for household expenses.

Every Saturday her father waits for the girls in the street as they come back from the factory, so that they can hand over their wages and he can go to the wine shop. He comes home late, drunk, sometimes at dawn. One winter night in 1926 he doesn't come home at all. In the morning someone comes to tell them that he has been found head downwards in a ditch, at the end of the square, near a house of ill-repute. The girls throw on their clothes in a hurry, buttoning them up all wrong.

It's February, carnival time. They're summoned to the police station and off they go, pale and ashamed, looking straight ahead. Michin does not utter a word, Ninin's mouth is so pinched that her lips are like a narrow thread. In deference to their condition – that of unmarried girls – the officer spares them the details of the death and sends them on their way them with a brusque but fatherly wave of the hand. Later, he will talk with their brothers, revealing one key detail of this nasty business: Giuseppe was killed outside a brothel. Widowers have certain needs, it's a known fact, and when wine and women come into it... some quarrel, some dispute, did he have any particular enemies, their father?

His children do not know, but if they do have their suspicions, they keep them to themselves. There is a feeling, within the family, that the less you have to do with the authorities, the better. But the worst has already happened. There's no arguing with death.

Astonished, disbelieving, the sisters learn that Giuseppe

was killed by someone with a knife. This moment of plain talking is soon over. Almost immediately, the brothers put their fingers to their lips.

The body is laid out by members of the Confraternity of the Holy Shroud, of which the deceased had been a member, they'd been his companions in the processions at Corpus Christi and the feast of Saint Joseph. The uniform is a black cloak with a white ribbon round the neck, worn over your Sunday best, a dark formal suit. Suspended from this ribbon, a holy medal bounces merrily up and down to the rhythm of the march, during which expressions are solemn and gloomy, eyes lowered to stare at the asphalt of the main street, voices intoning the Ave Maria and Pater Noster and hands still as still, one holding the other's wrist and both firmly anchored to the groin, as though to cover the pudenda. From the darkness of the porticoes, two lines of people echo the prayers; the balconies are covered with pots of geraniums in flower, and decked out in velvet and damask.

But at the funeral of Giuseppe Davito Gara there are no flags or standards, though there is some marching, and the usual smell of incense from the priest's thurible. The sisters would like to be thirty feet underground, because people are giving them certain looks, curiosity mingled with ill-will. Ninin thinks about her father's final hours, in that place where she herself will never set foot, among women to whom she will never address a word: how much will she have to pray, how much penance will she have to do, to have him released from the damnation brought upon him by his violent death, which is also defiling herself and her sisters? Margherita walks with her head held high, swallowing so that they won't see her crying, eyes fixed on the middle distance so that she won't have to acknowledge something she already knows: that

Ermanno isn't there.

Here Michin takes the opportunity of pondering on the well-known habits of the male sex: going to the brothel on Saturday night and then to church on Sunday. Women are much less complicated, she concludes, there are certain needs they simply do not have. But perhaps that's because they're kept on a short leash, and what you aren't allowed to do is beyond imagining. It's a problem, though – where would a woman go to sin? She's already sin incarnate! All sins are hers! Certain desires, she hasn't even felt. Or rather, if they so much as crept into her mind, all she needed to do was think of her mother giving birth, with stifled screams in the cowshed and bloodstained sheets to be washed, afterwards. And just as well that in those days women would feed the last born until it was at least two years old, because as long as you were breast-feeding you couldn't get pregnant again.

Love, for her, has always been a fairy tale, like in those serial stories, they're fine for dreamers and girls with their heads in the air, but they're nothing to do with real lives like her own. In real life there's work, and the house and your sisters, and all kinds of daily trials and tribulations, you don't need to go looking for them, they'll come knocking at your door, just like today, never you fear. She's always been suspicious of nice-looking young men, she regards them with distrust: what are they hiding beneath those well-shaven cheeks, behind that bewitching smile and that smell of cologne? As a child she'd heard so many stories about witches, women by day and goats or black cats by night, but in her opinion it is men who are far more likely to turn themselves into beasts and devils.

Those years are now over, and she has neither taken a husband nor purchased any children, but here she is with bloodstained sheets. One thing's for sure, you can never be certain of anything in this life. Except for your fate: dodge it as you may, somehow or other it will get you in the end.

What really happened that night during Carnival, no one will ever know. Perhaps her father had had that knife plunged into his stomach while he was in that house of ill-repute, and dragged himself, or had himself thrown, into the street. Or perhaps he was attacked while he was outside, in one of those pools of darkness in a turn in the alley, or a big gloomy doorway, or the entrance to an inner courtyard where the only beings to hear his shouts were mooing cows. Giuseppe must certainly have reeled forward for several metres, drunken and wounded, in a desperate search for some Samaritan. But Samaritans are few and far between in such towns, and clearly that evening they had other things to do. They found him early in the morning, head downwards in the ditch, besmirched with congealed blood and vomit, without a penny to his name, as cold and hard as the stones in the mountain stream. How did he spend his last moments on earth? Did he ask God's forgiveness? Did he die of loss of blood, or did he drown in those few inches of water which would not have been enough to wash him clean? Nothing will ever be known for certain. If there was an autopsy, the daughters were never informed of the results. Who had robbed him, his killer or some passing thief? Had he been murdered by a local man, who like him had gone to spend his Saturday pay on women and wine, possibly one of those who had said the rosary over his coffin, the night before the funeral, and had marched with him to the cemetery? Or had he had the misfortune to meet up with some puffed up member of a fascist action squad, who'd disposed of the old bumpkin without a second thought? This would explain the curious fact that no one had seen or heard anything at all…

During those days of shame and mourning, before the

coming of Lent and its privations, every evening there's been uproar and drunken songs in all the streets, and Ninin feels as though the devil himself is there among them, beating his great big drum beneath their window.

There is an inquest, but it proves inconclusive: that night the brothel had been crowded, the women hadn't noticed anything out of the ordinary, they'd just got on with their business, the wine was flowing, it was a holiday, it was none of their business, the madam is under the protection of the secretary of the local Fascist headquarters, who doesn't have much trouble convincing Mecio and Noto that it isn't worth making a fuss. There's no trial. It's better that way. It would have been disastrous. The sisters would have had to go away to another town. Sell off that couple of rooms, get themselves crooked by grasping buyers they wouldn't know how to deal with, and begin again from scratch, wherever that might be. Justice was a pipe dream they couldn't afford.

For years people in the town will whisper that Giuseppe had come to a bad end, or sometimes you could just see it in their eyes. But no one will ever say it openly before his daughters, who pretend not to know anything about it, Ninin with angry pride, to the point of almost convincing herself, and Michin with growing impatience, as though playing a part in which she believes less and less as the days go by.

'What do other women think?' she asks her sister in irritation, 'that their men all give that house a wide berth? That they're all holy innocents in this town?'

'Sshh,' says Ninin. 'Don't let them hear you.'

With the passing of time they will say that his death was a dreadful accident, which is certainly undeniable. That he died a sudden death. That the All-Powerful had punished him for his sins (Ninin, in moments of anger).

For some days Margherita thinks of breaking off her engagement with Ermanno. She tells him as much. She's giving him his freedom. He kisses her hand, with its little seamstress's calluses and index finger with its thimble, and assures her that he is no coward; he'll always be there at her side. He doesn't say why he wasn't at the funeral.

From then onwards none of the sisters, Ninin first and foremost, can abide Carnival.

Noto starts working at Fiat, and cycles from Ciriè to Turin each day, some forty kilometres there and back. It's a good job, and he's happy. Maria writes from America, short letters which hint at her loneliness rather than spelling it out. Ermanno gets given the American stamps for his collection. One day there's a letter from Pietro, Maria's husband: she's had a little girl, at last a healthy *bebi* after two miscarriages, but this time too things haven't gone quite as they should, Maria is ill and can't get out of bed. It's some kind of paralysis, the doctor says she'll never be back to normal, she'll never be able to work again. The sisters are worried, 'come back home, sell up and come back here, at least you'll have us nearby,' they write. Almost two years go by before Maria, by that time a fully-fledged poor thing, does indeed come home, all by herself, and begins her new life as an invalid, seated by the stove, at the age of thirty-five.

Noto is *'talking'* with a girl, also called Maria. That makes for a lot of Marias in this story. In family memories the name is so omnipresent as to take on the value of a generic name for a woman; in the absence of any further specification any woman could be a Maria, like the mother of God and of us all, the eternal feminine.

This presents problems for the storyteller: how do you

distinguish between so many Marias?

This Maria in particular, who works in a florist's shop, is a lovely bright girl, and well-brought up, and Ninin feels warmly towards her. One day she sees that she's been crying. She asks her what's up, and the girl, who now regards Ninin as a virtual sister-in-law, though somewhat older than herself, confides in her. That evening when Noto comes home from work Ninin greets him with a *'Ciau papalino!'* greetings little father, a phrase combining her regret that he has behaved badly, her pleasure at the prospect of having a nephew and a brusque invitation to him to do his duty, and soon. Noto and Maria tie the knot.

Ermanno on the other hand is undecided, still thinking things through. His family, the Chiesa, owns a sawmill and would like a daughter-in-law who is rather better off; he, for his part, is accustomed to postponing things, he is still young, part daydreamer, part philosopher, convinced that a man should not make choices in a hurry but must weigh matters up, take things easy and enjoy the moment. He's a pleasant man, a moderate, a hedonist – 'a rosewater fascist', as Ninin puts it when you can speak freely again, that is, when Fascism has fallen – who is half-heartedly considering making a career for himself in the party. But that entails a bit of an effort, and he doesn't see life as a one long grind, more like the foyer of a grand hotel, or the concourse of a modern station, in which you can wander around lost in your thoughts, admiring architectural details and proportions, smoking a cigarette, sipping a drink, observing people as they come and go, imagining a future as vague as it is pleasant.

In the meantime, almost every evening he goes to see his betrothed and her sisters in their kitchen on via Conte Verde, he takes them a bit of coffee and sugar, on high days and holidays he takes them cakes and enjoys a good chat.

'He's a bit of a *giacufumna*,' observes Michin. 'Hush now!' says Ninin, scandalised. Always impeccable, he thinks of himself as a paragon of poise and masculinity – how can one liken him to one of those men-women, one of those fusspots who shuffle round the house in aprons and poke about in saucepans? In time Margherita will discover that Ermanno is born to be an eternal son, accustomed to being coddled and having breakfast in bed, and she, his wife, will have to become battle-hardened because she will have to fight a lone battle against her parents-in-law. The couple marry in 1934, after six or seven years of engagement. The young wife goes to live in the Chiesa household, where she feels herself a stranger and where, for love of her husband, she cannot fight her corner with either words or deeds.

Meanwhile out there in California Pietro has died, and the family are desperate to get the little girl back home. When at last she arrives it is as though the two older sisters have purchased a ready-made daughter (and the real mother, from the depths of the dark well in which her mind is sunk, can see and feel and experience jealousy – and once, by way of protest, she even runs away from home, getting as far as piazza San Giovanni, dragging her bad leg, before they catch up with her and take her back home again).

The child grows up, enveloped in a cloud of no-nonsense love, rough-edged, but plentiful and unmistakable. With her, Ninin – the cross-patch, who has brought up the whole family and earned her spurs on the field of battle – lays down her arms and becomes a dog that barks but does not bite. Michin on the other hand is a stickler for niceties and gives her constant dressings down, and yet it is with Michin that Maria Grazia forms the most instinctive bond, because around that woman, with her ringing voice and constant song, who goes from scolding to joking in one split second, the air is always humming with a sense of playfulness.

Michin refers to her as *sumia*, or monkey, and *culo neir*, black bottom. On the occasions when she catches the child glancing in the mirror, she cheerfully informs her that if anyone tells her that she's beautiful, she mustn't believe them: they'll be pulling her leg.

Any domestic shortcoming (a badly sewn-on button, a household chore undone) will be met with abrasive allusions and pitying considerations concerning her future husband: 'I pity the poor man who takes you as a wife!'

Maria Grazia is doubly offended: is it possible that her aunt really thinks she will be a bad wife, because of one badly sewn-on button? Because, yet again, she's forgotten to put on the water for the soup? More to the point, what need is there to allude to that man of whom there is still absolutely no sign, that complete unknown the very mention of whom can cast her down?

If the older sister is all indulgence (Ninin's love has something of the doting quality of the aging Elizabeth, who no longer expected the miracle to happen), Michin does nothing but goad. Nonetheless, aunt and niece listen to the latest pop songs on the wireless and learn them by heart; they sometimes go to the cinema together on a Sunday afternoon ('waste of money', comments Ninin sourly). Seated side by side, chewing *sucai*, those black pastilles flavoured with violets, they watch propaganda films, comedies, historical dramas with Clara Calamai or Amedeo Nazzari. They dream along with the stars of the thirties, Greta Garbo and Marlene, and the so-called 'white telephone' films, so modern and sophisticated; so unlike them, as they sit in their cheap woollen coats in the wooden seats in the stalls.

But best of all is hearing Michin sing, she's got a lovely tuneful voice, and she makes faces and operatic trills to accompany the words – whether pompous or childishly carefree – of fatuous ditties in praise of the empire (*Faccetta nera, aspetta e spera*), or mawkish and exotic favourites (*Creola, dalla bruna aureola*) distracting Italy from what is happening elsewhere, or indeed even here under everybody's noses, and from the preparations for the war.

At times the two older sisters come to blows over her, Ninin screeches: 'Leave her alone, she's just a child!' and Michin strikes back: 'Don't you worry, I'm not touching your precious idol!' Maria Grazia is always on Michin's side, Michin is absolutely right to accuse her of negligence and incompetence, she couldn't be righter! But she says nothing, she doesn't dare to intervene, and like all children she is alarmed by that bickering between adults, though luckily it dies down as speedily as it flares up.

Gradually, almost without anyone noticing, Maria Grazia becomes an adolescent.

In '39 they move house. They sell the two rooms on via Conte Verde and divide up the proceeds equally between the six siblings. The three unmarried sisters, Ninin, Michin and Maria, can't find anything cheap enough to buy. No question of getting into debt, who'd pay it off anyway? So they will have to rent, first a flat on the main street, corso Vittorio Emanuele, with its ancient porticoes, and then after a few months two rooms on via Vittorio Veneto where they still live, in a house which is expensive but which has the double advantage of being near that of the Chiesa family, where Margherita lives, and of having its generous windows opening on to the district known as 'the Park', because in the good old days it had been the park belonging to the Villa Doria, now the town hall and chief wonder of the place. Divided up into lots, the Park is still green and tree-lined, but now dotted with villas large and small, surrounded by gardens; looking eastwards, you could feast your eyes on blue-leafed conifers, red maples and glossy magnolias.

In the meantime, war has arrived. Ration books have come on the scene. They have a second-hand wireless, bought from a family who live in the Park, you can even listen to 'Radio Londra'. At the end of '42 Ermanno dies of tuberculosis, leaving Margherita with Giulio, a little boy of seven. Ermanno's call-up postcard arrives a couple of weeks after the funeral: 'Too late,' comments Michin, 'death will have to make do, it can't claim him twice over.'

For years now Michin has been bleeding more than she should. It's a woman's problem, the sort of thing that doesn't get talked about in public, often not even in private, among sisters. And until it becomes too troublesome that's how it is kept, private, not even a visit to the doctor's. But now she is feeling really weak, the pain is beginning to tell. The doctor says they'll have to operate. So be it.

'Soon you'll be having the operation and then you'll be better, it's just a question of days,' Ninin assures her.

Shortly afterwards, it begins to snow.

The sick-room is colder than the room next door. There's no stove in it, whoever heard of a stove in a bedroom? When the landlord installs the heating, over twenty years into the future, Ninin will be scandalised: 'What a waste, what's the point of all that heat when you're asleep? Doesn't do you any good, either!' and when you're not asleep you get up, blow on your fingers and set to work, it's only ne'er-do-wells who rot in bed!

'In bed you warm up with the eiderdowns and covers, with the warmth of your skin and with your breath,' pronounces Ninin, and that is how it's always been for her. Her only luxury is the hot water *boule*, and that's only when you're not well.

The *boule* is made of copper, like a big flattened egg with a stopper that's also made of copper, which you manipulate with the help of a ring; you fill it with boiling water, you turn the ring until the stopper is well and truly closed and you hold the egg with the apron round your hands, and a cloth if the apron is not enough. You slip this boiling egg between the covers, where it creates a cosy hollow, like a hot stone in snow, leaving the rest of the bed as cold as ever. Then when you get into bed you push it cautiously down to the bottom and put your thick woolen socks on top of it, absorbing the heat through the soles of your feet, and that's how you stay for a bit, your body mid-way between ice and fire, your head in exile on the arctic steppe of the pillows, your breath frozen and your toes toasting, waiting for the warmth to spread itself evenly and for sleep to come.

When Maria Grazia comes into the room Michin – who has been waiting for her, who heard her come in a little time ago and imagined her going into the kitchen and opening the sideboard – pulls a heavy arm out of the covers and feels for the pear switch which is hanging between the bed and the night-table.

The bed is made of dark, heavy wood, with flowers and other decoration carved into the headboard. Beside it stands its twin, where *magna* Ninin sleeps; between them stands the night-table, with its grey marble slab, and above, keeping watch over them from the wall, a lurid print of the young Christ working in a carpenter's shop alongside Saint Joseph, while the Virgin looks on from the door of the house. The greenish-blue background is no doubt intended to represent a bosky Palestine, but it looks more like the woods around Rocca. The faces of Christ, Joseph and Mary are smooth and rosy, of quite unearthly beauty, with expressions which only saints can wear, and if anyone came into this house looking like that Michin would start to laugh and Ninin would take offence, imagining she was being mocked. In the bedroom there is also a big three-door cupboard and a chest of drawers. And three chairs with straw seats, where the sisters put their clothes when they go to bed, so they'll be ready for them when they get up the following morning.

Maria Grazia on the other hand sleeps on a camp bed on the other side of the landing, in the living room, and her mother sleeps on an old sofa which is slightly shorter than she herself, so that when she goes to bed she pulls up a little bench to put her feet on when she's tired of lying there with her knees bent.

After a bit Michin's fingers find the pear switch on the electric wire and press it, flooding that corner of the room with yellowish light.

Maria Grazia steps through the door and sees Michin lying there in the glow, her white face like a bony mask, her two eyes like black holes and her mouth a bluish slit. Her skeleton-thin hands lie on the dark blanket.

She lets out a little moan of fear.

Michin pulls herself up a little, and it clearly costs her some effort.

'Hurry up,' she says, 'come in and close the door, it's cold,' and her niece narrows her eyes, praying that her *magna* might be again as she had been before, the Michin who had gone to wait for her in Genoa harbour. The one who joked, who sang full-throatedly that it didn't matter if she wasn't beautiful, she'd got a lover who was a painter and he'd paint her lovely as a star! And Ninin looks at her askance, because there are certain words ('lover'!) which you don't say in front of children.

'Well? What's got into you? Have you seen the big bad wolf?' says Michin. 'Come in and close the door, it's freezing in here.'

Maria Grazia pulls the door to and walks towards the sick woman without looking at her, her eyes on the snowdrops withering in the glass on the bedside table.

Maria Grazia knows that *magna* Michin is ill, it's been going on for some time, Ninin is constantly saying: 'Be nice to her, leave her be, we mustn't tire her, say a pater, an ave, a *gloria* for her,' while Michin winks at Maria Grazia behind her back and asks for news from the factory, who said what, when Secondina is getting married, why the Catlinette, the little Catherines, have quarrelled, and if they'd warmed up her soup on the stove or made her eat it cold again.

Maria Grazia knows that Ninin is worried, but when is Ninin not worried? Michin is ill. Illnesses can be cured. Winters pass. Wars end. Maria Grazia shakes off misfortune like rain drops, in her thoughts it is already spring, the war has ended, there's white bread again, and fruit, and stew on Sundays, and Michin will be restored to perfect health.

The future, the afterwards, the happy tomorrow, that's the only place to be, at that point towards which every instant of every day is busily straining. As she pedals along with her heart pounding in time with the boom of the distant bombs, she too is already out ahead, elsewhere, seated at table in front of her soup, and saying: 'What a scare I had last night, the English came so close, there was a great flash near San Maurizio, for a moment the sky was all white...'

'Povra cita,' murmurs her mother, automatically feeling for her rosary in her pocket and touching the crucifix.

But Maria Grazia has never felt herself a 'poor child' in any way. Even fear, so far, has been a form of wealth, of excess, a bonus: the crack of a whip around your legs which sends you running down the street like a rocket, a thumping in the chest, a feeling of being more alive than everything around you, more alive than the trees, the road, the sky. The living centre of the universe.

But now, inside the house, while the sky is quiet and it's almost supper-time, now, at this moment, pushing its way through the layers of impatience and disbelief in illness which swaddle her like a baby in a cradle, a fissure is opening up in her sound young skin; and through it, fear comes rushing in.

As she crosses the room, walking towards the bed, step after step, Maria Grazia is suspended in the vast space of a word.

Timur.

Timur, terror, tumour, how like the three words are.

Michin has a tumour. A timur, a terror.

That's why things are as they are, that's the reason for it.

A tumour, she knows, is something you have inside you, something that sets itself up within, you can't see it from the outside. But now Maria Grazia has seen it. It has taken the form of a death mask on Michin's face, the hideous replacement of a loved face with a skull.

And as she walks up to the bed and listens to Michin speak, and answers her questions with a monosyllable, now for the first time she feels something new and horrible for Michin, a sense of repulsion, accusation, rebellion, because beneath her normal face she is hiding those scary, yellow bones. This is not her Michin, this is someone else, someone who frightens her.

A foretaste of pain rings in her ears, an awesome tidal wave which threatens to bear her away, outdoing all her powers of suffering. She wants to escape, like in a dream when you try to run but can't, your legs won't do your bidding. Suddenly she feels small and defenceless, and very sorry for herself, but also guilty, because it is not she who is suffering, but Michin. Michin wants to die.

People die, her father died without a word, leaving her among strangers, *barba* Ermanno died less than three months ago. Ermanno had been her protector; he had been the only man she'd ever known who smiled. When she brought home her school report, he would give her a couple of lire by way of reward for her good results. A few years ago, before the war, when chocolate was still available, he'd given her an Easter egg, she'd seen them in Reviglio's shop windows but never thought she'd have a whole one to herself. Ermanno is dead, he'll never be giving her another present, Margherita is wearing black. People die, even if you love them, they still die. They're merciless. It's like dying in war. War is everywhere, throughout Europe, throughout the world. But Michin too? Why her? Where's the need?

Maria Grazia is alone in the half-light of that chill room, her breath white in the cold. She feels as if she is about to suffocate, there's not enough air. What will become of her? Michin is spiteful, she wants to die. And what is Ninin doing about it, apart from looking on? No one is doing anything, no one will save her from the war, from the bombs, she'll be left all alone, so she too might as well be dead. Michin isn't there any longer, Michin has already gone away, she doesn't want to stay with her, she doesn't care about her, she's off. Possibly, if Maria Grazia manages to cry loud enough, and shout with all her might, Michin will reconsider matters and come back.

'Might we know what's wrong with you tonight?' asks Michin. 'Cat got your tongue?'

It's just a figure of speech, they haven't got a cat, but if they had it would certainly be dead, in view of their dire need Ninin would undoubtedly have throttled it and put it in a pan.

But at the mention of the cat, as though that was just what they were waiting for, the floodgates of misery are suddenly thrown open, and Maria Grazia breaks out in desperate sobs. She hears her mother saying *'povra cita, povra masnà'*, and sobs even more desperately than before.

Now Michin opens her arms and draws her to her chest, all swaddled with blouses and thick woollen shawls, and Maria Grazia carries on crying, half lying on that bed, enveloped in that soothing warmth, in that familiar smell, shaken with sobs; Michin's breath smells of medicine. Crying has a rhythm of its own, it comes and goes, now in long waves, now in short violent bursts, 'That's it, cry away, it'll do you good,' murmurs Michin.

Weak though she is, tempted as she is to wallow in her peaceful apathy, she nonetheless starts singing in a keen, mocking voice: *'Come pioveva! Come piangeva!'* (How it poured! How she bawled!)

They'd sung that song together so many times, while bringing in the washing, folding up sheets, arms outstretched: *C'eravamo tanto amati, per un anno e forse piu, c'eravamo poi lasciati, non ricordo come fu...* we'd loved each other madly, over a year or more, then suddenly we parted, now I don't know what for…

Then the darkness is ripped apart and Maria Grazia begins to breathe normally. She wipes her eyes and finds, despite everything, that she's still ravenous.

The hunger my mother suffered during the war. Those

sugar sticks, up there in their glass vase on top of the wardrobe. Those Californian apricots, and the potato and pasta soup with little bugs floating on the surface between the all too rare dots of butter, to be fished out with the edge of your spoon. And Michin saying: 'Come now, don't be so picky, what doesn't kill you will make you stronger.' Even though my family was not given to mulling over such matters, right from my earliest years these memories of hers become my own. What child has not wished to dry a mother's tears, to sate her hunger? The child-mother is closer, yet more unattainable, than any child that we may ever have.

In times of trouble and despair my mother will seek solace in food, a well stuffed ham roll will be the medicine required whenever her husband plays fast and loose with her, and coffee and a brioche and a bar of chocolate will be the fuel to get her going at the dawn of a new day, leaving yesterday's sorrows behind. A simple cure but one which will always prove effective.

Was it in order to feed my mother up, to sate her wartime appetite, that at the age of eleven I become a self-taught cook? Is that why, to this day, I enjoy cooking for those I love, and am gripped by an irrepressible and unbecoming desire to feed any kind of dog, cat or hungry animal of any kind?

Firm steps on the stairs, a door opening on the other side of the landing. It's Ninin, home late from work, she'll have taken the seven forty-five train. 'Pull yourself together,' Michin orders urgently. 'Have you put the soup on?'

Maria Grazia slowly shakes her head.

'Shame on you! I can't believe it! Every evening it's the same!' complains Michin. 'Go and peel the potatoes, and make it sharp!'

The evening soup: five or six evenings out of seven, pasta and potatoes, poor quality pasta, bitter tasting, and half rotten potatoes, cooked in salted water with a bit of butter added at the end. She will loath such soup until the end of her days and once the war is over she will never touch it again. In theory Maria Grazia should remember to peel and cut up the potatoes and put on the water the moment she gets home. But she almost always forgets, so that when Ninin gets home, after eleven or twelve hours in the factory, she has to do the cooking into the bargain.

It is Ninin who takes the sick woman the steaming plate which mists up her glasses.

Michin emerges from the covers half-asleep, and immediately the pain gets worse. She props herself up on her elbows while her sister arranges the pillow behind her head. Ninin places a painted wooden tray on the bed, the one they use, when there are guests, for serving coffee in the little cups with gilded rims that they bought in Ciriè market. Now what's on the tray is a small bowl of soup, a spoon, a folded napkin, a bit of bread and half a glass of wine.

Ninin pulls a chair up to the bed and watches her sister eat.

'Maria forgot to put on the soup again, the lazybones,' says Michin, blowing on her spoon.

'Leave her be, poor thing, it doesn't matter,' says Ninin. 'You've told her off, she was crying when she came down.'

'Of course, I'd quite forgotten,' mumbles Michin, 'no one must ever scold your precious idol.'

This is what they say more or less every evening, but tonight Ninin discerns a note of weariness in her sister's tone which wasn't there yesterday, or at least not so markedly.

She scrutinises her with her short-sighted eyes and her heart turns to stone.

'It feels as if it's going to snow, doesn't it?' says Michin.

'Yes, it'll snow tomorrow'.

Michin turns her head towards the wall. 'I don't feel like going to work tomorrow'.

'Don't you go,' says Ninin after a moment. 'You should stay at home. It's cold, the winter's back.'

'I'm sorry,' says Michin, face to the wall.

'For that tuppence ha'penny they give you!' shouts Ninin suddenly upset and angry. 'You're better off at home! It's an insult, that pittance!'

Then, embarrassed by her outburst, she presses her hands together, gets up, sits down again, gets up again and draws up the chair.

'Is it really so bad?' she asks her.

Michin shakes her head. She looks so calm, so far away, that you can almost believe her.

'Don't you want any more to eat?'

'No, give it to the *cita*, she'll finish it.'

So Ninin picks up the tray, with the half-full plate, and goes back downstairs; holding back her tears, because the evening has hardly begun and she still has to do the ironing and sewing.

Several days later, Michin has the operation. They open her and close her, as Ninin will put it, as though she were talking of the door of a house which is about to fall down, now tenanted only by ghosts, you can almost see the doctor squinting into the shadows through the bloodstained breach created by the scalpel and recoiling when faced with the overwhelming presence of the illness, hastening to sew her up again to avoid it positively seeping out.

They send her home on a stretcher, in the courtyard a brawny nun picks her up in her arms and carries her up to bed.

'Poor Ninin,' she says to her sister in the evening, her lips so dry she can hardly move them, 'I'm leaving you with an invalid and a child.'

The following day she is dead. Her grave is white with snow.

The war goes on. Men have long been off the scene, they're either at the front or working for the Germans. Mecio has been unemployed because there is no longer any wool for making blankets, and the factory has closed its gates; he has gone to Germany, where at least he gets paid. But in Germany the cities are crumbling under the allied bombs, and Mecio comes back to Italy as soon as he can, better unemployed than dead. His brother Noto is working at Fiat, a factory which is doing important war work, so he's not called up, but that doesn't mean that the war will leave him in peace because the factory is a military target and the planes which Maria hears rumbling through the night may be on their way right there.

Then there's the armistice, and the Salò Republic, and partisans on the hills, and Germans extracting vengeance, and rumours of dreadful goings on. Ninin doesn't want to know anything about it, what's the point in knowing, it'll only upset you further, make you more afraid. She is still working several days a week, so there's a bit of money coming in. Enough, with their three ration cards, to buy a quart of olive oil, half a kilo of butter, the odd kilo of bread. You can find other things on the black market, but you need money for that.

Evacuees are arriving from Turin, a woman with two little girls, as well as a father and an older son, though you see them less often, the men are still in hiding and only come home at night to sleep. The sisters put these evacuees in the room that's partitioned off for use as a kitchen and living room, and they themselves sleep together in the bedroom.

One evening, when everyone is expecting something to happen and they've all gone to hide in the Chiesa's cellar, they hear first gunshots and shouting, then heavy footsteps in the street; there are an awful lot of people, a whole troop, they come into the house, the Chiesa's and the one next door, our own, you can hear the noise of doors being forced open, bang bang, on the ground floor, the first, the second. The women leap up in alarm, they don't know what to do. It's their house, everything they own is there. What are the invaders going to do – plunder, burn?

'I'm going to see what's going on,' says Margherita. 'Somebody must.'

And before they can stop her she has gone upstairs and outside, the place is swarming with soldiers, a whole column of Germans in retreat, they've come from Turin on the side roads and they're on their way to the mountains and the frontier. There has been shooting all along the way, and the places where it has occurred will be marked with memorial slabs. A couple of hundred metres down the road a boy, all on his own, has opened fire on the Germans and now he's lying in the road, just beyond the level crossing. In times to come his photograph, set into an ugly memorial stone, will intrigue children not yet born (those of the Fifties and Sixties, because later generations will no longer play in the street): a young face with lovely full lips and an Alpine soldier's cap perched jauntily on his head; in front of those smooth cheeks, a bunch of yellowing plastic lilies and roses. Who was he, what is he doing there, why is he staring at us? He will become an obscure wayside divinity, a mysterious figure bleached by sun and dust. They say that he did not die instantly, but was there in his death throes for hours, and no one could go near him because the Germans had set an armed guard to watch over him, so no one could go and give him aid.

What can Margherita have said to those soldiers in retreat, and in what tongue? The routed enemy must certainly have been somewhat crestfallen; they were just ordinary soldiers, the officers had made a beeline for the villas in the Park, with their promise of more bourgeois comforts. Anyway, after a few minutes she comes back and says that they can all go back home, which is what the sisters do, and she's used gestures to persuade the soldiers to occupy just one room, the one that has recently been given over to the evacuees (who are spending the night in the cellar) and to leave them to sleep in their own beds, though of course sleep is in fact quite out of the question. It is a night of fraught truce with Germany, the women locked in their room, on the other side of a ridiculously vulnerable door which rattles, and this fraught truce is threatened from time to time when the German who is stretched out on the landing turns over noisily in his sleep. The noise of the rifle butts being banged down on the tiles, for instance, will take some forgetting, as will the sound of the soldiers' boots on the bedroom floor.

The next morning Margherita and Maria Grazia go out to get bread from Reviglio's, it's safer to do things in pairs. It's cold outside. The town is under occupation, Italy has been liberated but the invaders are still here. It's the first of May 1945. People don't say much, and what they do say, they say under their breath. Once they're back home, the women make an omelette with the eggs that the Germans have commandeered from farms they've been through, and then the Germans leave, taking whatever comes to hand, the car belonging to Commendatore Cellino, the owner of the factory making the concrete pipes which are stored in the courtyard, and the bicycles belonging to people who hadn't hidden them in time (the one belonging to Maria Grazia is safely stowed away under a pile of firewood in the attic).

When all that remains of the Germans is their muddy footprints on the stairs, and the blood of the boy who died down there in the street, Ninin goes to church to light a candle to the Madonna, who is not just Mary the mother of God but also her sister Michin, and her mother Domenica and even her father, whose unfortunate end must for the moment be overlooked. By now, for her the Virgin and God are multiple beings, their composite personae containing all those loved ones who are no longer here and who now, in time of war, combine their loving powers to watch over the living and keep them safe from harm.

The war is over, so they say, but hunger most certainly is not. One Sunday when Maria Grazia comes home from nine o'clock mass, she finds Ninin anxiously awaiting her return: 'Come on, we've got to go to the grain store to get corn, everyone's there, come on!' The doors of the grain store are open wide, some people have already helped themselves, most generously.

'They must have taken hundreds of kilos of the stuff, they'll be selling it off on the black market,' grumbles Ninin to herself, hastening to fill up bags and pillow cases, jostled by the crowd as it comes and goes.

Later people will be obliged to own up to this anti-social action, and Ninin too, always fearful if not respectful of a law which shows no particular respect for her, will own up along with the rest – though underestimating her takings, like everybody else. Those who have sinned will not be punished, they'll just have to take their corn to Reviglio's so that it can be made into bread. As a result, they'll get less with their ration cards, but Ninin isn't worried because Margherita's sister-in-law now works in the office where they give out the ration books, and amidst the recent confusion one or two extra ones have found their way into their household.

In people's memories, the bread made with the corn from the grain store will always be linked to the youngest of the refugees, a little girl who is barely two years old and who, on smelling those rolls fresh out of the oven, sits down on a step and sucks her fingers with a hopeful air, announcing, with her freshly forged new consonants, that she is 'berry hungry for some brite wed'. For her, who has known nothing but war, even that wholemeal bread, which smells of corn and is not black and evil-smelling like the bread you get with your ration card, is real, good bread, and therefore 'brite', or white. It is her first mouthful of peace.

Maria Grazia, the *masnà,* the child, has not really been affected by the war, she has been brushed by its cold breath but has not felt its chill touch directly on her skin. As her mother and the *magne* have prayed and hoped so ardently, a barrier has been thrown up around her, a protective plot has been hatched. In 1945 Maria Grazia is eighteen, a girl with clear, solemn eyes that give nothing away, and regular features, with a hint of a dimple in her chin, and hair, in photographs at least, that is a cloud of curls, a shoulder-length froth of foam. A more youthful, more angular version of certain pre-Raphaelite women, with fleshy lips and rapt expressions, both sensuous and chaste, austere and soft, a symbol of all the mysteries of womanhood.

Unaware of herself, and diffident (Michin: 'If anyone tells you you're pretty, don't believe them, they're teasing you!') and if ever a vain thought did dare to show itself, it would be promptly stamped on as a source of shame. What, after all, is beauty? *'Dui di d'mur bel'* according to Ninin's lapidary definition: a couple of inches of pretty kisser. You can't eat beauty, it doesn't last, it's thoroughly treacherous. There's something animal about it, it's a sort of fleshly mask which attracts youth and makes it buzz, as coloured flowers do bees.

The war has prevented Maria Grazia from embarking on those timid sentimental apprenticeships which were formerly the prerogative of nice young girls: walks, Sunday outings, dances, country fairs. All such events were now put on hold, postponed until some misty future; there may have been the odd fete, the occasional outing, but even so the raw material was lacking, either called up or somewhere else or in the maquis – absent, in any case.

'I was a fool,' she was to say, many years later, 'I didn't know a thing, I was really *fola*.'

'Fola', what a lovely word: quite apart from folly, it puts you in mind of foolish, and fable.

While Italy is celebrating the end of the war, the young men who've been away from home so long are drifting back. For many, the return journey will be a long one, it will be months before they will see the mothers, sisters and fiancees who are awaiting them. Maria Grazia isn't expecting anyone, there are no men in her family and hence no soldiers to write to, to suffer pangs of anxiety and uncertainty for; which means that she doesn't yet know who she's waiting for. Who, of those coming back, will be her man?

And these young men are different from the young men before the war. Her mother married a fat elderly man with a moustache, who awed and frightened her; you don't get that kind any more. What you get now are thin, smooth-cheeked, sinewy young men, who smoke unfiltered cigarettes and dance

American dances, they want to enjoy themselves and make up for lost time, they give women brazen looks, but women too are different, they wear short flared skirts, laugh loudly and smoke as well. They also have the vote.

She won't be voting on 2 June 1946, because she's not yet twenty. Ninin will go, and she'll vote for the monarchy, because there's still the king and queen, like God and the Virgin, father and mother, only atheists and communists can imagine a world turned upside down, without God and without a king. When the republic wins, after a brief period of indignant worry, Ninin calms down and sees almost no difference, even if in her vocabulary the word 'republic' will always mean chaos, the loutish, unbecoming desire to do something your own way rather than staying in the ranks.

Maria Grazia, who daren't look in the mirror for fear of being caught up in the delusion of her own beauty, is quite ready to fall for someone else's couple of inches of pretty kisser. In that summer of '45, the first summer without a war, the pretty kisser of her future fiancé is coming back from Germany to Italy, and, though she doesn't yet know as much, she's expecting him.

The man about to return is the one for whom, in Michin's prophetic words, she will be like the rising sun. Irony notwithstanding, she was right. My mother will be a true stroke of good fortune for my father, a stroke of genius, the best throw of the dice he'll have in his gambler's life.

Grey Skies

That's what his elementary teacher calls him. He's earned this nickname because of the smoky look in his hazel eyes, which betray a constant impatience, and flicker with resentment and sullen indignation whenever the master dispenses the humiliations reserved for unpromising pupils.

There they are, two hardened adversaries, he behind his desk in his black overall with a stiff collar and blue bow, the teacher, legs apart, planted firmly in front of the blackboard. He's clutching the cane in his right hand and bringing it down imperiously on to the palm of his left, *thwack thwack,* a foretaste of blows to come, a sound which will cause the whole class to stiffen in alarm.

The master looks down upon him from above, towers over him, as a hunter might tower over some simple-minded small wild creature. And the look in Grey Skies' eyes does indeed have something of a nervous animal intent on flight, but puffing itself up before it does so in the vain hope of alarming its aggressor. The master – a bull about to charge – lowers his broad blank forehead, and suddenly the boy is transformed, he breaks out into a smile of surrender and complicity, a smile without any trace of guilt or original sin, sunny and pagan and radiant. Grey skies, swept clean by a sudden burst of wind, become radiant expanses of beckoning blue. Faced with that angelic little faun the master is wrong-footed, he blushes with a rush of pleasure that's akin to love.

To cane or not to cane the little dunce? To strike him, or forgive? To take up the invitation contained in those eyes, which promise to bear you away to worlds as light and airy as the painted clouds found on church ceilings? Or not?

And then, another lightning change: quick as a flash, a mocking mirror appears for an instant in that golden gaze and the master glimpses himself in it, shrunken, comical and deformed.

Thwack goes the cane.

'He's bright, but he won't concentrate,' says master to her mother, just as millions of other teachers say about millions of other children. And he's not pleased with the pedestrian way he's expressing himself, either, nor with the banality of the observation.

My grandmother, a tiny woman dressed in black, gives him a timid smile, so like yet so unlike that of her son. As meek and speedy as a lizard, she observes the master from below, instantly taking in his red nose, the bags under his eyes, the none too clean black shirt. Fascism is going great guns, the master is a bachelor and makes good this flaw with a surplus of political zeal, expressed above all of an evening in the wine shop, over a bottle of wine.

'Potentially, your son is gifted,' he carries on. 'He's lively and responsive, but he's got no staying power, no self-discipline! He's a slacker and a liar! He's touchy and rude and crafty!'

He would like to say more, and say it better, but the words won't come.

Respectfully, smiling apologetically, she holds her peace. Like a sponge, she sucks up all the blame. She stares at his shoes, which could do with a bit of a clean.

'What's needed is a guide, a mentor, a firm hand!' the master says, warming to his task.

Like everyone else in town, he knows quite well that the boy's father is away, working in France, he lives in a family of women, so he can carry on just as he likes.

'He's got a lot going for him, he could even…' here the master pauses, he could what, that peasant's son? If the woman in front of him were a sweet-scented, soft-handed member of the middle classes he would suggest private lessons, a teacher who would straighten out and put a brake on that chaotic sensibility by nudging him in the direction of study, but the one we're dealing with is a little woman whose nails are black with grime, who has no money to waste on private lessons, so all he can say is: 'He could make a good peasant or a good craftsman, but without some guidance, some firm hand, you'll find yourself landed with a ne'er-do-well, or worse!'

She says nothing and smiles on.

'You women are spoiling him! Hand him over to your brother-in-law, he'll teach him a trade. A boy needs a man's example!'

My grandmother waits expectantly, encouragingly, for what's to come, as though to say: 'Go ahead, I'm all ears!' The master puffs and pants, it's a bit like dealing with someone simple-minded. She herself is riveted by his habit of making a fist with one hand and bringing it down on the other, a tic which becomes more frenzied as the conversation heats up.

My grandmother's eyes are wide and bright; always quick to acknowledge suffering and to forgive all and sundry, she is also as unerring as radar in detecting the slightest hint of humanity's common denominator, the ridiculous. She stares at the master with her grey eyes, leads him to suspect that she might have knowledge of a certain disagreeable episode in which the older man has been made to look a fool by the young boy: asked on several occasions to discreetly procure him a bottle of wine from the local wine shop, the boy had dug into the change. That was why he was so eager to perform such errands!

The master pulls himself together, regains some of his dignity. He wipes his forehead with his handkerchief and folds it up carefully.

'Do as I suggest, rein him in, my dear woman! At all events,' he concludes, lighting a cigarette, 'he'll be moving up a class, he's made it by the scruff of his neck, as usual. What more can we hope for? Everyone does the best they can, but there are natural limits,' he adds for his own benefit, though loud enough for her to hear, despite the fact that – much relieved and grateful and walking crabwise – she is already scurrying towards the door.

There are a lot of things I don't know about my father's family, but one thing is certain: the female side is the fulcrum around which daily existence gravitates. Here too, as in my mother's family, it is a group of sisters who holds the family together, and who decides where and how they live.

His name is Angelo, but for his gambling companions, as both child and adult, he is known as Gilin; for all the women in his life he will always be Angelo, even when his wife's pleasure in pronouncing that word, 'Aàngelo,' with the stress on the first syllable, will turn into a strangled shriek of shrewish irritation: 'Angelòo,' with the stress on the last.

His family comes from the Vaude, a region of long, low, green hills running towards the Canavese, but at some point they settled on the plain nearer to Turin, at Cirié, which is just a few kilometres from the Vaude. Angelo's mother is called Maria – every family has at least one per generation – and she's the third of five inseparable sisters, indeed if possible they become more inseparable as time goes by. During the first years of my life they are all living along the minor road which runs to the west of Cirié, towards the river Stura, then crosses it to join the main road which skirts the once royal domain of la Mandria, and on to Venaria and then Turin. They live just outside the little town of Cirié, in what is still almost the countryside, with houses arranged edgeways along the minor road, with courtyards of beaten earth or gravel in front of them, and a kitchen garden or a bit of meadow separating them one from the other, and one side opening on to cultivated or fallow fields. A close-knit nebula of Mattioda sisters extends over a couple of hundred metres, with children, husbands and grandchildren. The family also includes a brother, Pietro, who has also settled somewhere nearby, and who, loyal perhaps to the matriarchal customs of his tribe, will father three daughters.

My grandmother Maria, the middle sister, is the only one who's thin. The other four are rotund, chubby, even huge, though they wear their embonpoint proudly; only in old age will it become an inconvenience, a weight which binds them to the earth. 'People say that a woman is good and fat, but never good and thin,' they comment peaceably. Maria on the other hand is tiny, slender, a mere slip of a thing, the poor sister among the rich, making do with hand-me-downs and the most modest tasks.

But at the time when my father is a boy, before the Second World War, both Maria and her two sons, Giovanni and Angelo, and the two more distinguished sisters, Apollonia and Giulia, still live in town. These are the two who have had an education, and they've risen through the ranks and practise a profession: Apollonia is a midwife and Giulia, who studied to be a teacher but has never taught, works as a clerk in an agricultural co-operative. They live in a house with fine wrought-iron balconies, at the southern end of what was once the drive up to the seventeenth-century palazzina Doria, and which now links the old town centre with the train station. Their windows, on the second floor, look out over the last plane trees, with the little fountain in the form of a fascist boundary stone in front of the red station building. On Sundays you can watch the whole town out for its weekend stroll without even putting your nose out of doors. In winter, on the other hand, when the trees are bare and the sky is clear, you can glimpse the blue and white mountains among the branches, apparently balanced on the boundary walls of the grand villas which stand on the other side of the avenue. My grandmother lives in the same house, but on the ground floor, in two rooms whose only view is on to the courtyard.

Apollonia and Giulia have always lived together, first as young girls and then again when Giulia is widowed, after a brief marriage. Alone and in mourning, the younger sister moves into the house of the older one and her husband, Giovanni, the brother-in-law upon whom the master had cast his eye for the breaking in of the young and unpromising Grey Skies. But Giovanni is a man of few words, a misanthrope, who feels nothing for Maria and even less for her two sons. Although he teaches woodwork at the Craftsmen's Guild School, frequented solely by young boys, Giovanni is in fact more of a ladies' man, provided the ladies in question are creatures of habit and easy to handle; he lives a modest life of peace and quiet with his wife and his sister-in-law Giulia, themselves as heavy and solid as the furniture in the living room, while there is something wild and disorderly in Maria which rubs him up the wrong way. Giovanni and Maria, neighbours and relatives by marriage, are undeclared enemies, but it's an open secret, one of those unspoken truths on which family ties depend, made up as they are of enmity as much as of love; he glowers at her from under his thick grizzled eyebrows, she prances off and grins behind his back.

Of the five sisters, four (the fat ones) are *matres dolorosae*. Delfina, the oldest, whose husband died soon after they were married, has just one son, a deaf mute. Of the two daughters of Margherita, known as Ghitin, one is severely handicapped and will die in her teens. Apollonia and Giulia have no children, and it saddens them.

Apollonia, known as Polonia, the second born, is the most florid of the lot, her soft boneless body home to the family's strongest personality. Newly married, before she becomes such a commanding local figure, she works in the factory and loses a baby out of fear – or so the family legend has it. In the spinning–mill there are certain belts which 'water' the looms, that is, they turn the wheel of the loom using the water which comes from the mill. These belts, three or four inches wide, run along the factory ceiling and come down from above to each machine; they're visible to the naked eye, completely in the open and endlessly and frantically in movement. One day a worker's hair gets caught up in the belt, and the woman is lifted, shrieking, up above her loom. What happened to her? Family lore does not enlighten us on that score, but tells us only what happened to Polonia, who was right on the spot and fainted dead away; she is taken to hospital bleeding furiously, but there is nothing to be done, the baby is lost.

They tell her that with her constitution it will be difficult, if not impossible, for her to have children, any further pregnancies may cost her her life and she, having been so wrapped up in her own potential motherhood, now turns her passionate attention to the other women in labour and starts to help the midwives. Someone, perhaps a doctor, suggests she might become a midwife. She's definitely gifted! That will be her way of bringing any number of babies into the world! This is how Polonia finds her vocation and her career, she studies, gets her diploma and brings children to others, since she cannot buy any of her own. She becomes a 'bringer' of babies. She 'delivers' them, or perhaps actually 'makes' them, with her own pink hands and the mysterious instruments she keeps in her big black bag. She is a small, round goddess of fertility, who delicately but firmly extracts new life from the black womb of the earth and carries it safe and sound to the world of the living. Pale and fraught husbands, whose wives are about to 'buy', will turn to her with reverence and respect, and then repay her with gifts, because they know that everything – the right heartbeat, the perfect shape of the tiny fingers, the little quiff of hair there will or won't be on the little head – depends on her, on her goodwill and knowledge.

Polonia practises her profession with cheerful pride. She can be seen cycling around the countryside at every hour of the day and night, a round black blob on two slender wheels. Spurred on by her mission, she pedals along ditches, along unmetalled roads. Those who have cars will come to pick her up, others, those who are in more of a hurry or more afraid, and richer, may come by cab. She bends over the women in labour with her placid smile, her little shining eyes, and the unborn children see her from inside the womb and are drawn to her and come out without any nonsense, she handles them adeptly, tiny wrinkled buttocks safely lodged in the palm of her hand. How many cords can she have cut? How many grown adults now strolling around town have felt the touch of her hand upon their throbbing fontenelles?

Polonia is always out in the square at fascist meetings, next to the mayor, the doctor, the pharmacist. While the men talk of empire and of glory, she casts her eye over the Balilla and the Young Italians Girls and recognises them instantly, the ones who popped out without any trouble and those who had to be yanked out by the feet after twelve hours of labour, those who were breast-fed and those who took the bottle, those who ate rusks and those who were dragged up on bread and spankings. She knows and feels things about each child in the town, a pride and a happiness which are hers alone, an anguish which no one else can know or share but which everyone, in some way or other, acknowledges and honours.

Giulia, the younger sister, is the favourite and most cultured, she reads women's magazines and knows exactly how to behave. She came of marriageable age just when there were very few men about, shortly after the first world war, and had to make do with a tubercular reject who gave her no children and died after less than three years of marriage.

Does her widowhood weigh upon her? She's dreamed of a house of her own, of course, of children of her own to dress and tend, of a windowsill all her own from which to vaunt starched Sunday blouses. But perhaps the married interlude was just too short for her truly to become accustomed to the married state, and cohabitation with her sister seems a return to a better known, more natural kind of life. Rather than a widow, Giulia is an eternal *signorina*, a lovely velvety girl who plucks her eyebrows and wears long undergarments of pink silk and corsets with a thousand ties beneath discreet dark clothing, who knows how to serve coffee exactly *comme il faut* and greet important people with just the right gracious lowering of the head. She has a passion for high class linen, ribbons and lace; and also for fashionable novels, those by Liala, Delly, D'Annunzio, Pitigrilli, and Countess Lara, and these, on her days off, she reads from morning until late at night, when her hair, free at last of its combs and hairpins, is spread out on the pillow on which, before her brief marriage, she embroidered her initials as a married woman.

Every weekday, morning and evening, she goes off on her bicycle to the agricultural co-operative, where she sits down at her extremely orderly desk, dips her pen into her ground glass inkwell and fills great pages of the register with her regular ornate script. The men treat her with respect, she does sums and hands out receipts and looks at them kindly and slightly flirtatiously from above her double chin. Then she clambers back into the saddle and goes home, where lunch or supper await her, together with the wireless, a bit of delicate mending and *Vita Femminile*, or *Woman's World*, a journal for women and young ladies who are distinguished by their high-flown sentiments and rustling garments. The heavy housework is done by Maria the peasant, in exchange for meagre pay.

The sisters' bicycles spend their nights recovering from the day's exertions leaning up against one another in the dark, narrow hall. Their black leather saddles, polished by their owners' round posteriors, are soft as a baby's bottom. The parcel racks are as broad and solid as a pack-horse's saddle bag. Just as decades of footsteps have worn down the stone in the centre of the steps, so, above, in the flat on the second floor, the sisters' sleep has carved out soft shell-like shapes in the middle of the beds. Theirs is a household of women, in which husband-cum-brother-in-law Giovanni lives like a boarder or lodger, his days punctuated by the ritual of meals, the tasty, substantial dishes provided by Polonia and the afternoon teas by Giulia, who is as greedy as a child. Were it not for the lack of children, their cups would overflow.

By way of recompense, they have their nephew.

The only member of the family who has managed, by some miracle, to produce two handsome healthy sons, Giovanni and Angelo, is Maria, and of the two, the more handsome is the younger, Angelo. In him, Polonia and Giulia find a legitimate outlet for their thwarted mother love. Angelo grows up as the nephew of the Mattioda sisters rather than as his parents' son. Maria, his mother, accepts this and takes a back seat, as though she acknowledges that the sisters have more to offer than she has, and perhaps foreseeing that her son will have need of their support.

Maria's husband, Lorenzo, is away working in France and she is alone with two children, living on the money he sends her and the pittance she can make from such little land as she owns. Maria is a peasant by birth and calling, she is the only one of the five sisters to carry on in her parents' footsteps, to walk barefoot along the furrows, to have hands that are made to touch the earth, the grass and the trees, and a face with the kind of wrinkles that only peasants have, spending their lives in the sun and open air as they do. Permanently on the move, Maria waddles from the kitchen garden to the town, arrives there with her hair all over the place, weighed down with tomatoes and lettuce, then sets off again immediately on errands for Polonia and Giulia. She acts as a sort of servant to them, mopping their floors and washing their linen along with her own on the stones by the mountain stream, on the road to Devesi where the washerwomen meet. She accepts these labours so meekly that they do indeed treat her as a servant, criticising her both openly and covertly for her lack of organisation and general haste. Even though they are her sisters, they belong to a different social class in terms of income, aspirations and ways of living, their view of the world in general. If Maria has remained a peasant, Polonia and Giulia are now fully-fledged members of the bourgeoisie, having adopted middle-class comforts, tastes and manners.

This Maria has something in common with the other one, my grandmother Maria, poor thing, who is housebound and has problems with the left half of her body, which tends to drag. Both belong to the weak side of the family, both are vulnerable, almost silent creatures, yet somehow shielded by a strength that is all their own, and when they do speak they say little or nothing about themselves, and gaze out at the world with large impenetrable eyes. Unlike the invalid, however, this Maria can move around freely, she is in full control of a strong if tiny body, and the earth is on her side. The kitchen garden is her universe, and the trees her friends.

Her bunches of flowers were one of the mysteries of my childhood. My grandmother does not pick flowers as other people do, one stem at a time, avoiding weeds and blooms that have had their day. My grandmother tugs up whole handfuls of greenery, daisies, clover, nettles, dry leaves, all together, and they all end up in a chaotic cluster in an old rusty tin in a corner of the kitchen. Not a bouquet but a bit of meadow.

Her sisters regularly peruse catalogues of hyacinths and roses. 'What a mess she makes,' they say as they shake their heads. 'Totally lacking in discrimination.'

It's almost as though she doesn't want to upset nature by putting asunder that which the earth has joined. Over time, for me those bunches became the hallmark of her token, silent rebellion, of her remaining doggedly true to herself and alien from what the world expects and approves.

When she isn't working the land or washing clothes, Maria the peasant is rushing tirelessly up and down the town, greeting all comers; she is intimately acquainted with every shop entrance, every stone on the street, every knot in the bark of the plane-trees along the avenue leading to the cemetery which is where the smartest and most interesting events are held, namely funerals. After the dear departed has been buried amidst a flurry of rosaries and prayers, Maria the newshound rushes home to the sisters and tells them all about it, who was there and who wasn't, imitating this person and that, their voices, their gestures, their tics and manias, with a quite unexpected skill. The sisters laugh their fill, like smart ladies in their boxes at the theatre. These are her moments of triumph.

My grandmother Maria, with her sad grey eyes, is one of those who harbours the ambiguous gift of laughter within themselves. Like Michin, my mother's much loved *magna*. If Michin was cheerfully satirical, always ready to mock and sting, Maria the peasant relied rather on gestures, and like all great mimes would taunt the human race with pitiless pity. Should the two of them ever have pooled their talents, they would have covered the vast range of the comic in its entirety.

Of her two sons, the older – stocky and solid, with a deep voice – takes after his father, while the younger one takes after her, being made of a less sturdy, less dependable clay. Angelo grows up under the soft warm wings of the *magne*, untouched by the disapproving grunts emitted by his uncle Giovanni and the occasional angry outbursts of his father, who in fact is almost always away. Gilin is apprenticed to a shoe-maker, then goes to work for a cobbler in Turin. Work never really becomes second nature to him, like his mother he prefers to wander where his fleet feet take him but, unlike her, he wanders empty-handed. Duties and timetables mean nothing to him, the only thing that gets him going is novelties, and freedom. In those unsophisticated times, it doesn't take much to amuse young men: filching your neighbour's fruit, spying on the priest who's having it off with his housekeeper, doing target practice, taking the chain off the irritable schoolmaster's bicycle, to watch him falling off when he climbs on to the saddle, drunk. Everything is a game, and games are Angelo's passion, his calling in this life. Cards, bowls, dice, a world of child-men ensnared by the magic of their own making.

He and his friends are known in the local wine shops and those of the surrounding villages. At the end of the month one of the two *magne*, usually Polonia, will go around town, getting down from her bicycle at every wine shop and asking the governor whether her nephew has anything to pay. The sisters set great store by their good name and don't want family debts. Polonia pulls out a big purse from her black leather bag and counts her money, her peaceful face wrinkled by a smile, and often some woman will emerge from the back of the shop to greet her and give her news of the last-born child, and the governor will give her a discount and a packet of freshly roasted coffee. Polonia is satisfaction and serenity personified, it's live and let live with her, she's a woman of the world, on intimate terms with half the town, she knows their joys and sorrows and their secrets, unwanted children, children lost and ill, violent husbands and embittered wives, tragedies and betrayals, what are her nephew's little defects in comparison, those of a handsome, carefree boy so many women doubtless wish were theirs? While she is on those missions of redress her face expresses nothing but indulgence, an indulgence so trusting and unshakeable that it's almost catching.

'It's Polonia the midwife's nephew, the Mattioda sisters' boy,' as they refer to him, and everyone knows who they mean.

Meanwhile Angelo's father is back from France, he got sent off when war broke out, because now French and Italians are not on the same side. Apart from giving their orders to his wife and son (the younger one, because the older one has been called up), he hasn't got much to do, he tends that bit of vineyard he's still got up on the Vaude, going off in the morning and coming back in the evening, drunk and unsteady on his pins. He suffers from diabetes, and every so often he has a funny turn and falls down and someone has to be called to pull him up, he's certainly no tower of strength for Maria to lean upon, but he is a man, and as such he has the prerogative of laying down the law – and murdering. A cat which Maria was feeding on scraps gets shot for having dared to steal a piece of meat, but Maria can't bear to put it in the pot, and ends up burying it in the kitchen garden, hiding her tears. With Angelo his father is gruff and heavy-handed, but he's too slow to do him any real harm.

In the summer of 1943 the postcard arrives. First it had been his brother Giovanni, called on to fight in the Greek campaign, now it's Angelo's turn. Shortly after 8 September, bristling with rifles and submachine-guns, the Germans arrive at the barracks in Asti where he's been doing his military service, and order the flummoxed and nervous recruits to surrender (the officers having almost all vamoosed immediately after the announcement of the armistice, by wireless, on the evening of the eighth).

Very little is known about the time he spent in Germany. Come to that, the same could be said of all the key moments of his existence, of his deepest feelings, of his triumphs and defeats, of his joys and sorrows.

Gilin is secretive, mysterious. It's not that he doesn't talk, it's that his talk is pure fabrication; he often breaks off what he's saying and rarely finishes a sentence. He's a liar, everyone knows that by now, but he doesn't always lie out of self-interest, or because he's driven to it (though he may do this too, and often). He is also quite capable of lying for no conceivable reason, for the sheer joy of it, out of pure devilment. Perhaps he is a liar because the difference between truth and falsehood quite simply escapes him, or doesn't interest him. Perhaps he is just a bit of an artist, an innocent, that may be why he is so popular with women, who continue to love him even when they have stopped believing him.

He has inherited his mother's gift for laughter and for mimicry, and her mildness. He prefers peace to war, flight to fight. He knows how to be agreeable, charming, good, earnest; for five minutes he can be anything at all. He holds within him a perpetual promise – never fulfilled – of gaiety, of open spaces. Imaginative, perhaps even talented, at one point in his life he thinks of becoming a painter, but the colours dry up in their open tubes before he has even approached the canvas.

Grey Skies has no staying power. His face clouds over at the slightest difficulty, words and gestures fail him, he is trounced by impatience and ill temper. Wherever he may be, very soon the earth beneath his feet begins to feel too hot. Wherever he is, he dreams of being somewhere else. His means of transport (a bicycle, then a motorbike, then a car) are like paws to a hare, an integral part of his body, indispensable. The only time he is happy – a cigarette in the corner of his mouth, one elbow protruding from the window – is when he is driving towards some as yet unspecified goal. He strays through his one dimension, which is the present. He should have been born a dog, a gypsy, a cloud.

What we do know: he was taken to somewhere in northern Germany. He worked as a cobbler, then on the land, for some peasants who gave him almost enough to eat and were almost good to him, Germans though they were; then he worked in a sugar factory. Life was hard, all right. You went hungry, sometimes you received the odd bit of bread, it was almost always women who provided it, but also other prisoners who worked as bakers and who hid it under their jackets when they returned to the camp. Then there were various gruesome episodes, whose full implications were obscured either by shame, or by his habit of leaving his sentences unfinished: massacre by rifle-fire, laceration under bombardment, a man trying to flee the lager drowning in a sewer. 'Drowning in shit to escape a life of shit – war is one great lump of shit.' *Scheisse, Kartoffel, Kamaraden, Achtung, Rauss*! *Ta ta ta ta*, machine-gun fire.

And here his eyes would light up with surprise; in his memory, power and powerlessness, splendours past and horrors present send out a single iridescent glow: 'Oh my, those Germans! What a pack of bastards!' (for a moment, something like a moist dog's gaze would flicker in his eyes). 'You can't imagine what bastards they were! *Ta ta ta ta*! Lord, the things I've seen! But at least the Germans knew how to earn people's respect, that's more than we ever managed.'

His wife, in irritation: 'They lost the war, though. Luckily.'

Him: 'Bastards.'

This is his way of saying what cannot be said, of remembering what cannot be remembered. And then suddenly, with a mixture of admiration, irreverence, sentimentality and irony: *'Deutschland, Deutschland uber alles!'*

She (eyes to the heavens): 'It's pointless to try and talk to you.'

He (getting up): 'I'll be on my way, then.'

Hundreds of thousands of Italian soldiers are taken off in that autumn of '43. He vanishes into the crowd. He is just one of many, a little soldier boy who's never held a rifle in his life and will never learn to hold one, because they've already disarmed him before he's had a chance to fire a round, and he probably hands that unused weapon back to those who gave it him with a certain sense of relief.

Recruits like himself thought that they were going to war; they screwed up their courage by singing, drinking grappa, whistling at girls and trying not to think of home. He is just one among many non-heroes, he speaks in dialect and wears a medallion with the Virgin round his neck, hoping his mother's prayers will do the trick and see him home safe and sound. As in the wine shop and on the village streets, he finds himself in a world of men, almost all older than himself, to be admired and obeyed and curried favour with; here there are no women to soften the blows. Hardly has it begun than his military apprenticeship turns into something else, something unexpected: people are no longer going to war – so what exactly are they going to, then?

The Germans are armed to the teeth and look as if they mean business, they're super-manly with their bayonets and rifles and panzers, and the little prisoner soldier boys are just frail unarmed bodies beneath their uniforms, as docile and obedient as so many women, seized by iron-fisted warriors who drag them into a dance of death. The Germans give orders, and they're not orders like those from your sergeant, who may rap you over the knuckles if you don't obey, but orders from a German, who may shoot on sight. The Germans make them march, *marsch!* and woe to anyone who hesitates, you'll get it in the neck with a rifle butt, they cram you into trains already bursting at the seams. As long as you're in Italy, despite fear and discomfort, there's hope, you can sense it on the faces of the women who crowd into the stations to see their boys off, throwing them bread and fruit, picking up their notes to send them on home. But once you've crossed that border, there's no knowing where you're bound for, or whether you'll arrive.

These journeys last for weeks, which seem like years. Like everybody else, Gilin sleeps on his feet, lolling against the wall of the corridor or jammed between his fellow soldiers, because there's nowhere to lie down, he does his business in a tin receptacle which is then emptied out of the briefly opened door, and watch out you don't get it all over yourself, or over someone else's feet, which will lead to a torrent of swearing. He eats what he is given, or not at all. The worst thing is the thirst. In the morning he tries to be among the first to lick the metallic-tasting hoar-frost on the wagons' metal joints. Soon, although it's only October, it becomes very cold, this is the North after all, and even though they're packed in like sardines, animal warmth is not enough, their breath forms thick white clouds and their teeth chatter. On the few occasions they're allowed out, trousers have to be dropped in haste and you have to do your business then and there, along the tracks, because you've only got a minute, with German women and children staring disdainfully at Badoglio's traitors, insulting them and throwing stones. Where are they, what country are they in, where railways have neither timetables nor destinations, and trains stop for hours in the open countryside, and you can hear dogs barking in the distance, and the plodding step of the guard going up and down along the tracks? What can Gilin be thinking of, locked up as he is, smelling the stench of his own unwashed body alongside that of so many others, hearing the rumbling stomachs, and the prayers, the curses and the silences? He's thinking of the food he hasn't got, of the woollen pullovers in the chests of drawers at home, of *magna* Polonia's rabbit stew (no, that's the one thing he mustn't think about), about the fellow soldiers he's seen die, his feet, which hurt, the Virgin, his mother's face, the chocolate they gave him in the barracks, death, which will come one day… He's crying, the tears course down his grubby face and he is not ashamed, how could a man feel shame after he has shat into a tin receptacle and besmirched his trousers? And he's only a boy, brought up by women on bread and butter and sugar. But here there is no one to see him cry, and after a bit he wipes away the tears.

The journeys to which the Third Reich has treated deportees and internees serve their purpose well, no two ways about it: when they get out at their destination, the passengers are prepared for what awaits them. They find themselves not a few hundred kilometres, but light years away from home, over the course of the journey they have been stripped not only of their citizenship, their language, their habits, their family connections but also, most importantly, of the notion of time itself. Yesterday, today and tomorrow no longer exist, there's only an almighty present, devoid of memories or plans, without any hopes which go beyond the moment.

It is probable that Gilin is better suited to that particular type of present than the rest of them. It suits him to have no yesterday, and no tomorrow.

As an alternative to prison, the soldiers have been told that they can go back to Italy and fight for the Duce and his Salò

Republic. Almost all have refused, Gilin among them, though without knowing quite why, except that he likes to go along with the crowd, stick with the herd: anyone who separates themselves from it, who goes off on their own, is lost. He's seen what happens if you try to escape, or lag behind on the march: a bullet between the shoulders, or in the neck. People feel a genuine terror at the idea of abandoning the pack, becoming visible, a human target standing out against the grey background of the lager. At the edges of the camp, along the surrounding wall, there are a few metres of waste land, marked off by barbed wire: the death strip, the dead line. The guards in the watchtowers have orders to fire on anyone who sets foot in it, without even bothering to say '*Achtung, Scheisse Italiener*'.

One way and another, Mother Germany does not insist on sending them to fight. What she needs is slaves to be worked to death in the mines and factories, not treacherous combatants. Officers are asked whether they are willing to work or not, soldiers are spared the embarrassment of the choice. In a large unheated room, Gilin sews leather with hands aglow with chilblains. At midday there's a pause, the Germans go to eat, the Italian, Polish and Russian prisoners scratch at their lice-infested bodies and smoke a cigarette, if they've got one. A middle-aged German woman gestures to him – yes, him – to pick up a crate and take it to the end of the room, warily placing a bit of bread and margarine on top of it. He stares at her, full of hope and fear. She doesn't respond to his look, but dismisses him abruptly. The bread tastes wonderful, he bites into it with such eagerness that his gums begin to bleed. From then onwards he waits for her every day, and sometimes she comes and sometimes she doesn't, and when he glimpses her grey hair in the distance his heart begins to pound and his mouth fills with saliva. Their lightning meetings have all the suspense of a clandestine love affair; for that bit of bread and marge both are risking prison, perhaps life itself.

The internees are overseen by a vicious old German who kicks them and insults them, calling them *Scheisse Italiener*, but they are so weakened by hunger that they can hardly muster the strength to hate him, and accept his kicks and insults as though in a daze. This old man is called Hans, he suffers from arthritis and has three fingers missing on his left hand. The overseers in the lager are all elderly or maimed or both, like Hans; all able-bodied men are at the front.

One day Hans accuses Gilin of not working fast enough and knocks him to the ground. Instead of getting up, Gilin begins to cry. Hans stares at him stonily, his expression ever more contemptuous; finally he grabs him by his jacket and starts slapping him.

Wallop! *'Bist du ein Mann?'* asks Hans.

Wallop! *'Du bist kein Mann!!'* he answers himself.

Maddened beyond bearing, the old man loses his head and starts kicking him. Gilin thinks his last hour has come, he will die here, he who is not a man, dispatched by Hans's boots, his skull shattered, here where they make shoes, and while he is thrashing around on the floor, trying to protect his face, he beseeches his tormentor to stop hitting him: *'Pare! Pare dami nen! Gut Mensch! Gut! Gut! Basta, basta!'*

Hans stops. He's red in the face, breathing heavily; he's asthmatic. He presses his hands against his chest.

Gilin shields his eyes; he pulls himself up, feels himself over: one of his cheekbones is swollen, his lip is split.

Hans glares at him; he's panting, trembling, he's about to do something terrible, either he'll start to weep or take out his pistol and shoot him dead. And then Gilin, his guts twisted with fear, leans his head to one side, lifts up an arm and gives the German a gentle stroke.

He has addressed his tormentor as *pare*, father, perhaps just as a conditioned reflex when being thrashed (his father too could deliver a hefty blow, should he succeed in laying hands on his son).

Then he helped Hans to sit down on the bench and waited for him to regain his breath.

From then onwards Hans alternated thrashings with acts of kindness, allowing Gilin to rest every now and again and embarking on long, furious, bitter speeches which their recipient neither understood nor responded to, at most he looked his persecutor in the eye and smiled at him and smoked the cigarette the old man offered him. Inhaling deeply, he pondered on what he might do to that fingerless bastard of a German, how he would hold a pistol to his temple and make him eat his own shit before he fired. Once or twice Hans poured him some coffee laced with brandy from a pocket flask, and Gilin, his head swimming from that drop of alcohol on an empty stomach, smiled at him like a lover and said: *'Gut Mensch! Gut Freund!!'* his eyes bright with tears.

The plank beds in the huts are infested with bed bugs. The men talk of food from morning to night, it's their only interest. They remember their womenfolk's cooking, the traditional dishes, they intone recipes like prayers, spells, love poetry. One of them catches mice and roasts them, though the smell is not encouraging. Some steal brazenly from their weaker brethren, claiming part of their potato ration. Gilin is not one to put up a fight, he gives in straight away, then attempts to reclaim his portion by bartering it for Hans's cigarettes. Some men in his hut are bakers and come back of an evening with loaves stashed under their jackets, and he almost always manages to wangle a slice. At night, while he lies awake scratching himself and pulling up the blanket, which is too short, so that either his feet or his shoulders are uncovered, he thinks of the soft bed and groaning table back at home, swearing under his breath: 'Bastard! Coward! I hope you rot in Hell!'

Who is this bastard? Hans? Mussolini? The *Fuhrer*? Some fellow prisoner? No matter. 'Bastard!' At last the swearing trails off into sleep, becomes almost gentle; night steals over him, all shivering as he is, and carries him away.

He always dreams about certain places at home, ditches, meadows, the room where he used to sleep with his brother, one of his mother's dresses. He dreams of smells, from *magna* Polonia's kitchen, the hay in the fields. The road to the Vauda, with the long hill and the trees. In his dreams he is often running, trying to escape, he's afraid, though he doesn't know why, he's still hoping to save himself, but he has a long way to run. He never dreams about the camp.

Since he's been in the camp, he has become Italian. Until then, Italy had been just a word for him, one tedious concept among many, spouted at rallies by the master at school and the mayor, but now that Italians are queuing up to take a kicking from the Germans it becomes clear that he too is an Italian, even if he would have rather have been a German. The word 'Italy' becomes an insult, a second skin, a lump in the throat he'd like to cough up, but can't. Suddenly, his house, his family, his father, his mother, his brother, his aunts, all have become Italians and there they all are, so far away, among the trees, as though they were on the moon.

They have allowed him to write home, just a few sentences, and his prisoner's number. Months later he receives a parcel addressed to him in his mother's shaky, spiky hand. He clutches it to his chest, tries unsuccessfully to hide it under his jacket. He shoots his fellow-inmates harsh, suspicious looks: they must know that he will guard his treasure with his life. The parcel contains rice, tobacco (the packages have been torn open, and rice and tobacco are now mixed), a pair of grey woollen socks knitted by *magna* Polonia, chocolate and a postcard.

One evening the Allies bomb the part of the camp where they make soldiers' boots. In the morning six men from his hut don't come back, they've died in the bombing raid. Luckily for him, on the early shift, he's already left by the time the bombs fall.

They organise rescue squads, the prisoners are sent to dig among the rubble, one or two men are brought out alive, but more often it's dead bodies, or bits of them. Gilin digs along with the rest, his muscles aching and his face grey with dust, his spade brings up bits of brick and plaster, bits of machinery, sheets of leather. Then a shape emerges from the rubble, it's a man's arm, Gilin gives a strangled shout, grabs hold of it and pulls it towards him, and out the arm comes with no difficulty whatsoever, all on its own, without the rest of the body to which it had been attached. Knocked off-beam, Gilin sways to and fro, loses his balance, sits down clumsily still clutching that blackened hand, and calls upon God, as though he knew Him well, calls upon Him loud and pointlessly, several times, until a guard gives him an unceremonious kick, and then Gilin throws away that hand and severed arm, opens his mouth, breathes deeply of the air which smells of shattered brick and burned flesh, and faints dead away.

When he wakes up he's ill with a fever, vomiting and delirious. They put him in the infirmary where he spends a few days shaking and groaning and spitting up bile. Against all the odds, he recovers. He's skeleton thin, pale as a ghost and hollow-eyed. His smile looks empty, vacuous. A priest befriends him, brings him food, preaches long sermons which lull him to sleep. He's from the South, this priest, and quite often you can't understand what he's saying, but when he says his prayers in Latin Gilin closes his eyes and feels as if he's back at Sunday mass, head nodding, on the pew in his local church, pleasantly bored. He knows that every time he cries or smiles the priest will give him something, even if it's only a blessing, if he has nothing else to give.

It's spring. The fields are black with mud and the branches gleaming and bare, but you can smell spring in the air. A long and patient roll call in the bitter cold, they stand there for hours until they no longer care where they are sent, just as long as this endless wait is over, and the hours have passed which will take them up to the moment when they can collapse on to the ground and sleep.

Gilin and a few others begin to follow a big-boned woman, whose grey hair is constantly escaping from her scarf. They follow her down endless muddy roads and swear beneath their breath because they're tired, and do not realise that they are blessed by fate.

Those who preceded them have been sent to the steelworks which are the fiery heart of the Third Reich's war industries; those who come after them will be sent to Hitler's secret workshops deep in the heart of a mountain which is whelping bombs and devouring prisoners. Another group will end up in the mines in Schleswig, digging underground tunnels ten hours a day. These are places from which only a very few will return to tell the tale, accursed places where slaves exhausted by their labours will drop dead on the spot, or be transported, tottering, to showers and then thrown into a pit, to be replaced by other slaves who will last a few months or weeks.

Gilin on the other hand is lucky; his luck is called Lotte, she is a widower and has lost two sons in the war. She, together with various other women and old men, runs a large and thriving farm, and she has been allowed to take on a dozen or so internees to help her with the cabbages and beet fields. She feels particularly sorry for the younger ones, and at midday she allows them to lie down in the straw and brings them potatoes and bacon fat, and sometimes a bit of real meat. She lets them wash, and sometimes gives them her sons' old clothes.

The guards who supervise the prisoners, morning and night, backwards and forwards from the huts, are becoming older and older, now they're arthritic seventy-year-olds embittered by the effort they're supposed to make – too much for them at their ripe age – to appear certain of a victory in which they no longer have much faith. With guards like that, half-blind and lame, it's not hard to drag your feet on the way back and snaffle a beet and turnip or two to boil up for supper. Gilin and his companions begin to put a bit of flesh on their bones.

Then suddenly they're no longer internees, they are pronounced civilians. No more guards herding them to and fro, now they can come and go in the camp as they please, they're free to take one road rather than another provided they show up on time. They're even free to spend those few marks they can get their hands on at the wine shop, but they are foreign workers, paid in *lagergeld*, the camp's own paper currency, which is practically worthless.

Alerts become increasingly frequent, and everyone scuttles like flustered insects, internees included, even though they can't get into the camp's one shelter, which is for Germans only. One night the bombs tear off the shelter roof like the lid of a tin of jam, and the prisoners toil away in the smoke and dust dragging out the dead guards' bodies. This time Gilin does not faint.

But the next day he is bereft on hearing that the farm too has been bombed, Lotte and her fellow farmhands are dead, goodbye big-boned, blue-eyed German mother, goodbye potatoes and bacon fat and snoozing in the straw.

They send him to work in the sugar refinery, the war carries on with its work of destruction but the survivors have to eat, and they want sugar. The loathsome smell of beet clings to his body and clothes, but sugar is nutritious and it's easy to steal a handful. People are saying that Germany is losing the war. They say that the Americans are coming, that they have landed in France, that they're in Italy, moving up from the South, but no one has seen them yet.

And outside, in that vast lager which is Germany at war, there are still women, young Poles and Ukrainians who are being rounded up and sent to work in factories, girls of eighteen or twenty who want to joke and make love despite everything, who are still unbroken by the war. Some of them have undoubtedly made eyes at this handsome Italian, slender he may be, to the point of scrawny, but his eyes are still dark and bright, and his hair good and thick. One of them may have courted him, and he may have let himself be steered into some dark corner of a warehouse in exchange for half a loaf of bread or a packet of fags.

It is Gilin's second German spring. There are buds on the branches. Above his head are the steep skies of the North. Grey skies where the clouds sometimes roll back to reveal patches of blue, around him are rich dark fields, and, down there in the city, tall narrow red brick warehouses overlooking a branch of the sea and a green island.

The Baltic, with its grey-green waves, makes him dream vaguely of travel. He takes off his shoes and walks on the beach, feet in the freezing water, sand between the toes. It's his first sight of the sea, there's plenty around Italy but he has never seen it. He has paddled, rather than swum, in the mountain streams, in the clear cold pools formed by the Malone, above Corio. He's not afraid of water, he's drawn to it. He takes off his clothes and in he goes, feeling an inexplicable joy that is almost pain. He doesn't care what, if anything, lies beyond the sea. It is the sea itself which gives him that cold, clean, stinging feeling of being immersed in something immensely powerful, a force which he cannot bear for long, so he comes running out of it to warm himself, his skin tingling as though assailed by a thousand tiny needles.

The war is almost over, but the bombing raids are coming ever more thick and fast.

And then, suddenly, things become even more confused, if that is possible. The Russians arrive in the town with the red warehouses, shattered now, amidst the dry brick dust which hangs so lazily in the air; here and there some shred of everyday life emerges from the chaos, terrible and strange: a picture frame, some chair legs. A saucepan. An exercise book. A half-naked girl lying beside the road, her fair hair daubed with mud. Now the Russians are no longer prisoners but armed soldiers, and on the winning side, with the wolfish eyes of those who have once been victims and who cannot wait to embark upon rape and plunder of their own.

With the arrival of the Russians everything becomes complicated, you no longer know who must be obeyed, who feared. You want to give yourself up, but to whom? Germany has lost, the war is over, but they're still prisoners. Now it's the

Germans who are running away, and there are empty houses and you go in and grab anything you can, you can kill their chickens and make broth with them, with those German fowl.

But then they are transferred to another camp, and then another, and time passes and there's no question of going home. The camp is dirty and there's not much to eat, as usual, but there are almost no supervisors, and in that strange new state of freedom Gilin meets other Italians, and together they eat what they have stolen or exchanged outside the camp, and drink and talk, breaking off only to touch one another, to link arms, to pat one another on the back, like long-lost brothers together again at last.

He bumps into Hans, the old bastard, who is now trying to pass himself off as Polish, but Gilin recognises him and tells on him to his new friends, tells them about the kicks and punches, but not about the cigarettes, and the others decide to give him his just deserts. That evening Hans is dragged into a thicket and roughed up; when at last he stops moaning Gilin gives him one more slap and stands back to look at him, his dream of making him eat shit and then shooting him suddenly a thing of the past; right now he's frightened, he shouts out: 'That's enough, leave him alone!' and he starts hitting his own head with his fists, but the others get angry and he runs away and hides, because he's afraid that after doing for Hans they'll turn on him.

For a few days he stays in the hut with the blanket over his head, he's not well. He's not the only one, some people have died of overeating, they've literally bust a gut, after such a long period of undernourishment.

At last, at the height of summer, he and a couple of friends (new friends, because the group which did for Hans has broken up) leave the camp very early one morning and decide to make it home on their own, on foot, if the worst comes to the worst. Like so many others in their situation, they spend weeks wandering through central Europe, which has become one great shambles, going in the wrong direction and travelling on trains which chuff at random between frontiers old and new, over shattered bridges, past occupying armies. He leaves at the beginning of July 1945, and reaches home around mid-August.

When his mother sees him she goes very pale and loses the power of speech and weeps quietly for hours. Giulia almost faints and has to be offered smelling salts. Polonia almost deserts a baby in mid-stream, cutting the cord in haste and leaping on to her bicycle, a hundred kilos of lightness streaking across the fields.

Everyone says that Maria – Gilin's mother, that is – has been lucky. Giovanni, her other son, has come back safe and sound from Greece – unlike so many others, and accounts of that campaign beggar belief – and has lain low, waiting for this wretched war to end. He goes up into the mountains for a bit, but comes down again after a fortnight saying that he's had enough of fighting and shooting at people, and from then onwards he works as a carpenter in a sawmill on the road to Devesi, where at night – since he can't stay at home, for fear they'll come and get him – he sleeps on a camp bed between piles of wood, and by day, if someone from the Salò Republic shows up, they hide him under a pile of wood shavings. So Giovanni escapes the round ups, and now Angelo is back from Germany. Ultimately the Virgin has spared both of them. As long as she lives, during the *Marian novenas* of the month of May, Maria will cover the high altar in the church of San Giovanni with lilies from her garden, and will light candles to her plaster namesake with the blue cloak and the golden halo.

Gilin's father goes on a memorable binge and offers people round after round. The ecstatic *magne* feel the need to splash out a little. They want to fatten their nephew up, they go out and buy fresh butter, meat and eggs on the black market. He's become like a child again, with eyes too big for his face and a tendency to weep, and his clothes are all folds, much too big for him. Polonia has to refrain from picking him up and checking his weight after every meal. And this time she doesn't just go round the wine shops to pay his debts, she opens an account for him at the *Caffe Centrale*, so he can go there and enjoy himself, poor soul, after what he's been through.

For a few days they all clamour to hear about the kind of war he's had, where he's been and what it was like, and he answers in snatches, as always, he winks, implies that it was… well, it wasn't the kind of thing you want to talk about.

'Relax,' they say to him, 'forget it, Angelino, Gilin. Eat, drink and be merry. *Sagrinti neri.*'

Sagrinesse: to worry about something, to get worked up, to agonise.

Each time Gilin's gaze clouds over, they beseech him pityingly, hands full of gifts: *'Sagrinti nen! Por cit, sagrinti nen!'*

Is that how things went?

Now his daughter has fallen under the spell of the past – but it's too late. Always supposing that any reliable information could be prised out of him, Gilin has ceased to speak.

There is only the most fragmentary information about the places where he had been in prison: I know that he had spent some time north of Berlin, near the sea, but nothing more precise.

One summer's day I find myself on the Baltic coast; I've driven along the pleasant green road which runs from Berlin towards the sea and the island of Rugen. I won't refer to my holidays pompously as research exactly, I'm here by chance, I've always loved the vast and fickle northern skies. But during my travels I visited the concentration camp at Sachsenhausen, which is now a museum. Before I left, I read diaries and personal accounts and listened to interviews, it seems to me that by now I am thoroughly acquainted with the camps and that nothing can take me by surprise, but no sooner do I arrive there than I am proved wrong. Sachsenhausen is one vast cemetery formerly inhabited by living beings, a geometry of dread which visitors leave in silence, not daring to look each other in the eye.

Was that what Gilin's prison had been like?

One bright, light-filled August morning on the Baltic coast, I read in the guide book that the little town of Stralsund had been heavily bombed during the war, even if you'd never know it, it's so neat and pretty and its old buildings have been so well-restored, or more probably rebuilt from scratch. And then I phone my mother, as I do every day, yesterday she'd been to visit my father in his old people's home.

'I asked him whereabouts in Germany he'd been a prisoner,' she told me in the urgent tones of someone who has a novelty to impart.

'And?'

'He said: "Stralsund".'

It is with a sense of estrangement that I now gaze at the tall red brick warehouses overlooking the sea in the little town of Stralsund, bathed by the August sun.

Had he never mentioned this name before because he didn't want to, because he didn't remember, or because we never asked him?

What an unexpected meeting, Gilin, between my present and your past. It's odd enough, admit it, for us to meet up at all, to find you where you're being looked for. It's not like you to keep appointments, it's more your style to forget them. It's not much to get excited about, Stralsund, it's just a word, but a word more real, more precise and concrete than almost any other word you ever spoke. Perhaps there is nothing miraculous or even surprising about all this, perhaps it's pure coincidence; but you spoke the name so firmly yesterday, while I was in that very town and you were sitting in the little garden with the other batty old men under the *chimonantus*; it could have struck me as a mere summer flash in the pan, knocking me off balance for a moment in the dappled light of the forests of the North, in front of that grey-green sea, that Baltic sea which was the first you ever saw.

I'd spent a long time imagining your spell in prison, I spent almost as much time thinking about it as you did living it – two years. That was the period of my life when I felt closest to you. On your traces, a few steps behind you though never catching up – but closer, nonetheless, than at any other time.

At all events, Gilin will neither confirm nor deny any account of these matters, since he no longer speaks.

A stroke has deprived him of both speech and thought, like a bomb blowing up a bridge, shattering some vital link, and there's no way of rebuilding it. The collapse of the bridge on the river Kwai. All I remember about that film is that I saw it with him as a child, and we learned to whistle the tune together, tone deaf as we were. In my mind the river Kwai is a yellow tropical river, heaving with danger, in a place you will not find on any map.

Now we with the power of speech are on this bank, waving to one other, powerless to reach him, and he is there on the other bank, alone. Does he understand our messages? He makes signs, and sounds, he wants to say something, but what?

It's a mystery.

This is a stroke that chimes in well with his personality.

But he can utter the odd syllable, a name, a verb, and he repeats those few sounds, insufficient though they clearly are, he hurls them insistently, sometimes angrily, into the abyss that lies between us. He becomes agitated, he tires himself out, he tries to dam up the raging cloudy river Kwai with those absurd and paltry pebbles of meaning.

In the early days after his stroke, this senseless struggle was all but unbearable for his family as well as for himself. Then gradually we become used to it, as do the nurses and other helpers. At first we can't help trying to help him, interpreting what he seems to say: what is the meaning of 'postage stamp', repeated obsessively together with the name of an old acquaintance, who's been dead for at least ten years and not seen for twenty? Does he want to write him a letter, phone him, have news of him? Has he forgotten that he went to his funeral? He didn't visit him in hospital, because he's always steered clear of illness and sick people, he was too sensitive, he preferred to give them a wide berth.

'All right,' we say to him, 'We'll phone Pinot and give him your kind regards.'

That's not enough.

'What is it you want? To see him? You can't, not in your state. And anyway, he's…'

After twenty minutes we can bear it no longer and we tell him Pinot is dead. 'So you can't send him a postcard or go and visit him. Pinot has passed away.'

Sottovoce at first, as you do when talking of the dead, above all in certain places where you can already hear a sort of background whir, a kind of whetting of scythes; then more loudly and clearly, until you find your voice is rising rise to a shriek: 'He's dead! Don't you remember? *Kaputt!*'

Kaputt does the trick. His eyes cloud over with understanding.

'When?' he asks.

'Ten years ago.'

Gestures of mournful surprise. Shakes of the head. Then:

'Cigarette.'

(Certain words have remained with him.)

Once the cigarette is lit, and Pinot forgotten, we start off with another word.

After a bit you get used to it.

Gilin and his life. Two strangers sewn cheek by jowl into the same sack. They get along all right as long as the going is good, then they begin to irk each other, they fall out, and it's open war.

More than once, when he's over fifty, he falls down with a piercing pain in the chest, arms outstretched, face twisted as though he's giving a stifled shout, in the pose of a first world war hero who has been shot through the heart – although in his case this is not caused by machine-gun fire or shrapnel shards but a perforated ulcer. Things get worse over time, illnesses take him by surprise, gastric acids and glycaemic markers, obstructed veins and obscure internal haemorrhages, surprising manifestations of mortality to which he reacts as might be expected: with cunning, with indifference, with diversionary tactics. By challenging fortune, who has always been his friend, he has offered her a loophole. But man does not live by good luck alone, particularly when old age trundles up and mobility saunters off. Escaping his own ills and his own body proves more of a problem than walking out, as he has always done, ditching *magne* and mother and wife when they got to him.

Then he tries to forget, which is another kind of going away.

From time to time a state of forgetfulness, increasingly dark and ineffective – punctuated by trips to hospital and intervals when he is semi-comatose – is broken by threats from pitiless doctors and domestic blitzes by his daughter, who bursts in waving the results of various tests and empties sugar bowls into the dustbin, possibly reminding him of Hans of old and thus reducing him to a state of temporary docility.

White as a sheet, he surrenders, performs an act of contrition, weeps the odd tear, swallows the odd tablet and waits for his wife to go out before filching a biscuit from the larder. What with the repetition of this cycle, together with other natural processes of deterioration, and artificial heart valves, not enough blood here, too much somewhere else, the occasional broken bone – words forsake him…

And yet good fortune has not entirely abandoned him. He's a tough nut to crack. At his age, with his medical history, most people would be dead. Wiser, more sensible, more conscientious folk, who've stopped smoking and drinking and choked down bitter medicines and bidden farewell to the joys of life, would already have given up the ghost after a lengthy period of suffering. Far more deserving men have fallen victim to dreadful accidents or gaps in the health system, mistaken diagnoses, bureaucratic delays, faulty equipment. For him everything always goes without a hitch, he's whisked into hospital, dealt with by exemplary surgeons, the x-rays are always easy to read. The nurses love him, their underlings coddle him.

He's become an internee again, this time in an old people's home. He divides his life between his bed and his wheelchair, parked in summer in a shady little garden and in winter in a large sunny room, between a ficus and a glass case with a photo of the trip to the Vatican his fellow internees had taken a few years ago. He looks at television, or perhaps the wall. Around him are a dozen others in their second childhood, sucked back into their own inner world.

His wife comes to see him, as does his daughter, if less frequently. When they appear he weeps, to signal his unhappiness and the injustice of his imprisonment. His visitors take not a blind bit of notice, either because they scent the theatrical nature of his tears, or because they have hardened their hearts against him, as he himself used to claim when he was still capable of claiming things at all. He weeps, and in the meantime he eyes their bag, from which they hasten to produce a buttered roll with anchovies or salame. Then the sobs suddenly cease, and he eats with a prisoner's relish. Even here, it seems there are people who are good to him even though they are the enemy, and even here they give him almost enough to eat, even though it is far, far less than he would like.

'You're looking well,' his wife Maria says to him. 'You've lost weight, your eyes are nice and clear, your hands are less swollen.'

He looks at her grimly, chewing the while.

'Your colour's good,' she notes. 'Before, you were all yellow.'

He tries to convey his suffering through his expression, but he's sensitive to compliments, and once he's polished off his sandwich, his pyjama top liberally sprinkled with crumbs, he is seized by a desire to perform some outstanding feat. He gets up, making rowing movements in the air with his arms, stands for a moment balanced on his dangerously thin legs and then clings on to the wheelchair, taking a step or two.

It's a miracle!

His wife is full of admiration, but she's also scared. At his age, to say that he has brittle bones is more than a mere figure of speech, it's the literal truth.

The nurse comes rushing up and puts him back into a sitting position. She's an attractive dark-skinned girl of about twenty-five, clearly big-hearted, with a lovely soft voice and a great shiny mass of hair which won't stay tucked up in her cap.

'Come on now, *Aangelo*,' she says, rearranging him in his chair, 'there's a good fellow, Angelino.'

Then she strokes the top of his head, quite bald by now, and plants a sudden kiss there too.

His sky is now cloudless, and his face lights up with a beatific smile. It's still him, the same old Grey Skies, in one of his moments of grace, though time has had its way with his features. The women of the family, his ancestors and my own, now make an appearance on his face, in the way he folds his hands on his chest, in the moist corners of his hazel eyes. As he is now, in the grip of old age, immobile on a chair, veering haphazardly between a baby's easy crying and the great toothless smile which cleaves his round face in two, although he does not know it, he looks like Maria, his mother, like *magna* Giulia and above all like chubby, smiling Polonia, her cheeks lined with tears, as she could sometimes be seen during her later years.

My Childhood's East and West

They say that uncle Giovanni changed, just like that, when I was born.

They say that right from my earliest weeks he bent over my cradle like the Three Kings in the stable in Bethlehem; that he held his breath to avoid misting up my still unfocussed baby's eyes; that he carried me around holding me at arms' length, red in the face with the effort of trying not to awaken me or crumple my swaddling clothes, holding me out stiffly before him like a monstrance above the altar.

My great-uncle, *barba* Giovanni, was a solemn, crusty man, with a high forehead, a crew-cut, an unsmiling mouth and a perfectly kept moustache, neither too thick nor too sparse. He was tall and thin, without being exactly gaunt, and he dressed as people used to dress before the war, even though the war was long over. He wore grey or brown suits, shirts with stiff collars and a waistcoat whose front part was made of dark cloth but whose back was of smooth, shiny material, both in the same dark, dull colours as the suits themselves. Only in summer, and inside the house, could he be occasionally glimpsed *in desabiglie*, as aunt Giulia put it, that is, in his shirt sleeves.

At the time of my birth he was living with his wife Polonia and his sister-in-law Giulia in that second-floor flat overlooking the big avenue, near the station. He was a creature of habit, and led a well-ordered life. Early in the morning, when in winter it was still dark, he would cross the wider part of the avenue, which was near its end, where the road from Turin divides into two, with one branch going into town and the other towards Val di Lanzo, and he'd take the Ciriè-Lanzo, the local railway so-called after the two main places through which it passed, even if its official title was the Turin-Ceres.

It was a small local line, with little trains with hard wooden benches, whose windows shook in time with the wheels, and which were subject to powerful draughts. Each day he would sit on one of those benches, bolt upright and inscrutable, a black leather brief-case propped up beside him with the lunch prepared for him by Polonia, contained in a hermetically sealed and still piping hot mess-tin wrapped up in newspaper.

The newspaper might be *Vita Femminile*, an edifying publication for mothers and young ladies, with letters, recipes, advice on etiquette and patterns for shawls and embroidery. Or it might be the well-known *Domenica del Corriere*, an illustrated weekly whose back page reports 'the' event of the week, ranging from the catastrophic or the heroic to the merely intriguing. Or, again, *Il Risveglio*, the local paper which keeps interested citizens informed about current marriages and deaths. Such is the reading matter shared by the three members of the family and passed from one to another in a very specific order, *La Domenica* and *Il Risveglio* going first to him, because he likes leafing through them while the pages are crisp and still uncut, and *Vita Femminile* first to the women and then, when the issue is past its prime and has already been superseded by another, passed on to him.

But Giovanni does not read in the train, reading is for the evening, after supper, and for holidays. In the train he sits straight-backed, staring severely ahead of him, answering his acquaintances' greetings with mere nods of the head. He rarely exchanges a word with another passenger, but sits there in frowning silence, staring fixedly out of the window, lost in thoughts which must strike the onlooker as positively momentous. He is regarded as antisocial. His answers are curt and do not encourage further communication. A few words about the weather and local goings on, and the rest is silence. Men chatter on around him, playing cards, smoking cigars, snoozing, wrapped in their overcoats, of a winter's morning, pulling out pocket flasks and nattering on summer nights, on the way back.

Ever the Stoic, he puts up with them.

The train takes little more than half an hour to cover the twenty kilometres separating Ciriè from Turin, stopping at every station: San Maurizio, Caselle, Borgaro, where other commuters get on. Giovanni gets off at the terminus, at the small station on corso Giulio Cesare, which will later cease to be used, but which at that time is all a-bustle, the whole of Val di Lanzo gets off there, people who come to Turin to work or study, and go back to their towns and villages in the evening, every day except Sunday, when the traffic, at least in the summer, is in the opposite direction, in the morning from the city to the places in the valley, with travellers in search of cool air, mountain streams, meadows and hostelries, and back again in the evening when it's time to go home.

From corso Giulio Cesare Giovanni turns immediately right, avoiding the ever chaotic Porta Palazzo, one vast open-air bazaar, then goes through the little streets with the secondhand shops and a bit of the walled city of the Cottolengo, its streets lined with high, all-concealing walls behind which nuns, devoted to the poor, the sick and the afflicted, go silently about their business. He emerges on to corso Regina Margherita at the Rondo della Forca where once, it is said, dead bodies dangled from the gallows. He crosses the corso and turns left down corso Valdocco, which after a few blocks becomes corso Palestro, a dignified, tree-lined street with the Craftsmen's Guild School at number 14, an institution founded over a century ago to teach orphaned or abandoned boys a trade.

At the end of his journey – always the same – through the centres of Turin's nineteenth-century social piety and the work of its holy priests, Cottolengo, don Bosco and don Murialdo, Giovanni enters that vast, severe, box-like college building with its great windows and corridors forever echoing with steps. He goes to a cubby-hole where he leaves his briefcase, takes off his jacket and puts on a brown smock and then a leather apron, all scratched and stained with grease. In the evening he does the same thing in reverse, puts on his jacket and seizes the handle of the squat black briefcase, lighter because the mess-tin, carefully washed and dried, is empty now.

His day is spent in a world that is exclusively male, among boys of twelve to nineteen; he teaches them to work a metal-turning lathe.

Is he a good teacher? Does he enjoy his work? What do his pupils think of him?

For them he must have been a rough-and-ready presence, oppressive at times, like those nineteenth-century walls on a winter's day, cold and insurmountable, but at the same time solid, protective and steadfast. Certainly they respect him; they fear his lowering gaze, his narrowed lips, his bony finger raised in annoyance at carelessness and work poorly done.

They don't expect to have their ears boxed, or pulled, because he expresses his annoyance through brief verbal outbursts, mutterings and furious looks. He may adopt an expression of outrage, like the god Mars, but he never lifts a finger against them, and rarely raises his voice.

In the evening he goes back to his household of women, which always smells sweetly of cooking and talcum powder, and a vague sense of excitement at some new birth, a beacon casting light over the ocean of children who are waiting to come into this world. When they talk of him in town they refer to him as the husband of Polonia the midwife, that Bazzoli who married the Mattioda woman, the brother-in-law of that Giulia who works at the co-operative.

His marriage with Polonia is a peaceable affair, a success, all in all, apart from the bitterness caused by the absence of children. If his wife can make good this lack by acting as a stork on a local level, he must make do with his pupils, the budding craftsmen of the future, and perhaps he is indeed fond of some of them, but none of them becomes part of his life, none of them comes to call on him as Polonia's babies come to call on her when they are grown up themselves, with their children and grandchildren, who are also Polonia's babies, because for generations children continue to be born at home, welcomed into the world by a slap from Polonia's expert hands.

Some time in the Twenties, Giovanni and Polonia take in her younger sister, Giulia, who has been left a widow at the age of twenty-six. It's not right for a young widow to live alone, even if she's a working woman, or rather especially if she is. An employee like herself, who has dealings with men on a daily basis – peasants arriving with carts full of sacks, wholesalers in vans, silver-tongued brokers with indelible pencils in their pockets – should have a safe haven to return to of an evening, where she will not be preyed upon or gossiped about.

For the first few years, with her hairpins and her novels scattered around the house, with sweet papers as bookmarks, Giulia may have got on Giovanni's nerves. But then he realises that the two sisters together fill the house up nicely, together they stop it feeling draughty in a way that one alone never could. Giulia's chatter makes Polonia smile, Giulia's ups and downs keep Polonia busy; in a way, she is a replacement for the child they never had. At least she and Giovanni are not alone of an evening, staring at each other over a bowl of soup. And two housewives make light work: the tablecloths are always spotless, the napkins perfectly folded, his slippers neatly lined up behind the door awaiting his return.

For their part, beneath the deference tinged with compassion with which women of their generation treat the male sex (masters of the universe but incapable of sewing on a button, laid low at the slightest hint of a fever), the sisters make room for him in their personal world. They put up with his tetchiness and establish a routine of sweet-tempered mockery, upon which he becomes thoroughly dependent, as upon a tranquilliser.

Of an evening he can be seen seated in the kitchen. Austere, unmoving, helping to wind the wool, elbows neatly tucked in, arms bent at ninety degrees, hands ensuring that the skein is kept taut. Or absorbed in shelling beans into the little enamel basin, which sings out quietly with every bean that falls, or peeling fruit for jam, sleeves rolled up, with a knife freshly sharpened on the whetstone. Whatever work he does, you can be sure that he will do it meticulously, indeed pedantically. He is their right-hand man. There are moments, when you see them all together, when Giovanni looks like another Mattioda sister in drag.

The extent to which he has become part of that little female world can be gauged by his habitual exclamation: *'Ammi mi povra dona!'* ('Woe is me, poor woman that I am!') As in some operatic aria, some nineteenth century melodrama, our family sighs, declaims, laments: *'Ahimé, povera donna che son io!'* And it is he, *barba Giuanin*, who utters these words most often.

On his feet in front of the frost-flowered window, hands crossed behind his back, or perched on the diminutive seat used when polishing his shoes, eyes on the middle distance, brush in the air: '*Ammi mi povra dona*!' says Uncle Giovanni, sad as only a woman can be, teaching me of sorrow's feminine declension.

On other occasions he lets slip the phrase while he is reading the paper, as a bitter, outraged comment on the doings of the day. Or when he's listening to neighbourhood gossip, scandalous or petty as it's prone to be, and he intends to keep his distance from it. *Ammimipovradona* enters my vocabulary as a single word, whispered or growled in his bass voice; in my memory it is associated with his moustache, his waistcoats, the smell of soap that comes from his shaven cheeks.

Born in 1890, he was sixty-two when I came into the world.

Uncle Giovanni looms out of the past already an old man, his crew-cut pepper and salt from the word go. I have a clear memory of some of his possessions: a silver snuff-box containing that particularly strong tobacco which made you sneeze so violently, a minuscule cannon in turned metal, a long yellowish ivory cone, part of an elephant's tusk. As a young man he had apparently been in Abyssinia, called upon by his brother, a priest, Don Giacomo, to work among the *moru*, the *sarvai*, the savages. But Africa was not for him; he soon came back to Italy, to put down roots among his womenfolk, the Mattioda sisters: Polonia and Giulia, as I see them in a youthful photograph, eyes smiling above cheeks round as brioches, their vast bodies draped in huge garments with wide stripes, which fall straight down from the window-sill of their breasts. Giovanni has elected to take refuge behind those reassuring bastions of flesh as though in some sheltering fortress.

Uncle Giovanni barely endures humans of any stripe, but two categories in particular earn his especial loathing: relatives and children.

Among his relatives, the one he can least stand is his sister-in-law, Maria the peasant. She comes and goes as she pleases, without knocking, her shoes all muddy from the kitchen garden and her nails black. Maria who's in a permanent tearing rush, who never stops, who laughs and mimics, who takes everything lightly: when cruelly berated by him she makes herself small and scuttles off, like a lizard among stones. Giovanni would like to catch her by the tail, but she gets clean away before he can be anywhere near her. Maria raises her bright eyes to gaze at her brother-in-law – in alarm, rebellion, mock fear? – and promptly vanishes. But she always comes back. She pops up out of a crack in the wall, materialises out of the evening shadows, grey upon grey, a little saucepan in her hand, a bunch of carrots still wreathed in soil, her pockets tinkling with lost buttons and rusty nails. With his soldier's love of order and personal and domestic cleanliness, he is deeply offended by her unkempt appearance and the chaos she brings in her wake. Unlike her buxom sisters, Maria seems to have remained thin in order to avoid taking on the weight and solidity of their new-found prosperity; with her peasant's fatalism, her edgy deference and her scathing humour, for Giovanni it is as though Maria were taking the whole family back a couple of generations, to those benighted times when men, women and animals all slept together in the straw, with no sense of shame or decency.

If the sisters treat Maria with the slightly condescending and protective indulgence usually reserved for the simple-minded, for those who end up being everybody's doormat, he on the other hand has declared a state of mulish trench warfare, which will end only with the death of one of the enemies, or both.

Maria brings two sons into the world, and the sisters select the younger one as the focus of their affections. At first, perhaps, Giovanni too allows himself to be beguiled by Angelo, who until the age of three is dressed as a girl, as was the custom in those days, and the *magne* take him to the photographer to have his photograph taken in a little high-waisted cotton dress which shows off his dimpled knees. In that little dress with its white collar, a bow in his hair and his little ballerina shoes, he is a boy-girl baby, with his mother's blazing eyes, only even darker, and the smile of someone who knows that he is loved.

As he grows up, though, Angelo known as Grey Skies arouses different emotions in Giovanni and the *magne*. The women are ready to grant him his every whim, full of indulgence for what Giulia winningly refers to as his 'pranks', while Giovanni begins increasingly to keep his distance, though without directly intervening. He sees his nephew growing up more pampered than a colonel's horse – a horse which needs reins, and a good going over with a curry-comb, whereas all the women do is offer him sugar out of the palm of their hand. Quarrels and carping ensue, Giovanni accuses his nephew of being a *fagnano*, a shirker, a liar, the *magne* accuse Giovanni of being spiteful, unfair on the *por cit*, the poor boy.

Why poor? Here the two sisters exchange looks which say everything that can't be said in so many words. Poor because, rather than of them, he's had the misfortune to be born of the parents he's got, namely a barefoot peasant woman and a clodhopper who's still wearing clogs. Polonia and Giulia have put their all into making good these unfortunate beginnings and continue to do so.

Giovanni is quite aware that both these women give him money on a regular basis, but since both earn their own livings – Polonia earns more than he does, sought after as she is in the town and surrounding region – he is in no position to object to the way they treat their nephew. This maddens him still further.

'He'll be the ruination of you both!' he prophesises, while energetically tearing damp newspaper into large balls which will be put into the attic to dry and then burned in the stove, a wartime economy measure which persists for a few years after the war is over. 'You stuff him like a *pipi* , a chick; his mouth is getting bigger and bigger, and one of these days he'll gobble you up as well!'

When Angelo is called up and taken prisoner by the Germans and interned in Germany, and they don't have any news of him except a postcard, and then nothing, Giovanni hopes he'll never come back, it would certainly be better for them all.

'He might be befriended by some German woman, or a Pole or a Russian!' he adds, for the benefit of Polonia and Giulia, who are stopping their ears in order not to hear.

One day he repeats this bit of wishful thinking about Angelo's non-return to his sister-in-law Maria, but without the pious mention of the good Samaritan from the North. Maria looks him unblinkingly in the eye, then lowers her gaze, apparently absorbed in counting the paving stones (they are on the town's main street, he has gone out to buy some oil, the bottle with its cork top is poking out of his shopping bag; she is clutching her apron to her chest, something seems to be moving beneath it).

'All will be done in accordance with God's will,' she murmurs after a moment, 'what we want is neither here nor there.'

Then she turns round and goes off, clutching the corners of her apron, which has now become frenetic.

'Have you been crying?' Polonia asks her later. 'Your eyes are red.'

'It's nothing really. Gina gave me a rabbit and I broke one of its paws while I was coming home.'

'And that's why you were crying?' says Polonia. 'It's only a rabbit. Bring it in, I'll cook it for Sunday lunch.'

'Poor beast,' sighs Giulia. 'On Sunday the priest will be coming, will one rabbit be enough?'

Giovanni sits at table in complete silence, he does not utter a word during the entire lunch.

But in fact Angelo does come back, and begins to 'talk' to one of the local girls, the one called Maria Grazia, the niece of that Ninin Davito who works at Magnoni's.

In those days, if a young man and a young woman are 'talking to each other', it's all as good as done, it's virtually official, the mothers will be counting the trousseau sheets and the fathers, if they have a house and land, will be building an extra room for the young couple. Maria Grazia has lost her father in America and the land, on this side of the Atlantic as on the other, has been eaten up by death and war, and her mother has been cloven by paralysis. She has precisely nothing to her name, apart from the *magne* who brought her up, and only one of them, really, namely Ninin, because Michin died of a tumour in '43 and Margherita has other fish to fry, since she is a widow with a young son.

So it is Ninin who goes with her to what in other circles would be regarded as the official engagement meal, which is held at the house of Polonia, Giovanni and Giulia. The young bride to be is too embarrassed to eat, she smiles and blushes and sits there stiff as a ramrod, afraid that she might put her elbows on the table and not know how to use her knife. Ninin is scandalised and impressed by the quantity of food that's on the table, and by the eating habits of her future in-laws.

'My goodness, they put a whole slice of ham into their mouths at once!' she tells Maria, poor thing, who has stayed at home with her little book of stories of the saints. At home, a slice of ham has to eke out a whole loaf, virtually a supper in itself. And anyway they wouldn't know how to go about laying hands on any ham, times being what they are.

And yet the meal goes well. Polonia and Giulia have been amiable and friendly, and just sufficiently indulgent to reassure the future bride of their goodwill. Maria, the mother of the groom, is seated at the end of the table and doesn't say a word, but smiles at the guests whenever they catch her eye. After a glass or two of wine, Lorenzo, the bridegroom's father, has begun to praise the bride's beauty and youth, making her more nervous than ever, while Polonia's husband is looking daggers at him and Angelo looks increasingly cast down. Luckily Polonia has started to tell a story with a happy ending about premature twins, and everyone starts to smile again. There are also cakes – real sweet cakes with cream, and genuine coffee.

His family likes the girl. It doesn't matter that she hasn't got a bean to her name.

'Well, he's no prince if it comes to that!' says Ninin. 'He's got patches on his trousers! If it weren't for those *magne*, what would he have? A drunkard for a father and a handful of earth up on the Vaude!'

The handful of earth is a thankless bit of land planted with vines, and the odd fruit tree which has run wild.

But one evening my mother, who is not yet my mother, sees a shadow emerging from behind the gate post. Slightly alarmed, she gets off her bike and ties it up.

'Grazia,' the shadow's voice calls quietly.

Without knowing it, my mother was expecting this. She wants to escape, to go into her house and have her supper, just as on any other day.

'I'd like a word with you,' says Angelo's mother, slightly out of breath, taking her by the arm.

They walk in silence along the dark road that runs between the little villas and their sheltered gardens. There is a smell of autumn, burnt leaves, damp earth.

What does my grandmother say to her? It must be difficult, for a woman who isn't good with words, to say something she doesn't want to say. However her mission goes, my grandmother knows that she will be the loser.

She must undoubtedly have told my mother that she was a lovely girl, that she was beautiful, that anyone would want her; and that he wasn't a bad boy, that his heart was in the right place. But that she could find herself another boy with a better job, someone who had studied, perhaps. At school the master had said that he was intelligent, he just didn't concentrate.

Then, having uttered all the platitudes, she stares down at her shapeless shoes as they move forwards over the gravel. She feels my mother's arm now pressing down upon her own, putting up resistance. She takes my mother's frozen hands in her own and blows on them, to warm them.

She feels guilty, keeping her there in the cold.

They've reached the corner, and now they're turning back. Maria the peasant is in a hurry, she hasn't got much time.

She stops under the lamp, looks my mother earnestly in the eye, that look must say it all. Their breath makes little clouds in the dark air.

'Chiel, chiel,' says my grandmother, and that's all she can say.

'Chiel a l'e parei,' she says at last, throwing up her hands, hoping the gesture will say what words cannot.

'That's how he is,' she repeats. And she smiles at my mother apologetically, sorry she cannot do any better.

'Poor Grazia,' she adds, stroking my mother's face, suffering at her own lack of ease. Faced with my mother's silence, my grandmother feels sorry for her, and also feels a sense of fatalism, that same feeling that so often causes her to shrug her shoulders, because, when all is said and done, there's little we can do.

A squeal of bicycle brakes makes them jump. My mother extracts herself from my grandmother's grip and turns to look towards her house.

'Off you go,' says my grandmother, 'it's getting late. Think about it, though. And I'm sorry; I'm so sorry.'

My mother isn't sure whether Maria the peasant is sorry because she's made her late for supper, or because she has tried to sow the seeds of doubt concerning Angelo, or simply because she brought him into the world at all. My mother is a bit worried, but not very. Despite her docile, thoughtful character she is convinced, like all young people, that old folk have nothing to teach her about how to live her life, because old folk are tired and always thinking of the past and no longer have the strength she feels within herself. Suddenly she is sorry for that little dark-haired woman whose eyes are glinting in the lamplight, and who always looks as if she wants to run away, like a dog expecting a good kick.

'Don't worry,' says my mother. 'I'm going to marry him, because I love him.'

My grandmother hugs her hard, sighs and vanishes into the night as suddenly as she appeared.

Maria Grazia and Angelo talk to each other for four and a half years, though they don't have much to say. They see each other two or three times a week, they go out, to the cinema, sometimes they go dancing, they hold hands, exchange the odd surreptitious kiss. He promises that he will settle down, they'll have a car, they'll have fun. They make a fine couple. Angelo is a provincial James Dean with an insolent expression and a rebellious quiff, shirt open to the waist and wide trousers with all manner of tucks and pleats, she still has a wide-eyed look and wears her hair loose on her shoulders, pre-Raphaelite style, but she is becoming the sort of woman who turns men's heads, helped in this by the increasing availability of certain postwar foodstuffs and little Fifties hourglass dresses. He buys himself a pair of American film-star dark glasses and shows them off on the stony banks of the Stura, where boys bathe under the bridge, their chests pale and their arms dark, as if they were wearing imaginary tee-shirts. In those days there were pools deep enough to swim a few strokes, when it has rained you could even dive in from the bridge, a feat which causes the blood to freeze in the *magne*'s veins when it is reported to them, because, the only time he's done it, he's cut his head and comes out looking shaken and pouring with blood. Biting her fingers, Maria Grazia looks on from the river bank. Girls don't bathe because they haven't got costumes, they make do with dipping their feet in the water, lifting their skirts to reveal more or less daring expanses of leg. (Boys don't have costumes either, they splash around in their underpants, or in old rolled up trousers.) She makes him promise that he'll never dive again, and this will be one of the few promises Angelo has ever been known to keep. He'll never dive off the bridge again, but he will continue to swim around in the Stura, taking his little daughter with him, unbeknown to her mother and the other women of the house, until the water becomes tinged with all the colours of the rainbow with the deadly waste from IPCA.

Then, thanks to a word from Polonia, Gilin gets a job at the paper mill. Grazia continues to work in the weaving mill, but Giulia tells her that they are looking for workers at the town hall and encourages her to apply. It's five years since the war ended, and the new decade begins, there's a bit more money around, the war seems a long way off, particularly to the young. It's 1950, and at last we can draw breath.

In May '50 they marry and go by train to Venice for their honeymoon. She travels in what she has worn for the wedding, an olive green silk suit, because the preposterous idea of spending a fortune on an outfit that you'll wear just that once has not yet come into its own: a wedding dress is an investment, it will be your best dress for years to come. But they stay in Venice just three days rather than the intended six, because on the evening of the third day he leaves her alone in the hotel and goes off for a stroll. He comes back late, she's already asleep, and the next morning, restless and gloomy, he tells her they might as well go home, after all, they've seen Venice, haven't they? It's all very expensive, and they're almost out of funds. She's obliging and easy to please, she's not too upset by the idea that he's bored on his honeymoon; everyone knows that men aren't specially keen on walking around and looking at churches and palaces and views and feeding the pigeons in St. Mark's Square. She doesn't ask any questions about the money, she doesn't know how much the *magne* have given him, and anyway it's true that Venice is expensive, the drink they'd had at Florian's had cost as much as a meal. So they take the train back and see the stations they'd come through on their way fly past their window in reverse order: Padua, Verona, Desenzano, Milan and finally Turin, where they get out and take the little Ciriè-Lanzo train. Maria would like to get out at every stop on their way home, the trip to Venice has made her suddenly curious, she wants to see unknown places, but this desire, like so many others, will have to be postponed, put off until a tomorrow which may never come. Angelo soon recovers from his momentary despondency and is soon his usual dashing self, ready to hug her and make her laugh on every occasion. Now they are husband and wife, one single being in the eyes of all, beginning with the priest who married them and who, only a few months later, caused her further embarrassment in the darkness of the confessional by asking why no child was yet on the way.

The couple go to live in her house, on that second floor on via Vittorio Veneto which overlooks the tree-lined courtyard; the concrete pipes have now been removed, to be replaced by the demijohns belonging to a wine-seller who has set up his storeroom there. The house in which Maria Grazia lived with her mother and the *magne* was enlarged after the war, and the two rooms opening on to the landing have become two sets of living spaces, each with an internal bathroom. One of them is occupied by my family, the other is rented to a young couple, he's a police sergeant from the South who's been posted to Piedmont, and she's a housewife.

So Angelo finds himself cohabiting with three women, his

young wife, her mother (who must have struck him as being as harmless and insignificant as his own) and Ninin, the only member of the household who is in any way alarming. Ninin is not at all like the *magne* Giulia and Polonia, she's more like *barba* Giuanin. She even has a pair of slight moustaches, just like him. Sharing those four en suite rooms with her, where the only place that isn't part of the system is the balcony which links them all, is a bit like living in a barracks with reveille, at six in the morning, with the bugle replaced by Ninin's piercing tones. But Angelo is not so easily cornered; he is a master escapee, a dab hand at flight, he can melt away with the best of them. Scarcely has Ninin launched into her tongue-lashing than he's out of the house.

Although they don't really get on together, Ninin is in agreement with Maria the peasant on at least one point: *chiel a l'e parei,* that's how he is. She utters the words in a different way, though: not indulgently, but accusingly.

But what sort of a *how* are we talking about?

'He's been deported, don't forget,' says my mother.

'What's that to do with anything, he's not the only one!' retorts Ninin, who is disinclined to forgive her new-found nephew for his lack of gravitas. She remembers all too well that he was *like that* even before the war, when Polonia Mattioda was making the rounds of the wine shops to pay his debts.

Still, out of love for my mother, Ninin does not insist. She says nothing. She vents her irritation on her sister Maria who listens to her with her crooked smile, but there's no knowing how much she actually takes in. Gilin is unreliable, a *masnà*, a child, an outrage! He takes off his shoes and throws them all over the shop! The hours he gets back at night! And the cinema, and his friends; and as for the idea of work – out of the question!

In point of fact, Gilin goes to work at the paper mill every day, even if not all that enthusiastically – were it not for that grating reveille he'd probably have stayed in bed – and he brings home his pay packet. Meanwhile Maria Grazia – or Grazia, as everyone calls her by now except Ninin – has been taken on at the town hall, but she doesn't like the work, her colleagues are spiteful gossips and she misses the spinning mill and Alfonsina, her friend and fellow worker at the loom. She often comes home red-eyed. Ninin is worried on her behalf, what a shame, such a good position, she hates to see Grazia in this state, but what's to be done? It is Margherita who comes up with the solution: some years ago she opened a small grocer's shop, but now that she's remarrying she'll hand it on to her niece.

At forty-two, a widow with a fifteen-year old son, Margherita has married a widower of forty-seven who has two children, one of them still a little girl. This would seem to be just a sensible arrangement, bringing together what remains of two families broken by mourning, but for Margherita her years with her second husband are the happiest she's ever known. He's called Pasquale, but after the war he kept the name he'd used as a partisan, Carletto. He's tall and solid, greying at the temples, with a broad forehead, and even if he is a communist he inspires trust and respect, even in Ninin, for whom communists were and are dangerous subversives. But Carletto goes to mass on Sundays, he's been mayor of Ciriè since the end of the war, he wears double-breasted jackets with aplomb and has a good job, he's a foreman at IPCA, the paint factory on the banks of the Stura where it is about to launch a project for the beautifying of its waters – modestly at first, and then all systems go – with the red white and blue waste from the manufacturing process.

Margherita and Carletto, and their children, live at number 13 via Vittorio Veneto, in the spacious apartment left her by her first husband Ermanno, just a stone's-throw away from her sisters and Grazia and Angelo, who live at number 15. The little grocer's shop which Margherita has handed on to her niece is some fifty metres further down the street, on via Remmert, and it enters family life at the same time as I do. I am still in my mother's stomach, in a warm darkness as yet unprofaned by ultrasound, a question mark in the hands of God, or more prosaically of Polonia, when – with enormous relief at leaving her previous job, and immense trepidation at the one she is beginning – my mother takes possession of her shop. It is there, among sacks of Agnesi pasta and crates of oranges, that I spend the winter before my birth, while my mother becomes bigger and bigger, the *magne* saying to her: 'Eat, *cita*, eat, you're eating for two,' and they don't need to say it twice, the memory of wartime hunger is still fresh, and amidst all those foods that catch the eye, let alone the other senses, yesterday's hunger joins forces with today's to see her devouring salame rolls and slices of cheese and juicy oranges fresh in from Sicily.

Uncle Giovanni's impatience with his nephew extends to his whole new family. He tells my pregnant mother, on her way to visit her midwife aunt, that he intends to purchase an Alsatian dog and set it to roam free when relatives arrive. From then onwards my mother knocks on their door somewhat apprehensively, hoping that it will be one of the aunts who opens up.

Then one late morning at the end of March Maria Grazia takes to her bed, and by evening there I am, a pink baby with a dark fluffy head, just like any other newborn except for the fact that I have emerged from the dark cave with a squashed nose; to everyone's relief, this rights itself before the week is out. A month later I will be baptised in the local parish church, wearing a white hand-embroidered christening robe and a cap edged with genuine Burano lace purchased by Aunt Giulia at the Lace Fountain in Turin. Giovanni is present at my baptism, dressed in an elegant grey suit, his eyes fixed on me and lightly veiled with tears.

It seems he put up no resistance, he allowed himself to be completely won over from the start; as though he had waited for me for years, and at last here I was. Among the many babies brought into the world by his wife, I was the one destined for him, and him alone.

A girl – it could not have been otherwise.

(In those same years two male cousins of mine were born, the sons of other nephews of Polonia and Giulia. Giovanni did not so much as notice their arrival. Not only did he not evince the faintest interest in their existence, but when they were old enough to disturb him with their cries, he did not hesitate to brandish his stick and threaten them.)

I am the great event of his old age. With me he becomes uncle, grandmother and mother, at last allowing himself to experience all the joys and sorrows he had perhaps been envying women all these years. He doesn't hide his emotions. It doesn't matter if people laugh at him, he is royally indifferent to what the world thinks of him.

His wife Polonia says that nowadays, when he gets in from work of an evening, the first words he utters on coming through the door are: 'Have you seen her today?'

'He doesn't ask me how I am,' says Polonia laughing. 'He asks after the baby – she's the only one who counts.'

Right from my very first spring I am transported in his arms, on long May and June nights he comes to take me out; he can be seen walking the streets with a white bundle, concentrating fiercely, as though that short stretch of street leading from our house to the avenue of plane trees were a war zone, bristling with danger. Then we go slowly up and down beneath the trees, until we come to the little square in front of the elementary school, which at that time of year smells marvelously of lime.

I spend my afternoons in a small triangular patch of vegetable garden wedged between two streets behind my mother's shop. They put me there, in the shade of a tree of heaven and a privet hedge which will scent my entire childhood, and my maternal grandmother Maria, poor thing, sits beside me with her little black book, the lives of the saints. By the end of my first summer I am brown as a berry, arms and legs burnished by afternoons in the open air.

When I am about two, and have learned to run and there's no way of keeping me in one place, a memorable incident occurs. While Uncle Giovanni is exchanging greetings with a neighbour, I climb up on to the edge of the fountain with the Fascist boundary stone and fall in.

The aunts see him arrive, breathless and deathly pale after two flights of stairs, the baby all wet and grizzling in his arms; after the first fright has worn off, they come to his aid. They change my clothes and I calm down instantly, but he is in a state of acute alarm, talking nonsense, tearing his hair (what little he has, that is) and spattering his waistcoat with the contents of the tiny glass of brandy his wife has poured for him – a measure to be used only in extreme emergencies.

As time goes by, before it sinks into oblivion, this episode passes into history, worthy of illustration on the front cover of *Domenica della Sera*: me face down in the fountain, my pink dress billowing out to reveal my white knickers and kicking legs, Uncle Giovanni in the foreground, mouth twisted into a howl, arms raised to the heavens in a gesture of horror and entreaty. In the background, the citizens of Ciriè reacting wildly to a tragedy foretold: a woman stifling a scream, a group of terrified children pointing in my direction, a man taking off his jacket as he prepares to come and dive in to rescue me. At the end of the avenue, in front of the school, the fire engine, evidently approaching at some speed. No need to worry, though: up there in heaven, above the tops of the plane trees, next to the bell tower of the church of San Giovanni a small, gleaming Virgin with a faintly mocking expression is waving a merciful hand in our direction.

It goes on much in this vein for months, for years, the aunts recounting the dramatic episode with tears in their eyes and chins quivering with laughter.

No glimmer of a smile from him, though; ever.

Then comes the time of kisses and coloured ribbons.

He's retired, he no longer takes the train each morning to go to 14 corso Palestro. He's folded up his stained, scuffed apron for the last time; it now reposes in the lumber room. He carries on shining his shoes on a regular basis, seated on the little stool reserved for this activity, but he puts them on only on Sundays, or on the rare occasions he goes into town.

With the money they've set aside over a lifetime, they've bought a piece of land just outside the town, with a rough and ready farm building on it, wedged between the lodgings of the other two Mattioda sisters, Delfina and Margherita, on the minor road running towards the west and the river Stura.

Maria has been settled in the farmhouse, which is fairly large, for quite some time. Before they'd purchased it, she'd rented it; she lives in two rooms on the first floor and the rest of the building, rooms on the ground floor and a large hayloft, has now been refurbished for use by a family of peasants. The aunts and Giovanni build a little house propped up against the old original brick building, a white cube with four rooms and a corridor and bathroom below, and a large empty space used as a loft above.

When I am four or five this house, as yet unfinished, becomes my 'second home'. The walls are still whitewashed, and painted. The kitchen, which has one wall facing south and one facing west, has furniture from the Thirties, with clean, straight lines and rounded corners. The furniture in the living room, which faces north and west and where the blinds are almost always down, is more massive and elaborate. The uncomfortable sofa with its metal sides and unwelcoming overstuffed cushions embroidered with beads, and the dark wooden sideboard with its carvings of flowers and leaves, inspire a certain respect, but also a vague sense of boredom. This room is never used, except on very rare occasions when we have visitors, and it also serves as a pantry, because it's always cool, and freezing in the winter (there's no heating in the house, apart from a stove in the kitchen). It's the land of milk and honey: the large square table, the shelves and even the windowsills are permanently groaning with provisions, packets of *grissini*, salamis sweating into their greaseproof paper, pans and plates where stews and casseroles and jellies and cakes are hidden beneath blue enamel lids.

Behind the house is the woodshed, a small rough brick building leaning up against the north wall. Inside it's dark and dusty and streaked with cobwebs, heavy with the smell of cut wood, old rusty blades, turpentine and DDT.

In this house the points of the compass are as full of life

and meaning as those on ancient maps. The north is the land of shade and damp, of green mould on stones, a window opening on to night. The south is the sun pouring in on the table at midday, lizards basking on the boundary wall. The west is open fields, adventure calling. As befits an old people's house, this one does not have an east; the east wall is blank, built up against my grandmother's original farm building. You never see the sun rise, except reflected in the leaves of the plum tree in front of the window, on the yellow fruits which cluster on the branches and fall on to the gravel.

In front of the house, in the land of the south, there is a courtyard dotted with slender, tenacious purslane plants with red and yellow flowers, and a bench up against the wall, for sitting on to watch the fireflies on summer evenings. Beyond the courtyard there is a piece of land known as 'the garden', bordered by a row of vines. In the garden there are tomatoes, courgettes, onions, basil and other herbs, and strawberries; and above all flowers, which are Aunt Giulia's passion, she chooses and orders them from catalogues and then seeds and sometimes little plants themselves arrive by post. There are pink lilies speckled with black, known as crown imperials, green-hearted white anemones, pompom dahlias, delphiniums with great wrinkled spikes of pink and indigo and violet, broad blue borders of ageratum. There are and will be, over the years, asters in September, cosmos as ghostly as rice paper and rustic zinnias at summer's end, graveyard gladioli and mysterious columbine before which I would stand stock-still, enchanted. And roses, of course, scented roses whose like has vanished from this earth. And a blue clematis which clambers around the red brick uprights of the gate.

Beyond this garden is the house of their sister Delfina, with its own little gravelled courtyard, hedges and garden, and beyond that the kitchen garden belonging to Maria the peasant, with its long rows of lettuces, peas and potatoes, and cherry trees, apple trees, a struggling apricot tree, and pear trees which produce hard, worm-eaten fruit. My grandmother's kitchen garden is messy and muddy, and there are no flowers, apart from a few unkempt tufts of marguerites; what there is, thrown into the ditch and under the trees, is a profusion of old broken baskets, seed packets, rusty bill hooks and other mysterious bits of equipment in various stages of decay. Around them grows thick, healthy grass, teeming with worms and insects, in summertime deliciously cool to damp skin, and between the toes. Beyond the kitchen garden is the open countryside. This is my borderland, and from here, like Livingstone in Africa, like Lewis and Clark in Louisiana, I venture a little further into the unknown every day, making a mental note, for future reference, of rows of mulberry bushes from whose low stumps you can climb to hide yourself among the branches, streams whose banks are starred with white wild garlic flowers, and shady spots where thread-like field mushrooms grow.

Sometimes Uncle Giovanni goes with me on these walks, sometimes he sits under a tree and follows me with his eyes. One summer evening we go as far as Devesi to see the fair with the stalls and nougat. On the way back he carries me on his shoulders, and I float proudly through the air like a little *maharani* on an elephant, gripping his collar and his ears, while he has his hands gripped tightly round my ankles.

If the months of our glorious heyday could be compressed into a single day, it would be towards the end of summer, when the yellow heads of the camomile are puffy and ripe. Maria the peasant brings great bundles of it in from the meadow and now a sweet-scented golden pile is spread out on the ground on an old blanket, and the aunts are seated, handkerchiefs on heads, in the half-light, on the strip of land between the wall of the house and the surrounding wall. They put a handful of camomile into their aprons, strip off the heads of flower after flower and throw them on to a tray placed on a rickety old table. Then they lean down and take another handful from the pile, wheezing a little as their heavy bodies lean forward. They talk to one another, slowly and quietly, looking at us out of the corner of their eye as we stroll around the garden. I've asked for a little basket so that I too can do some picking, and have been given one; he follows me like a faithful equerry, my own personal bodyguard.

'What has our little peasant maiden picked today?' asks Aunt Giulia, who delights in using pet names and diminutives and outdated mincing phrases from her youth, and always tells me that I must be *a model child*, which puzzles me, because for me models are those tissue paper things you use to make clothes from, so what is a model child, a tissue paper one?

'Ammi mi povra dona,' says Aunt Polonia, taking the words out of her husband's mouth, 'whatever is going on here?'

I have made a massacre of miniature vegetables, courgettes the size of my index finger, tomatoes as hard and green as marbles.

'That's no way to pick vegetables! You have to let them grow! What a waste! And you didn't say a word!'

He lowers his eyes, tightens the belt on his old grey trousers.

'All this fuss about a couple of little courgettes,' he grumbles.

'A bit of commonsense, that's all you need!' protests Aunt Giulia. 'If the child hasn't got any, you're going to have to din a bit into her!'

Indulgent as ever, though, the *magne* are already laughing

at our exploits.

'Come on,' he says, 'let's go and wash our hands.'

We go to the old pump next to the well, and he pushes the lever backwards and forwards, head lowered, while I lean over to catch the water flowing out of the pipe. It's lukewarm at first, then cold, then freezing on my hot hands. I collect some in my palms and throw it in Uncle Giovanni's face, screeching with joy. He shakes his fist at me and dries himself off with the big handkerchief he always keeps in his pocket. Small droplets glitter in his moustache.

'With the *magne* and *barba* Giovanni you can do what you like, because you're the oil,' Ninin says to me crabbily when we're back home.

'What do you mean, the oil?'

'Oil always stays on top.'

The two houses of my childhood have distinct boundaries; they are as different and complementary as weekdays and holidays. In the weekday house there are rules to be respected: don't lean out over the balcony, it's time to get up, finish the food that's on your plate. In the holiday house the rule which out-rules all others is… me.

Ninin is no fan of this system of upbringing, and she lets me know it. Although I adore the easy-going life style in the house of my aunts and uncle, in my heart of hearts I am on her side. I may be the oil, but I know I can't live without the vinegar.

The camomile is taken up to the attic to dry out in the shade of the eaves, under the red tiles. The *magne* have gone in to make supper. We two are sitting on the bench, outside, in front of the kitchen window. Maria the peasant comes back from the kitchen garden, her dull grey printed dress hanging limply around her scrawny body. She's scuttling along, as always, her apron full of herbs.

She bends down to empty her apron at the garden's edge, at the foot of the vine. She opens an old sheet of crumpled paper, smoothes it out and spreads it with handfuls of courgette seeds still sticky with rotting yellow pulp.

He stares at her balefully, narrowing his eyes. Then he suddenly whispers: 'Go and pull that paper out from under those seeds! Go on!'

For a moment, I hesitate. Uncle Giovanni's cheeks are grey, unshaven, his mouth is as severe as ever, but his tone of voice – anxious, conspiratorial – causes me to shudder with delight.

'Go on,' he says, giving me a shove.

And off I run, with all the lightness of my five-year-old legs. Maria is not even three steps away and her seeds are already scattered over the gravel.

I trot back in triumph, laughing heartily; but he drags me away, and we hide around the corner of the house.

I cling on to his grey trousers. He looks down at me, a finger on his lips: 'Sshh,' he says.

That's where we stay, hidden behind the wall. I can't resist the temptation to peek out: in the courtyard, my grandmother is on her knees picking up her seeds, and I stare at her grey bent back, at her quickly moving hands, already slightly twisted by arthritis. She doesn't complain, she doesn't ask who did it, she doesn't look in our direction.

When she has finished, she gets up and walks away, head bent, without turning round.

Uncle Giovanni is now his old self again. He's in a bad temper.

'Come on, we're going in, it's time for supper.'

I don't know whether or not I have been forgiven for what I have done. Going into the house I am alarmed by a shadow that has formed in the corridor, and I rush towards the kitchen with a shout which, in its turn, alarms the aunts.

In my house, supper consists of the remains of lunch – insufficient for tomorrow's mid-day meal – followed by the usual milky coffee which, as Ninin the *vivandiere* so often says, fills all the gaps.

In my aunts' house, on the other hand, supper consists of fresh salad from the kitchen garden, with finely sliced onion and chervil, a tender, peppery herb resembling a delicate piece of fine embroidery. There are roulades of ham filled with Russian salad, wrapped in tremulous gelatine made of skimmed broth, flavoured with bay leaves and cloves; hard boiled eggs stuffed with tuna and capers, which I push to one side, finding them too salty, and which Uncle Giovanni retrieves from the side of my plate. One of *magna* Polonia's renowned specialities is stewed rabbit, marinated in wine overnight and then slow cooked in milk, on the stove, until the flesh is so tender that it falls off the bone even before it touches the plate. And a soft, puffy apple cake, with a generous dose of vanilla which slightly stings my tongue. At this time of year, Aunt Giulia, who has a sweet tooth, puts ripe fruit in the oven with a mixture of egg, sugar, macaroons and chocolate, together with nutmeg and knobs of butter. This mixture disconcerts my childish palate and brings me out in pink spots.

I'm an easy child, I eat everything that's put before me, I have no bad habits, no likes or dislikes and my aunts praise me for it.

'Such a good girl, a model girl,' (more visions of folded tissue paper, of paper dolls with paper dresses to cut out). I'm learning Italian, until I was four all I spoke was dialect, and the *magne* make it a point of honour to be my teachers. At table, it is announced, we are to speak only Italian, but this threat instantly falls by the wayside, and we all slip back into dialect. I learn with alarm that the things that Uncle Giovanni wears on his shirt are not *bertele* but *bretelle* (braces). Will I ever master the subtleties of this foreign tongue which must become my own?

I already know how to read, but certain words fill me with a deep sense of wonder. Who is this Mr Manners Aunt Giulia is constantly talking about? Where does he live? What does he look like? Is he a person or a thing? Mr Manners says you mustn't put your elbows on the table when you're eating. Mr Manners is demanding and hypocritical, there's no pleasing him. Furthermore, he's always hanging around, not just at meal-times, he's also dragged up when we go into town to do the shopping, and I have to be quiet and good and not tug at Aunt Giulia's dress, begging 'to go home, I'm tired!' Above all I have to say hallo to the people with whom she stops to talk, unknown old ladies who chat for hours while my legs go numb and positively twitch with boredom, old men who smell of camphor and tobacco and sometimes add to my misery by pinching my cheek, and then have the gall to laugh at my silent glare.

My grandmother Maria does not eat with her sisters. She lives separately in the two rooms on the first floor of the next-door house, with that terrible strident dark old man who is her husband and my grandfather, and I don't think of her, I've already put her out of my mind. At least for this evening. I don't yet know that you never forget anything of what you have done to others…

Eating demands all my attention, I look at my aunts and try to imitate them, for Polonia and Giulia eating is a pleasure and a ritual, they don't throw themselves upon their food but savour it slowly, enjoying its tastes and colours, commenting on it, comparing it with dishes from the past, subtly evaluating its flavours. They teach me how to hold my knife and fork, to cut up one mouthful at a time and lift it gracefully to my mouth. They pour a little wine into my water, which becomes ruby red, I lift the glass and look through it, the lamp with the milk-glass shade sets it on fire.

They're two hedonists, these paternal great-aunts of mine, two country-mouse philosophers who know how to get the best out of day-to-day life; they know that a little bit of sugar helps the medicine go down.

Towards the end of the meal, when I am full and feel that I couldn't swallow another mouthful, the pleasures of the tongue give way to those of the eye, and I am lost in contemplation of the pudding plates, with their slightly faded but still wonderful patterns of purple plums, golden peaches, crimson cherries, green and light blue grapes. There is also one plate which is kept specially for me, decorated with a curious-looking gnome who lives in a red mushroom, with a smoking chimney emerging from his white spotted cap. At home, all plates are white, and their sole purpose is to hold food. But here many objects suggest a concern for beauty – even if there is sometimes a hint of the naïve or the grotesque – and this opens my mind to new horizons.

After supper, and a brief stroll around the courtyard – now the shadows have swallowed up the garden, transforming it into another place, dangerous and strange, one into which I dare not venture on my own – we all go back to sit around the kitchen table, the *magne* with their sewing, Uncle Giovanni with the paper. But I can't bear to let them pursue their own activities for long, and soon I start clamouring for their attention, forcing the women to put down needles and thimble, and him to fold up his paper. I persuade *magna* Giulia to go and get the object of my evening longings, the treasure that's kept stored in the cupboard in her bedroom. It's a Lazzaroni biscuit tin, full of coloured ribbons, braid and assorted trimmings. I proceed to plunder it, unrolling lengths of red and green and lilac satin ribbon, which I thread into the buttonholes of Uncle Giovanni's shirt and waistcoat and wind around his head and neck, till he's all frills and furbelows. He sits stock-still, happily allowing himself to be thus garlanded, and the aunts express their amazement at how strange you get as you grow old, allowing yourself to be festooned by a small girl and even taking pleasure in it. They laugh at him, and he sits there solid as a rock, without moving a muscle in order not to spoil my game.

'Uncle Giovanni,' I say to him, contemplating my work with pride, 'you look really handsome!'

And, seated on the table in front of him, my dangling legs thumping against his chest, I put my arms around his head and plant two smacking kisses on his crew-cut hair.

He looks at me with eyes moist with adoration.

'Bombonin,' he murmurs.

'Bombonin,' I reply.

'Prussot,' he says to me.

'Prussot,' I say back.

The aunts split their sides laughing. A *prussot* is a small pear, the kind that is so good when cooked in wine. *Bombons* are almonds covered in frosted sugar. In our mother tongue, terms of endearment are inspired by modest titbits from the good old days.

Then, exhausted and half-asleep on the table, I am carried up to bed. I sleep in Aunt Giulia's room, in the double bed one side of which her body has sculpted into a valley. For a few minutes I feel out of place, floating in a land which is neither here nor there, perhaps on the borders of the scented forests where the flowers on the painted pudding plates grow. The strips of light which flash over the ceiling whenever a car goes down the road seem so many mysterious portents announcing my departure for neighbouring worlds. Then I fall deeply asleep.

The following morning we sit in front of our bowls of milk, Uncle Giovanni and I, and Giulia pours us a little coffee from an enamel jug. I bite into a slice of bread spread with a thick layer of yellow butter and sugar which, a few hours later, will give me *urticaria*, but it's so good that it inspires me to come out with an unusual request. 'If my parents die, will you adopt me?'

'Sshh, don't say such things,' protests Giulia, visibly delighted.

'Why not?'

'Because you don't talk about people dying. And certainly not your mother and father.'

'But will you?'

'Yes,' says uncle Giovanni, wiping my fingers on his napkin, 'yes, we'll adopt you.'

Then they dress me and my uncle takes me home. We walk along side by side, hand in hand, he adjusting his steps to mine, along the minor road which runs into town. At every car that passes – and there are not yet that many – he pulls me to him, and we wait until they've passed. When we enter the courtyard he calls up, and Ninin appears at the balcony.

'I've brought her back,' he says brusquely.

'Good morning,' says Ninin in a formal tone, wiping her hands on her apron. 'Do come up and have a coffee.' Uncle Giovanni is the type of man of whom she almost totally approves, that's why she invites him in. And that's why she does not expect him to accept.

And indeed he answers: 'I haven't got the time.'

Then, as an afterthought: 'Thank you.'

I cling on to his hand; imagining unprecedented scenarios of vast potential (Uncle Giovanni in my house, two parallel worlds converging) I beseech him: 'Come on, come on in.'

'Up you go,' he says to me without letting go of my hand.

'Come up and see,' calls my father from upstairs, 'there's a surprise.'

Next to him – fresh out of bed, in trousers and tee shirt, his belt undone (but wasn't he supposed to be going to work this morning?) – I see a small black four-footed shape dashing around.

With a shriek I shake my hand free of Uncle Giovanni's and fly up two flights of stairs. We've got a dog!

For a moment, Uncle Giovanni is dumbfounded. Alone, forlorn, abandoned in the courtyard, he looks as though he can't imagine how he came to be here.

'A dog's all we need,' grumbles Ninin from upstairs, before she goes back into the kitchen.

Uncle Giovanni turns on his heels and marches off, defeated and dignified.

The dog is a little mongrel with claims to Pom ancestry. He's black, with a white star on his chest, white boots, a tireless curly tail and ears which are now erect, triangular and alert, now soft and drooping above an eager face and panting mouth. He is called Pucci, and he likes to sleep on the sofa when

Ninin has her back turned. As soon as he hears her moving around anywhere in the house he jumps down and goes about his business with an innocent air. She runs her hand over the sofa, feels that it's warm and goes off in search of the broom: 'Wretched animal, wait till I get my hands on you!'

But, like his master Gilin, Pucci is a born dodger. He's a free spirit of a dog, no lead or collar will ever find its way into our house. Pucci comes and goes precisely as he wishes at every hour of the day and night, blissfully irresponsible as only a dog – or perhaps only this dog – can afford to be. My father envies him, which is why, every so often, he tries to put him in his place. When Pucci has been away for two or three days, Gilin will go in search of him and ultimately find him, hollow-flanked but bright-eyed, in pursuit of some bitch on heat. He will be dragged home by the scruff of his neck, and he'll wolf down any amount of food and then curl up in his basket on one of the old felt covers which Gilin filches from the paper mill, until Ninin wakes him – she can't bear to see anything sleeping in broad daylight, not even a dog.

Once, though, he doesn't come back. Gilin doesn't know how or when he got lost, all he knows that he'd been in the car with him and suddenly he wasn't there. We search for days, hiccoughing with despair, and at last we find him in a nearby villa, where he has been depriving the legitimate recipients of their meals. The legacy of those buccaneering days is a permanent smell of dung, which clings to him even after he has been given bath after bath in the courtyard, so Gilin has him shaved by a barber friend of his and taken home all pink and trembling, half the size of his former self without his thick black coat.

On another occasion he gets stolen, together with the blue station wagon he'd been left to guard, parked outside a bowling club at Venaria. After more vain searches, Gilin comes home a broken man. The next day the police call by and accompany him to the stolen vehicle, but the first thing he asks about is the dog, and the dog's the first thing he mentions when he gets home: 'I've found him! I've found Pucci!'

Merry barking from the dog, tears of joy from me.

'If only it was him they'd stolen,' says Ninin, drying plates. *'Sensa sust!'*

Brainless. Not an ounce of common sense.

Indeed, between the three of us – myself, Gilin and the dog – common sense is sorely lacking. With me it's largely a matter of age, as I grow up I'll surely be bound to acquire at least a modicum of the virtue; even the dog will outgrow this heedless phase and seek an alternative to his current picaresque existence. Only Gilin will remain true to himself over the years.

If even a dog may weary of not having a lead, perhaps it is not because freedom is not sweet, but because the price to be paid for it is beginning to strike him as too high: for instance, when Gilin decides to assert his ownership or to amuse his friends, and forces Pucci to do circus tricks, to dance, to bolt down a bread roll to the last dry crumb, to drink pure alcohol, which lights a fire within him that cannot be quenched even by running around the courtyard in mad circles and howling like a banshee. Or when, fed up with canine insubordination, Gilin resorts to drastic training methods, and the dog returns, dusty and exhausted, after having run after his master's car from Barbania to Ciriè, a lung-bursting journey of ten kilometres to teach him to obey.

The dog is with Gilin that summer's morning when I've just turned ten, when my father has come to take me to the sea so that I can say goodbye to Uncle Giovanni one last time.

They've been travelling for hours, stopping only in village bars which open early to eat a sandwich or have a coffee. Pucci loves travelling by car, his head out of the window, his nose combed by the wind and his tongue hanging out. It's not clear whether the dog is imitating his owner or vice versa, the fact remains that Gilin does exactly the same, window open and elbow out, dark glasses giving him a dandified air which is somewhat belied by his slightly heavy, almost forty-year-old physique. At that time the Turin – Savona motorway is still a dotted line, a single lane which breaks off and carries on by fits and starts, which is why my father and Pucci have crossed half Piedmont and the Ligurian Alps on main and minor roads, have driven up hairpin bends and over cols, hooting viciously here and there to wake up hamlets still drowsing in the pearly light of dawn. Dog and master are proud of their car and regard it as a second home.

It's some time now since we've had a station wagon – now we've got a Fiat Millecento van, with room in the back for boxes of fruit and vegetables. My father left the paper mill a few years ago and now he helps my mother in the shop, a fact which causes Ninin to engage in long, impassioned moans and pre-dawn banging of wardrobe doors.

'Now he doesn't have to go to work, he's always hanging around and giving himself airs!' she says, plucking a chicken whose tragic wrinkled neck is dangling between her knees, while I stare in horror and fascination at this small domestic spectacle of death.

'Now he can get up whenever he fancies, and take his time about it! He leaves the soap in the water after he's washed, just look, what a waste! And he lays on the perfume like a cheap tart!'

With these words she delivers a blow of the chopper to the pathetic corpse stretched out on the chopping board, sending its head bouncing over the kitchen floor.

The dog, who has not missed a trick, sidles hopefully towards the dead creature, with its staring eyes and withered wattles, but is firmly pulled up short by a stentorian: 'Keep off, you!' And it is up to me to pick up the severed head, holding it by the comb with my fingertips, because nothing of a chicken gets thrown away, the parts that don't go into the pot go into the pan for making soup. And that tiny bundle of bones, once boiled, will be split open to extract a brain the size of a walnut, which will end up on my plate, together with the heart and liver, because they are prized morsels, a whole chicken for barely a gram of grey matter, a little crunchy heart the size of an acorn.

'He's struck it rich all right,' Ninin carries on. 'We're putty in his hands. No one is going to put him in his place; he leaps into his car and off he goes! He's the monarch of all he surveys!'

Another fierce chopper-blow, firmly detaching a thigh.

To me: 'You could peel the potatoes, I'm running late. And he's always inviting people to supper at the last minute.'

So I get peeling, as thinly as possible, because one of the small virtues that have been inculcated into me before I could even talk is to treat the fruits of the earth with respect, precision and economy.

If during the war the Italians had *Radio Londra,* which dispelled the mists of government propaganda, I have the daily broadcasts from radio Ninin. At school the mistress and her assistant talk of family, of how good and cheerful our mother is as she stays at home and cooks and cleans, and how we need to respect our father, who is strong and wise and comes home tired of an evening because he's working to look after us. At home, radio Ninin provides a ringing commentary on our everyday life in which the mother spends the whole day scurrying around the shop and comes home tired and worried, while father and dog saunter in and out at all hours of the day and night.

For some time now there's been a bit of interference on radio Ninin, with half-finished sentences and sudden silences. Something more serious has taken over from the reassuring daily diatribes. There are evening whispering sessions between her and my mother. Some years ago, in my preschool prehistory, Ninin had found the time between one thing and another to teach me the alphabet, and in the evening in bed she would read me a page of *Pinocchio* before I went to sleep. She would talk to me about her own schoolmistress, the woman with the long cane which would reach right to the furthest row of desks, she'd tell me the story of the fox and the wolf. Now I can read without help, I leave the adults in peace, I've found a little big world of my own in which I can take refuge whenever I like, and in this I resemble my father and Pucci. We are three escapists, three wool-gatherers.

That summer morning of my eleventh year, the two of them leave when it is still night, the mood is tense and stormy, last night at supper there was a great argument. But being on the road, the sense of freedom it gives, the sight of the sky as it grows light, the early morning cool, the feeling of adventure they always have when they're on the move, particularly at that time of day when everyone is still half-asleep and they're the only ones awake, all this has put them in a good mood. When they knock on the door they do so boldly, like two comic strip heroes, Batman and Robin who've come to carry me off with them on some astounding undertaking.

I'm on holiday in Porto Maurizio with Aunt Margherita and Uncle Carletto, who have rented a first-floor flat in a house overlooking a little square in the old part of town for the whole of July.

They could quite well have gone there on their own, their children are grown up now; they don't have any trouble fighting off boredom. If they wanted to have me with them, it was simply out of that generosity which radiates from happy couples, who produce surplus energy which can also warm or light up others. You need only watch them walking along the avenue of pines, or sitting at a cafe table, to sense their mutual respect and liking, to observe their small gestures of consideration; he makes sure she has the best seat, she straightens his collar. Middle-aged, distinguished, they seem to me to be members of another social class, like the prince of Monaco and Grace Kelly. From time to time, in order not to show them up, I make a serious effort to behave like a blue-blooded princess myself, and my aunt says to me: 'Come on, perk up now, what's got into you?'

My aunt is teaching me to speak a Turinese version of Italian that is more polished than my broad country dialect. With Carletto I speak Italian, a language I know well by now but which for me is still official, not innate. Margherita also teaches me how to behave at table in public, to put my napkin on my knee rather than stuffing it into whatever I'm wearing; to place the cutlery on the plate when I've finished. Carletto always addresses her with the greatest courtesy, which strikes me as extraordinary because relatives usually bark at each other, and not just in my family either. With strangers, be they waiters, those sitting next to him on the beach or complete unknowns in the queue for an ice cream, Carletto is quietly authoritative and patient and never looses his temper. At home they address each other as 'Mother' and 'Father', and in my company as 'aunt' and 'uncle', and often also in the third person: 'What would Aunt like to eat today?' which to me sounds like some ceremonial language, a kind of discreet public courtship, as though they were afraid of wearing out their names by using them too often, and kept them wrapped up in those 'aunts' and 'uncles' like silver spoons in woollen cloth.

We spend the mornings on the beach, where I am allowed to swim for an hour (not more, because it is believed that staying too long in the water can be harmful, particularly for children), and I spend the rest of the time reading, playing marbles on my own and above all running for miles along the wet sand and among the rocks, looking for shells. I don't make friends easily, I have my own sweethearts at home, they're called Walter and Ugo, they're brothers, and they have recently broken my heart by moving from our courtyard to a villa in the Park. Before them there had been Roberta, a dark-skinned child of my own age who lived on the same landing and was the daughter of the police sergeant, whose move to Asti marked my first (and fleeting) *chagrin d'amour*. I was four years old at the time. Now that I am about to go to secondary school, the emptiness, the anger and the confusion aroused in me by my small friends' departures has set unknown depth charges echoing within me once again, a prelude to the agonies and ecstasies which lie in wait for me around the corner of adolescence. But for the moment I am almost safe in my childishness, soothed by my aunts' serenity, lulled into a state of drowsiness in which I grow up almost unawares.

In the afternoon we take long walks, with me as an advance guard and them some way behind. One of our favourite walks is along the tree-lined seafront promenade linking Porto

Maurizio to Oneglia. I never weary of the routine, nor do I resent the discipline. I'm grateful for Carletto's decorum, even a little intimidated by it, and by the tact with which Margherita beguiles, rather than forces me, into obedience. When, in the late afternoon, we sit down at an open-air cafe, I invariably forgo the privilege of choosing the drink they offer me, and answer the question: 'What would you like?' by saying: *'Fa l'istess,'* I don't mind, and my aunt teases me for always ordering a *falistess*. Because I'm shy and touchy, Margherita calls me 'cactus flower', a nickname which both embarrasses and gratifies me, like being tickled, a pleasant ordeal which makes you laugh. I'm sufficiently important to warrant a nickname!

'It's so good of you to have her,' my mother said to my aunt before we left. 'Especially just now.' And to me: 'Try not to be a nuisance!'

'She's such a quiet child,' my aunt replied, 'it's a pleasure to have her.'

'Right now, though, I haven't...'

'Don't worry about money, we'll take care of that.'

Margherita has become my mother's confidante. It is to Margherita that Grazia unburdens herself, from her that she seeks advice, to her that she confides everything she cannot tell Ninin, for fear of unleashing her wrath, even if Ninin knows everything anyway because, as she points out firmly every so often, she has eyes to see and ears to hear. 'And a mouth to speak,' my father will add.

So, that morning before nine o'clock I hear barking on the landing, and then a knocking at the door. Familiar voices, of man and dog, come into the flat and mingle with those of my uncle and aunt.

I come out of the bathroom in my pyjamas, toothbrush in hand (it was she, Margherita, who introduced this crucial bit of equipment into my life, before that I made do with rinsing out my mouth and rubbing a sage leaf over my teeth, if there was one to hand).

My father is standing in the middle of the room, smiling, Pucci is hurling himself around in a frenzy at his feet; as soon as he sees me he leaps up and licks my face.

'Here I am – I've come to spirit you away!' he says, arms outstretched, face wreathed in smiles, as though he had travelled half way across the world to reclaim his lost daughter. The dog jumps up on to the sofa, still squirming madly. Uncle Carletto raises an eyebrow. My aunt tells me to get dressed.

'Put your bathing costume under your dress,' my father whispers, inching towards the door.

While I'm getting dressed I hear them saying that Uncle Giovanni had felt unwell yesterday, they'd called the doctor, it was serious, they hadn't even taken him to hospital because by now, you know the way things go, it was only a question of hours, he'd asked to see the child.

'So suddenly? What do you think caused it?' asked my aunt.

My father lowers his voice, I can no longer hear him, only the odd word, 'arguments', 'money', 'the aunts', 'a stroke', and when I go back into the room the conversation languishes, my aunt and uncle exchange silent glances, my father looks out of the window, the only sound is Pucci, lapping away at a bowl of water my aunt has put down for him.

I gulp down my white coffee, my father has a black coffee with lots of sugar, my uncle, who has not said anything so far, now comes out with: 'And how are you proposing to sort out this mess?'

My father doesn't answer. He spoons the sugar out of his cup and puts it in his mouth, as though he needs something sweet to make the bitterness go down. 'I'll come up with something,' is all he says.

'You have to face up to your responsibilities, a lot of harm has been done and that is that, but in future things will have to change,' says Carletto, as calm as my father is edgy.

My father gives him a nasty look, then gets up so hurriedly that he knocks over the chair.

'Are you ready?'

I'm ready, and so is Pucci. My aunt, who has gone into the bedroom to pack my suitcase, comes out with my things.

We say goodbye to them on the little square, in the light of a summer morning, against the green background of a pittosporum hedge; she, in a yellow and white striped sun-dress, is beautifully brown, he is bare-headed and wearing a short-sleeved shirt. They tell us they'll phone us to get our news. They look solemn and worried. The shops on the sea front are just starting to raise their shutters.

The moment we are out of sight my father smiles at me, pushes the dog's nose away – Pucci is breathing down his neck from the back seat – drives in the direction of the beach and parks crosswise in the middle of various piles of rope, in the space reserved for the local fish market.

'Come on, let's have a quick dip.'

I've put my bathing suit on under my dress, but I still hesitate. He winks at me, as he so often does when trying to recruit me as an ally against adults, against others. Pucci too seems uncertain, and before obeying his peremptory order ('Down!') he stares at my father with desperate canine urgency, his moist gaze seeming to ask: 'Are you my master? Are you? Can you be?'

So here we are on the sand, among old early risers who are having their ankles massaged by the waves, pulling their sundresses up over their thighs. We proceed in the direction of the deceptively limpid looking sea, only to have the soles of our feet land in the inevitable patch of tar. Like many dogs, Pucci has an ambiguous relationship with water. He is both drawn to it and fears it, he feels the desire to hurl himself into it but at the same time is profoundly distrustful of such an elusive element, which cannot be bitten into or grasped in any way. He casts himself into the waves and does vigorous battle with them, unsure whether he wants to be in the water or out, swimming doggy-paddle, more or less as I do. I too am a self-taught swimmer. One day my father, as my prospective teacher, has ordered me to follow him: 'Look, it's easy, you just go like this,' and then, forgetting that I am supposed to be in his wake, has streaked on as far as the buoy, a wooden platform painted blue on which a couple of girls in two-piece costumes are sitting, dangling their legs in the water. When he realises that I have actually splashed all the way there, he turns extremely pale, more worried about what he would tell his wife than about me, who is after all safe and sound and spluttering. And yes, my mother is indeed waiting for us on the shore, glowing and lovely and flustered in her apricot-coloured elasticised bathing suit, its bra cups stiff as cardboard. 'Grazia, Grazia, she can swim!' he informs her triumphantly.

She: 'Have you no sense of…'

He: 'Your daughter's learned to swim, and you're not even pleased?'

This happened a couple of years ago, during the first and only holiday my mother and I spent together during my early childhood, that Sunday he'd come to pick us up. Other things happened during that fateful holiday fortnight, but I have not been told about them, or not yet.

My father too has an ambiguous relationship with water, when he's nowhere near it he can't wait to be in it, when he's in it he can't wait to be out. And indeed no sooner are we in than we're out again, the dog shaking himself over a crowd of protesting supine figures basting themselves in the early morning sun, us drying ourselves as best we can with our clothes, because we've forgotten to bring a towel. 'Doesn't it feel good with your clothes on your wet skin?' Gilin says to me, waving his arms blissfully in his damp shirt.

He lights a cigarette and off we go, windows down, my father occasionally remembering to shout into the wind: 'Mind your head,' when we are passing a lorry on a narrow mountain road. We stop in a mountain village to eat an omelette sandwich and he buys a little bottle of lavender to give to my mother but which he himself will use, because he's the only one in the family who uses scent, as Ninin has often pointed out to me and the dog, the most loyal of her listeners. On the last stretch a satiated Pucci curls up on the seat with his nose on his tail and closes his eyes, and I too fall asleep in the heat.

By the time we arrive it's already afternoon, and I can't remember why the holiday ended sooner than expected, at least for me.

Old people die. It's a fact of nature, like the seasons. The first to depart during my childhood was my grandfather, the only one I knew, my father's father. He was a rough man, a bogeyman, with a voice like thunder, always armed with willow canes. I don't remember him ever taking me into his arms, or saying a pleasant word to me or my cousins. He was like some dried up old tree lingering in a courtyard, black and half-shrivelled but still clinging to the soil, until one day a storm snaps it in half, and now it's not there any more; and nor is he, and no one seems to mourn him, not even his wife Maria.

Next it is the turn of my maternal grandmother, Maria, poor thing. And now the time has come for *barba* Giuanin, my Uncle Giovanni.

Surrounded by a court of devoted and adoring attendants, I – who owe my secure and loving childhood to the elderly – resign myself to loss, indeed become inured to it. One by one they fall, apparently without any demonstration of grief on my part, or only the most fleeting. On I go, towards my life, and they are gradually left behind, first one and then another fading away into the past. But after some years I begin to understand that their death is a delusion. They are not dead, they are departed to another world, that isn't here not there, it's inside myself, the world of shadows that you can't hug anymore and that lure you to an immaterial dimension.

I don't believe in heaven, but if by chance it did indeed exist, it would be where they are.

We go straight to my aunts' house. There is a smell of medicine and alcohol and a sense of emergency. They look at me in silence, Aunt Polonia's little black eyes are like two tiny pools when the ice is melting, her round face crumpling and trembling; leaning forward on her chair, she gesticulates wildly from behind her handkerchief. Giulia gives me a hug, sobbing into my hair, and I can tell that she is anxious and nervous in a way that will become habitual. Rather than actually seeing them, I sense other silent presences in the room, a spinster niece who does good works with the sick, and a vast black cassock – Uncle Giovanni's priest brother – against which the dog is hurling himself, barking fit to burst, barely restrained by my grandmother Maria.

'You took your time,' says Giulia.

'You wouldn't have wanted us to be killed en route,' snaps back Gilin. And, to his mother, 'Leave that dog be.'

'That's enough! Get out! Shame on you!' and it's not clear whether she is talking to the dog, who slips out of the room with his tail between his legs, or my father, who darts a black look in the direction of the formidable old priest.

The room is in semi-darkness; the blinds are completely down, only the faintest glimmer of the dazzling afternoon sunlight filters through. He's lying on his side of the bed, almost invisible in the half-light, his hands on the sheet.

They thrust me forward in his direction.

For years now – ever since I started going to school – things between me and Uncle Giovanni have been changing. I'm growing up.

I have twenty-four classmates and a teacher. I learn history, geography, arithmetic, grammar, I learn curiosity and anxiety, distrust and disenchantment and any number of emotions which keep me occupied. Every day, after school, I do my homework. The courtyard, the centre of gravity for the children from my block, becomes my country, I am a citizen *d'la curt*, of the courtyard, that is where I fight my battles, work, marry, divorce, gain power and lose it.

At some point before my seventh birthday, when I have already been at school for several months, my mother, never a one for speechifying, takes me aside after lunch one day and says to me solemnly: 'Listen, I don't have time to check your homework, school is important and you'll have to work hard without my constant chivvying, do you understand?'

Yes, I tell her, I won't need any chivvying. It's my first important vow, one of the most solemn and portentous events to occur in my life between the ages of six and seven, when things start to speed up, like a roundabout after its first time round.

From my mother – who, after thirteen hours in the shop, tends increasingly to fall asleep in the arms not of her husband but of a novel – I have inherited a love of reading. I study her, wrapped in the embrace of her invisible lover, her lovely face intent, her loose black hair fanning out over her nightdress, the last cigarette of the day between her fingers. How could I not long to join her in that world which has her in its thrall? I had my own personal book collection even before I learned the alphabet, assembled scientifically with tokens from Agnesi pasta, every ten sacks of *macaroni* or *fusilli* a book by Stevenson, Verne, Alcot. I no longer need Uncle Giovanni, or Ninin, or Maria, poor thing, to read me stories about Pinocchio or Alice; I read on my own, every evening, in bed, until Ninin, who sleeps in the twin bed and shares my bedside table, tells me for the umpteenth time to put out the *basur*, the lamp with the shade.

In a word, I'm growing up, I'm outgrowing my childhood day by day, soon I won't fit into it at all. Physically, too, I am no longer Uncle Giovanni's *bombonin*, the slight little girl with plaits and a little dress with flounces who survives on a bit of soup and a slice of bread and butter. I'm a chubby, awkward preadolescent girl, with short hair and permanently rumpled clothes, drooping hemlines and missing buttons; and, as Ninin puts it, I'd eat a table-leg.

The old idyllic times are now far off, and it will be years before I start to think of them again.

He's stretched out, motionless, his cheeks hollow, his mouth half-open, his face strangely pale and yellowish. He's breathing unevenly and with difficulty through parched lips.

I don't recognise him. He's a stranger and a faintly alarming one at that, but there's no escape, the hands which are pushing me towards him are still on my shoulders, giving me courage.

'Here's the child – we've brought the child to see you,' Aunt Giulia says to him.

He doesn't move; he stares into the void.

Polonia emits a lengthy sigh.

I hear my grandmother whispering to someone who has just arrived: 'Don Giacomo has just given him extreme unction.'

Then the head moves on the cushion and his eyes seem to come back to life, searching for something in the shadowy room.

His gaze alights on me, but whether he can see me or not there is no telling.

His breathing becomes more laboured, and suddenly I am pushed away: 'Come on now, take her home, take her home to her mother,' and everyone around the bed seems suddenly frantically busy, even if they also appear to be almost motionless. One bends over him, moistens his lips, the doctor, who has now arrived, opens his big black bag, and from the kitchen comes the tinkling of the glass syringe, as it boils on in its metal case, forgotten on the stove.

In the Sixties, around these parts, funerals are much as they have always been, with people emerging from the welcome coolness of the parish church to be stunned by the blazing sun in the warmest hours of a July day. Slowly the mourners form an Indian file and fall into step, in a silence broken by whispers, as they proceed towards the cemetery which is just outside the town. The women have their heads covered with a *cuefa*, the veil they wear at mass, and the men are sweating into their *muda*, their good suits, buttoned up to the neck, with ties which smell of mothballs. The children too will be dressed in their best, though in dark colours.

I walk with my head bowed, right behind the big hearse which proceeds at a walking pace, with the back doors open so that you can see the coffin, on which flowers and greenery flutter as though to greet the following procession. I'm uncomfortable in last year's blue cotton dress, now too small for me, I'm sweating, and I hardly dare raise my arms for fear that the sleeves will split. I cast my eyes down, sadly observing my increasingly dusty patent leather shoes, and I know that my mother is going to ask me when I'll learn not to drag my feet, look what a state my shoes are in. I'm not thinking about death, except as something that happens to grown-ups, to the old. The cemetery holds no surprises for me, I've been visiting it almost weekly throughout my childhood, on the arm of one or other of the aunts.

Behind me are my mother and father, grief-stricken but still handsome, enjoying a momentary truce. And uncles, aunts, cousins and assorted relatives.

Polonia is not among them, though, she can no longer walk. She follows her husband at the end of the long procession, in a black car, a bouncing ball of bitterness on the leather seats. The hearse stops at the entrance and waits for her, the procession parts to let her pass and she gets out, unsteady on her feet, assisted by an array of eager hands, her own arms outstretched towards Giovanni's coffin, as though even now, at this late stage, she hoped to call him back, to keep him from that unexpected journey on which he had embarked too speedily, without a briefcase, without a coat, without even an umbrella.

For some time now my mother has been changing, she's no longer the meek wife, the little greengrocer bent over her crates of lettuce, who blushes at the commercial traveller's compliments. Now she sends me to the tobacconist's more often to buy her a packet of unfiltered Nazionali Super, and slips into the next door bar to bolt down an espresso. She's lost weight, her voice has become more forceful and she's going to driving school. One day, when my father has offered to give her a lesson, on some country road, it's not at all clear how, they run over the dog. When they take him home he seems more or less dead, except for a faint but distinct beat in his side. After a few days of recovery spent lying on an old cushion, Pucci pulls himself into a sitting position, licks my fingers and my tears of joy, and is reborn.

One August day, when I go back home from the courtyard, I find my family drawn up in ranks on either side of the table laid for lunch, he with his hand raised as though about to slap her, she grabbing a piece of bread and throwing it in his face. Discountenanced, he beats a stormy retreat. Ninin, fists clenched, observes the scene from the kitchen door, a carving fork in her hand. In her view, it is a woman's duty to accept men's unpredictable behaviour and forgive them for it, and she often tells my mother so, but practice is another thing entirely. In practice Ninin stalks fiercely through our four little rooms, sharpening the knives of her animosity for this ne'er-do-well, this sluggard, this *lajan*. Ninin is like a rock, split by the conflict between what's right, and what one secretly desires; but when it's a question of my mother, the rift is miraculously healed and the rock made whole again.

After Giovanni's death, while Ninin gives her household goods the benefit of her unvarnished opinion of the injustices of fate ('It's always the best who go! You're left with the pains in the neck!'), Grazia and Gilin have a series of private conversations, no easy matter in a house which is open to the four winds, particularly given my father's slippery nature. Telephone calls are made – from the shop, we have no phone at home – and whispered appointments are made, like at the doctor's.

One afternoon they set off together in the Volkswagen beetle which has replaced the Millecento, to go to Turin on one of these mysterious appointments, and come back thoroughly crestfallen: my mother tells me that they've lost the dog, most likely at a traffic-lights at Venaria or possibly the next one, it was still hot and the windows were open, that minx of a dog must have jumped out without their noticing, they were deep in conversation, they had other things to think about and they were almost home before they noticed.

'Don't worry, we'll find him,' my father assures us. 'That wretched creature will think twice about running off after I've got my hands on him.'

But this time searches and inquiries are to no avail, any more than my prayers to Saint Anthony, who helps you find things you've lost. Unlike Lassie, the collie in the series on children's afternoon tv, whose refrain is, precisely, *Lassie come home*, Pucci does no such thing. A few months later someone says they've seen him near le Grange, and my father goes to check up. I'm not around, I'm probably at school, and in any case by now my father comes home only from time to time, he lives his own life. Later he will tell me that the dog in question was indeed Pucci, chained up in the courtyard of a farm, and that the creature had pretended not to recognise him.

'Leave him be, he's better off where he is,' says my mother; for her, the dog has made an understandable effort to save his skin by moving to a saner habitat.

So within a few weeks I lose both Uncle Giovanni and the dog. Two bereavements, the second undoubtedly more painful, but both soon buried beneath the present's forward march.

Treasure Hunt

Among my childhood photos – small, black and white, with scalloped edges – there is one which shows me and my mother in the little courtyard behind the shop, a small space which no longer exists, having been engulfed by concrete: a triangle of beaten earth and gravel wedged between two roads crossing via Dante and coming together a few metres further on, in the little square between the station and the start of the large tree-lined avenue. That little courtyard was the place where the scenes of my earliest childhood were played out, before I started consorting with other children in the big courtyard in our block. I was often there alone, or in the company of my (usually silent) maternal grandmother, who, despite her poor state of health, was supposed to be looking after me, as well as the little kitchen garden situated at the tip of the triangle. The oddness of this space – the fact that it ended in an acute angle and was hidden from the road by a thick privet hedge and a row of ailanthus? – made it seem unique, mysterious, a place for dreaming in, and these dreams have stayed with me. Beyond it was the noisy road, public and open – but here, behind a green and fragile barrier, within hearing distance of the general public, we could be entirely, and blessedly, alone.

Perhaps this is the first example of the lessons I was given, wordlessly for the most part, throughout my childhood: that all intimacy is tenuous, deep rather than wide; that it's better to see than to be seen; that it is as well to erect an iron curtain of reserve between ourselves and others if we wish to safeguard some precious quality which has no name. Even under the same sky, outer and inner space are two different things, to be kept separate.

In the photo of myself and my mother, against a background of a hedge and a small wooden gate, I am about three, so she must be about twenty-eight. It's summer, I am wearing a little white dress and buckled shoes; she is a beautiful young woman in her prime, wearing a printed cotton dress and sandals. Her black hair is drawn back over the nape of her neck; apart from a tuft which falls over her right eye, it leaves her unlined face entirely visible, her mouth clear-cut and shining, a sign that she has put on lipstick that day, perhaps specially for the photo. My mother is crouching down and holding me against her; I am half sitting, half leaning on her, using her left leg as a kind of seat. Our heads are on a level: despite the difference in age and size, we are equals on the ground that bears us. The photo is given a satisfying sense of structure by the soft double curve of her bent body and the arm around me, placed on my little dress, my unseen hand in hers; the broken line of my own body, set into hers, serves as a counterbalance. All in all we form a figure which is almost perfectly round, our shoulders seeming to merge, our two heads rising above that single harmonious curved line. As luck would have it, our two figures somewhat resemble those of the Virgin and Saint Anne in Leonardo's cartoon, with two important differences, the first being that there are just two of us, there's no infant Jesus. Here it is I who would be the holy child, as we see from the way my mother is making herself a seat and throne. Furthermore – and here is the second and more significant difference – while in all his versions Leonardo depicts Saint Anne casting a loving look at the young Virgin, in our photograph my mother Maria is fixing the photographer (almost certainly my father) with a calm unfathomable smile, lips parted, and it is I who am looking away from the lens and turning my head towards her to gaze at her adoringly. Eyelashes lowered, rather than actually looking at her I appear to be lost in the golden mist of her presence, apparently proclaiming to anyone who might care to listen: 'Behold, this is my treasure.' Like Leonardo's drawing, this photo too, even if it portrays just two figures and not three, is the image of a double motherhood.

People are always talking about mother love, almost always misguidedly. In the Sixties my young female friends who were studying medicine would read academic texts asserting that mother love had its seat in the mammary glands, and they were obliged to parrot as much to their professor. Perhaps it is scarcely surprising that during those years women should have wanted to steer clear of mothering, which they saw as something negative, as a pathology. At the end of the decade, Elizabeth Badinter bravely proclaimed that a mother's love for her child is not a matter of glands but rather an add-on love, an acquired emotion, the fruit not of nature but of nurture. There had been a time, after all, when well-off women handed their babies over to wet-nurses, scarcely caring whether they survived or not, and it was only post-Rousseau that they began to feel a touch of pride in putting themselves at the service of their offspring. Thus mother love is neither physiological nor immutable over time, but changes from age to age, according to social context. Like fashions in dress, religion, public and private habits, how we feel about more or less everything, in a word…

Today, though, I wouldn't be quite so shrill as to claim that if you're not a mother born, you become one under pressure from society. When I imagine my mother leaning over me in my cradle, I cannot but think that some feeling of attachment stirs within her, let's call it instinct, which leads her to love and take care of that tiny, vulnerable, ill-smelling creature which, despite the trouble it brings with it, arouses her tenderness.

But that is not the only voice that speaks in her. My mother is tired, she is busy, she is lacking in strength. Furthermore, perhaps, she is beginning to have doubts about the man she has married, a man who makes daily promises he promptly forgets, who has no past, no memory. What future can they build together?

It was an easy birth, she worked until midday, as always, pushing her huge stomach before her – her ballast for some time now – and then she'd gone to bed; Aunt Polonia had arrived and labour had begun, and she'd bitten Margherita's caressing hand and shrieked at the sight of the scissors Polonia was brandishing – and at six in the evening there I was, kicking heartily. She forgot her pain and took a week off before going back to stand behind her counter.

I know that my mother was severely depressed for at least six months after my birth, perhaps longer. She's putting on weight – she's always hungry – but she has no strength, she's permanently on the point of tears. She probably feels guilty, not because she's neglecting her work or her daughter – she's definitely not – but because her feelings strike her as weak, inadequate. No unconditional, triumphant beatitude descends upon her from the skies to lighten her load; at times she seems indifferent to everything except her swollen legs. When she is woken by my cries, three, even four times before dawn, beneath maternal devotion slithers the thought of silencing her nocturnal tormentor once and for all.

'If she weren't mine,' she confesses to Margherita, 'I'd be tempted to throw her out of the window. Does that mean I'm a bad mother?' Margherita laughs: 'Don't be silly, that's how they all feel!'

The aunts help her to look after the baby, 'take the weight off your legs, poor thing,' they say to her, an invitation never to be taken too seriously in our household, and eventually she's her own self again, she returns to her normal weight, regains her colour and above all her strength.

How does my mother's depression affect me? Do I notice it? Later she will tell me that I was a healthy, hungry baby, but that feeding me was painful, she suffered from mastitis, her nipples were cracked and bleeding. Together with her milk, I literally sucked her blood. It's hardly surprising that she dreaded the moment when it was time for me to have a feed; not for her that sensual pleasure others talk of. Furthermore, getting up at night to feed me exhausted her, the hours she had to spend in the shop were non-negotiable, from seven in the morning until eight at night, with a two hour lunch break.

Nonetheless, Maria is happy to have a daughter. Later, whenever she talks to me about it, that's what she stresses: she's happy to have brought a girl into the world. She says that when she looked at other mothers with baby boys in their prams, she felt secretly sorry for them; they couldn't have been nearly as happy as she was.

I am born a girl into a family of women and I represent the future and continuity with the past. My mother, nourished by the love and strength of the generation that preceded her, sees in me the logical – and fortunate – continuation of what came before. All she has known will be repeated, but in happier circumstances, minus death and the war. I am a lovely story waiting to be told.

This is why she feels a secret sense of superiority vis-à-vis mothers of boys. Her pride and joy in me are not precisely formulated, they are feelings which swim around beneath a placid surface. When Emma Bovary is told she has given birth to a little girl, she turns her face away and goes into a swoon. My mother smiles. I am just what she was hoping for, the bearer of all her expectations, I have her total backing: she was expecting me. The psychic nourishment I receive from her is more precious than milk and blood.

But her body takes some time – at least six months, perhaps a year – before it can bid me welcome. The maternal instinct rises slowly from the muddy waters of depression; she undoubtedly feels very much alone, she feels sorry for her own painful breasts, for her state of exhaustion. I am her loveable little tormentor. It's just as well she shares me with so many others.

Somewhere, in letters from an emigrant, I read a sentence which often comes back into my mind: 'When you are hungry, you have no time for love.' My mother is not hungry – or rather yes, she is, she's always hungry, that's why she's always eating. And she certainly does love me – but like some happy story to which I, a suckling, am a mere preface, one which she'd be quite happy to skip.

Perhaps all she needs after my birth is a bit more rest, a week doesn't seem much. But in our house physical illness and exhaustion receive short shrift, and the shop can't get by for long without her, work, as always, comes first. So my mother loves me in the intervals between one bout of exhaustion and another, and puts off the moment when she will be able to love me at her ease, the moment when she will begin to take pleasure in life again.

Am I aware of this? Sometimes I think that my gratitude towards her has its origins in just this year of my life. Right from the start I do not take my mother's love for granted, but regard it as a gift. Perhaps, too, right from the start I respond with an excess of passion to something in her which is tacit, dormant. I also take on her part of the dialogue, I talk to myself, I talk of her to myself.

Then my mother recovers, her nipples, scarred by my eager nozzle of a mouth, heal up, her legs begin to move more willingly. She feeds me until I'm thirteen months old, something which was fairly common at the time but which is quite an undertaking for her, from which she emerges triumphant. She has had time to get used to my infant body; in the meantime I stop wearing nappies, and smell sweet. I'm healthy and easy-going, I cause no one any worries. I imagine her smiling at me contentedly, touching my smooth, firm skin, feeling a sense of joy in me… when she's got time. Now, perhaps, if she were the wife of a doctor, or a head of department at IPCA like Margherita, she might have devoted herself to me entirely, become a perfect Rousseau-inspired mother concerned with me alone, and perhaps have had other children… who knows, perhaps if some solid, trustworthy man had asked it of her, or somehow quietly insisted on it, Maria Grazia might have renounced her economic independence because, at twenty-five or twenty-six, she was not yet fully formed, she was still malleable, amenable, ready to adapt to circumstances, to wills that were stronger than her own. She was not yet what she would be at forty.

I try to imagine my mother slithering over well-polished floors in pattens, checking my nails and lengthening my dresses, her mouth full of pins, forcing me to sit still on a stool.

I would have irritated her, she would have smacked me. She would have been on edge, dissatisfied, and she wouldn't have known why. And I see myself as a little girl bending over a cradle on which Aunt Giulia has lavished yet more lace, to contemplate a toothless creature, a rival and an acolyte, to be broken in and vied with, and I can catch that smell of lye and disinfectant which wafted around in the kitchens of some of my friends at elementary school…

I was indeed about to have a brother, or perhaps a sister, but he or she ended up as an undignified gobbet of blood one day when my mother was more tired than usual, and felt unwell after having run up the stairs. Her body flatly refused to bear another child. After that, she later told me, it was she herself – she meant her conscious mind – who didn't want any more children, and she decided to take action to make sure that that was how things stayed. In those days, she was to tell me, men were careful, and the couples of her generation had one child, two at most. The time of large families was over, farewell to living like rabbits all in a single room: the time had come to work, to shuffle off ignorance and poverty and make sure your children got an education. But that miscarriage had to be kept secret, like the one her own mother had had on her return from America, because, however unintentional, in the Fifties such an event was still cloaked in shame.

But the image of a Maria Grazia as a full-time wife is purely hypothetical. Would she ever have dragged herself away from *magna* Ninin and her mother, to lock herself up in a little house or one-family flat? I don't think so. Indeed, it is quite possible that she married my father – without knowing it, of course – precisely because he *was not* a mature and confident man, who would carry her off and claim her all for himself, but a grown-up child who had come to join her in her family of women…

As things stand, she does not have to choose between work and domestic confinement. Luckily my mother has married a *lajan* and lives with a sick mother and a grumpy old *magna* with a miserable pension! She can't afford to play at being the housewife. It's Ninin who takes care of domestic matters – when I was born she stopped working at the factory, and at just over sixty she's still full of aggressive energy. My mother lives in the shop and for the shop; because the shop, in the early Sixties, is our only hope of rising from the working class into the lower middle. Maria Grazia gets up at six in the morning, rushes around from seven until one, gulps down her lunch and falls into a heavy sleep, from which she is rudely awakened just before three, then it's back to her counter until evening.

Still, what bit of luck – I will sometimes say to myself when thinking of certain mothers not all that much younger than herself, all but engulfed by clinging, clutching children who constantly bawl to gain their full attention – that my mother worked so hard and had an old-fashioned attitude to life! That I'd never seen her naked, that she'd never given in to my whims, that I'd never scraped the bottom of the barrel of mother love! Her work – whose importance was part of the air we all breathed – created an aura round her, put an almost sacred distance between her and me. In the afternoon, when she was resting before going back to working in the shop, I would be as silent as a mouse, furious with the neighbour, a mother of six who was permanently submerged by her domestic duties, but who chose that very moment, in apron and curlers, to appear at the window overlooking the courtyard to summon her brood with a series of piercing shrieks (they never bothered to reply), disturbing Maria Grazia's sleep with her stentorian tones.

Even then there were mothers who were browbeaten by their children, even the girls, and insulted if they did not accede to their requests ('I want an ice cream! Give us fifty lire! And I mean now, you stingy old cow!') I felt superior to my insolent contemporaries because – as I put it to myself when I was about eight – I *respected* my mother. I had something precious which they did not have. 'But if they let themselves be treated like that, then they deserve it!' I added, expressing my final judgment on doormat mothers. An admiring if worried shadow passed over the aunts' faces (children are so canny!) Because it is typical of adults to forget what they once knew, instinctively and infallibly, as children, about power and its misuse.

Right from my earliest years, I regard my mother as the Law incarnate. During the day Ninin and my grandmother chide me for my shortcomings and take note of my misdeeds. In the evening, on her return, my mother is given a detailed account of my crimes, and she administers due punishment, a telling-off or the odd smack, with Ninin and my grandmother as anguished onlookers, wringing their hands. At some point, Maria Grazia rebels: after a long day in the shop, she doesn't want to be obliged to act the martinet with her daughter. From that moment there's an amnesty and, in the evening, peace descends. But Maria Grazia is still what we today would call a strict mother, she's not at all inclined to go back on her word. In the power struggle which is inevitable in any relationship between two human beings, it is clear to me that she has the upper hand. I'm grateful to her for this, above all because her power strikes me as just. I want to be worthy of her approval. I admire her energy and her clear, concise answers. I bask in the way others stop to listen to her and, when I see her in a crowd, I feel a secret delight in noting that she is the best-looking.

The spiritual nourishment my mother gives me earns her

my respect and gratitude; over the years it becomes my moral skeleton, just as her milk has become my muscle, bone and blood.

Paradoxically, in my eyes, work – which is both slavery and freedom for my mother – becomes her passport to nobility. She may be a greengrocer, but for me she's a queen: My Lady Mother – as some mothers are referred to in novels I'll read when I'm older – who moves, speedily and majestically, through the world of things which count, giving instructions to those who gravitate around her. There is a loving distance between the two of us, full of echoes and ambitions, into which I can withdraw without getting lost, breathe without breaking faith. She will never be the mother-friend that some of my school friends have, who sits on my bed and rummages through my thoughts, nor indeed the dogsbody, slightly dog-eared through use, of most of my contemporaries. And throughout my life I shall feel a sense of relief, surprise and gratitude that I was born of her, and no one else.

I don't remember any household hints, or recipes – my mother will be taught to cook, after the age of fifty, by me; instead, I see her unloading crates of oranges from the van, or seated at the till or bent over the chopping board, with that tuft of hair which has escaped from her severe bun and is tumbling over her forehead; struggling with a large parmesan cheese which is to be cut into neat pieces and squared off with a chopping knife, or a Parma ham to be expertly boned. She has no time for trivialities, for the fripperies of life. She's deep in the world of real things, slap in the middle of it. Over a period of ten years, when I am growing up, Maria Grazia casts off her shyness, learns to negotiate the world, to face up to difficulties and be self-sufficient. She becomes a grown-up woman.

She's not an absent mother – she works a few metres from home, and as soon as I am able to walk I can go and see her whenever I like – but she's present in spirit rather than the flesh. It's difficult to get near a busy woman, and often I make do with simply looking at her, feeling her presence; the sound of her voice, the idea of her, they're everywhere, in our house, in the roads around it, in my life and in our conversations. *Magna* Ninin, my grandmother and my father are always talking about her. Ninin calls her Maria, my father calls her Grazia when he's trying to ingratiate himself and Maria when he simply needs her. My grandmother doesn't talk much and appeals to her mainly with her eyes.

Maria Grazia is the one who keeps us going. She's the ticking clock which gives a rhythm to our day, the goddess Reason who won't take any nonsense and is untouched by childish wiles; but she is also the even-handed force which brings opposites together, the lynch-pin in the unlikely shared existence of my thoughtless young father and Ninin, the stern custodian of duty. My mother lights us all up like the sun, which is there even when you can't see it. She is the rock on which we stand; my father, by contrast, is lunar, lunatic, breezy and unreliable.

Madame de Sevigné, a fond mother, wrote to her daughter, Madame de Grignan: 'Madame, I love you not because you are my daughter, but because you are you.' Here she was admirably clear-headed (though I also sense a desire to ward off any suspicion of mawkishness). It is a bit of rare good luck to have a lovable woman as a daughter – a never-ending source into which love can for ever dip and never find it dry; an endless banquet of emotions.

Then there's Violette Leduc, who aborted the only child

she ever conceived, but passionately loved her mother, an impossible woman, and a number of other impossible people into the bargain: 'Of those I have loved, I wanted no other children than themselves. They were my love.'

In civil status terms I've always been just a daughter, never a mother. But in truth civic status is not the whole story. I am acquainted with mother love because I have lived with it; my mother loved me, but, more importantly, while loving me, she left me free. And I, who was on the other side of that love as on the other side of a very thin skin, or osmotic membrane, loved her back, with filial love. Although, in fact, can we apply adjectives to love? Filial, sisterly, marital, passionate – each adjective seems to lop something off love's mysterious complexity. What I am trying to say is that I loved my mother not just with filial love, but in many other ways: as the ideal woman, as the captain of my ship, as the nearest and at the same time furthest link in the chain of women of which I was part, and which bound me to life; as a child to be nurtured, a being to be protected – and not just from a certain age, when the roles are reversed, and power and responsibility fall to me.

It is said that childless women lavish their thwarted mother love on animals, that spinsters replace children with dogs and cats, as though animals were poor substitutes for humans; as though our domestic pets did not have a right to a love all their own, of an almost religious kind, since they are what remains to us of that Other which once loomed over us in all its awesome wonder: bears, lions, forests, northern lights, omnipresent death… And do animals in their turn not love us back with a child's blind pig-headedness and a mother's protective anxiety? Ever since she was a kitten, my cat Manì has expressed her love by licking my face as though I, so much older and bigger, were *her* kitten. This fledgling mother, the size of my fist, would look at me with concern: 'Will she make it, this hairless creature of mine, with neither claws nor whiskers, practically deaf, low on night vision and lacking the most elementary of feline faculties?'

We bear within us atavistic attitudes, prenatal memories of ages not yet lived. Old and young, big and small are not just relative concepts but inseparable parts of our whole being. I too as a child, like Manì the fledgling mother, used to lick my mother's face and hands; I did it as humans do, not with my tongue but with my eyes. I was a mother at the age of three. You can see as much from that photo. I don't just let her hug me, I'm not merely the recipient of her affections: there is a tiny echoing motherliness in me too, a hint of protectiveness and of pride in my treasure. Even then, as throughout my life, I feel older than my age.

Like Violette Leduc, I might say that those I have loved have been my children. Starting with my mother.

One evening in my early childhood, before I've started to go to school, probably as a result of tireless pestering, Gilin promised me that the next day, early in the morning, we'd go off with the caravan of fairground folk who've been camping on the avenue for the local saint's day. They had wagons with little windows with washing hanging out of them, and patient-looking animals between the shafts, donkeys and possibly the odd horse. The prospect of settling into one of those diminutive dwellings where everything seemed like a game, and sharing a wandering existence with those mild-looking creatures, would have struck any four or five year old as exciting. Obviously the next day nothing happened, except that the fairground people left without us.

Perhaps my father thought that I'd forget about his promise

during the night. I didn't. Not only did I remember it perfectly well the following morning, but that small episode remained lodged in my mind for ever after, like one of those pebbles of memory which for some reason are always rising to the surface, unburied by the unstoppable landslide of the present. At an age when you are always turning round to see how far you've come, that summer evening (it must have been summer, the local saint's day was in August) seems to me to mark a small turning point in my personal history, the only one for which I can claim some expertise.

Thanks to the searing disappointment of not having left at dawn on a donkey-drawn cart, some days later I announce to the world, or at least to a duly astounded and attentive audience of aunts, that my father has reneged on his promise, and that if you don't intend to keep a promise you shouldn't make one. It's the first time I've pronounced a considered judgment on an adult, not just childish whingeing but an out and out moral verdict. The grown-ups listen to me without a word; they do not say as much, but they clearly think I'm right. They sigh and avert their eyes from an inconvenient truth, as they have always done, and offer me a sweetie by way of compensation.

As I remember, I myself was surprised by my assertion. No doubt I too, like all children, parroted what I heard around me, or guessed at what was meant by grown-up's silences and omissions. I knew quite well – it was in the air I breathed – that my father's black curls and sparkling eyes were a snare and a delusion, that he was not to be trusted, that *magna* Ninin disapproved of him and that he caused Polonia and Giulia to sigh. Still, the sentence came out of my mouth like one of those things you don't know you think until you've said them.

There are some thoughts which come into the world already grown and fully formed, like Athena from the head of Zeus.

The fact that this metaphor should have come into my mind at this particular juncture gives me pause. Zeus and Athena, father and daughter. A somewhat hare-brained father, this Zeus, who got up to all kinds of mischief and didn't think twice before turning himself into an animal to satisfy his lust; and produced a daughter who was armour-plated, coldly virtuous. The exact opposite of her feckless father, she is all moderation and good sense; he is sensual, she virginal; he's histrionic, she's always down-to-earth; you won't catch her with a smile on her lips.

What can they have been thinking of, those Greek ancestors of ours, those shepherds, to come up with such a thing? Zeus will not have been the first nor the only god to have given birth (the idea will recur across the ages and among many peoples), but a daughter emerging from his head? Is this not tantamount to saying: women give birth to children with blood and guts, but fatherhood is a more elevated matter altogether, it's (just) an idea? But why then is this daughter the exact opposite of her father? Incidentally, she's motherless, not that anybody seems to care. This armed goddess, unflappable and grave, is never caught off her guard, like her progenitor or winged Hermes, never caught half-naked like her brother Apollo or her sister Artemis; she's never without her warrior's helmet, the one you see on the boxes of Minerva matches my mother would send me to buy at the tobacconist's, together with the Nazionali Super without filter.

From a very early age I know it's crucial to underplay my paternal birthright. When *magna* Ninin wants to lob a particularly cutting reproach, she throws in a reference – to my fury and indignation – to the fact that I'm my father's daughter. All the old people in my life know that my father's not quite the full shilling, but they keep quiet about it with varying degrees of good grace, either because they hope things will change, or not to hurt my mother, who is blinded by love – they all keep quiet, except for *barba* Giuanin, who emits muffled roars like those of some asthmatic lion, and *magna* Ninin, who shouts the truth to the four winds, but only when there's no one around, like John the Baptist in the desert.

In the empty house – empty except for me, the dog Pucci, at a later date the cat Malachia, and my grandmother Maria – Ninin's prophetic and threatening voice rises above the sound of the water splashing in the sink to proclaim that *someone* is a liar, a skiver, an egoist, etc. And we, who are both there and not there – my grandmother, the dog, the cat and I – feel sheepish, ashamed on behalf of that *somebody* present and absent in our midst, and if we look at each other askance, it is to reassure ourselves that we belong to the chosen race, and not the damned.

But it is not enough to think it and to tell each other as much in silence: we have to prove it.

We children and domestic pets, we paralytic grandmothers in our second childhood, we have to toe the line, to plight our troth to the merciless god who rules us all, namely Duty. Needless to say, we cannot fully satisfy him. In his eyes, and in those of his awesome prophet *magna* Ninin, we will always be sinners, since we will have forgotten or broken or dirtied something, will have been greedy, slothful, disorderly and, worst sin of all, lazy. This is why we are not so different from that *someone* who has wormed his way into our company like the son of shadows among the sons of light; and, as it happens, one of us is actually related to him: me.

Of course, dumb creatures though we are, we know that *magna* Ninin is right. We would never dream of questioning her words, their truth is self-evident. Furthermore let it not be forgotten that we all love the same woman. We are as one, Ninin, my grandmother, myself and the cat in our veneration for Maria Grazia (I'm not so sure about the dog, Pucci is more my father's child, an awkward condition from which he will redeem himself by flight). It is she who forges us into a tight little army of faithful, eager for her smile.

After the wedding my parents go to live in the bride's house, or rather: Gilin goes to live with his wife; Maria Grazia stays where she's always been, with her mother and *magna* Ninin. Gilin quite simply adds himself to a household of three women – a matrilinear arrangement which must strike him as entirely normal, since his family too tend to cluster around women; but it is also inconvenient, possibly even worse. In that small space he's always within range, under surveillance. All the more so since the young couple's room is wedged between the kitchen and *magna* Ninin's room, which, when I'm born, also becomes mine. There are no corridors in our house, you go straight from one room into another – unless you use the balcony which runs the length of the apartment, overlooking the courtyard with its lower buildings which will soon become garages, and its cherished trees, two tall Atlantic cedars and a magnolia, the only true splendour and adornment of that modest block of flats.

The 'matrimonial bedroom', or rather the furniture it contains, has been made by Giovanni the carpenter, Gilin's brother: bed, chest-of-drawers and three-door wardrobe, all in blond wood, all rounded curves, with hand-carved flowers and broad petals tumbling down their corners. And two over-stuffed little armchairs, on which nobody ever sits but on which people put clothes and linen. There is something reassuring about the naïve ugliness of this furniture; the large mirrors on the chest-of-drawers and wardrobe doors, and the window and French window, make the room very light; in my memory, it is forever bathed in summer brightness.

But it's certainly not very private. In point of fact privacy is an unknown concept in our house, whose suite of rooms, all looking east, towards the rising sun, is marched through by Ninin well before there's any sun to contemplate, as she awakens us with a noisy banging of doors. Thus my father is obliged to vacate the premises as fast as he is able, and take himself off to the traditional male redoubts, the street, the bar… At times, even the factory must have seemed like a safe haven. There at least he could draw breath between one corvee and another, or smoke a furtive cigarette with a friend.

Not that he didn't smoke in the house! These are the Fifties, everybody smokes. At table, in the cinema, on screen and off, over the cradles of the newly-born. Even my mother smokes, braving Ninin's more or less tacit disapproval (smoking is definitely a vice, a generic term for all pleasures which cause you to take time off work and which cost money).

But it's not true that our house contains no private space. There is one – my grandmother's room, a little room which had been made by partitioning off a bit of the living room, the only one that's not east-facing, looking out over the trees. It's small and narrow, lit by one tiny window so high up you can't look out of it. That's where my maternal grandmother keeps her things: a single bed, little more than a camp-bed, a bedside table, a chair; the rest of the space is taken up by an old sideboard and other household objects which are no longer used but which no one dares to throw away, after all you never know. My grandmother sleeps there, she retires there of an evening to read her pious books – the only ones she has, I realise, perhaps because no one has ever thought to give her any other kind. Now, of course, when I am approaching the age at which she died, it's too late to put things right. She read to us when we were children, and my friends from that time, Walter and Ugo, remember those readings; I think that this must have meant that she was a good, expressive reader and also a willing one. Books were her private world, a parallel world which made this one possible to live in; as for her daughter and grand-daughter after her. I comfort myself by imagining her borrowing the odd novel from my mother, possibly on the sly.

Personally, if I want to be alone I go to the top floor, to the loft, a realm of cobwebs and shadows and dusty disused objects. These lofts – ours is wide and deep, the last one at the end of a corridor faced with bare brick and rough planks – form a sort of suspended limbo land where the laws of the daily grind do not apply. On breezy days, when boldness is in the air, I clamber up on to a crate and manage to reach a little window opening on to a lower part of the roof above the building's new wing; I climb out. Wobbling precariously on red tiles, it seems to me I have a view of the world which can be had only from here; I feel like a hero from Jules Verne, an explorer of unknown lands, engaged in deeds that are as thrilling as they are vague, and I imagine that I have a strange power over those far below me, as I watch them getting on with their earthly doings, unaware of my gaze. Sooner or later, of course, I am found out, and forbidden to return to my perilous vantage point; but it's not that which stops me, it's my growing body, as it becomes more and more difficult to ease myself through the little window under the eaves; and my body begins to feel anchored to earth by its own weight, and hence it feels a kind of limitation which suggests that it too belongs down there with all the rest; and there's a troubled memory of a lightness which was, and is no more.

Even if you've left it decades ago and think you have forgotten it, in some corner of your memory, which comes to life again in dreams, the place where you lived when you were little always remains *the house*. When I dream about the houses I've lived in during the course of my lifetime, I always see them subtly transformed into that one, the first I ever knew, and the origin of all those that came after. So this is the model that tends to reappear in dreams: an apartment without corridors, with rooms that open one off the other and which are reached from a treacherous landing, marking the border with the outside world. A long balcony overlooking a courtyard, like the deck of a windswept ship suspended above the waves. But once I've made it through these in-between spaces , once I'm safe and sound *inside*, it's there that I'm most truly myself, right at the core of my being – not always an easy place to be. It's there, in those four-and-a-half rooms, and preferably in the kitchen – the innermost of those spaces, which looks outwards from a place of safety, absorbing the light from the sky and the coolness of the trees – that I find myself from time to time, at night, in dreams where almost nothing but at the same time a great deal happens, and which leave me stunned, on edge; indeed perhaps rather than dreams they're apparitions.

There are always just three of us in that kitchen: Ninin, my mother and me. Although Ninin has been absent for decades, at some point she reappears, to tell me that she's dead; I both believe and disbelieve her, aching with a protective love which seeks both to reassure her that she is alive, and at the same time to continue to see her in her final, venerable, vulnerable state, that of a shade. Since then she has been back in my dreams, austere as ever but also more serene and smiling, and almost completely silent. And with the years I have realised that she had undergone a total transformation: she was no longer Ninin, or at least not just Ninin: she was my mother, who had turned into her as she grew old. And the other woman, the one who in my dreams still has my mother's face, is in fact Claudia, who has long shared my domestic space and has become as precious and vital to me as my mother had been when I was little.

Ninin, a grey-haired old woman who seems to have loomed up out of the mists of time, the steward of a border area which I approach with reverence and awe, and Maria, my mother, with her lovely face, still that of a young woman, and her black hair: both have become symbols, or perhaps avatars, as we would say nowadays of my psyche: inhabited, for ever – my modest, mortal 'ever' – by two women, one old, one young, who are for me the two faces of love.

It's the end of the Fifties. We're at the height of the economic miracle, and the shop is going well. People have more money, they buy more. All of a sudden, we're coining it.

Things that were once familiar vanish from one day to the next, and others take their place. Pasta and rice, which used to come in fifty-kilo sacks and be sold to customers in screws of grey paper nimbly done up by clever hands like so much grocer's origami, will now be sold in specially-made paper bags or blue cardboard boxes. Goodbye big white cotton sacks with 'pasta Agnesi' written on them in red, which *magna* Ninin then reuses as kitchen cloths or sheets, sewing them together with big stitches which scratch your back. Tuna will no longer be sold by weight, wrapped up in oozing grease-proof paper, but in sensible little tins; fewer and fewer women will make jam at home, and will buy it not in five-kilo tins – like the potentially lethal rusty ones my grandmother Maria the peasant has in her kitchen, and uses as vases for her clumps of wild flowers – but in little tins to be used up all at once, or kept piled up in the pantry, which is what the well-groomed women in the adverts do, to make themselves feel they're the perfect housewife. Another foodstuff that disappears without trace, except possibly on provincial market stalls, is a kind of sweet in the form of a compact dappled mass which is cut into slices, and which leaves a pasty taste in your mouth suggestive of various fats of dubious provenance, mixed in with hazelnuts, cocoa and vanilla, the precursor of the all-conquering Nutella. Fresh milk holds its ground, brought to the shop twice daily, on the dot of seven in the morning, when Maria Grazia's eyes are still heavy with sleep, and at five in the afternoon, the key moment when housewives are beginning to think about supper. In Turin there is already a Central Dairy which produces milk in hygienic bottles with red tops, but for years we in Ciriè continue to buy milk from the cowhand who arrives with his can on his back, smelling of the stable, and pours the foaming white liquid into your bucket, which until quite recently was made of alluminium (nowadays they're plastic). Customers bring their empty bottles from home, and the owners' attitude to cleanliness – indeed, their value as human beings – can be judged by the state of their containers: gleaming glass is indicative of a good housewife, evil-smelling smeary ones of a *plandra*, a lazybones, who will probably complain that the milk goes off immediately: hardly a surprise, given the state of the bottle!

Milk has a front-rank place in both our home life and the life of our shop, and the two are indissolubly linked. The buckets and measures (one litre, half, a quarter) have to be cleaned out with boiling water, and our fridge – for yes indeed, we have a fridge – contains bottles with a hermetic cap in which the cream rises to the surface; this is then speedily lapped up by my father, who adores cream, and whose passion for milk in general – particularly ice-cold milk – is unconfined. The milk which is not immediately sold, if there's enough of it, is put into big shallow pans and curdled with a few drops of lemon juice, and after two or three days the thick yellow cream which has formed is spooned off and put into jars with ice and water; this improvised churn is then shaken until the fat thickens into globules of butter, which is then squeezed out by hand and fashioned into little pats, also to be kept in cold water. This is work that can also be done by old and young alike; at once boring and exciting, its final outcome, foreseen though it may be, is nonetheless somehow miraculous. Once the sour cream has been skimmed off and the butter made, the quivering white mass of curd is collected with a ladle and placed in perforated cheese drainers, these too made of white plastic, whereas once they used to be metal. The greenish whey is left to seep through for a day or so, and then the cheese settles, fills in the gaps, becomes compact. Then, white, cool and slightly bitter, it is turned out on to a clean tray and taken back into the shop for sale. Nothing is thrown away, the wartime hunger and poverty which were so recently our lot are not forgotten: unsold spinach is trimmed, washed seven times, as custom requires, boiled, then dabbed dry, and snapped up like hot cakes by customers who are too *plandre* to do all this themselves; withered apples are put in the oven with a generous dusting of sugar, and pop up again on, lightly caramelised, their split skins oozing a sweet lava of flesh, on the counter of ready-cooked goods.

But the change which makes most impression on my

childish mind concerns dipping biscuits, rather than bread, into white coffee. It may not have really been so, but in my memory it is as though 'sweet things' burst into the house from one day to the next, you couldn't open any cupboard or sideboard without finding some toothsome morsel, even in my grandmother's little room, now just a boxroom, there was a sideboard groaning with treasure: cream biscuits, butter biscuits, wafers, savoy biscuits, macaroons, *langues-de-chat*. It is hardly surprising, then, that during those years I cease to be the self-controlled, restrained child that I used to be, and become a greedy guts. This happens when I suddenly find myself on the big rock candy mountain, but perhaps, during those same years, something else also plays a part, something my mother already knows, namely, that food gives you strength. Food takes sugar and energy into your blood; food is the fuel that enables you to face life, it's a way of saying: yes, I'll take up the challenge.

From this time onwards, in our house only Ninin will remain faithful to the habit of dipping bread into white coffee; a roll and coffee, and that is supper. My bowl, by contrast, is full of biscuits. My mother gets a real meal, with soup, a steak or something left over from lunch, and my father looks after himself, often bringing a tomato, a pepper and a head of celery from the shop – always the best of the bunch – to make a kind of dip.

'Only the best for that *pet sernu*,' comments *magna* Ninin. For years I wonder what this extremely familiar expression actually means, applied as it always is to self-important fusspots who regard themselves as too refined for the rough-and-ready world of family life. Finally, deciphering the obvious, I realise that it simply means what it says: a 'pet' is a fart, and *sernu* is the past participle of the verb *serni*, to choose. A chosen fart, one that's been self-selected.

My grandmother's room is now a boxroom because she herself is no longer with us. One morning, while she was combing her still black hair over the bath, she had a sudden fall. Over the following, last three days of her life she neither spoke nor opened her eyes. They say she did not suffer. They say that I broke out into inconsolable sobbing at the funeral, that they didn't know how to calm me down. I don't remember anything about this crying, nor about my grief, which must have been somehow clean-cut, leaving no scar, like the loss of milk-teeth, so soon replaced by others.

Then I forgot her.

Her little room, long and narrow and always in semi-darkness, with its worn old tiles, speaks to me of the olden days. In a few years time, when we knock down the wall and enlarge the living room, it will disappear. It will live on only in my dreams, a twilight place, well suited to the mysteries of childhood.

My grandmother Maria – whom I refer here to as 'poor thing' to distinguish her from all the other Marias in my family saga, but also perhaps because this was how others referred to her – died at roughly the same time as television made its appearance in our house; together with the fridge, the washing machine, and the biscuits. She never entered the modern world, or if she did she instantly withdrew from it into her silence, the weak light of the lamp on her bedside table, her lives of the saints. Perhaps she too was a saint, and we never noticed; an obscure saint without followers, with her mild half-smile, that poor cloven grandmother of mine.

The shop is going well, *madamin* Maria Grazia, as the commercial travellers call her, is learning to adopt the forceful gestures and firm voice of a woman who knows her business. *Magna* Margherita helps out at the till at the busiest times in the morning and evening. The moment has come to expand, to quit that inconvenient little shop and take on a nice big well-lighted place. You can't afford to fall behind, now that the world is bursting with televisions and fridges and biscuits and adverts.

In front of our house they've just finished building an ugly great block which has pretensions to being more than mere council housing: office workers, dentists and professors live there. Three wings of four and five storeys, a treeless, cheerless inner courtyard and, on the fourth side, the crowning glory of this architectural undertaking, the *skyscraper*, a nine-floor behemoth overlooking via Dante, clad in blue mosaic whose tesserae soon become detached and end up jingling in the pockets of us children. There are new commercial premises on the ground floor, with great big showcases. My mother decides to take the plunge and rents two adjacent spaces and, later, a third.

The new shop will have an ultra-modern counter, all glass and steel, for ham and cheeses, and tall metal shelves which my mother calls *'gondolas'*. One of the showcases will be for fruit and vegetables, and it will be replenished every morning and afternoon, apples, pears, grapes, celery and peppers laid out with care, as in a still life. Our fridge – deep as a small lake – contains hake and other frozen fish, stiff and opaque with their coating of ice, bumping against each other with a dull thud whenever a human hand goes in to fish one out.

My mother has more work and more responsibilities – and some debts, too – but how much more will she actually earn? Gilin does not go into things in depth, he doesn't quantify – that's not his forte – but he seizes his opportunity. His wife needs him, this is the moment to quit the factory. Perhaps there's also a touch of wounded male pride: what, his friends may have said to him, your wife's running a classy shop and you're still just a factory worker? Her head turned by the recent outbreak of abundance, her mind on other things, Maria Grazia instantly agrees, she's convinced that the air in the shop will do him good, it will bring out the best in him. Perhaps she is still deluding herself that she is not alone, that she is sharing her everyday joys and sorrows with the man-child she has married. Sometimes, when she casts her eye over those seventy or eighty square metres so rapidly filling up with merchandise – so small in comparison with the supermarkets of the not too distant future, but so big in comparison with her own previous little shop – she takes fright, asks herself whether she can make it, on her own. As a couple, perhaps…

Magna Margherita purses her lips, raises an eyebrow, tells her we've got to think carefully about this, but Gilin simply can't bear the factory any more, he's given in his notice, so Margherita says nothing, she knows that family peace and quiet sometimes require a degree of compromise. His aunts smile, putting on a show of conviction which they don't feel, or at least not as wholly and radiantly as they might like: 'Come on now, give the boy a chance, he's wasted in that factory, what with timetables and bosses and all that kind of thing, he's the sort of man who likes to be his own boss, he's thoroughly likable, he knows how to handle people, he'll get on well with the customers'. Our two local Cassandras, Ninin and Uncle Giovanni, will have moaned and groaned and obscurely prophesied all manner of disasters – and gone unheeded.

The shop is a full-time business, a powerful centre of gravity which demands total commitment, work and yet more work. By its very nature it is no place for my father, whose character is distinctly centrifugal. He gets into the shop late in the day, so it continues to be Maria Grazia who has to get up early, who goes down at seven o'clock, when it's still dark for much of the year. If she's five minutes late she'll find the cowhand waiting for her, smelling of stables and cigars, and the odd self-righteous local clutching an alluminium can and saying: 'Overslept this morning, did we?' As it turns out, the customers don't take to my father quite as much as the aunts had assumed they would, imagining their smiles and eagerly proffered purses – as current usage makes quite clear, customers want to be *served*, and my father feels very little inclination to serve anyone at all. Impatience incarnate, he's not likely to put on much of a show of self-control when choosing a kilo of pears – not those, those at the back, they're firmer – for some demanding termagant. Emboldened by the fact that he's in his own home, he loses his patience – his tongue is never entirely under his control at the best of times – and answers back, in ways most don't find funny. As we all know, humour is a subjective matter.

But there's one thing in the shop that holds a strong attraction for him, a gleaming honey-pot of a device – the till. There it sits, the grey metal cash register with its brand-new keys, queening it in a corner near the door, ever ready to give out that short *ding* that precedes the emergence of the little black drawer from within its depths. Bored and humiliated by his confinement, Gilin often glances in its direction – and when he sees that the drawer is temporally accessible, unguarded by chary female hands, the temptation is too great. He doesn't take the lot, just the odd note, a coin or two. At that time those lovely silver five hundred lire coins are still in circulation, with a portrait of a woman on one side and ships with billowing sails on the other, how could anyone resist the *invitation au voyage* they seem to offer? With a handful of those in his pocket, on occasions he will saunter out of the shop, drunk with the possibilities of a day that's scarcely begun, get into the car, whistle for the dog, which hurls itself blindly upon him, and set off for somewhere, anywhere, there's always something beyond the *here and now*, a bowls pitch, a wine shop, an anchovy sandwich, a pack of cards. This is a man's world, so different from that of woman, a world where you can swear to your heart's content, come and go as you please, turn traitor without fear of reprisals.

Gilin has many friends, but none of them for long; sometimes friendship turns to deep rancour, and the mention of a name will give rise to dark looks and obscure recriminations. Then all seems to be forgotten, so and so is back in favour, at least for a while. Cycles of friendship and betrayal, estrangement and rapprochement follow one another at the margins of family life, never spoken of and certainly not explained to the womenfolk, but capable of involving everyone, womenfolk included, because the consequences of something we know absolutely nothing about, occurring on an unknown day somewhere we've never heard of, wash up on our very own doorstep and shake the house to its foundations.

And that's how it happens, that is, no one knows how, nor where – or rather, yes, they do know where, even if they've never been there, it's called Saint-Vincent and it's in the Val D'Aosta – and nor do they know who he's with. It happens in the summer I turn nine, while my mother and I are at the seaside, at Loano, with my little friend Roberta and her mother, who lived on the same landing as us when I was very little. It's the first holiday my mother has ever had. Indeed, holidays themselves are a fairly recent development, the factories shut down in August, some people go to the seaside, others to the mountains, and some go back to their homes in the South. The previous year I had been sent up to Mezzenile, in Val di Lanzo with *magna* Ninin, to breathe the good pure air, an air laden with any number of fresh, mysterious smells: hay in the sun, moss, damp stones, espaliered *rosin*, little roses with a lot of thorns, the colour of dawn, which smell of apples. By the sea, on the other hand, the air smells of sun cream and fried fish, and everything – the shadows in the little streets, the afternoon warmth – is sharper, more clear-cut.

My mother can afford to leave the shop for two weeks because she now has an assistant, a thin girl with a nose like the beak of some exotic bird; she goes by the unusual name of Dilva. So she serves in the shop, with back-up from *magna* Margherita and Ninin.

Maria Grazia's first holidays; and also her last, at least for the next fifteen years.

The facts, part imagined, part plausibly reconstructed, go more or less as follows: a certain character has recently made an appearance among Gilin's friends, let's call him Demarchi; he's an older man, about fifty, and a 'cut above' us, he has a small mineral-water business with a warehouse on the Turin ring road. In a vain effort to disguise his bald patch, he sweeps the odd remaining tuft of hair over his head from his temples; he wears a jacket and keeps a pen in his pocket, he has bad breath and never smiles, but looks at whoever he's talking to with a puzzled air, as though he couldn't make you out (at least that's how he struck me when I met him on several occasions, a few years later). All in all he is a serious businessman and *paterfamilias*, albeit a little edgy and elusive. At first sight, what attraction he can have held for someone like my father is hard to grasp. But clearly this Demarchi is a changed character when he's among friends, he becomes a boon companion, a demon businessman with a comb over, the Tex Willer of the local casinos in a double-breasted suit. He organises wild nights at Saint-Vincent attended by my father while his wife is away on holiday, like a good husband in an Italian-style comedy.

This Demarchi is not a loner, various nameless shadows cluster around him, perhaps not even my mother knows exactly who they are, or has forgotten. Where my father's concerned, it's hard to put a finger on reality; that's also the case with his friends.

The only friends of his I know, and not well either, are people from our town and the surrounding countryside: all, or almost all, respectable people, with jobs, a wife at home, children, regular hours. There's the odd maverick among them, for instance a certain Fredo who occupies a front rank position in my father's personal mythology, a bachelor whose hair gleams with brilliantine and who engages in shady deals. But the others are workmen, office workers, one or two have farms, one is the manager of the local Savings Bank; they are brought together by the conviviality of the billiard table, which is a great leveller. Their headquarters is the bar Piazzo, right on the corner of our own via Vittorio Veneto and corso Martiri della Liberta, where the avenue of plane tree begins, below the aunts' old apartment. On Sunday mornings, while the wives are at high mass, a small group of men wearing their best jackets can be seen, seated in front of the counter, playing cards and drinking Cinzano, spitting out olive stones on to the floor in the hopes that someone will come in and slip on them. This is a man's world – they bet and steal each other's cars, take each other on at bowls and probably see who can piss furthest; they drive slowly along certain Turin streets where prostitutes are waiting behind their bonfires of blazing tyres.

All these years later, I find it hard to distinguish what I know of them from what I've heard, sensed it or reconstructed it, and what I've seen in the cinema. My father's cronies are the *Amici miei* of the remotest provinces, sunk deep in those distant Sixties which are the prelude to today. Their doings put me in mind of the *Decameron* or the *Soliti Ignoti*; their stories are of mammoth bean feasts and drinking bouts, of vicious pranks and numbskulls hoodwinked. The thick-head is a key figure in their universe, he is crucial to their enjoyment, someone has got to be bottom of the pack, and they take it in turns to play this role, my father included. But the true facts were never known or discussed at home, because the only other male member of the family who takes part in these expeditions is Pucci, who does not speak.

During those July nights in 1960, while Maria is sleeping next to her daughter in a rented apartment in Liguria, her personal fate takes a crucial turn but does not bother to alert her to this fact. On his return Gilin looks thoroughly gloomy and chastened. It's clear that something has happened, but even when he explains it to her – and Gilin's explanations are well-known to make the unclear downright obscure – she still can't really understand what has happened.

At first it must have seemed like yet another act of bravado, everyone knows he likes his bit of fun, it's his friends' fault, can't they see that some places are just not for the likes of him? He is allowed into the casino because he has put on his light grey summer suit, and on his identity card it says 'shopkeeper' rather than 'workman'; and during those years the law is indeed paternalistically concerned with protecting the proletariat from the dangers of gambling, as though they are children, but doesn't give a hoot about shopkeepers, they're adults, members of the lower-middle class who are enjoying their recently acquired pelf, so let them get on with it. What exactly happened during those nights, how many of them had there been, what had got into my father's head when the gambling spirit had leapt on to his back and spurred him on? His is a minor demon, a lesser imp which lives off subterfuge and is set off by random sparks; he can scarcely have believed his luck when, for the first time in his life, he finds himself in a large, luxurious unfamiliar gaming room, the temple of the mythical game of roulette, part of a savvy, world-weary crowd, people with money who relish the thought of gambling it away. He must have felt something approaching admiration and respect, laced with romantic rapture, for those hard-faced men as they cast their chips on to the green baize with an insouciance which he will never have the time to learn, mainly perhaps because of the absence of the raw material in question, namely money.

My father has a soft spot for desperadoes, outlaws, comic strip baddies. His brain, like that of an eleven-year-old child, lights up with sheer love for males who feel no sense of fear or respect for anything in this world. If only he could be the bandit who always gets away! Not Vallanzasca, too risky; Tex Willer would be better, he always makes it.

One day, decades later, a woman astrologer friend is looking at the stars which were present at Gilin's birth and will tell me that the sun and the moon were occupying the same position in the heavens. For him the sun and moon, the two opposite poles of an eternal dichotomy, are superimposed upon each another, merged into one. Her diagnosis: he's a kind of primitive! For him reality and imagination are one and the same, they're not separated by that more or less clear-cut line which marks the boundary of our own mental health, however precarious.

In a sense, my father lives in a place where all is possible, in a forest where paths cross *before* they could possibly cross, *before* they've even been marked out. His natural home is primordial chaos, where everything is all mixed up together and light has not yet been separated from darkness; the place where alpha and omega are still one, and perpetual motion has neither beginning nor end. That's why Grey Skies is never at peace. This is where my own restlessness has its origins, those rushes of blood through my veins which make me want to get as far away as possible from wherever I am. I wasn't born a primitive, but from him and his mother, my paternal grandmother, I have inherited the knowledge of that primordial place where alpha and omega are still one, and the wind never stops blowing.

How many moist and hopeful glances did Gilin cast upon that green baize table at Saint-Vincent? We cannot know. But we may imagine that his gambling demon – already somewhat intimidated by being kitted out in jacket and tie – fairly soon realised that it had taken on more than it could chew. I can see that gambling imp, that fitful fiend – a Peter Pan afraid of crocodiles and Captain Hook, which forgets how to fly from time to time, and hurtles heavily down to earth.

For a time he must have tried to hold his head high among the Saint-Vincent fast set by putting his trust in the gambler's deathless credo: today's good luck will send yesterday's bad luck packing. The whole thing cannot have gone on for long, though, and not just because the deathless credo is so much hot air, but because it simply isn't his scene. The casino regulars are not his friends, they do not speak his language; not only have they got deeper pockets, they've also got other vices, other tastes, they have another way of lighting their cigarettes, and far more powerful cars. He probably copied them for a bit, trying out new poses, new makes of *eau de Cologne*.

He will take up with new friends – let us not forget that for him the word 'friend' is extremely broad and imprecise – whom he's probably met at the gaming tables. Especially painters. Painters will fascinate him for several years, inspiring a short-lived passion for painting, about which he knows nothing (not that you need to know anything about things to do them, but he doesn't even know how to clean a brush). He buys himself canvases and oil paints, and turns the aunts' attic into an artist's studio. He sets up an easel and palette among the old furniture and bundles of yellowing newspapers but never produces a single painting. I too spend a few afternoons of my early adolescence daubing those abandoned canvases with colours which have to be forcefully squeezed out of tubes that have been left half-open and then dried up. He doesn't even do that; all he leaves behind him are hardened brushes and a smell of turps.

The money he loses at the casino during those years is all too real, and Gilin, as always, abhors reality. He'll shuffle the burden off on to those who are more accustomed to bearing burdens: my mother and the other women of the house. Then he forgets everything that's happened, he simply puts it all behind him. My mother puts fifteen years of her life into paying his debts; for him, matters are solved much sooner.

Yet it would seem that he knew how to beguile his painter friends, and in a way he showed good taste: I've still got a few paintings he brought home, landscapes, a seascape, two still lifes with flowers and a woman with a child. Perfectly decent figurative works, the kind of quiet paintings you can live with for decades, while at the same time absorbing and forgetting their peaceful beauty. How he came about them isn't known – it's unlikely he would actually have bought them – but they strike me as the only assets he retained from his male friendships; in all else he was the loser.

The one reality to emerge with stark clarity by the end of that summer, the only certainty amidst so many details, blurred as always – amidst pleas, prayers and promises – is that he's going to have to pay up. After some weeks or months the debt, previously merely alluded to, takes on the form of a small piece of paper which Maria Grazia signs, what else can she do, she can't say no to him. She's married him, no one forced her into it, there's no turning back.

There's no longer any way of finding out whether it was a protected bill or an open cheque, and anyway it no longer matters much. But we do know how much it is for: five million three hundred and fifty thousand lire. That piece of paper is worth roughly ten years of Gilin's worker's wages; it's worth eight or ten Fiat 500s (depending on the model) and almost one Ferrari coupe Farina 250 GT. The point is, though, my mother hasn't got that kind of money, and nor has anyone in her family. If you put all the aunts together and shook them, all that would come out of their pockets would be small change. Gilin has already done his best; it's impossible (and pointless) to calculate how many banknotes have already been extracted from Polonia and Giulia's cotton overalls and pink satin bras.

That bill, or cheque, will land Maria Grazia in court, because she has committed an action which Italian law regards as wrong, while all other laws tell her that she could not have done otherwise: the words of the priest when she married, the aunts' concern, the rule – accepted by all, in real life and cinema alike – that a woman must stand by her man, come rain come shine. She will not be found guilty, because her lawyer – tall, thin, elderly and distinguished – will prove that she had no idea what was going on, she's a young provincial wife, naïve, hardworking, who knows nothing of the world. She acted in good faith, as a decent woman should. And anyway, if during those years the wives of *mafiosi* were found not guilty, so too could my mother.

At all events, those five million lire are paid off. They have to come from somewhere, and to the question: but where?, there is only one answer: from the shop. That's where the money is, the big money, because by now all the aunts have is their pensions. And the house.

The law, which has acquitted my mother of a crime committed to save my father ('to save his bacon', in Ninin's earthy phrase) is to be seen in all its splendour and consistency by enjoining her to pay off his debts in full. Are couples one flesh, or are they not? So now the young provincial wife, ignorant of the ways of the world, must fork out five million plus if she wants to carry on going down into her little shop each morning. The banks will lend it her – with a suitable guarantee, which in this case too is called a shop.

It's not the first time Maria Grazia has found herself in deep waters: she's been separated from her mother, she's lost her father, she's been through the war, *magna* Michin has died. But in all those cases she has been completely powerless, all she could do was go along with them. Now on the other hand she has to take a stand, make a choice. I imagine that the person who helps her understand all this is that tall man with white hair, the lawyer from Turin, in his office on corso Matteotti or perhaps piazza Lamarmora, where you could glimpse the tops of the trees through the windows, behind the heavy curtains.

'Signora,' he must have said to her – this lawyer never

takes liberties, he never talks in dialect, with her he is distant and severe, albeit almost fatherly – 'if you want to save your business and your daughter's future, you have no other choice: you will have to pay those debts. Otherwise you'll have to resign yourself, take a step backwards, declare yourself bankrupt and let the creditors take all you've got. There will be nothing left, you will have to go back to being an ordinary working woman to keep your daughter, who will be in no position to study. If you take up the challenge you will have to carry on with your trade and have a fine headache for years to come.'

My mother regards herself as lucky to have found that lawyer. He makes an appearance in her life as a wise man, perhaps the imaginary flawless father whom we all ask for help at some point or other, and who usually does not respond, because he does not exist. Maria Grazia asks the lawyer whether she will make it. And the wise old man smiles at her and says: 'You are young and strong and full of energy. You are a courageous woman.'

So now begins my mother's bitter ten-year dalliance with banks and moneylenders. Life seems to go on as normal, but in reality everything has changed. Maria Grazia gets up at six in the morning – or rather at five three times a week, now that she goes to the main market for the vegetables, rather than to the wholesaler's, so as to spend less and have more choice – and she soon starts listing the things she's got to do and the sums she's got to pay. She has a permanent slight ache in the pit of her stomach, which intensifies at around three in the afternoon, the time when banks like to make phone calls and tell you you're overdrawn. There are two banks in Ciriè, the Cassa di Risparmio di Novara and the San Paolo, and my mother is all too familiar with the two sets of stairs that go up to the manager's office, rather as my grandmother the peasant knew the way to the headmaster's room whither she was so often summoned. Perhaps it helps that one of the managers is a friend of my father's, but that doesn't alter the interest to be paid. Friendship doesn't go into banks.

She also has to behave civilly to a certain unctuous grey figure, who sometimes appears at our house and stays on to supper, singing the praises of Ninin's genuine home cooking – insensible to flattery, she glares at him throughout the meal – and then renews the promissory note after receiving a dog-eared bundle of banknotes from Maria Grazia's pinafore.

But my mother makes it, as the lawyer had said she would. She pays off all her debts, and the debts on the debts, and meanwhile the shop expands with two further show-cases, and Dilva is joined by another assistant, the touchy Fernanda, from Friuli, who has lovely arms like a statue, and then by a third, who is young and podgy, and who will be given her notice because she has a regrettable habit of doing her shopping while bypassing the till. Meanwhile I have gone on from elementary to middle school and then on to the grammar school, in Turin. Like most children, I decide not to follow in my mother's footsteps; though many years later in fact I do just that, and hers strikes me as a most satisfactory calling , the others I have tried have been far less to my liking. As though only by doing what she has done – by handling real things, things that will perish, things which have a colour and a smell, doing sums which have got to come right, overcoming a thousand little problems each day – can I find some sort of truth, and peace, and indeed happiness; and in this alone, not in any of the more high-flying and prestigious activities I've turned my hand to in my time.

Maria Grazia finds freedom by taking on a debt that is not her own. It is thanks to this permanent leakage – which seems to grow rather than to diminish over the years and which has gradually to be stemmed, stubbornly, day by day, bit by bit, so that she must sometimes have felt like whoever it was who had to empty the sea with a spoon – that my mother can definitely no longer be described as a wife. People are endlessly saying that freedom lies in choosing to be a slave. Here I think they may perhaps have been referring specifically to God but, like all fine phrases and aphorisms, this one too contains a goodly portion of truth.

Maria Grazia did not find freedom by enslaving herself to God, or to an idea; she found it by enslaving herself to work.

In our house that is more or less how it's always been, there's no noticeable change. Things are certainly made easier for my mother by the fact that she doesn't have to change tracks: working is what her aunts have always done, Ninin and Michin and her own mother, before she got ill. Ninin in particular. Work takes on a meaning of its own because it means the survival and dignity of your nearest and dearest, the daily triumph of order over chaos.

The shop is not just a means of earning your daily bread, and a future, it's much more than that: it's an undertaking, an adventure at whose end lies either salvation or ruin. It's a war – against faulty fridges, carping customers, over-ripe peaches, wilting celery, installments to be paid, aching feet, a gossipy concierge, bad-tempered assistants and so on, down to the least of such problems, a mouse which has sneaked into the storeroom and is nibbling at the potatoes – and my mother is its unsung heroine. Each morning she leaves her cosy bed not with the conviction that this will be another normal day, but rather that risk and uncertainty, as always, lie in wait. Each night she falls asleep thinking: 'I made it through today.' Before he is banished to live with the aunts, my father joins her only when she is already deeply asleep ; she's been reading a novel, and her last thought will have been: 'I must have sweet dreams, I have enough nightmares during the day.'

It always works. For years, like Descartes, my mother is mistress of her dreams. At night she strolls with the *magne* through flower-filled gardens, she is a child with a young mother who has been made whole again, she laughs and sings with Michin, she makes love with a nice man she doesn't know and who, like my young father, has a Lambretta – and it's all too good to be true.

When she got married, Maria Grazia probably thought she'd start leading a more normal life, that is, a less tiring one, like her friends, all of them married, who lounged in their husbands' shade. All, that is, except Alfonsina, her oldest and most faithful friend, dating from the times they worked together on the looms, and she married a younger man. Alfonsina's husband is what many would describe as one in a million, all he thinks about is work and home, he doesn't drink or gamble or even smoke and he loves her so much, perhaps too much, and Alfonsina – who's half his height – advises him and cares for him as though she were his mother and, every so often, sighs. She can't complain, she says, she has no reason to – but having him always attached to her apron strings! Maybe other women would like to have a man permanently glued to their apron-strings, to be fed and almost suckled like a newborn babe. She just finds it stifling, she says as she fans herself, taking a deep breath: 'Am I being unreasonable?' she wonders.

Maria's other two friends are also shopkeepers, Lidia sells twinsets and linen, Bruna sells cut flowers and potted plants, and both have shops on corso Martiri, quite near us. The three of them, plus their husbands, go out to New Year's Eve celebrations and the local fair – the one with the merry-go-round people and the caravans – and the men go off to the shooting range and if they strike it lucky there'll be a group snapshot, all looking a bit surprised, wide-eyed because of the flash, the women with rouge and perms, the men in shirt-sleeves, slightly balding and with a hint of a pot belly, but still young. It's odd to think they're not yet forty, but their clothes and hairstyles and attitudes are those of adults, and therefore old, at a time when youth's boundaries were far more clear-cut than they are today.

At a time known also as the *patatrac*, the crash, when my father's *futa* (blunder, misdemeanour) begins to roll over us like a slow-moving avalanche which drags us along for years, my mother realises that she has no friends, apart from Alfonsina, who lives in Nole, just a few kilometres away in fact, but since they've both got their own lives to lead they don't see each other much. Alfonsina is the only friend in whom she can really confide and talk about her problems. Bruna and Lidia don't want to know how my mother feels, they put on the right faces as they listen to her, but their eyes say: that could never happen to me. She for her part feels somewhat ashamed when she talks of what has happened to her, even though she wasn't the one who lost the money. When a husband slips up, it's his wife who takes the rap. And when the wife puts herself forward and takes up the reins, other less forceful wives are bound to take their distance.

I can't remember what Lidia and Bruna look like, only that there's something aloof about them. I see them in their stifling little shops, even Bruna's, permanently scented as it is with greenery and flowers. They are closed-in places where I have to sit around for quite long periods, fizzing with impatience, a clumsy wide-eyed wader all too eager to take flight.

The protective walls of lower-middle class respectability have tumbled down. From now on my mother will breathe fresher air – colder, perhaps, but undoubtedly healthier.

It starts in the summer I turn eight, and ends six years later with her de facto separation from my father, with her exploration – cautious and unthinking at first, then increasingly enterprising and determined – of her free will as a woman and the costs it will entail. Faced with the alternative of going down with her ship or taking command of it, she soon realises that while the first option will earn her disdainful pity, the second will inspire a grudging admiration tinged with envy. The more confident she becomes, the less Gilin pitches up in the house or shop, and the more the local matrons, with their end-of-month perms and brown nylon stockings and slippers, observe her, gimlet-eyed, hoping to catch her out. For them, every commercial traveller, with his catalogues in *borse a soffietto* and clothes smelling of cigarette smoke, is a *'barba'*, the well-off, elderly 'uncle' of a younger woman. Maria Grazia has plenty to be getting on with, and soon shakes off any spiteful gossip. All hints of injurious comment are strangled at birth with a shrug of the shoulders: 'If you had as much work as I have, you wouldn't have time to speak ill of your neighbour.'

But Maria Grazia is not alone: the aunts are with her, Ninin and Margherita and also my grandmother Maria the peasant, who offers her own shy, wild camaraderie, *'povra cita, povra cita'*, and offers to run errands for her.

Although she's solid as a rock, Ninin at seventy is no longer a young woman. One day she falls on the stairs, and in order not to break the bottle she's carrying, she clutches it to her chest. Whether this is indeed the cause, the fact remains that she develops a nodule on her breast and they operate, and remove a bit. From that time on – Ninin has never worn a bra in all her life, she's got nothing to warrant such a thing – under her vest she wears a little cushion stuffed with cotton, made by Margherita, a sort of homely, low budget prosthesis. She makes a good recovery, and lives on for another fifteen years, working almost until the end. Ninin is the rock on which our house is built, but she is too old world for Maria Grazia to be able to speak freely with her. Ninin rants and raves, maybe in fact she's afraid; she knows so little of the big wide world, money and debts and bills…

Ninin the indestructible, the untamed shrew, *la pasionaria,* wanders around the house brewing up dark thoughts of lethal accidents, mortal illnesses striking out of the blue, even a providential murder. Nor is this as remote a possibility as it might seem, in view of the fact that one day Gilin notices that someone has taken a potshot at his car, probably a warning from some dear friend who is even more impatient than he is, and who is armed with the real thing and not just a fairground weapon. Poor dusty green beetle, still smelling of dog – even if Pucci is long gone – its back seats invisible beneath a mountain of shoes, rugs, bowls, socks, greasy paper bags of food, comics… For a time it even served my roving, roofless, workless father as a home.

A powerful character, like Ninin herself, the old Volkswagen will survive until I'm old enough to use it for my first driving lessons. These, though, will be its curtain call.

It is now, during these years, that *magna* Margherita answers the question Maria had put to her on 12 April 1935 on the quay in Genoa: 'Are you my mother?'

In the shop, or in the sparkling kitchen on via Vittorio Veneto, in the house next to our own, or in her living room which smells of wax, Margherita listens, makes coffee, doles out advice and staunches tears. She too knows a thing or two about family troubles, with that first husband – perfectly nice, but who died of TB – and the years of enforced and purgatorial cohabitation with the relatives, for the sake of a son who is now grown-up and causing troubles of his own, he seems to be a bit of a Peter Pan, in the morning she has to drag him out of bed to go to work, and he's got a cushy job all right, sitting comfortably behind a desk in the land registry office just a few hundred metres from his home, a short stroll beneath the planes and limes in the little square in front of the school.

Giulio's not a bad boy, but he's easily distracted, and sometimes, instead of going to sit behind that desk – recently Margherita has caught him at it – he goes to play pintable football in a bar in San Carlo, a meeting place for truants. At his age, almost thirty! And someone sees him, and now he's in trouble at work because he's on sick leave too often, without much reason. Also, to get into the students' good books, or rather those of one particular female student with back-combed hair who's a bit brighter than the rest, he's been paying for drinks, and put coin after coin into the juke-box…

Margherita speaks of these things only with her husband Carletto and her niece Maria Grazia; word mustn't get around. The boy's still young, he has time to fall into line, the less gossip there is the better. It's possible, indeed probable, that Margherita feels that sense of pain and guilt which mothers of fatherless boys so often feel for their children, even if it's not their fault. Margherita, with her queenly bearing, her head held high, her regal smile, must sometimes have wondered what she has done to deserve this son, so unlike her, who does things that she so signally fails to understand… and perhaps felt guilty at having this very thought.

'When you have a child, you never know who you're bringing into your home,' said a woman who had wisely refrained from doing any such thing. Perhaps my aunt too thought something of the sort, because she was a clear-headed person and rarely sentimental. She may even have said as much to my mother; I hope so, for her sake. I hope they told each other all those unspeakable truths which come to your lips when you feel completely safe and can speak out without fear of any come back. I hope they confided in one another about their problems to their hearts' content, perhaps laughing until they cried, because that's how I remember Margherita, with laughing eyes.

All in all she has been very lucky to marry Carletto. Her second husband makes up for all her previous bad luck, and now that he's about to retire she imagines them spending more time at the seaside, indulging in a bit of *dolce far niente*, because he's lost weight recently, he needs a rest. None of this happens, though, because shortly after he retires Carletto is diagnosed with bladder cancer and dies in November 1966. At the time it is whispered that his illness is linked to his work at IPCA, though people are not yet saying so aloud; Margherita herself talks of it without anger, though with alarm, as something that couldn't be prevented, like being struck by lightning or run down by a derailed train. He has died from the work he's doing, and what is more natural and necessary than work?

IPCA, or Piedmontese Aniline Dyes Industry, makes dyes, as one might expect; it's been known for some time that they're harmful, there have already been some deaths and the Turin Chamber of Commerce has issued a report which says that 'the environment in which they are produced is extremely unhealthy, the places of manufacture are very run-down and working conditions themselves are extremely poor. The workers are transformed into so many unrecognisable masks, their faces daubed with an odious, sticky, multi-coloured paste; after a time, their skin itself takes on these loathsome hues and is further affected by sundry external irritations.'

These words were written ten years before Carletto retired, when he was still going through the IPCA factory gate on every working day. But it takes time for people to complain, and even more time before they're listened to; years after his death there will be an epoch-making court case, albeit no justice. But Carletto will know nothing of this, and nor will his wife, and perhaps by that time they wouldn't have cared about it anyway.

He, on the other hand, has known for some time that he's ill, and what is wrong, as Margherita discovers after his death, when she comes upon a bookmark and some pencil underlinings in the medical dictionary that's kept in the immaculate glass-fronted bookcase in the living room.

After the death of her second husband, Margherita will not stay among us for long, less than two years. One October day in '68, a Saturday, she does not go down into the shop because she has a headache. My mother and Ninin exchange looks: in our house you don't have headaches. On Sunday afternoon we go for a walk, as usual. In Maria Grazia's van, just the three of us (Ninin stays at home to rest) we drive to some country path and walk among the yellowing poplars and dry, grey rows of maize. I, who have inherited my paternal grandmother's love of picking things, plunge into brambles in search of red berries and colourful branches; my mother and Margherita hang back, talking quietly. But at a certain point my aunt stops, begs us to go home, she looks very pale and clearly does indeed have a headache. Still sceptical despite herself, Maria Grazia drives us back. On Monday Margherita's voice is croaky and she can't get out of bed; she's taken to hospital, where they say she's had a brain haemorrhage and it's too late to operate, there's nothing they can do. They send her home.

For years my mother will reproach herself for not having taken that headache seriously. The very idea of thinking she was a *pita!* A *pita*, in our house, is a finicky little woman who allows herself to be waited on hand and foot, who's always complaining and gives herself airs. It's the feminine of *pitu*, a turkey cock; a *pita* is a farmyard fowl, puffed up, stupid and ridiculous.

It's words like this that make my native dialect a treasure trove that's quite unlike the official language. How can you proclaim the faults of a woman who is insufficiently robust, adaptable, hardworking and generally strong if you don't have the words for them, if they do not exist in your everyday speech? Certain it is that none of the women in our family were *pite*.

Margherita dies the following Friday, the day of her sixtieth birthday, without regaining consciousness. She departed as speedily as Carletto had tarried.

When I think of Margherita, the woman after whom my mother has named me, I see her as she was one day when I ran to her, weeping, to take refuge in her arms. I was eleven or twelve at the time and was beginning to teach myself to cook. I was making shortbread on the living-room table which, when opened out, became a large working surface impregnated with centuries' old flour, on which *tagliatelle* and *agnolotti* had been kneaded by generations of Davitos. *Magna* Ninin was casting a critical eye over proceedings: far from approving my noble efforts, she regarded them as positively depraved: 'You put in that much butter? Another egg? Another? I can't believe my eyes!'

Unappreciated and frustrated, with a shrug of irritation worthy of my father, I abandoned my task and ran off to shed my tears in Margherita's scented decolletage. She called me 'cactus flower'; she forced me to laugh at myself and go back to my biscuits at peace with myself. Margherita was like lemonade with lots of sugar, sweet and sour at the same time. She was the only one in the family who had perfected the art of the smile. And all of a sudden she was no longer there.

Things have also changed for my paternal aunts. With Giovanni's death, the happy times are over. As long as he, the grumbler, was around, they remained good-humoured, so as to make him laugh; now that he's dead, the sisters became downcast. He was like an old wooden post to which they had been moored, two buxom buoys floating peacefully on the domestic waters of incipient old age; now, without him, they drift off slowly towards decrepitude.

Giulia in particular, although she is the younger, is showing worrying symptoms of a tragi-comic malaise. She gives herself over to melancholy, reclines exhausted on the chaise-longue, like a nineteenth-century neurasthenic; she sighs, clad only in her flesh pink satin underwear, too overcome by *mal de vivre* to bother to get dressed. Her sister sighs as well: 'Oh Giulia, don't be like that!'

Dragging herself across the kitchen on her little wasted legs, leaning heavily on the chair which serves her as a crutch, Polonia puts an apple pie into the oven, later to be cut up wearily by her sister. '*Ammi mi povra dona*' says Polonia, and her thoughts turn to her husband, and the tear which nowadays is ever more frequently to be found ready and waiting in her bright little eyes, rolls down cheeks which have become as soft as dust, negotiates a wrinkle, trembles on the light down on her chin and finally falls upon her small pink hands, on the wedding ring she can no longer ease off over her arthritic joints. Her hands, which are the liveliest part of her, go up to her face like two concerned relatives huddling around a teetering widow to hide her unseemly grief. She wipes her face, she blows her nose, she spits a gobbet of phlegm up into one of those squares of newspaper she keeps in her pocket for this purpose, so as not have to dirty a real handkerchief. She regains her composure.

Meanwhile Giulia stares into empty space, not even bothering to wipe the crumbs away from the corners of her mouth. Her grey hair hangs down her back in a thin plait. Can diabetes be to blame? If at least she could stop eating all those chocolates and hiding the scrunched up silver papers in the drawers of the sideboard in the living room, as though everyone hadn't noticed!

Polonia can't manage on her own any more. There are certain things she can't ask of Angelo, who now lives with them: she can't ask him to help her wash herself, get dressed, do the washing (her bloomers make him laugh) or the shopping, but someone has to go and buy bread, potatoes, oil... Of course there's still my grandmother, Maria the peasant, who lives nearby in the two rooms on the first floor of the farm building, right next door to my father's attic-studio. But ever since they removed a malignant growth which was growing under one ear, my thin, brisk grandmother has become thinner, and less brisk. The operation has left her with a crooked face, with her cheek pulling to one side. I don't remember ever having seen her cry, but her eyes are misted over, they no longer shine. Her hands – which are much darker than Polonia's, and more gnarled, to the point that they look as though they belong to a member of another race – are less fidgety nowadays, they're often joined in prayer, but otherwise she's not much changed, except that she knows that her time is almost up. She carries on anyway, making no noise and troubling no one, just as she's always done. Everyone has their own troubles, she knows that.

So Polonia calls on one of the many Marias, a spinster niece who lives on the other side of the patch of meadow. And this umpteenth Maria, whom we may call Maria the servant, in view of her spinster status and the fact that she doesn't do outside work and so is at everybody's beck and call, comes round to earn the odd penny by doing the cleaning and the washing and the shopping. Dependent as she now is on an outsider, albeit a relative, Polonia feels increasingly ill at ease in her own home.

And meanwhile Giulia, indifferent to everything, throws herself down on the *dormeuse* and complains about life.

Until one day, all of a sudden, she wakes up. She washes her hair and draws it back into a bun. She gets dressed. Before she fell into that state of lethargy, she recalls, she had put bulbs in glass pots in the dining room. Yes, there they are: in the cold room, on the marble windowsills, the hyacinths have put down roots, white skeins like hair, floating in water. The pale buds are swollen, about to burst into pink and blue inflorescences whose intense scent will spread throughout the house, drowning out the smell of cooking and that faint whiff of old age which, despite Maria the servant's best efforts, continues to waft in from the bathroom and sleeping quarters.

'Look, look Polonia,' she says, showing her a flower which already has a hint of colour, 'isn't that lovely? We've got so few, next year we'll have to order more.'

And Polonia nods, half pleased, half anxious, because she has learned to fear her sister's reawakenings almost as much as her lethargy.

Giulia goes into town, meets any number of acquaintances, stops to talk to them. Every shop window speaks to her of urgent purchases, her feet in their black leather shoes deformed by bunions paw the ground, skip rapidly along. She returns home laden with bags and boxes, and then it's Polonia's turn to sigh and groan: it's all too much! But Giulia takes no notice and begins to put away lettuce, salame, cheese, then stops to do something even more important, to make a coffee, then she goes to look in the cupboard and decides there and then that its time to update her wardrobe, what a lot of things there are she no longer wears!

Heedless of her sister's dismay and Maria the servant's grumbles, Giulia sweeps through the flat with her broom like a human tornado, shifting furniture, emptying drawers, planning urgent purchases: new curtains are needed, elastic, buttons, stockings… Most of all, though, Giulia speaks. As though to make up for lost time, for those months of silence, my child of a great-aunt – small, fat, nattily turned out, her head set on her round shoulders with scarcely any neck between – launches into spirited whirlwinds of conversation with anyone who comes within earshot, like a brazen young girl who'll dance the mazurka with any gentleman on offer. Polonia suffers in silence, half laughing, half crying, then blows her nose, shakes her head and tells herself there's nothing to be done. 'Old age is not for cissies,' she murmurs to herself.

Once the object of the whole town's respect, dignified and genial, here she is now, a heap of old flesh parked on a chair, in need of everybody's help, including that of her nephew, just to keep her clean. Sometimes, however unwillingly, she has to wake him at night to help her to the bathroom.

Nowadays my father lives with them, not with us. After his nomadic phase, in the beetle, he's set himself up in their place, in what used to be Giulia's room; Giulia herself now sleeps in the double bed, in the space left empty by Giovanni. Now there are two dips in the mattress, of roughly the same depth.

The *patatrac* – the famous piece of paper bearing the figure of five million – was not the last event in my father's career as a gambler, only the most spectacular: a sort of earthquake, 9 on the Richter scale, followed by others, less violent and spread out over time, which slow down those who are trying to help him and mow down the oldest and weakest of the earthquake victims. Can it be mere chance that Giovanni has a seizure just when there is talk in the house of selling up? Can it be coincidence that I put on ten kilos even earlier, in the seven or eight months after the *patatrac*? I forge myself a breast-plate, I make myself heavy and unyielding; my uncle, God rest his soul, simply withdraws from the fray. My paternal grandmother, shortly afterwards, begins to cast her tongue over that poisoned morsel which will then settle in between jaw and ear and, from then onwards, prevent her laughing.

I don't mean that my father should be blamed for all the deaths in the family; Gilin is not a murderer. But he did give fate a fillip, that's for sure. Sooner or later they would have died, indeed perhaps sooner rather than later, and I would undoubtedly have become the stubborn creature I became. But there can be no doubt that the family events of those five or six years leading up to my adolescence were marked by the paternal earthquake.

Like Mina in the song, who *makes promises, promises, always the same promises,* at a certain point my mother too realised that her married life was becoming a little too repetitive: he'd come home contrite, ask for money, confess to shady episodes in which he was the innocent victim of circumstances and false friends, he'd cry, make those famous promises, repent, go off absolved with something in his pocket – and a few days later the same thing would happen all over again.

So Maria Grazia goes back to the lawyer, the paragon of a father she'd never had, in his setting of velvet curtains and huge desk with leather accessories, and he utters the words which authorise my mother to give voice to what she thinks and dares not say, to imagine what until yesterday had been unimaginable.

'Your husband will never change, *signora*. You must go your own way, you must save yourself while you can. You must separate – you must send him away.'

'But I've got a child, your honour.'

'Quite so! Think of her future.'

She talks about it with Margherita, with Ninin. She even talks about it with Angelo, who doesn't refuse categorically, that's not in his nature. He goes off to live elsewhere, and where would that elsewhere be if not the home of the Mattioda aunts?

They're the ones who've always paid off his debts, however small, and now they continue to do so. And so it comes about that first the house where the grandmother lives is sold, and then that of the aunts, that cube built just a few years ago for their old age – sold to relatives who live not far away and have a butcher's shop on a minor road on the edge of the little town. My great-aunts receive a sum which is just a fraction of the value of the house, but they are to be allowed to stay there for the remainder of their days – and my father will be able to appease his creditors, including perhaps the irascible owner of the pistol who took a potshot at the beetle.

I am fourteen by the end of this performance, and my mother

is a separated woman, a dubious, almost sinful condition in those days when the word 'divorce' still had a whiff of sulphur about it in the provinces, even if this is just eight years before the 1974 referendum in which Italians will give the divorce the thumbs up, definitely one in the eye for the Catholic church.

We don't go to church much, just to mass on Sunday morning, because that's the done thing. My memories of the excruciating boredom of interminable pre-first communion and confirmation catechism are with me still; the thought of confession, too, still weighs upon me, with its set phrases: father I have disobeyed, I've answered back, I've had impure thoughts, I repent and am sorry, three paters, three *aves*, three *glorias*, amen.

One Sunday, in the gloom, in front of a grille pearled by the breathe of innumerable supplicants, a strange thing happens. The priest behind it is a massive faceless figure, and on this occasion he's not satisfied with the ritual formulas: bad thoughts, what bad thoughts? Have you committed any impure acts? A big man sitting in the dark, a fat girl kneeling in front of him. I am fourteen, he is fifty, possibly older. Until a few years ago I hadn't known what impure acts were, but now I do. But I also know that all my sins are venial, indeed perhaps they're not sins at all, and the ritual being performed by me and my plodding inquisitor strikes me as grotesque. Perhaps, in a flash, I sense that real evil and real good, however little I may know about them, have nothing to do with the words we are exchanging. Suddenly a question forces itself upon me: what does this fat-head want from me? By the time I've got up from the hassock I've realised I'm now too big to go to church.

I tell my mother as much. She doesn't argue, anyway she herself goes only to avoid attracting attention, and after a bit she too stops going. But my absence is enough to set tongues wagging. And if I don't care, then why should she? The air turns blue with Ninin's curses, but after a bit, as always, she goes along with what my mother has decided.

It is the first time that my mother has sided with me, has followed me down the path that I have chosen, and it will not be the last. Over the next few years I shall teach her to cook – an art I now practise with some success, despite the objections put up by *magna* Ninin, whose innate Calvinism is ultimately conquered by my budding epicureanism – and to read French fluently. From now on Maria Grazia will devour novels and history books in two languages, something of which I am extremely proud.

In the meantime she's learned to drive, which means she can go to the central markets three times a week in her new light grey Volkswagen minivan, which can carry up to eight hundred kilos of merchandise, but which she will frequently load up with ten or twelve, driving slowly to avoid the potholes, her heart in her mouth at every sighting of the traffic police.

From the pretty child I was until the age of eight – however unwilling to be clad in little tulle dresses – I have turned into a podgy, pig-headed pre-adolescent. I'm studious – my mother has instilled in me the idea that education is a privilege not to be trifled with – and I'm a girl of few words. Adults think that I'm shy, but they're mistaken; I know how to make myself respected by my contemporaries, and when I can't be in the limelight I'd rather keep out of things altogether. Throughout my life I've been the object of unconditional love, and this makes it possible for me to bear my status as a chubby chops, mildly mocked by the other children. It's as though I'd always lived incognito among people, children and adults alike. I feel that no one really knows who I am, and this suits me fine. I sense that over the years to come I shall have to muster all my resources to face a world I know nothing of, and of which my forbears too were equally ignorant. I overtake them. I forget them. I return to them. What wisdom do they hand down to me? What answers do they give me? None at all, of course, except for the love with which they nurtured me. Perhaps that's all I need.

If in times gone by I was free to flutter about among my old sweethearts, now that my elders and betters have begun to die off and I am growing apace, I find myself claiming the freedom to roam from one house to the other, to mark out the geography of my childhood each day, unsupervised. Thinking back to those times, that's how I see myself: along the road that goes from my house to that of the aunts, or along country paths; going on long daily walks at a fair lick, thinking, daydreaming, constructing complex adventures going on and on, like television serials. I come upon beings – hardly ever human – which capture my attention: dogs, lizards, trees, abandoned mills. I walk in winter and in summer, without any set idea where I'll be going, I explore the countryside around my little town, I go wherever I want and no one asks me where I've been when I get back.

My mother doesn't ask me to account for my time, she trusts me, she knows I'll do my homework and study my lessons – and that is exactly what I do. Quite simply, my mother gives me free rein to do precisely as I please. It's only much later, when I listen to other girls, and women, that I realise that Maria Grazia's faith in me was indeed extraordinary. Yet she also gave me an even rarer gift: she never chided me for being fat, or ugly, or not very feminine. Perhaps she hardly had time to notice, just as she didn't have time to check on the progress of my studies, or perhaps she just liked me as I was. She never wanted me any other way.

She and the others gave me the gift of freedom. It's only years later that I realise how different this makes me from most other girls and women.

And it occurs to me that freedom is also a matter of space. In my mind's eye I see the countryside where I grew up, with the familiar dangers – ruins, brambles, wells, fast-flowing streams – which made my walks like journeys into outer space. I see my mother in her minivan driving cautiously through a sea of winter mist, wheels skittering over the frozen asphalt. Might she sometimes have imagined that she was in the Russian steppe, or with some smugglers in the mountains, as in the novels she was reading? I ponder on the fact that, in her mind, the clear-cut borders between what you must and mustn't do, between what is respectable and what is not, have fallen into disuse, like rusty old barriers which no longer set anything aside from anything else.

When she's in the euphoric phase of her manic depression, or bipolar disturbance as we prefer to call it nowadays – but at the time none of us had a name for her mood swings, they were just something that happened to her – *magna* Giulia never stops talking. She barely breaks off to eat, and sleep – just a few hours, and very lightly – to wake up as though electrified, a prey to energies which have boiled up anew.

Polonia groans and puts her head in her hands.

Then she takes it out on her nephew Gilin, her Angelo, and it's as though she were fifteen again, a 'lovely young woman on the threshold of life', as her girl friends at school would write in her autograph album, not hesitating, amidst all manner of curlicues and pansies, to give expression to desires which might seem suspect today but which at the time seemed utterly innocent: they wanted to kiss her 'laughing lips', they sang of her 'shapely body', they wished – as sisters – to embrace her 'rosy child-like flesh'.

At the age of sixty, Giulia is on the brink of a second adolescence. After months of sentences that have been mangled or left unfinished, she is once more seized with a delight in language; her speech is eloquent and burnished, and punctuated with exclamations and gales of laughter.

And her nephew allows himself to be addressed as 'My little Angel, my joy, my little treasure', he listens to her, positively encourages her to talk even when his eyelids are dropping with sleep, because he knows that in the small hours, when her voice alone breaks the silence of the night, apart from the odd car speeding along the road outside and the effortful rustle made by *magna* Polonia as she stirs in her sleep, he will finally persuade her to go to bed, and he himself will be able to sleep as well, exhausted maybe, but rewarded for his labours with the odd thousand lire note.

Unlike their more illustrious predecessors the Materassi sisters, my great-aunts do not regard their nephew as the dream lover, the eternal masculine – and indeed my father is no such thing. He's handsome, but he's not manly, he's no Don Juan and he is not known for his affairs; the company he prefers is male, his famous friends, who never lose their allure even after he's suffered badly at their hands. At the same time, though, it must be said, Gilin knows which side his bread is buttered and remains close to his aunts, who continue to pay off his debts for him: an eternal prodigal son who eternally goes back to his mothers, that's how Polonia and Giulia have wanted it, that's what they've made of him.

Now my father is working for Demarchi, in his drinks and mineral water business. Perhaps the businessman with the comb over feels guilty for having introduced a former workman to the casino and is trying to make up for it by offering him paid employment. At all events, and despite the inevitable occasional unpleasantness between him and his boss, each morning Gilin now goes to the depot, a turreted city of bottles in Turin's most desolate suburbs, he loads up the van and sets off for the new supermarkets which are opening up in other suburbs. He's probably stopped going to the casino – his demon has gone back to humbler gaming tables in various inns and wine shops – and he's hanging around again with his old friends who play bowls, a game at which he is extremely skilled, and he almost becomes a champion; almost, because to become a champion you need a certain persistence, even in bowls. Anyway, he wins several gold medals, which he displays with pride and which periodically disappear, sold for a bit of small change.

Money, or the lack of it, is his constant preoccupation. The aunts, who collect their pensions each month at the post office, keep bundles of bank notes in the chest of drawers among hankies and undies, and when the two pachyderms are snoozing in the kitchen or engaged in conversation with the dwindling number of visitors, he has got into the habit of rummaging among the linen and detaching the odd note or two from the bundle without their noticing – or being sufficiently niggardly to complain.

One day he initiates his daughter into the mysteries of this game, which he calls 'the treasure hunt': 'Look, this is how it's done.' And he thrusts a greenish Christopher Columbus or a pink Michelangelo note under her nose.

His daughter stands hesitantly in the doorway.

I look on and don't say a word.

I walk back home, and as I do so something strange occurs: as I leave the old gravelled courtyard behind me, and the red brick columns supporting the iron gate, and walk along by the little wall from which the hedge of tea rose protrudes, I suddenly feel I'm walking in the past. The roses are now faded, as though they were last year's. The grass of the lawns along that stretch of road are dusty and yellowish, like a damaged print of an old film I've seen too many times, and which has nothing new to tell me. The excitement I once felt when going to see the aunts has disappeared, as has my delight in the flowers, the kitchen garden, the living room and all that it contained, Giulia's old books, the attic I'd sneak up to in order to pursue my archaeological activities. The aunts and my grandmother seem suspended in a time which has already ceased to be, almost as though they had outlived themselves.

At the age of fourteen I see them from far off, as though a time machine had suddenly catapulted me into the future. Decades later, the same machine will carry me backwards, in search of them.

When I began to write about my family, starting with Ninin, I was obeying a long felt need: to gain access to the very core of those I loved, though I can never quite find it; to recreate their presence, to make them live again. Perhaps these pages are the equivalent of those ancestral portraits enshrined by certain so-called primitive peoples in the places where they live: to whom they devote an altar, even a whole room. It's said that offering food to the dead serves to appease them, stops them from coming back to disturb the living. But I'd like it if they came back, it wouldn't disturb me at all; by writing this, I've tried to persuade them to do just that. And the custom of laying the table for the dead lives on, on the evening of the first day of November, with wine and chestnuts. Claudia would put an unopened bottle of wine on the table, and I would suggest she open it: it's not polite to expect the dead to handle a corkscrew with their hands of air. Then next morning you can tell yourself that the level in the bottle has gone down, just a little.

Not everything I've written here is true – names and dates and facts, yes, but I've invented things here and there, where I didn't know enough, I've altered the odd fact and reconstructed the order of events where I was unsure about it; and of course I have interpreted the whole thing in my own way. My family did not make history, and the only person it interests is me; so it's of no importance if a certain event took place on a such and such a day, or the day before or the day after. Some years ago I carried out some on the spot reconnaissance, in the mountain villages and country cemeteries, in search of impressions, names and dates of births and deaths; and – how could I not? – I did some research on the internet. But above all I questioned my mother, and was thus witness to her gradual mental decline: with the years, and then with the months, her replies became increasingly cursory, and vague, until towards the end she didn't answer at all, because she'd lost her memory. It's too late now for all the questions I'd failed to ask.

As I was writing, I found myself encountering not only them, but also myself, because I too was in that past, or at least in part of it; and, more importantly, because they are present in my life, within me, at all times. It was inevitable that I should find myself in them and tell myself from time to time: that's it, I am as I am because he, she, they, were as they were.

But I would certainly never claim that family destiny was all-determining: that would narrow things down too much. I know that I'm the product of the unexpected, seamlessly fused with the foreseeable.

If, for example I modelled myself upon my father because I was both close to and antagonistic towards him (in some ways I am a kind of cast of him, my solids correspond to his voids), I certainly did not do so with a good grace. In view of *magna* Ninin's battle-cry, 'You're your father's daughter all right', *I had to* prove that I was not like him, I *could not* want otherwise, it would have been a betrayal of my mother's side of the family, they were the rock on which I built, I was dependent upon them for my very survival (I'd always known, right from the start, that if I'd been dependent on him I wouldn't have had a chance).

I've often caught myself addressing him: you're an irresponsible good-for-nothing, here I am having to make good all your mistakes! It's your fault that I too can't be irresponsible, and God knows, at times I'd like to be!

I'm sensible (or at least I think I am, which possibly proves precisely the reverse). I'm economical, I hate waste, I turn out lights when I leave a room, I eat up leftovers, I pay my bills on time. As if that weren't tedious enough, every time he appears at my side – when I'm paying off the debts that he continues to run up until the ripe old age of eighty, when I'm checking his blood sugar level, when I talk about him with his friends who, having spent ten minutes with him, find him delightful company – I am transformed into a haughty, sour Minerva, a figure of fun.

If what I've inherited from my mother's side of the family enables me to live a decent life, it's when I take on Gilin's mantle that I know success – when I rid myself of the goddess of reason's heavy helmet and make people laugh, not caring how.

It's my impatience that's my greatest bugbear, my desire to banish all constraints, to take short cuts, to burst the world like a balloon – and yet never to allow myself to do so because he did it all before me, the old reprobate! I've never allowed myself to indulge in impatience at its most glaring, but it's always there, under my skin, and it's done me a certain harm (or good, depending on your point of view), for instance deflecting me from the academic career that I briefly contemplated at the age of twenty-one, twenty-two, because I realised I'd have been driven mad by all the pomp and circumstance, the trappings, the traipsing around with briefcases. I'd have thrown them down the steps of the Palazzo Nuovo and done a runner, just like him!

Yet in everyday life I was forced, willy-nilly, into the dismal role of the thrifty woman, the woman who mends, who saves... the tiresome ant!

How could I reconcile these opposites, allow my maternal and paternal sides to live side by side within me without one stifling or aggravating the other?

By writing.

This form of deviance, which first reveals itself compulsively when I am about fifteen, will prove absolutely vital to my wellbeing. Above all, it frees me of the serious illusion that there is just one of me, the one that others invariably see. People who write not just professionally, but also as a bad habit, as I do, know quite well that 'I' is any number of people, and they don't necessarily get on together – indeed, whole new worlds may be born of their disagreements, unexplored spaces in which the inner universe never stops expanding.

For years I'm dogged by a certain dream: I'm burying my father's corpse in the courtyard of our house, among the old silver cedars and glossy-leaved magnolia. It's an oppressive dream, from which I wake exhausted, burdened by the mass of that dead body which I have to hide, or I'll be accused of having killed him. I never dream that I've killed him, and perhaps I haven't – but anyway, he's dead… I'm reading a lot of thrillers at the time, and the part where the body has to be got rid of is the part that most troubles me.

One day I awake from this dream with a new energy, and I write a story in which my mother kills my father, and then asks me to help her throw the dearly-beloved deceased into the well. Then she goes off on a trip with a woman friend, leaving me alone with the burden of proof and my own sense of guilt.

This story proved my deliverance. I found it exhilarating; my few readers found it chilling. I still regard it as one of the best, most sensible things I've ever written.

Among other things, it also happened to be true.

After ten years of separation, my mother took Gilin back. He was still working in the mineral water business, and seemed to have turned over a new leaf – a stopgap new leaf, glued on with spit, but anyway – and she'd never even looked at another man. Ninin was no longer with us, and Polonia was on the point of joining her. My mother was alone; I'd gone to live in town, I was a busy young woman, I'd got a flat, a job, lovers, even a cat.

My mother had had a husband, and she took him back.

In so doing she'd brought him back into the family, into that family which, thinned out by death, had been reduced to her and me (along with such loves of mine as were destined to endure). Every now and then she would justify herself: 'What would people have said if your father had ended up as a tramp?' 'I don't care what people say!' I'd snap. She: 'You'd have had to look after him yourself, in the end.' Me: 'I've had to look after him right from the start!' In fact, I knew that this was bound to be my fate, living as I did in a country which didn't allow divorce between parent and child, the family country par excellence. In Italy, you don't get rid of your father.

You can get rid of your husband, though. Even if you're living together. Over the years, my mother too has forged herself the life of a mature woman, with cats, books, women friends, the cinema, travels, even the odd love affair… My father, on the other hand, is old, cantankerous, greedy, incorrigibly *lajan*… who's going to take him to hospital, who's going to worry about his future as a long-term invalid? His daughter Minerva, her helmet askew above a disapproving eye.

Writing that story did me a lot of good. I saw myself as a ridiculous victim, and I laughed at myself. I saw my mother as she was, a potential murderess and hence at last a woman complete in all her parts, with the cynicism, egoism and intellectual coldness necessary for pursuing her goals in life. For the first time I looked at her askance, casting aside love, or perhaps with a more adult love, understanding something that made her more human, and me more free.

And my father more dead; poor Gilin.

He's the only one of them still alive, if that's the word to describe the life beyond life he lives, with ever greater difficulty, in the old people's home in the hills of Monferrato.

My mother too has gone, leaving me amazed, incredulous: how can this be? Where has she gone?

I still dream about her, together with *magna* Ninin, a young woman and an old one, both very beautiful, the two faces of love.

A strange thing has happened in connection with Ninin.

In my childhood and youth she was such a familiar presence as to be almost invisible, but now that she's dead she has become more vivid. Never one to put herself forward, over time she has began to appear to me as I describe her here – as the true family figurehead, around whom the lives of the various members seemed to take on meaning and flavour, as does my own. Furthermore, I've often found her where I least expected her – in the people I've chosen to be closest to. I see now that there was something of her in the people I sought out for myself; that I would never really be able to love anyone who was not as loyal, combative and rough as she, and that what I found irresistible, above other more lovable qualities, was a certain awkwardness, a harshness of character which tries to contain itself but always fails, and bursts out into grumbling, and putting the world to rights…

Once we'd laid down our arms, I delivered Gilin the fatal blow when I realised that my sense of humour did not come just from him, but also from my grandmother before him, as well as from my unknown maternal great-aunt Michin, and probably from any number of other unknown sources; just as, in some mysterious and roundabout way, the limits of my life are the very shape of my choices. I would have wanted no other life nor shape.

Spending their time as they do, unearthing and dusting down minute fragments, archaeologists are clearly driven by a powerful passion. The magic moment, of course, will come when two pieces match up and something appears which is not yet quite a shape, but a pointer towards one. To find connections, to glimpse a pattern, to join up ideas: are the pleasures of the mind less intense than those of the body because they are more abstract? At times it seems to me that the reverse is true.

While I was on my search for my now vanished family, I sometimes felt that I was coming to understand something more of myself, and perhaps even of the vast and poorly charted field of human endeavour as a whole…

I don't like to refer to them as 'my dear departed', that's too depressing! I prefer to think that they have emigrated to another dimension, that they've set off on the *Colombo* in search of another America, one that's still brand new, and from time to time I come upon them again in a curve of time, I see them from a distance and try to attract their attention by waving wildly. Sometimes they see me, sometimes they don't, and I have the impression that they're smiling at my haste, and sometimes they make me suffer, as all lovers suffer, always, at least a bit, even when they are happy.

Author's Note

All the names, places, dates and facts in this book are true; but the tone, the internal rhythm, the slants of memory, all these are fiction, reality recreated and invented, as in any narrative.

If there is any reader who still remembers those of whom I speak, I hope they will forgive any errors or omissions, and regard this story simply as a novel.

I would like to thank my agent, Rita Vivian, who believed in this book from the start and championed it warmly and effectively. Giulia Ichino made me feel welcome and appreciated, and Marilena Rossi helped me to cast light on passages which were still shrouded in darkness. And, lastly, my thanks to Alessandra Maffiolini, who has been my playmate in the magic world of vocabulary and punctuation.